An Overnight Sensation

The Torch Singer
Book One

Books by Robert Westbrook

Howard Moon Deer Mysteries
Ghost Dancer
Warrior Circle
Red Moon
Ancient Enemy
Turquoise Lady
Blue Moon

Coming Soon!
Hungry Ghost
A Howard Moon Deer Mystery

The Torch Singer Trilogy
An Overnight Sensation
An Almost Perfect Ending
The Saint of Make-Believe

Left-Handed Policeman *series*
The Left-Handed Policeman
Nostalgia Kills
Lady Left

Other Books
Intimate Lies:
F. Scott Fitzgerald and Sheilah Graham – Her Son's Story
Journey Behind the Iron Curtain
The Magic Garden of Stanley Sweetheart

An Overnight Sensation

The Torch Singer
Book One

Robert Westbrook

SPEAKING VOLUMES, LLC
NAPLES, FLORIDA
2020

An Overnight Sensation

ISBN 978-1-64540-128-5

For Gail

Prologue

The Love Nest
St. Valentine's Night, 1956

It was the biggest scandal of 1956, and they liked scandals back then almost as much as we do today.

3 DEAD IN HOLLYWOOD LOVE NEST! That's how *Confidential* magazine had it, a cover story complete with a sultry photo of my mother, a publicity still from 1947, back at the height of her career when her legs were said to be insured for a million dollars and men went mad with lust at the sound of her name. The dead were famous enough to merit an exclamation point: a sexpot singer, a blacklisted movie director, and a U.S. Congressman who had recently been forced from office due to lurid revelations of an extra-marital kind.

I was only twelve at the time, but I'd grown up fast in show business. I knew a love nest wasn't something made out of twigs, with three little chicks inside and mama bird giving everyone a nice fat worm.

This particular love nest was my home.

*****

I was asleep when the first gunshot woke me.

It was midnight on Valentine's Day night and the sound of the shot jerked me awake from an erotic dream. I was about to kiss my darling Penny, who was fourteen and fascinating, two years older than myself. I didn't want the dream to end, for Penny had just turned to me with lips that said yes. I wanted to stay with her forever. But my eyes flickered open.

I lay in the darkness of the bedroom listening hard, uncertain of what I'd heard. Rain was beating on the roof and the big fir tree outside my window creaked and whooshed in the wind. I could smell the wetness of the night outside, wetter than a dream. It had been raining for three days, the kind of Pacific storm that brings down California hillsides and houses built where houses were never meant to be. The streets were flooded, the gutters awash, the rain gurgled and dripped in a thousand little rivulets.

Our house was big and old and solid, with thick stucco walls and a red tile roof, the kind of architecture that was popular back in the days when California was still said to be Mediterranean. My bedroom was on the second floor in the back overlooking the pool. After a while, I heard a car go by on the street out front. The tires of the car made a wet squishy slap against the pavement, then gradually faded into the distance. The sound was reassuring, familiar. The sort of sleepy far-off sound from the adult world that makes you feel safe when you're a kid lying snug in bed, trusting to the order of things.

An Overnight Sensation

I decided I hadn't heard a gunshot after all. I was a dramatic kid and I had to watch myself. Still, something was wrong. I'd fallen asleep with the radio playing and it should be playing still, KFWB, Color Channel 98, the Top Forty station we all listened to in 1956. The last thing I remembered was the doo-wah chorus of my favorite song, "Why Do Fools Fall in Love?" —a question that eludes me still. I fumbled for the bedside light, but when I clicked the switch nothing happened. I tried a few times before I realized the electricity was off.

I didn't like having the electricity off. It made the darkness somehow darker. Just as I was getting seriously spooked, I heard a second gunshot. *Boom!* It came from my mother's part of the house.

There was a treble element to the sound, a shrill bang, as well as a bass echo that reverberated afterwards, dying slowly. This time there could be no denying what it was. I sat up in bed, but I couldn't hear anything now except my heart which had moved up from my chest and was thumping in my eardrums. I was so scared all I wanted to do was pull the covers over my head and hide. But at last, reluctantly, I forced myself out of bed. Walking blind, I made my way barefoot to the bedroom door. The darkness was so thick it was like floating in a sea of black velvet.

"Mom?" I called out experimentally into the hallway. I stepped cautiously onto the landing at the top of the stairs, feeling my way forward with my hand against the wall, inching along step by step. Everything was unfamiliar in the dark. I was thinking I had gone too far, that I must have missed my mother's door, when my hand brushed against the knob.

"Mom?" I called again. "Are you okay?" When there was no answer, I tried the doorknob. Being a famous beauty, she didn't always spend the night alone and sometimes she locked the door. But tonight, the knob turned and I made my way into her suite of rooms. There was a yellow glow of candlelight coming from the far end of the hall, flickering uncertainly, throwing deep shadows.

"*Mom?*" I called, more anxiously.

I moved forward like a sleepwalker in a dream, passing the doors to her dressing room, her walk-in closet, her bathroom. This was my mother's private world, a mysterious feminine realm that smelled of perfumes and cold cream and a musky hint of fur from the closet—mink, the animal of choice in my childhood.

My footsteps slowed as I stepped into the bedroom. At first my eyes refused to believe what I saw there. I couldn't take it in all at once. I could barely breathe.

My mother's bedroom was large and white and full of lovely things. White was her favorite color. White curtains, white tables, a white sofa, a big white bed with a white canopy of gauzy material that flowed down from a white frame. It was a bedroom for a storybook princess, for my mother was a woman who still clung to fairy tales despite the jaded requirements of a Hollywood career. But tonight, the fairy tale had come to an end.

There were two people on the bed, my mother and Uncle Max. I wasn't sure at first it was Max because he looked so different. There was a good deal of blood. I smelled the blood even before I saw it, a warm cloying smell that made me gag.

They were lying on opposite sides of the bed. My mother was naked. I hadn't seen her like that since I was a small child and I would have been embarrassed if I hadn't been so scared. She lay on her back with her right arm hanging carelessly to one side. Her long blond hair fell down her creamy shoulders. There was something broken about her, like a discarded doll. Yet even dead she was beautiful. She had always been the most beautiful woman I knew. It had been a source of pride for me as a child to have a mother who was so beautiful. It was like she was carved from some perfect piece of marble.

Uncle Max was naked too, but he wasn't so beautiful. He looked old in death, his skin was sickly grey. Gentle, aristocratic Max who always gave me books on my birthday, hoping to wake me from my California stupor. He was on his side, one leg dangling off the bed. Max was where the majority of the blood came from. His head lay in a pool of dark, gluttonous red, a corona of death that had spread out onto the white sheets of the bed.

The two people on the bed didn't seem entirely real to me. Growing up in Hollywood, you get used to grown ups playing make-believe. For years, Uncle Max had been the King of Noir at Warner Brothers. He'd made dozens of black and white features full of babes and bodies with torrid scenes on rainy nights just like this one. Max liked to joke that melodrama was his middle name. I kept expecting him to sit up in bed, wipe off the ketchup, and say, "Hey, Jonno, I got you going there, didn't I?"

But he didn't say that. He didn't move. No one moved. Time itself had come to a stop.

That's when I sensed someone behind me. I spun around with a cry. It was Fred Landson—"the Congressman", as my mother liked to call him, a reminder of how far she had come in the world. I hadn't noticed Fred in the darkness. He was sitting on a small white antique chair near the front window deep in the shadows of the room. It was a feminine sort of chair, not meant for a man his size.

Fred was bent forward with his elbows resting on his knees, his face in his hands. In his left hand, he held a pistol with the metal butt rubbing against his cheek. I had seen this particular gun before. It was a 9mm Luger that Fred had taken off a Nazi officer and brought home from the war. He had shown it to me once, trying to be friends.

"I flubbed up, Jonno," he said quietly, staring at the floor. Fred was the sort of denatured 1950s male who said flub instead of fuck, even at a time like this. "I'm sorry, son."

I was too frightened to answer. I could only breathe in shallow bursts, more like panting. Even under normal circumstances, I had always been repelled by Fred. He lacked grace. He was tall and gangly and bony. His face reminded me of a rock fish, the kind I sometimes caught off the beach at Malibu, all spine and mouth. I wished he didn't have the Luger and I hoped he wasn't going to shoot me. I began backing away, very cautiously. Self-preservation is a recurring theme in my family genes.

"Don't go," he said in the same quiet voice, sitting up straight to look at me. "I won't hurt you, son. I'm through hurting people. Please, just stay with me awhile."

Reluctantly, I stopped my backward slide.

"I shot 'em both," he said, as though he couldn't believe himself what he had done. "God knows, I didn't mean to do it. You gotta understand what it was like for me, walking in and finding them together like that. I just went nuts, I guess. You gotta help me now, Jonno. I need you to help me, son."

I wished he'd stop calling me son. I wasn't his son, nor did I wish to be. Still, I managed a sick kind of nod. As long as he had the gun, I was ready to agree to pretty much anything.

"I gotta get away from here, Jonno. Gimme half an hour, son, that's all I want. Half an hour. Then you go ahead and call the cops. Okay?"

I nodded more vigorously. I would have given him forty-five minutes if he'd asked.

"You know what I regret most?" he said. "I regret that I never had a chance to take you fishing on my boat, Jonno. We could have gone to Catalina together. You and me, we could have been pals."

Even in my state of terror, this was a little hard to swallow. That after killing two people, what Fred Landson regretted most was that he had never taken me fishing.

He must have seen it in my eyes, the disgust I felt for him. Fred had always been what in California passed for a winner. But I think for the first time in his life, looking at me, he knew he was defeated.

He smiled and shook his head. It was the saddest smile I ever saw. "Naw, that's okay, Jonno," he said, looking away. "Never mind, son, it was just a thought. What's a half-hour head start? The cops will only get me anyway, in the end."

I was starting to worry that he intended to kill me after all.

"Look, if you leave, I'll wait longer to call," I promised. My voice was hardly more than a raspy croak. "I'll wait until morning. You can get all the way to Mexico."

Uncle Max had made a movie once about a killer escaping to Mexico, which was why this occurred to me. At the age of twelve, most of what I knew in life came from the movies. But Fred only laughed at my suggestion. Maybe he had seen the same movie and didn't like the ending.

"Naw, I've got a better plan," he said. "Something fool-proof. You take care of yourself, son. Never forget this is America, and a boy like you can achieve great things."

Without another word, U.S. Congressman Fred Landson raised the Nazi Luger to the side of his head and blew his brains out. All over my mother's expensive white carpet.

It was foolproof, all right.

*****

I fell apart once Fred was dead. I was only a kid, after all. I screamed, I shouted, I wept. Everyone was dead, bodies everywhere, three down in the love nest, more than I could bear.

In my grief, I must have stumbled too close to one of the candles on the bedside table, knocking it over, because suddenly flames were racing up the canopy of material around my mother's bed. It all happened so fast. In seconds, the whole bedroom was on fire and I knew I had to get out. I ran down the hallway, down the stairs, and out the front door into the rain.

I grabbed my mother's car keys from the foyer table on my way out of the house and the next thing I knew, I was behind the wheel of her Cadillac driving like a maniac out of Beverly Hills and up the Pacific Coast Highway. It was Max who had taught me to drive and I was good at it, though not tonight. I got nearly to Santa Barbara before the cops pulled me over, a twelve-year-old in pajamas who was going eighty miles an hour on the wrong side of the road and crying hysterically. Naturally, they asked me some difficult questions, but I could only cry and shake my head, unable to tell them a thing. I was a little crazy, I guess. It was weeks before I could talk.

Even today, I can't say why I took my mother's Cadillac for a joyride instead of going to the police, except I'd felt an urgent desire to get away. But you know these things already if you've read the newspaper accounts, all the front-page blather that held America spellbound until the next big story came along. They said I was in shock.

Eventually the cops got the story out of me and this is the tale I told, once a small army of psychiatrists had finished with me and I could speak about it—what I saw that night on Valentine's Day 1956, the night my childhood ended. It's a pretty good story, I think, how I woke in the dark hearing gunshots, and over the years I've gotten better at telling it, turning up the narrative steam.

Of course, there's not much in it that's true, except for the dead bodies and the ugly weather, the rain pouring down. But you probably suspected that from the start.

Murder is a lot more complicated than it seems.

Especially the kind you get away with.

10

Part One

The Understudy

One

Krakow, 1940

She was born Sonja Wojtkiewicz, a snarl of consonants from the wrong end of the alphabet that's pronounced something like "Wait-Cabbage." She wasn't French as she later pretended, she was a Polish Jew. This is an important fact to remember. Hollywood was dreamed into existence by people with difficult names who, generally speaking, were running for their lives as fast as their feet could carry them.

For Sonja, fate came knocking on a Sunday afternoon in December, 1940 when she was seventeen years old, comfortably camped in the Royal Box of the Krakow Opera, watching a dress rehearsal on the stage below. It was the week before Christmas and snow had been falling steadily for two days, burying the old city beneath a soft fairytale blanket of enchantment.

She wasn't supposed to be in the Royal Box that Sunday afternoon, not even for a rehearsal. Cesar Psarzyck, the grumpy house manager, always tried to shoo her away from the public parts of the theater. But she was young, she was pretty, and a smile was generally all she needed to get her way. "Oh, very well," the house manager finally agreed, unable to resist her. "But Sonja, don't put your feet up on the upholstery. And please leave everything just the way you found it. Those chairs, you know, are a hundred years old.

Sonja assured him of her profound respect for all things old and decrepit, including the house manager. Then the second he was gone, she made herself as comfortable as a princess, using two of the red velvet armchairs as a make-shift chaise with her feet propped up and her wool cloak spread over her legs as a blanket.

Below her balcony perch, a final run-through of *Carmen* was in progress, an opera she had seen countless times. Her mother was one of the dancers in the chorus—a Spanish dancer complete with castanets, red skirt, and shawl, twirling to the music. In Sonja's opinion, *Carmen* wasn't quite the thing for Polish dancers, who looked ridiculous, face it, dressed up like hot-blooded Spaniards, their big Slavic bodies stuffed into black wigs and toreador pants.

The opera house—the Teatr Slowackiego—was a little jewel box, very pretty, even though the building had fallen into disrepair. If you looked closely, you could see that the red velvet curtains were frayed and the seats were shiny with age. Everything smelled of must and decay. The gilt was chipped, the heavy baroque chandeliers hadn't been cleaned properly since before the war, rats ran about quite freely in the wardrobe rooms.

But Sonja saw only enchantment. This was her private realm and, up to now, even the Nazis had left it alone.

Everyone liked music, after all. Often there were German officers in the audience; once, Governor General Hans Frank himself had come to a performance of Mozart's *Die Zauberflöte*, sitting in the very box where Sonja was now ensconced. Naturally, one had to be careful during times like these; occasionally, one saw quite horrific things on the streets. But for Sonja, life had settled down to an odd normalcy after the first terror of invasion. German soldiers sometimes smiled at her on the streets because she was young and pretty, and though she knew she shouldn't, she occasionally smiled back.

The music stopped in the orchestra pit below as the conductor, the tyrannical Adam Miezcrady, beat his baton against the side of the lectern and screamed at the fat Austrian diva who played Carmen, informing her that she had ruined the entire middle section of her aria. The singer shouted back that in her opinion the tempo was too fast, the orchestra too loud, and a donkey could do a better job conducting Bizet's score. For Sonja, quarrels of this nature were old hat and she paid none of it any mind.

"Measure four-fifty-one, if you please!" the conductor cried irritably. "One-and-two-and-three-and-four—"

The orchestra started up again on the required beat as Sonja followed along. She had the score of *Carmen* open in her lap, a huge dark-red volume that was battered with age. Sonja had borrowed the score from the opera library because she was hoping to convince the conductor to allow her to understudy the title role.

Wanda, the regular understudy, had recently been shot by the Nazis for buying food on the black market. Sonja had been stunned by the news. She herself shopped on the black market whenever she had the money, it could easily have been her who was dead. Poor Wanda! Sonja had wept for an entire day, and had spent a further day in bleak philosophical speculation, wondering what death was like. But by the third day, her thoughts had returned to practical matters. War inured one to such things and, though it was sad, a person had to go on. This was her first real break, and she didn't see how refusing to take advantage of it would bring Wanda back.

Growing up at the opera, a theater brat, Sonja had performed first in various children's parts, then in the chorus, and occasionally as a servant or herald (male or female, take your pick), the kind who appeared for two or three measures to announce an army or a rival suitor at the palace gate. But she was eager for a real role and the chance to understudy Carmen would be a major piece of luck, particularly since this was one of the few leading roles in opera literature written for her range, mezzo-soprano. She had a low voice, which was a disadvantage when it came to getting the best parts. Sonja's voice teacher had been trying to convince her that her range was lower still, contralto, but she refused even to consider such a thing. In opera, the great women's roles were for soprano and she intended to be a star.

Sonja had been practicing relentlessly to reach the higher notes and she was sure she could do it. Now she needed to convince Adam Miezcrady who had the final word on such things. He would be reluctant, she knew that. Besides the question of her range, she was young, she lacked serious experience, all the usual failings. But what choice did he have? With the German occupation, one couldn't just hire a singer from Warsaw or Prague. War had its advantages after all. One had to make do.

Sonja raised her eyes from the score and drifted into fantasy, imagining herself on stage singing the role of Carmen with such passion that the audience sat stunned in their seats, hardly believing their ears.

Who was this girl, this unknown understudy who sang like an angel?

How could she do it?

And listen to those high notes! She had always been a daydreamy child, imagining heroic tales in which she was the central character, the star.

Stretched across her makeshift throne in the Royal Box, Sonja had entirely forgotten the dress rehearsal that was taking place on the stage below. She was dreaming of glory, basking in a world that adored her, when the doors of the theater burst open and German soldiers flooded down the aisles.

An Overnight Sensation

*****

The Nazi soldiers came in a swarm, nearly a dozen of them, their boots shaking the old theater like an earthquake as they made their way down three separate aisles toward the stage. Sonja watched as Henryk Moniuszko, the choreographer, stood from his seat in the fifth row and began to object to the intrusion. "Gentlemen! Please! What can you be thinking of? This is our final dress rehearsal! We . . ."

Henryk was a prissy little man with a toothbrush mustache and high airs. He never finished his sentence. A Nazi officer pointed his pistol at Henryk's head and fired in quite an offhand manner. *Plip!* It was only a small explosion, not nearly as loud as the prop guns that were sometimes used in a performance. But Henryk collapsed like a sack of old clothes between the rows of red velvet seats. On stage, several dancers screamed. The orchestra stopped in mid measure, a wheezing cacophony of dying sound. Adam Miezcrady, the conductor, turned to face the soldiers, his eyes dark with scorn. *Plip!* Another shot from the same pistol and the conductor fell sideways, landing with his head near the chair of the first violin, his baton still in hand.

All this happened so quickly that to Sonja it didn't seem real. In opera, people died with more dramatic flourish. They sang arias as they lay bleeding on stage. In opera, you knew that something significant had occurred. But this . . . it was so ordinary and sudden, it had almost no impact. As Sonja watched, a number of soldiers came on stage with their guns pointed at the dancers and the fat singer who played Carmen. With the bright Spanish costumes and German uniforms mixed all together under the hot glare of theatrical lighting, Sonja almost expected the Nazis to burst into song. But the dancers and singers had their hands raised in confusion, and some of them were now crying and whimpering in several languages.

Slowly, hoping not to draw attention to herself, Sonja lowered herself to the floor of the Royal Box and crouched behind the protection of the balcony parapet on her hands and knees. From below, she heard the short burst of a machine pistol followed by more screams. This was so terrifying that Sonja crept backward into the dusty shadows at the rear of the box and curled up into a fetal position, making herself as small as possible. The carpet beneath her wasn't entirely clean. Her hand touched something sticky, repulsive, spilled champagne or orange squash from long ago. In her over-stimulated state, she thought it might be blood.

The Nazi officer began shouting orders in bad Polish, telling everyone they must raise their hands and leave the theater in an orderly fashion. The Germans always insisted on doing things in an orderly fashion, though their idea of order was utter insanity. Sonja hugged her knees and tried hard not to cry, but she was worried about her mother and the tears came of their own accord. From her hiding place, she heard hurried footsteps, chairs scraping, people in frightened motion. Someone knocked over a cello, probably one of the musicians as he climbed out of the orchestra pit. The cello made an absurd sound as it fell, a hollow woody twang.

The shouts and motion continued for some time. Sonja waited, trying not to make any sound that would give herself away. But now she had to pee. She had to pee terribly. Her bladder didn't know what a bad moment this was to need a bathroom. From the lobby beneath her, she listened as doors opened and closed.

"Anyone else?" a voice called in German. Growing up at the opera among an international crowd, Sonja spoke several languages fluently and understood bits of quite a few more.

"No, we have everyone," another voice answered, also in German.

"What about the balcony?"

Sonja's bladder let go. The fright was too much. It was a crime punishable by death for a Pole to hide from German soldiers. The soldiers were going to come and shoot her. She felt a warm gush between her legs.

But then she heard one of them say, "No . . . there's no one."

"Let's go, then. They'll need us in the square."

They were lazy, that's all. Sonja's life was spared because two soldiers hadn't wished to climb an extra flight of stairs. She listened to their footsteps as they left the theater below. She heard a door close in the lobby, then there was nothing. The opera house was perfectly still, except for the occasional creak and sigh to which old opera houses were prone.

Lying miserably on the floor of the Royal Box in her pee-soaked clothing, Sonja couldn't hear a single living sound.

*****

But was her mother all right? That was the question that tormented her as she lay in hiding on the sticky carpet, imagining the worst.

Throughout her life, it had always been Sonja who kept her scatter-brained mother from harm, who dealt with landlords when the rent was late, who smiled flirtatiously at shopkeepers when credit was needed, who kept their makeshift lives in order.

Her mother, Rozka, was a jolly, fun-loving girl who had given birth to Sonja out of wedlock, cheerfully disregarding convention. "My only religion is dance," Rozka liked to proclaim. "Otherwise I believe in nothing except love and laughter and being as free as the wind!"

Fortunately, free spirits were welcome at the Krakow Opera, as long as there continued to be an audience to pay the bills. Live and let live was the guiding philosophy backstage. No one had a zloty to their name, but that didn't matter. At the opera, make-believe ran amuck. Everyone was a creation of their own design, a character. That was what opera was all about.

Sonja believed herself lucky to have grown up among such a colorful group of rogues, everyone making a great fuss over her. But someone had to be practical, and by necessity—when she wasn't in an alternate universe daydreaming of great deeds—she was the designated worrier of the family, the one who made certain her mother got to rehearsals on time and didn't spend quite all their money on hats and rings and frivolous things.

"My girl is as bossy as a little general," her mother often complained. "But I don't know where I would be without her."

Which was why it was so difficult that they should be separated now, at this terrible moment when she was certain her mother needed her most. Sonja tried to remind herself that her mother was very good with men—this was her one great skill in life. Given half a chance, she would soon have that Nazi pig of an officer up in a private room at the Café Chopin opening bottles of champagne.

After the theater had been quiet for some time, Sonja raised herself to her knees and peered cautiously over the parapet to see what was happening. A work light was shining overhead, but the stage lights were off. The bodies of the choreographer and Adam Miezcrady, the conductor, had vanished. As far as she could see, there wasn't a soul in the theater except herself.

Sonja rose quietly and slipped out from the Royal Box into the hallway, looking about in every direction. The mezzanine lobby was dark except for gray late afternoon light coming through a dusty window at the front of the building. Sonja made her way past the mezzanine bar and crossed the lobby toward an arched window that looked onto the street. From this vantage point, she was able to peer down onto the front steps, the formal entranceway to the theater, and see what was happening outside.

It was snowing heavily and at first she could make out very little. There seemed to be some sort of commotion in the small square that faced the theater. Sonja could see a group of Poles standing dejectedly with their backs to the theater, and beyond them there was a line of German soldiers. All at once, the meaning of the tableau became clear. A public execution was in progress.

Sonja gave a little cry. Forgetting her caution, she stood and raced down the wide curving stairway that led to the main lobby below. She ran across the lobby and out the small door at the side of the box office into the December afternoon. Soft white flakes floated down from the darkening sky, blinding and cold. Sonja barely noticed. She flew down the front steps, bounding perilously over the loose snow until she reached the square. She forced herself to slow down as she made her way to the rear of the crowd, the gathering of people who were silently facing the execution.

All the spectators were covered in snow, Poles and Germans alike. Beyond the line of German soldiers, the small square consisted of a few wintry trees and benches where people liked to sit in the summer. Eight street lamps, wrought iron fixtures from the last century, stood along the walkway that led to the main steps of the theater, four lampposts on each side.

Sonja had passed this little park every day of her life; she had played on these benches, climbed these trees, skipped among these lampposts. Now seven bodies dangled from the lampposts, each by a short length of rope. The victims were stripped to their underwear and rags had been stuffed in their mouths to keep them from crying out final patriotic slogans. The dead no longer looked entirely human, more like puppets in some bizarre children's theater. Their hands had been tied behind their backs, but their legs dangled free.

"Don't look, Sasha," a voice said softly coming up behind her, addressing her by her childhood nickname. It was Julka the Gypsy, whom she had known practically forever.

"*Why?*" she whispered without turning to him. "Why are they doing this?"

"Why? It's because they don't trust artists. They don't want Poland to have a culture of our own. They want us to be slaves, nothing more. Close your eyes, Sasha. You don't want to see this."

But Sonja was determined to see. One by one, she recognized the dead. The first figure she saw was Krzysztof, a young music student who played bassoon in the orchestra and had sometimes flirted with her. He was hanging from the lamppost closest to the theater steps. Sonja worried about the rag they had stuffed in his mouth. There must have been a terrible moment before death, gagging in terror. But now he was almost peaceful, like a dead chicken hanging in a butcher's window.

Sonja's eyes went up and down the two lines of lampposts. She saw Grisha, the viola player who had always been so proud to tell people that he had studied in Berlin. And Bela, the French horn player who had sometimes pestered Sonja's mother for a date. And Thaddeus, an overweight fellow from the business office who no one had much liked. And Stanislaw, who played the trumpet and often showed up drunk to work. And Josef, the old man who guarded the stage door and was always so nice to everyone.

And then she saw her mother.

Later, Sonja realized that she had seen her mother from the start, her eyes drawn to the familiar form, but had simply refused to acknowledge the fact. Her mother had been stripped to her petticoat and her black wig was pulled from her head to reveal her lovely dark blond hair. She dangled lifelessly from the rope, her head lolled vacantly to one side. It was her mother, yet not her mother at all.

Sonja's eyes blinked furiously. She couldn't stop blinking.

"Sasha, for God's sake, you don't want to remember her this way!" Julka said from behind her shoulder.

Sonja stood stunned, disbelieving. She heard a scream and turned to watch as two soldiers dragged a young woman, a dancer from the chorus, toward the last remaining lamppost. Her name was Oda. She was new to the company, from Warsaw, and Sonja didn't know her well. Once she had heard her mother say that Oda would spread her legs for anyone, man, woman, or beast. But there would be no more leg-spreading now. Oda had been stripped down to her slip, half-naked, a final indecency, and she was shivering uncontrollably. Sonja watched as her hands were tied behind her back.

"Long live Poland!" the girl cried hysterically. The soldiers hadn't been fast enough to stop her, busy tying her hands. "Long live . . ." But that was all she managed. A German officer slapped her across the face with his gloved hand and then a soldier stuffed a rag into her mouth. A noose was put around Oda's neck, and she was strung up quickly onto the lamppost with no further ceremony. The girl struggled and jerked, dangling from the rope, kicking out with her unbound feet as though she were trying to run in place.

It took a long while for Oda to die. She would be still for a moment, but just when Sonja thought it was over, the body on the end of the rope jerked and shuddered in her death spasms, refusing to accept the finality of her end. Sonja stared at her until the girl was quiet, her head hanging brokenly to one side.

At last, she forced her eyes back toward the dangling shape of her mother. "Oh, Mama!" she whispered. As she watched, the German officer gave an order for the crowd to disperse. The sullen group of Poles at the edge of the steps began melting away into the snowy afternoon.

"They're saying we're to leave now," Julka told her, pulling gently on her arm.

But Sonja didn't move. A great surge of anger was welling up inside of her. It was beyond belief what these Nazi monsters had done, killing her mother, hanging these people she loved. Her anger kept building, growing like a wave.

"Sasha, please. It's dangerous to stay."

"You leave if you want."

"Listen to me. It's awful, but there's nothing we can do. Please, let's go."

Sonja barely heard him. All her attention was focused on the German who had slapped Oda, the officer who appeared to be in charge. He was a stout, red-faced Nazi, overfed and arrogant, stuffed like a sausage into his greatcoat. Sonja decided that somehow she would kill him. She would wait until the crowd had finished clearing, then rush forward and stab him in the eye with the pin she used as a clasp to keep her cloak closed. It would be a dreadful death. The German had a pistol in his holster; he was physically stronger, a man. But God would give her unspeakable power for just this instant. Nothing would stop her. One sharp jab of the pin through his eye into his brain and he would fall into a bloody heap in the snow. Then, mercifully, the remaining soldiers would kill her. She didn't mind that. In fact, she longed for death.

"Sasha! This is madness! We must leave!" Julka tried to pull her away but Sonja shook herself violently free of him.

The crowd had finally cleared. There was no one now between her and the German officer. He must have felt her murderous stare for he turned and studied her curiously, a pretty Polish girl who lingered in the company of an old man when the others had gone.

"Please, Sasha, we'll go to my flat. I'll make us a good strong drink," Julka whispered anxiously in her ear. "Listen to me. I know what you're feeling, of course I do. But Mama would not want you to die. You see that, don't you? Mama is looking down from heaven and she wants you to be safe."

"Leave me alone," she said.

The Nazi was regarding her now with tolerant amusement. Without warning, he did a clownish thing. He lolled his head to one side and raised his hand to imitate a rope, pretending he was hanging. The other soldiers laughed, finding the crude joke uproarious.

Now! she thought. Now I will spring like a lion and kill him!

She was going to do it. She had the pin in her hand, she was ready to rush forward. But then to her great shame, her courage faltered. She didn't want to die. Not today, not ever. She wanted to live. Every corpuscle of her being insisted on it.

Without a word, she turned and walked away. Julka took her arm and followed, greatly relieved. They shuffled through the snow together toward Pijarska Street pursued by the coarse laughter of the soldiers.

"I have the very last bottle of Scotch whisky in all Krakow," Julka was telling her. "We'll get ourselves good and drunk, I promise you."

Would they? Would whisky from Scotland ease the crushing sorrow that was like being buried alive? Sonja didn't think so.

As she walked away, she expected a bullet in the back at any moment. They could easily kill her still, just for sport. The Nazis didn't need a reason. Let fate decide, she thought. Kill me now, and I will accept it. Or let me live, and I will triumph. I don't care either way, I swear I don't.

But the bullet didn't come. The soldiers let her go. Perhaps they'd had enough killing for one afternoon, or maybe they were simply in a hurry to get back to their barracks. It was impossible to say.

Sonja, for whatever reason, was destined to be a survivor.

Two

The Journey South:
Eastern Europe, 1941

During the years of the German Occupation, the Polish resistance— the Polskie Państwo Podziemne, a loose association of partisan cells— maintained a secret route of travel to England, where a free Polish government-in-exile had been established under General Władysław Sikorski.

Initially, the underground route passed westward through France, but after the fall of Paris in June 1940, it was necessary to make a much longer journey south through the length of Eastern Europe and then proceed as hidden cargo in a ship, either from the Black Sea or one of the thousand coastal inlets of Greece.

It was never an easy journey, and for Sonja and Julka it meant seven months of hard travel in which the prospect of death was never far away. Sasha—as Julka called her, the childhood nickname everyone used— arranged their escape from Poland with the help of one of her mother's old lovers, a baritone at the opera who had joined the Communist partisans shortly after the 1939 invasion. In late January, 1941, on the coldest day of the year, Sasha and Julka traveled to the Czech border hidden in the back of a truck that was carrying filthy sacks of half-rotten potatoes. The trip took three days on back country roads, cramped and nearly suffocating beneath the heavy sacks, and once they reached the border, they had to wait another two days in a bitterly cold peasant hut before a Czech partisan appeared from the forest on the other side of the border and took them across.

For the next seven months, they proceeded in this fashion, passed south from one cell of partisan fighters to the next. Sometimes they remained with a group for several weeks, other times it was only an hour. Occasionally they traveled on their own, with instructions to seek the proprietor of a certain shop or farm once they reached a designated village. Secrecy was vital for everyone involved, for to be caught meant immediate execution.

They traveled by every means imaginable—truck, car, hay wagon, bus, boxcar, horseback, bicycle, and by foot. In Czechoslovakia, they crossed a mountain on skis, which was a challenge for Sasha who had never skied before and had to learn quickly. Julka, on the other hand, did surprisingly well—he claimed to have spent a winter skiing in St. Moritz in 1922, which Sasha knew was nonsense, one of his many inventions, but he had obviously learned to ski somewhere.

For the rest of her life, Sasha would remember the cold, the lice, the days when they went without a thing to eat. The constant danger put a numbing shroud of anxiety over every moment of the day. You never knew if you would still be alive at nightfall. There were times when she was so cold and tired, she almost wished the Nazis would catch them just so she could put an end to the struggle of trying to stay alive.

They kept going, town after town, through blizzards, road-blocks, through mud and rain and misery, a Gypsy and a Jew on the run down the length of Hitler's Europe. Luckily, she was blonde and fair as her mother had been, and she had al-ways been able to pass herself off as Gentile. Some Scandi-navian pirate must have come raping and pillaging southward into Poland at a distant point in her family tree, which couldn't have been pleasant at the time. But time proved its ironies, and the rape of long ago was providential now. She didn't look Jewish.

As for Julka, he pretended he had an Italian grandfather as an explanation for his swarthy complexion, though some-times he forgot and told people his ancestors were Spanish. In any case, he didn't look like a Gypsy any more than Sasha looked Jewish, and neither one of them intended to set the record straight. Why should they? In Sasha's opinion, the world was not such a fine place that one needed to worry over a few strategic lies.

"Do not be discouraged, my darling! We will get to Lon-don, by crook or by book," Julka often proclaimed in English when the going was rough, mangling the expression with his usual disregard of precise fact.

Hook or by crook," she corrected. Her English was better than his.

"Yes, yes, isn't that what I said? Crook, book, look, rook . . . what a funny language English is, all those vowels! Oh, we'll be eating steak and kidney pie in no time!"

Julka had begun to irritate her with nearly everything he said and did. Sometimes it seemed to Sasha that if the Germans didn't kill him, she might be tempted to do so herself.

*****

Ever since they left Krakow, Julka had been a source of worry. He complained about everything—the food, the cold, the bathroom arrangements (non-existent, for the most part), even the lack of respect they received from the often crude partisan fighters who didn't appear to care that they were highly cultivated persons from the great city of Krakow. More irritating still, he reminisced endlessly on the comforts they were missing—soft beds, fabulous seven-course meals he had once eaten in Paris and Madrid, hot baths and clean clothes, on and on.

"Julka! Please shut up!" she told him on more than one occasion. "I don't want to think about these things that we don't have!"

"Yes, my dear. But did I ever tell you about the time I was in the south of France?" And before Sasha could stop him, he was off on one of his raptures, remembering swimming pools and terraced gardens and dinners overlooking the Mediterranean.

Sasha couldn't bear it. Hard travel puts a strain on the closest friendship, and there were many times when she was tempted to abandon him. He slowed her down. She would have been able to reach London in half the time without him. One night after a quarrel, she actually began walking off by herself, but she turned back after several minutes. Annoying though he was, Julka was all she had left of her childhood and the journey would have been unbearably lonely without him.

Julka Jabolonski—Julka the Gypsy, as people called him—had been a Krakow fixture, the proprietor of the Café Chopin on Florianska Street, a smoky, chaotic tavern where the opera company liked to gather after rehearsals and performances to enjoy champagne dinners, raucous conversation, and only the occasional fist-fight. It was said that Julka had won the Café Chopin in a card game and it was popular with the opera company in part because he was so generous with credit, frequently allowing singers to pay off their bar bill with an aria or two—there was a decent upright piano near the bar, and it was often used. There was never a dull evening at the Chopin.

Sasha had begun going to the café early in her childhood, dragged along by her mother, often falling asleep near the ceramic stove on a pile of coats. Julka had made it a point to look after her, watching out so that none of his drunken customers tumbled over her make-shift bed. He had spoiled her shamelessly, feeding her anything she wanted from the kitchen as well as sarsaparilla concoctions from the bar.

Julka wasn't handsome, but Sasha had always found him a striking figure. He had a gaunt face with sharply pronounced cheekbones, jet black hair that fell to his shoulders in a theatrical manner, and intense black eyes. In Sasha's childhood, he had always dressed beautifully in dark suits of the best material and he was seldom without a Russian cigarette in a long ebony holder that he held between his tapered yellow fingers. She had believed him to be the most elegant man in Krakow.

It was unfortunate that he was a Gypsy, which in Krakow was considered even worse than being Jewish. But Julka had made himself an exception to the rule, the sort of Gypsy people wished to know, telling themselves how progressive they were, free of prejudice. Of course, it helped that he owned a fashionably seedy café where artists, poets, and singers liked to gather, and that he was never stingy when it came to opening up a bottle or two on the house.

Sasha had adored the funny old man from the start. By the age of eight or nine, she often walked to the café by herself to spend afternoons with Julka playing cards. He taught her all sorts of tricks, how to deal cards from the bottom of the deck and other ways to cheat, and they had hilarious games together, cheating and finding each other out. A prissy set designer once suggested that there must be something fishy about such a friendship between a pretty little girl and a middle-aged man, a Gypsy, no less, a bachelor who had never married. But the relationship was entirely innocent. Julka was simply a childish man, while Sasha on her part had been a precociously adult-like child. They met somewhere in the middle and enjoyed each other's company immensely.

But all this changed when the Nazi administration in Wawel Castle closed the Café Chopin as a potential gathering spot for degenerates and partisans. Displaced from the usual props of his life, Julka had become almost another person. He was only in his mid-fifties—he had always refused to tell Sasha his exact age—but suddenly he seemed quite fragile. Shortly after they escaped from Poland, he came down with a case of flu so bad that for several days Sasha had worried he might die. The illness couldn't have come at a worse time. In order to nurse him back to health, she was forced to leave the small band of Czech partisans with whom they were traveling and remain hidden in a boxcar on the outskirts of Ostrava, a polluted industrial town. Not only was this uncomfortable, it was dangerous as well, for the rail yards were patrolled by German soldiers.

By the time Julka was well enough to travel again, he was thin as a stick and Sasha was shocked to discover, that almost overnight, he had become a befuddled old man. This left Sasha as the one who must worry and plan for both of them.

Even after his recovery, they lost several more weeks in Ostrava before they were able to reconnect with the partisan
fighters whose help was needed to continue their journey
south. Julka hardly seemed to notice, caught in his reveries of
better times.

As they traveled from one group of resistance fighters to
the next, Julka told everyone who would listen that Sasha was
"a world-famous singer"—the sort of wild exaggeration to
which he was prone—and often at night, after a few glasses
of vodka, the men would shout and clap their hands and demand a song. Sasha gave it her best, singing *a capella* every
aria and old Slavic folk song she knew, sometimes making up
lyrics on the spot when she couldn't remember the proper
words.

The men plied her with vodka to keep her going, and
though in the past Sasha had been disdainful of alcohol, she
found it welcome now. Flushed with inspiration, too tired to
care if she hit the right notes, she sang with all her heart until
tears came to the eyes of the war-weary soldiers who listened
to her. It was an odd power to possess: to be able to make hard
men cry. Sasha discovered that her voice could touch the sor-
rows and longings that were buried deep in men's hearts, and
she liked doing this. She liked it very much indeed.

The partisans, of course, were fascinated by the young girl
who sang so beautifully, and this presented dangers of a different kind. They were still in Czechoslovakia when Sasha

came up with the idea of telling people that Julka was her father, hoping this would discourage the drunken men who stumbled her way. At night, when the singing was over, she slept close to Julka in crowded rooms—the more crowded the better—with his arm around her and a knife in a sheath strapped to her leg beneath her dress, alert to every sound. A knife wasn't much protection against men with guns, but she didn't intend to be raped or murdered without putting up a fight.

When it came to sex, Sasha let her guard down only once, in Budapest with a handsome young fighter who declared that he was a poet. His name was Attila—Attila the Hun, he liked to joke—and he was dark and pale and romantic in an ardently half-starved way. They were staying in a crowded safe house in the Pest part of the city and, though there were few opportunities for intimacy, she managed to lose her virginity in a utility closet leaning against a sack of laundry with her skirt hiked up around her waist. It wasn't quite the magic moment that Sasha had always imagined, but it wasn't so bad either. At least if the Germans got her, she wouldn't die a virgin.

Attila swore that he loved her more than poetry, more than life itself, and he asked her to stay in Budapest and be his wife. But she was already bored with him.

"We will die together fighting the Germans!" he declared grandly, believing this would impress her. "I will die gladly if you are by my side!"

Die gladly? How idiotic! Sasha thought.

Personally, she wasn't ready to die in the least, and she certainly didn't plan to be at Attila's side when the unhappy moment arrived.

She intended to use all her wits and cunning, and any other means at her disposal, to reach London and get the better of a world gone mad.

*****

In March, Sasha and Julka found themselves held up in a small farmhouse in the southern countryside of Romania for nearly a month by bad weather and six ragged partisan fighters who showed little interest in helping them continue their journey. The partisans were unfriendly and suspicious, and to make matters worse, they spoke only Romanian, one of the few Eastern European languages of which neither Sasha nor Julka had a smattering.

Only the leader of the group, a wild looking man in his late forties, knew a few words of Russian, which Sasha could understand well enough to carry on an ungrammatical conversation. "*Kogda mui uydem?*" she kept asking—when will we leave? But the man was a brute, more like a hairy animal than a human being, and he replied only with a grunt. His name was Boian and Sasha found it irritating that he showed no interest in her. She wasn't accustomed to men ignoring her.

One evening, after Boian had ignored her for several days, Sasha lost her temper.

"*Kogda?*" she demanded angrily, then repeated it with increasing frustration, the key word that she knew he must understand: When, when, *when?*

"When it is safe, not before," he replied unexpectedly in English.

Sasha stared at him in surprise. She and Julka often spoke together in English, practicing for when they would arrive in London, and it was disconcerting that this barbarous-looking fellow might have understood their conversations.

"I must get to London as quickly as possible," she told him, now that they could finally speak. She studied his impassive face and added: "I'm carrying important papers that I must deliver to British intelligence."

This was a lie. Sasha carried no papers at all, important or otherwise. But she didn't mind lying if it meant that Boian would agree to help.

The farmhouse was very simple, only two small rooms with a single wood burning stove and an outhouse in back. Boian paused to poke a straw into the fire and light a loosely packed cigarette before he answered.

"Ah, well, important papers! That puts a different light on it. Still, I think we'd better see these papers of yours before we do anything hasty." For a wild-looking brute, his English was nearly perfect.

Sasha was taken aback. "I'm not allowed to show them to anyone," she told him. "Certainly not to a person like you."

He smiled very slightly. "Then we'll get you across the border when I say it's safe, not before. I'm not going to risk my men just because you're impatient. Meanwhile, you can make yourself useful. This house wants a good cleaning, starting with the toilet. When you're finished with that, my men need their clothes repaired. You'll find needles and thread in the next room."

Sasha made an effort to control her fury. "The papers are in my head," she said. "I've memorized everything."

"Oh, is that so?"

"Yes, that's so. The Germans are building a secret weapon at Wieliczka, in the old salt mines outside of Krakow, and I must get news of this to London as quickly as possible. It's an atomic-powered weapon," she added, giving her imagination free rein. "Every day that passes will help the Germans win the war."

Boian laughed and said something in Romanian to the other five men in the room. Sasha didn't understand the comment, but she knew it was derogatory from the unpleasant snickering.

"Well, fancy that—an atomic-powered weapon!" he said once he'd had his laugh. "And how would a girl like you know about such things?"

"As it happens, it's because a German officer took me to Wieliczka and showed me the factory," she answered haughtily. "He was hoping to impress me. The Nazis have a thousand people working day and night on this weapon in a cavern hundreds of feet below ground where they are safe from Allied bombs. I saw it myself."

Sasha's lie had a small foundation. In Krakow there had been rumors flying for months that the Germans were using the ancient salt mine for some nefarious purpose, hiding their activity deep below ground where they were safe from prying eyes. The Romanian leader gave her a closer look.

"And what's the name of this Nazi officer who took you to Wieliczka? I know quite a bit about these things, so please tell me the truth."

"If you must know, it was SS Obersturmbannführer Liebehenschel," she told him. Herr Liebehenschel was an important SS colonel who Sasha had seen once in a motorcade on Florianska Street, though she had never actually met him, and he had certainly never taken her to Wieliczka. "I met him at the opera. He had rather a crush on me, you see, and used to send me flowers. A horrible man, of course, but I had a friend in the resistance who convinced me to cultivate his interest in order to find out what I could. It wasn't easy, but I did my patriotic duty."

She had Boian's attention, at least. He studied her in silence.

"It's useful to be an attractive girl," she went on. "But of course, you wouldn't know about things like that. I promise you that what I am saying is true. Do you think I would make up something like this? The Germans are building a terrible weapon underground and I must get to England to warn them and tell them what I've seen."

Boian wiped his nose on the back of his filthy hand. It was hard to say how much he believed of Sasha's tale, if he believed any of it at all. But she had apparently created enough doubt in his mind that at last he nodded and said he would get her across the border into Bulgaria as quickly as possible.

In time, Sasha would become more adept at telling her fanciful tale about the secret atomic-powered weapon being built at Wieliczka, and the German SS colonel who fell so hard for her that he was willing to risk the entire war effort in order to impress her. But for now, at least, she had achieved her goal. They would be getting out of Romania, a country she had come to loathe.

As far as she was concerned, there was no time to lose. That night, Julka had a coughing fit in which he spat up blood and Sasha knew she had to get them to England quickly.

*****

Two days later, Boian and two of his men drove Sasha and Julka for several hours on a back road toward the border, passing through a dense pine forest. The road became pro-gressively worse as they travelled south, alternating from thick mud to deep snow drifts. Finally, the road gave out al-together, covered with too much snow to continue.

Boian said that the border was less than a kilometer away and from here they must continue on their own through the mud and snow. The local people sometimes came this way to visit relatives in the village on the Bulgarian side of the bor-der. All they had to do was follow the wagon path alongside a fast-running creek; when they came out of the forest onto an open meadow, they would know they were in Bulgaria. Be-yond the meadow, they must climb a hill toward an aban-doned barn and from here they would find a road that would take them another kilometer to a tiny hamlet where they must look for the proprietor of the town's only tavern. This would be their next contact for the journey south.

Wet snow began falling as Sasha and Julka set out upon the slushy path through a forest of huge old trees that creaked in the wind. Sasha was concerned for Julka, that the hike would prove too much for him. But he appeared to be in par-ticularly good spirits today and assured her that he was fine.

"Ah, the woods on a snowy afternoon! Just like a Christ-mas card!" he said happily. "Did I ever tell you about the Christmas I spent on Christmas Island in the South Seas?"

She laughed irritably. "Please, Julka. You were never in the South Seas. And I am certain there is no place called Christmas Island."

"Oh, but there is, my dear, and I assure you I traveled there when I was a young man. The native customs are fascinating. No one wears a stitch of clothing and when one of the native boys wants to show that he's interested in a girl, do you know what he does?"

"I can't imagine," Sasha told him acidly, though in fact she was curious to know the answer

"He makes a little ring of flowers and puts it around his penis."

"Oh, please!"

"No, this is the gospel truth. And when a boy and girl kiss on Christmas Island, guess how they do it? They rub noses."

"You're thinking of Eskimos, my dear Papa. When you make up ridiculous stories, you must learn to keep your facts straight."

"No, I assure you this is what they do. They rub noses and say, 'Gula gula, bora bora.' Which in Christmas Islandese means, 'I like you so much I think we should fuck.'"

This was so ridiculous that Sasha had her first good laugh in many weeks. Her spirits lifted and for the moment it felt good to be traipsing with Julka through a snowy forest talking of silly things. But then the road turned, following the contour of the little creek, and they came out onto an open meadow that was covered with snow.

Sasha stopped so suddenly that she bit her tongue. "Wait!" she hissed at Julka, grabbing his arm. There were two German soldiers with rifles slung over their shoulders standing next to a jeep on a road on the far side of the meadow. At first she thought they might slip back into the forest, but the soldiers had already seen them and there was nothing to do but go forward and brave it out.

"I'll do the talking," she told Julka. "We're peasants, that's all. We're going to visit our uncle Ivan across the border in the village there."

They looked like peasants, at least. After months of travel, their clothes were little more than rags and their faces were stained with dirt and exposure that would take more than a few baths to remove. Sasha adjusted a dark shawl about her head and they made their way forward to where the soldiers were standing.

"Good afternoon, sirs," she said in the sort of pidgin German she imagined a Romanian peasant might know. "We go see uncle, yes? . . . across . . . across to village, yes?"

But Sasha knew from the start that this wasn't going well. The soldiers were young and loutish and looked as though they had been conscripted from the underbelly of some ugly city. They were clearly bored, patrolling a remote stretch of the border where few people came. Worse yet, they had been drinking. There was an open bottle of schnapps propped up on the hood of their jeep.

"Ah, look at the little blond number!" one of them said. "Let's have ourselves some fun, eh?"

"But she's filthy. You don't want lice, do you?" the other said more skeptically.

"We'll have her suck us off. Come on, Ernst, I'm horny as a pig. She can do me first, then you . . . then me again a second time. We need some fun out of this fucking war!"

Sasha kept her face blank, pretending she didn't understand. But she understood perfectly, and it was horrible.

"My papa," she said helplessly in her bad German. "My papa and I . . . we visit uncle. You are very nice soldier boys. Good boys," she repeated, hoping to make it true.

"Look, you suck my thing, then my friend's thing . . . then we let you go see uncle," the first soldier said, mimicking her pidgin German. "Otherwise we shoot you bang-bang dead. Both of you. You understand?"

She glanced at Julka who was staring at the ground unhappily but not offering any help.

"You understand?" the soldier repeated, taking her by the arm and forcing her to her knees. "Otherwise we shoot you bang-bang dead."

In case she didn't understand, he unbuttoned his fly and pushed his smelly limp penis against her face.

"You understand, Fraulein?"

What could Sasha do? They were alone at the edge of a remote forest with two soldiers who could kill them as easily as they could let them live. They might be young and loutish, but for the moment they had the power of gods.

Sasha did what was necessary to live; that's what she told herself later. Kneeling in the snow with her knees wet and cold, she took the flaccid penis that was against her face and put it into her mouth, using her hand around the shaft to pump him up until he had an erection. She did her work efficiently, wishing for it to be over as quickly as possible. The soldier was far from clean and his underwear smelled of urine and traces of shit.

He came quickly with a groan and a little laugh, flooding her mouth with his sperm. Sasha spat it out onto the snow and then, without moving, found the second penis in front of her, already hard. She did her work again, closing her mind, closing off her senses. She did what was required of her, that was all. She let herself be an impersonal machine.

She was aware that Julka was standing only a few feet away with his eyes averted. Every now and then she heard him sigh. But he did nothing to stop her, for to stop would have meant death for them both on this obscure stretch of the Bulgarian border.

The second soldier came in her mouth, and then—true to his word— the first soldier demanded that she do him a second time. This took longer, but at last he finished.

Sasha stood from her knees and, without a word, without once looking at either soldier, she began walking up the hill toward the far side of the border, aware that Julka was following a few paces behind.

Once again, she expected a bullet in the back at any moment. But the soldiers were laughing, in high good spirits after their exploit, and they let them go. "Come back this way, my little slut, and we'll do it again!" one of the men cried out merrily after her. "Next time I'll fuck you in the ass!"

As soon as they were in the forest out of sight from the soldiers, Sasha held herself against the limb of a tree and vomited into the snow. She did this several times, gagging miserably, then she scooped up a handful of snow and did her best to wash away the taste of sperm and vomit from her mouth.

"You know what I've been thinking, Sasha?" Julka said as they continued through the forest toward the Bulgarian village ahead. "Once we reach London, I'll resurrect the Great Jabolonski, the famous Polish spiritualist. Did I ever tell you about him?"

Sasha didn't answer. She was unable even to shake her head.

"A peek into the crystal ball!" he went on. "Séance by special appointment! Not cheap, mind you, not cheap at all. But the rich don't mind paying for their pleasures. Tarot cards, magic potions for every occasion, the I Ching, the Kabala—oh, I made a fortune with the Great Jabolonski in Barcelona when I was temporarily without funds and had to come up with something quick. It will be just the thing for London. We'll dress you up in something sexy and we'll positively rake in the money, my dear. In six months time, we'll be living at the Ritz!"

Sasha turned to regard him. At first she believed he was simply trying to distract her and make her laugh. But as he continued to describe his scheme to make money in London—the Great Jabolonski and his Beautiful Daughter—Sasha began to suspect that he had already forgotten what she had so recently endured for the sake of their survival.

Julka was telling her how they would put on a perfect show—the right costumes, subtle lighting, perhaps even music to create the proper mystical effect—when he started coughing hard into his handkerchief, as though his ruined body could no longer sustain the weight of his imagination.

Sasha refused to look at his handkerchief to see if he were coughing up more blood. She didn't want to know for there was nothing she could do.

Twilight was falling quickly as they trudged through the snowy forest. In the distance a wolf howled and the temperature began to drop. Sasha took Julka's arm and led him toward the village that was ahead on the road.

"Come along," she said wearily, taking much of his weight on her shoulder. "It's almost nightfall and we need to find somewhere safe."

Three

London, 1942

She sang open vowels in her low mezzo-soprano, meandering in and out of the Lydian mode. The melody was a ghostly hint of a part she had once sung in *Suor Angelica*, the girl's chorus, in which she was supposed to be a nun.

"*Aaaaaaaaaaa . . . oooooooooooo . . . aaaaaaaaah*," she sang fervently.

The result was quasi-Gregorian chant with a bit of Puccini thrown in for good luck. The effect was enhanced by the fact that she was half-naked and every man in the room was trying to ogle a better look at her.

Sonya Jabolonski (as she called herself in London, Sonya with a *y* rather than a *j*) stood in the candlelight of a Mayfair dining room chanting gibberish while Count Julka Jabolonski—the Great Jabolonski—led a séance to contact John, the dead son of Mrs. Harcourt, killed at Dunkirk. There was a good living to be made with séances in London in 1942, a huge number of dead souls to contact if one possessed the proper skill.

Sasha's job was to stand before the group at the start of the session and cleanse the air with the purity of her voice. This, at least, was the avowed purpose of her presence. Her real job was sheer theatrics. She was very pleasant to look at under-dressed in a diaphanous robe, faux-Greek, wearing nothing underneath, the contours of her body visible if you caught her at just the right angle with the candlelight coming from be-hind.

She told people she was seventeen years old, a small fib designed to stress the illusion of innocence. In fact, time didn't stand still, not even for Sasha, and she had just turned nineteen that October. She had become good at telling "sto-ries," as she liked to call them. Truth was beauty, she knew that very well. Unless you were struggling to stay alive, and then it seemed to Sasha that God gave you a special dispen-sation to tell any whopper you pleased.

Sasha had lost twenty pounds in the nearly two years since she and Julka had escaped from Poland, shedding the last pudgy remnants of childhood. She had become a great beauty—everyone said so, and it was true. She had thick dark blond hair that fell nearly to her waist, wide Slavic cheek-bones, and a complexion that blazed with life, a vital animal glow. Her eyes were hazel, a mixture of different flecks of green, blue, brown, and gold. But green was the color that predominated, and few men could resist her when she turned her eyes their way.

She stood with her arms raised, a devout look on her face, eyes lifted to some distant heaven, while the Great Jabolonski sat with the others at the table staring moodily into a large crystal ball. Count Julka Jabolonski and his daughter had appeared in London a year earlier, part of the flotsam of war, the jetsam of European devastation, and, between the two of them, they had already succeeded in leaving a swathe of broken hearts and empty wallets in their wake.

Of course, there were cynics who saw through them, who claimed Julka was neither a count nor Poland's most celebrated spiritualist. But who could say for certain? Poland was far away, lost to the Nazis, and it was hard to check on such things during a time of war. Meanwhile, reality was up for grabs, and one needed to make a living.

*****

The séance began at midnight, generally a safe hour, between the first and second wave of German bombs. Mr. and Mrs. Harcourt, tonight's customers, lived on the top floor of an elegant four-story building on Curzon Street, a good address, though not Belgravia. The top floor made Sasha anxious because it was a long way to run to the shelter if the sirens sounded. Mr. Harcourt was a banker of some sort, upper middle class rather than of the truly rich. Still, the dining room was opulent enough: a spacious room with a pretentious crystal chandelier and the usual sort of horsy paintings on the walls, country scenes of a fantasy England that had ceased to exist years ago, if it had ever existed at all. Heavy dark purple drapes kept the candlelight from spilling out from the window, or there would be an air-raid warden knocking on the door.

Along with the Great Jabolonski, there were seven people seated around the crystal ball staring into the mysterious refractions of light—four busty women and two smaller men, all of them well advanced into middle-age. Sonya didn't like the English very much. They seemed to her a cold people, dull and conventional.

When her part was through—a long final vowel that she let float into the room and fade—she withdrew from the dining room into the hallway. Behind her, she could hear Julka launching into his performance—*yes, I am starting to see something now! Who is that in the crystal with a message for the living? Is that you, John Harcourt?* But she had heard all this many times before and it had begun to bore her.

Sasha prowled restlessly down the hallway until she came to an open door that led to a drawing room where a single electric lamp was burning. The room seemed over-furnished to her, fancy but tasteless. There were too many uncomfortable-looking chairs, too many surfaces cluttered with framed photographs of dreary people who were probably all dead— they looked dead, even in the pictures.

Sasha's eyes fell upon a small silver cigarette lighter on one of the tables and a quiver of temptation ran up her spine. The lighter was small enough to fit into the palm of her hand.

If she could get it into her coat pocket in the hall, it would make an easy few pounds on Portobello Road. Unfortunately, London was expensive and she and Julka were in need of money. Séances paid well when you could arrange one, but the work was unpredictable, and meanwhile, they owed their landlord a week's rent.

Sasha stared at the silver lighter undecided, caught between longing and fear. Did she dare? What if she were discovered? She was certain these rich people didn't need the lighter nearly as much as she did. There was an ultimate justice on her side; the justice of need. But the British could be stuffy about such matters and she knew she must be careful.

Sasha had just picked up the cigarette lighter from the table when she heard a sound behind her.

"Well, well, my girl. Don't you stay for the spirits?"

Sasha turned with a strained smile, the lighter in hand. It was Mr. Harcourt, the banker. He was in his mid-fifties, tall, paunchy, nearly bald, dressed in a dark gray three-piece suit. He had a red face and a bulbous nose. A respectable figure, she supposed. But he had mean eyes that were set too closely together.

"Oh, I've seen my father do his magic many times. I thought I'd have a smoke," she replied, making an effort to calm her racing heart. She held up the lighter she had hoped to steal. "Do you have a cigarette, perhaps?"

His smile had a cunning edge. Was he suspicious? Sasha wasn't sure. "Of course, my dear," he answered, reaching for a silver case on the same table where the lighter had been. It was lucky that men enjoyed giving cigarettes to pretty girls. Sasha took a Player's from the box while Mr. Harcourt relieved her fingers of the lighter, pressed the lever and produced a small flame for her. When her cigarette was lit, he slipped the lighter into his own jacket pocket. Perhaps he was suspicious after all. Sasha inhaled greedily. She liked English cigarettes. They were a big improvement over the sawdust people were smoking in Poland.

"But you are missing the séance, Mr. Harcourt," she chided.

"Oh, I don't believe in that balderdash, my dear. Not a bit. My wife does, of course, but that's her business. I figure, if it comforts her, why not? Meanwhile, I was more interested in getting to know *you*."

His small hard eyes left her face to roam freely up and down her costume. Ah, that's it, she thought. This had nothing to do with the silver lighter. Sasha was relieved. Still, it was not pleasant to be inspected as though she were a Piccadilly whore.

"You know, that's a *very* intriguing outfit you're wearing," he told her. "I'm sure a lot of men have told you this. You're a remarkably pretty girl."

"Thank you, Mr. Harcourt. How nice of you to say so."

"I say, why don't you call me Edward. No need to be so formal. Is there, my dear?"

"Edward," she repeated. It struck her as a dull name for a dull man. But she smiled because she must.

"Where did you say you were from, you and your father?"

"We are from Krakow. It is the city of Copernicus. Have you been there?"

"Afraid not," he said with an unpleasant laugh. As though it were absurd to imagine a proper Englishman like himself in such a dubious place. "Your English is splendid, what? Where did you ever learn to speak so good."

Well, she wanted to say. *Speak so well.* But she resisted.

"I spent my childhood with an opera company," she explained. "My mother was a famous singer. Before the war, before the Germans came, the company was very international and we spoke many languages. Growing up backstage, I learned English, French, Italian. A bit of German and Russian too."

"My, my. Clever girl. Me, I don't have any head for languages at all. Though I can *parley-vous* a bit of Frog if I'm pressed."

"Can you, Mr. Harcourt?"

"Edward," he reminded.

"Edward."

"I suppose that's where you learned to sing, is it? Growing up at the opera?"

"Oh, yes. I had many lessons. Piano, voice."

"I suppose it's rather a come down, what? Doing this séance business?"

She shrugged. "It is necessary to survive," she told him. Then added, dutifully: "And of course my father has such amazing talent."

The banker smirked. "Mmmm, yes, I can see that. A real showman. You and your father are quite a team, aren't you?"

Sasha kept smiling, not certain she liked what he was inferring.

"You know," he said softly, leaning forward intimately, "you are a *very* pretty girl. You're so pretty, a man might lose his head entirely. Go quite beyond the beyond, if you know what I mean."

She smiled, doing her best to be pleasant because you can't offend the paying customer. But she put her cigarette to her lips to keep him from moving closer, holding the burning end between them as a barrier. Up close, she could smell whisky on his breath.

"Well," she said, exhaling smoke in his direction, "I must be getting back to my father. He will be needing me."

"Will he? You help summon up the spirits of the dead, do you, my girl?"

"Oh, I try, Mr. Harcourt. I do my best. Though it is my father who is the psychic."

It was a shame to waste a good cigarette, but Sasha reached over to stub out her smoke in an ashtray on one of the low tables. Mr. Harcourt made her uncomfortable and she wanted very much to escape. But the banker had other ideas. He grabbed hold of her wrist while her hand was still a few inches from the ashtray. Sasha flashed him an inquiring look. She recognized the expression that had come into his eyes, the hungry look of the sexually stimulated male. There was hard focus in his eyes, a consuming interest that she knew would quickly go slack the moment he got what he wanted.

"I tell you what, Sonya. What do you say we come to a small business arrangement, you and I?"

Up close, she could see his teeth were yellow, partially rotten. The English had the worst teeth in the world, no matter what their social class.

"A business arrangement? I don't know what you mean, Mr. Harcourt."

"Oh, sure you do, my girl. I've spent my life in commerce and I recognize very well when something's for sale. There's no need to be coy about these things, not when you're parading around in a dress I can see through well enough to know you're not wearing knickers. So tell me your price. How much do you want?"

She stared at him, frowning, not sure how to answer. The man disgusted her, she wanted to pull free of his grip. But she and Julka were refugees in a strange land, she had to be careful.

"My father is in the next room," she reminded him. "And so is your wife."

"Oh, I don't think your father will mind. And why don't you let me worry about my wife. I tell you what, I have to go up to Oxford next weekend. There's a small hotel where I like to stay, very nice. Why don't you come and spend the weekend with me, be my girl. I'll make it worth your while. What do you say?"

"I am not a prostitute, Mr. Harcourt, no matter what you think. I am a victim of the war."

He smiled impatiently. "Yes, yes, of course. The damn Krauts. But still, a pretty girl like you needs spending money, what? A chance to buy nice clothes, eh? Don't worry, my girl, I won't tell a soul. It will be our secret, just you and me. So tell me what you want and I'll pay it. Can't you see, I'm wild about you." He leaned closer and whispered in her ear: "I say, John Thomas wants you so bad, he's getting hard just thinking about your pretty little cunt. He'd like to fuck you 'til the cows come home!"

Sasha had never heard of such a thing. *Fuck you 'til the cows come home*! Though her English was excellent, there were still native expressions she didn't understand, and she worried that this reference to cows might hint at some strange English perversion, perhaps involving whips and the breasts.

When it came to perversions, she didn't trust the English a bit. But luck was with her. Just at this moment, the air raid sirens began to wail, rising and falling, saving her from the need to answer. Within seconds, the big anti-aircraft guns started firing from their position in Hyde Park, only a few blocks away. Sasha was never so glad for an air raid in her life.

"Oh, my God, it's the Germans!" she cried. "I must go to my father!"

Edward Harcourt released her wrist, momentarily defeated. "Think about my offer, Sonya. I'm a rich man and I'm prepared to pay well for what I want."

"Yes, yes," she told him hurriedly. But she was already moving, no time to waste. The first bombs were starting to explode in the distance, dull percussive thuds, and she didn't like being on the top floor of a building. Sasha had enough experience of air raids by now to guess that the Germans were bombing the electric station in Battersea across the river. But this could change. In a few minutes, the planes could easily be over Mayfair.

Sasha hurried back into the dining room where the séance had come to an abrupt end. Everyone was scurrying about looking for their coats and purses, with the exception of Mrs. Harcourt who kept her seat by the table. "Personally, I refuse to leave my flat for Mr. Hitler!" she said disdainfully. The British often referred to the German führer archly as Mr. Hitler, a bit of snobbery they employed to put the little corporal in his place. As far as Sasha was concerned, the Harcourts would make a splendid target for any German bomb.

"We must hurry, Julka," she said in Polish to the Great Jabolonski who was rising stiffly from the table. He seemed befuddled, still halfway in the make-believe performance of his séance. "Come, come, we must find your coat and get downstairs quickly to the shelter."

"Yes, yes, here I am. But get our money, Sasha. These damn people owe us ten pounds."

"All right. But hurry, please," she said, guiding him toward the hallway where they had left their coats. "That horrible Mr. Harcourt believes I am a prostitute—believe it or not, he wishes to buy my body for a weekend in Oxford. I tell you, I want to throw up and never see people like this again!"

Julka gave her a shrewd look. His eyes were dark and liquid, curiously childlike.

"And what did you tell him?"

"Nothing. I was about tell him off, actually. But the air-raid siren began, sparing me the trouble."

"Listen, my darling," he said quietly while she helped him into his coat. "People in our position, we need to be practical. I wouldn't want you to miss out on a splendid opportunity just because of me. These horrible people, as you say, happen to be quite rich."

She stared at him, horrified. "You're saying . . . my God, Julka, I don't believe what you are saying!"

He shrugged. "Come on, Sasha. We've discussed these things before. One needs to get along, that's all. One can't afford to be too finicky at a time like this. But of course, it is your choice."

"But you . . . you wouldn't mind?"

She had stopped to study his face. Even the air raid was momentarily forgotten. He blinked and appeared embarrassed, which was to his credit. But he was not embarrassed enough, not nearly.

"It would be for us, my dear," he told her hesitantly. "For our great goal. But don't do it if you can't. You know how deeply I respect your wishes."

Did he respect her wishes? She wasn't sure anymore. It was hard to remember that this was her friend who had once seemed so smart and funny and kind. But that was long ago, another life. In this new world of war and madness, he seemed happy enough to allow her to support them in any way possible. Of course, he put a fine face on it. He liked to say they were both free of bourgeois prejudice. This was the quality that had brought them so far, escaping Poland at a time when others were dying like flies. They had broken all the rules, they were free spirits.

The bombs were sounding closer by the minute and it was necessary to hurry. Sasha took him by the arm and led him urgently toward the front door. She didn't feel like a free spirit, only desperate.

Edward Harcourt was waiting for them in the foyer. Julka held back discreetly while she approached the banker.

"We were promised ten pounds," she said curtly.

"Yes, of course." Mr. Harcourt reached for the billfold in his jacket pocket and counted out two five-pound notes. He handed them to her along with his card. "You'll think about what I said, won't you, my girl? I've written down my private number at the office."

Sasha hated what she was about to do. Nevertheless, she boldly met his eyes. "I have already decided. I'll do what you wish."

He was taken aback. "You'll do it?"

"Yes. But perhaps you will not like the price."

"I told you, you can ask whatever you like. What is it?"

"Two tickets," she told him. "Two tickets to America, along with the required papers. That is my price and you can take it or leave it. I wish to leave this terrible war behind. I am fed up with idiots killing each other."

The banker appeared momentarily shocked, for the war in England was a patriotic matter, not to be spoken of disparagingly. But he recovered quickly.

"All right," he agreed. "As it happens, I have an old school chum at the Foreign Office and I believe I can arrange what you want. It's a deal."

She turned away, unable to face his yellow teeth another moment more. She could still change her mind. In her daydreams, she had always imagined arriving in America so differently, as a world-famous star basking in applause and adulation. This would be loathsome by comparison, whoring herself to cross the ocean. But one had to face the facts. Her mother was dead, the world had turned to smoke and ash, and she had no one to rely upon except herself. Just then, as though to accentuate the point, a bomb exploded less than half a block away, rattling the windows, shaking the foundation of the house. The explosion was a reminder of what was important and what was not. She and Julka could die in London if she didn't find a means for them to get away.

"Yes, it's a deal, Mr. Harcourt," she replied bitterly, turning back to him.

"Edward," he reminded.

He touched her bottom as she was leaving, as though trying out the goods, running his finger lightly up the crack of her ass. Sasha froze, struggling against a furious impulse to turn and slap him hard. But another bomb exploded, closer still, and there was nothing to do but take Julka by the hand and lead him away.

America! she thought, as she hurried down the stairs into the street of burning buildings and sirens wailing and death whistling down from the sky. *Oh, America! You had better be worth the price I am paying!*

My Awful Childhood:

The Perils of Paradise

One

I grew up in the shadowlands of Los Angeles, the *noir* part of town. Beverly Hills, to be precise—an anxious corner of the city full of the insecure rich, everyone struggling to hang on to their fragile moment of success, knowing it all slips through your fingers in the end.

The secret of this place, apprehended dry-mouthed at three in the morning, is that beauty, fame, and fortune are a mirage that vanishes the closer you get, pure puffery that can never last.

I know what you're saying: Poor rich boy! Still, if I'd had my way, I would have grown up somewhere else. Paris, maybe—now, that's my idea of glamour. Or better yet, a small island in the South Pacific where there are more coconuts than people. But children aren't given the choice. We land where our parents put us, and my mother brought me here.

At least, the Beverly Hills of my childhood was a more romantic place than what you'll find today. Our lives were ruled by dreams, however foolish. Occasionally you saw gods and goddesses driving in their convertibles along the palmy streets. Or at least, that's what I remember, looking back.

In the Beverly Hills of my childhood, there were hardware stores on Rodeo Drive, quite ordinary places, and five-and-dimes and soda fountains where you could sit at the counter and sip a Coke in a paper cone with shaved ice. The part of Rodeo Drive from Santa Monica Boulevard to Sunset had an actual gravel bridle path running down the middle bordered by low green hedges for people to ride their horses.

Our maids were Colored, we had Filipino gardeners, there wasn't a Saudi prince anywhere in sight. Many of our homes were Midwestern in appearance, as though they had set down in the Land of Oz from Kansas on the backs of tornados. Of course, being Los Angeles, we had a sporting mix of styles— English manors, Mediterranean villas, Moorish palaces, and quite a selection of Southern plantation mansions *a la* Scarlett O'Hara, big two-story houses with white colonnades and front porches where no one ever sat. Here and there, modernity was creeping in: a scattering of odd boxlike structures that generally had rock gardens in front rather than lawns, no need to mow.

In the Beverly Hills of my childhood, every house had an incinerator in the backyard where we burned trash, little free-standing crematoriums with protruding chimneys in which we sent our daily offering of smoke and garbage to the heavens.

I remember a shoe store on North Canon Drive with an x-ray machine shaped like an old-fashioned nickelodeon in which you could put your feet in the bottom, peer down through a viewer, and see your own skeletal bones. The idea was very scientific according to the optimistic notions of the times, to be able to look at your bones and judge for yourself if the shoes were the right size. If Superman had x-ray vision, so could we.

We believed in progress. We believed in frozen orange juice. We believed in cutting down orange groves in order to build a new kind of road where the way would always be free—freeways, we called them, because freedom was what we craved, ribbons of concrete and clover leaves on which we might travel faster and faster to any destination at all.

The war was over. We believed we could be happy in our paradise by the sea. There would be blue skies, nothing but blue skies from now on.

That was what California was all about.

*****

I have a photograph of myself from that time.

In the photograph (early color, sepia-toned with age), I've just turned seven years old and I'm standing proudly with my new pony, Errol, that my Aunt Mina had just given me for my birthday.

My mother had dressed me that day in a brand new Hopalong Cassidy outfit: black cowboy shirt, black pants, black cowboy hat, and a six-shooter cap gun inside a spangled holster. The pony had arrived as a complete surprise. Mina simply appeared that day in her Cadillac with the top down and Errol tethered to the back seat. It was a crazy thing to do, of course, driving through Beverly Hills with a pony in the back seat of a convertible. Mina had to sell that car eventually because she could never get rid of the smell of pony piss, but Cadillacs were easy to come by in those days, so she didn't mind.

She arrived that afternoon with a stuntman from 20th Century Fox, one of her old lovers, who helped us with the saddle and bridle, and fixed up a sort of temporary stable in our garage until a pen could be built near the swimming pool. Frankly, I'm not sure what my mother thought about all this, but she and Mina had a complicated relationship, so she smiled and pretended to be pleased.

In the photograph, I'm squinting into the sunlight with my hand on Errol's mane in a proprietorial manner, showing off my new possession—a Show Biz moment straight out of a fan magazine, a spoiled Hollywood princeling in the land of plenty. Lucky me, I had it all. My mother was a famous singer and my Aunt Mina was more famous still—Mina Bower, one of the great movie stars of the 1930s. What more could any kid want? With my cap gun handy, I was ready for make-believe battles with a make-believe world.

From the expression on my face, it's evident that I thought Errol was cuddly as a stuffed animal. I believed him to be a kind of Walt Disney cartoon that had been put on the planet solely for my pleasure. But the viewer can make out what I had not yet observed—Errol's colossal dong, a huge pony penis that hung nearly to the gravel path below, a hint of Errol's true nature to which I didn't have a clue. In the photograph, the pony almost seems to be winking at the camera. It's like he's saying: Oh, Jonathan!—what you don't know about me would fill libraries! Believe me, my little friend, life has surprises in store.

I'm sure Aunt Mina enjoyed her little joke—she'd named Errol after Errol Flynn because of his huge dong. Errol, I should mention, was one of Aunt Mina's lovers (the actor, not the pony), so she had inside knowledge of this anatomical detail. Of course, Aunt Mina should never have given me a pony in the first place. Neither my mother nor I knew how to take care of him, and our backyard was no place for even the smallest horse.

We found him dead two months later floating in our swimming pool. It was my fault—I'd forgotten to fill his water trough, an old bathtub we'd placed at the side of the garage, and as a result he'd escaped from his pen and drank chlorinated water from the pool. It was my first real test in responsibility, and I had failed the grade in a big way.

I remember crying bitterly and wishing I were dead. And then, being the California kid I was, I barely ever thought of him again.

*****

Like all kids, I accepted the world to which I was born as normal— that I should grow up in show business with a mother who was famous, the fabulous Sonya Saint-Amant, the object of male desire and female envy from one end of the country to the other.

I also took it for granted that, though I had a good many uncles, I had no father. My mother and I lived alone in our big California Spanish home on North Maple Drive. We were thick as thieves, my mother and I, constant companions and confidantes, and I presumed life must be like this for everyone.

Except for the occasional dead pony floating in the pool, my first years as a princeling were pleasantly drowsy. But then at the age of eight, everything changed: I was sent to military school in time to start the third grade, a hellish establishment that went by the name Black Fox. With a name like that, you'd except to find yourself in Hitler's secret mountain lair. In fact, it was quite a swanky place by the bizarre notions of the time with a sprawling campus on Fairfax Boulevard not far from Beverly Hills.

From a life of sheer indulgence, I was now expected to wear a uniform, march for hours in the sun, turn right-face, left-face, carry a toy rifle, and call the older boys "sir." Sadly, I never quite figured out my left foot from the right—I marched to the beat of my own drummer, which earned me countless demerits and made life a misery. Military schools, I should mention, were quite the fashion in the 1950s, not simply a place to ship off juvenile delinquents, and Black Fox was a popular choice in Los Angeles at the time. The majority of my classmates were the sons of movie stars, producers, directors, agents, and the like. Of course, everyone in Hollywood was extremely right wing back then, or at least pretended to be if they wanted to keep their jobs. I'm sure parents considered this fact—I know my mother did—that having your kid in military school would look good on your résumé when HUAC came calling, the House Un-American Activities Committee.

At Black Fox, we marched, we blew bugles, we raised and lowered the American flag with great ceremony, and we carried our play wooden rifles in order to get ready for the Russians. For birthdays, we generally went to movie studios and saw screenings of our parent's latest picture. Some of our parents had projection rooms in their homes, and this was considered even better than going to a studio, big status for the lucky kid who could boast of having a private movie theater of his own.

As for myself, my mother had one of her admirers at 20th Century Fox, so that's where my birthday parties took place. In those days—before Century City, before Rupert Murdoch—Fox had the best back-lot in town and we were often allowed to play in the fake Western town, shooting each other in mock battles in dusty streets outside saloons that had doors and windows leading nowhere. These parties made me almost briefly popular.

Birthdays aside, I hated every minute of Black Fox and spent my days in a dim haze of terror. There were a lot of fistfights, petty vandalism, and it was impossible to change clothes in the locker room without some pre-adolescent psychopath snapping a wet towel at your bare ass. We fought about nearly everything, even whose parents were the most famous. It sounds silly now, but at the time we invested these quarrels with the stubborn pride of childish one-upmanship.

I had good reason to worry when the subject of parents came up. In the early 1950s, my mother was known not so much for her singing (her style had already fallen out of fashion) but for the fact that she was notoriously sexy, the glamorously French Ooh-La-La Girl. Unfortunately, there was a famous calendar in which my mother had appeared naked. By today's standards, the photograph would hardly deserve a second glance: a coy nipple barely showing, a discreet bend of the leg that obscured private parts. But I was mortified. You can imagine what it was like to be in a military school full of nasty little boys and have your mother be someone who had undressed for the calendar year of 1951, January through December.

At first, I did my best to keep my mother's identity secret. But my name was Saint-Amant also—Jonathan Saint-Amant—and there weren't enough Saint-Amants in

Hollywood just then that I could pretend to be from a different branch of the family. I prayed to be invisible when the subject of parents came up. "Please God, if you have any regard for me at all, sir, don't let anyone find out who my mother is!" But of course, the news that my mother was Sonya Saint-Amant spread like a dirty joke from ear to ear and I never had a moment's peace after that. I had to listen to sniggering jokes about her tits and ass, and whether I had ever seen her pussy, and other comments of a similarly low nature.

"Jonno's mother doesn't wear clothes!" they'd taunt. "Jonno's mother goes around naked!"

What else could I do but slug everyone in sight? I fought endlessly that year, often coming home with a bloody nose or torn shirt. I can't say I was defending my mother's honor. I knew she could take care of herself. Rather it was my own honor I was struggling to find.

I hated Black Fox. But all clouds, as they say, have a silver lining. For it was during one of these after-school brawls that I came upon the start of a long breadcrumb trail that would eventually lead to the secret of my birth.

*****

The incident happened in the fall term of the fourth grade, my second year at Black Fox, while I was riding home in the school bus. There was a new boy on the bus, a fat kid named

Daryl whose father was a columnist from New York who had arrived recently with a job writing movie gossip for *The Hollywood Reporter*, one of the two powerful daily trade papers in town. Daryl seemed to think he was superior to the rest of us just because he'd grown up in New York. He was always going on about ice skating at Rockefeller Center and Sardis and opening nights on Broadway, a real pain in the ass.

Some of the older kids were smoking cigarettes in the back of the bus, blowing smoke out the windows as we made our way up Melrose Boulevard, past gas stations and crummy little stores. Two decades in the future, Melrose would become a trendy part of town, but in the 1950s, the neighborhood was low and ugly, caught in a kind of terminal L.A. slouch.

"Hey, you guys hear the joke about Bob Hope and Sonya Saint-Amant?" someone asked. It was Lew Tsaroff, a total jerk (we called him Jerkoff, naturally) whose father was a movie composer who specialized in heroic scores for gladiator pics. I stared nonchalantly out the window, pretending not to hear.

Lew continued to tell the joke, which was far from witty— the sort of humor that appealed to nine-year-old boys who weren't entirely toilet trained.

"So Bob and Sonya are walking down the street when suddenly Bob's shirt falls off —"

"That's stupid," someone said. I think it was Ralph Loomis, one of the few non-show biz kids (his father owned a chain of department stores). "I mean, how can his shirt just fall off?"

"It's a joke, asshole. Now listen . . ."

Probably you've heard this, if you were ever a nasty nine-year-old boy. Lew went through the whole thing, Sonya looking at the hair on Bob Hope's chest and asking, 'What's that?' 'That's my lawn,' Bob answers. Then a little later, Sonya's blouse comes off and her boobs fall out. Bob looks at them and says, 'What's that?' 'Those are my babies,' she says.

The clothes keep peeling off, as will happen occasionally in real life just as in dirty jokes. When Bob Hope's pants come down, he tells Sonya, 'That's my limousine.' And when her skirt vanishes, she says, 'That's my garage.'

When they're finally naked, Bob poses the big question. 'I tell you what . . .'"

Two voices piped up from the back of the bus with the miserable punch line: "I'll let your babies play on my lawn, if you let me put my limousine in your garage!"

It was an old joke, most everyone had heard it, and there were appropriate groans all around. As for me, I kept staring out the bus window as though I didn't have a care in the world. There were a few hoots and hollers in my direction. Someone said, "Hey, Jonno, does she let you put your limousine in her garage?" Even then, I didn't say a word. I showed almost superhuman restraint. I'd been through these scenes too many times before.

And that's when Daryl spoke up, the fat kid from New York. He was sitting one row behind me.

"Hey, you know, don't you?—Jonno doesn't even have a father. He's a bastard!"

I turned in controlled fury. "Why don't you just fuck yourself in the ass, you fat fucking fairy?" I suggested alliteratively, imbued even then with the poetic instincts of a future writer.

"At least I'm not a bastard! Who's your father, then?"

"My father was killed in the war, if you really want to know," I replied loftily. "He was a pilot. He was shot down over the English Channel. He was a hero."

"Bullshit he was! You don't even *know* who your father was. You're a bastard. That's what my dad says. He says your mother wasn't married when she had you."

There was no option but attack. I leaped backward over the seat that separated us and began pounding that fat fucking fairy with all my might. The fight got so bad that the bus driver had to stop and pull us apart. He ended up giving me a bunch of demerits, and I would spend the next month during the afternoon sports period marching up and down the gravel parade field with my sad wooden rifle. But I didn't care about that. What I cared about was that from now on everyone at Black Fox was going to say my mother wasn't married when she had me.

An Overnight Sensation

My mother was gone that week "playing Vegas"—in my childhood, I assumed this was like playing cards or Parcheesi, just a game that grownups did. Claire, our Colored maid, was looking after me and I didn't see my mother until the following Monday. I confronted her as soon as I could.

I found her in the library downstairs, a room with depressing green walls that she used as her office. She was sitting on the leather armchair with her feet up on a hassock, wearing an old dressing gown, smoking a cigarette—far from glamorous, her at-home persona. She was bitching on the telephone to Sol Weintraub, her manager, about the musical arrangement of a song she insisted was "drowning in goddamn violins." This was 1952, and my mother in her at-home state, *sans* make-up, was starting to show signs of puffiness around the face, as well as a bulge to her figure that caused her to be on a continual diet. She could still doll herself up and fool the paying public, but as the years went by, this magical transformation into a sex goddess took more and more effort. At home, she no longer bothered.

My mother hung up the phone (clunky, black, rotary dial) and her whole manner softened as she turned to me with her lovely green-hazel eyes. I was her Little Man, that's what she called me. Together we were a team, an army of two against the world.

She touched my cheek with the coolness of her hand. "Oh, Jonno! You've been fighting again!"

I stubbed out the cigarette that she had left burning in the ashtray. I loved her so much I almost didn't tell her my bitter tale of woe. But it was burning a hole inside of me. I couldn't help myself, it came spilling out.

"Someone at school said you weren't married when you had me!" I told her, full of tearful accusation. "He said I was a bastard."

"What?" Being a selfish kid, I had only been thinking of my own shame, not hers, how a story like this might affect her.

I told her again what I had heard. That she hadn't been married when she had me as decent women in the 1950s were supposed to be.

Her complicated eyes became very focused as she studied me.

"That's not true, Jonno," she said softly. "Of course, I was married. Your father was a wonderful man. He was a hero. He died fighting for freedom. You don't know what it was like in the war, I'm happy to say. Your father was a fighter pilot who was shot down over the English Channel. You should be very proud of him. Come here and sit in my lap, Jonno. Who said this to you?"

"Some new kid named Daryl. I beat the crap out of him."

"Oh, darling, I wish you wouldn't fight." She hugged me in a tight embrace and her body broadcasted a very different message than her words: *Yes, of course you must fight! You*

*must beat your way forward, fight to the end, anyone who in-
sults you, anyone who stands in your way.*

She kissed the back of my neck, which felt so tickly good
I'm sure Sigmund Freud would have had both of us arrested.
"I'm going to call the school," she said. "This is outrageous.
You shouldn't have to hear lies like that."

"Mom, don't call the school!" I pleaded. "It'll only make
it worse."

"Oh, Jonno!" she sighed. "I wish people would just mind
their own business."

"Tell me about my father, Mom."

"I've told you all this before, Jonno. Many times."

"Well, tell me again. What was his name?"

"His name was Jules Saint-Amant and he was French,
from a very distinguished family. Julka, we called him—that
was his nickname. Quite a number of French managed to
make their way to England in order to fight the Germans.
There was a whole section of the RAF that was French."

"What was my father's rank?"

"His rank? He was a captain."

"I thought you said he was a major."

"Yes, that's right. He became a major later, shortly before
he was shot down. To tell the truth, I never thought about his
rank very much. That's not what I remember. You know,
Jonno, Julka shot down so many German planes that people
started calling him the Great Saint-Amant. He was famous."

"Honest?"

"Of course. I would never lie to you about something like that. I first met your father in Krakow where my mother was a singer at the opera, a big star. My family was French, too, of course, just like his, but when you're a singer you have to go where the work is. That's why we were in Poland when the war broke out. You see, there's always been a special re-lationship between Poland and France—"

"Yeah, but I want to hear about my father," I interrupted, knowing my mother's stories could easily veer off into un-planned directions.

"Well, he was very handsome. Before the war, he . . . he was a composer, actually. That's why he came to Krakow, to stage one of his operas. Of course, I had a crush on him from the start. But it wasn't until I met him again in England that we fell in love. You can imagine how surprised I was to find him in England flying a Spitfire."

"You fell in love? So when did you get married?" I prod-ded, anxious to get the important facts.

My mother laughed. "Jonno! What is this? Of course, we were married. We fell in love and then we got married. That's how these things happen, you know. You would have liked him. And he would have liked you."

My mother had a beautiful voice, even when she was speaking, and her voice brought the story alive. It was a fine story, too, almost like a movie. How handsome Julka Saint-

Amant, the romantic composer-turned-warrior had shot down over two dozen Nazi planes in incredible dogfights, how wonderfully brave he was.

I loved hearing about this brave French fighter pilot who had been my father. But it was funny. Without knowing quite why, I didn't believe a word my mother said.

*****

I tried to ask Aunt Mina about my father a few weeks later. I often spent weeks at a time with her and Uncle Max when my mother was gone on long tours. Mina had never had children of her own, so I suppose I filled some empty space for her.

When Max was busy at the studio, Mina and I would often drive by ourselves to the ocean, to Trancas which is on the northern end of Malibu. Trancas has a wide, long beach and Mina loved to walk here at low tide when the sand was wet and hard and glossy under our feet. On the afternoon I have in mind, there was a cool wind blowing, stirring up the white caps on the water, and everything seemed to exist in perfect Technicolor: the blue Pacific, the white sand, the golden orange of the sun. I kept running circles around Mina and showing her sand dollars I found until she laughed and called me a sand dollar millionaire. My question, when it came, seemed to slip out of nowhere.

"Aunt Mina? Did you know my father, the Great Saint-Amant?"

Mina laughed and turned away.

"Oh, look! There's a sea lion!" she cried, pointing out toward the breakers.

"But what about my father?" I insisted. "Did you ever meet him?"

She turned to me, seeing I wouldn't be put off. Mina was a small, elfish woman, a pixie waif, and at the age of nine, I was nearly as tall as she was. What you remembered about her were her amazingly large, expressive eyes. I felt her studying me, deciding what to say.

"I tell you what, Jonno," she said finally. "I think you should ask Max about this."

"*Max*?" I replied. "Why Max? Did he know my father?"

"Just ask Max . . . oh, there's that sea lion again! Look how pesky he is! Wouldn't you like to be a sea lion, Jonno, and swim through the beautiful waves?"

"Aunt Mina . . ."

"Oh, Jonno! Let's run, run, run, my darling! Oh, let's be seagulls and we'll fly away!"

In a moment we were running down the beach along the glistening hard sand by the water, flapping our arms like wings pretending to be seagulls with Aunt Mina in the lead.

I loved running down the beach with Aunt Mina at Trancas. She was more child-like than I was, a better child in every way. But that was all she would tell me then about my father.

Ask Max.

Two

Yet I didn't ask Uncle Max about my father, the Great Saint-Amant, at least not right away. I'm not sure why I hesitated. I kept telling myself I was waiting for the right moment.

Max and Mina lived in Bel Air on a hilltop from which you could see the ocean all the way to Catalina Island on a clear day. It was an expensive location and I understood from the start, in the way that children do, that they were richer than we were and higher in the Hollywood pecking order.

There was something else, more subtle, that I picked up from my mother's attitude regarding them—that Max and Mina were somehow legitimate in a way that we were not. They were what passed in show business as aristocracy, while we were new arrivals, scrambling to hold onto our small place of fame and fortune, posing nude in calendars and such, eager to make a splash. By the time I was nine, I knew they weren't my real aunt and uncle, that this was an honorary designation. Still, there was some old connection between us, one that I didn't completely understand, that made it seem quite natural that I should spend so much time with them.

They called their house Casa Esperanza, for in those days Hollywood people often gave names to their homes, as though they were children or pets. Despite the Spanish name,

An Overnight Sensation

Casa Esperanza was New England to the core. Or rather a storybook version of New England as fantasized from California: a white, two-story, rambling clapboard home with blue trim around the windows that stood in the green shade of many trees on nearly two and a half acres of land.

It was a comfortable home with plenty of rocking chairs and over-stuffed sofas where you could put your feet up on coffee tables and no one would mind. The main building sat in a nest of vegetation that had been left partially wild—bougainvillea creeping up the sides, a tangle of flowers and vines that threatened to engulf everything. At the rear of the house, French doors led to a flagstone terrace, and from here an overgrown path meandered through a field of tall grass until it arrived at a swimming pool, a small guest house, and a tennis court that was bordered on the north by a windbreak of eucalyptus trees that dropped seed pods onto the court, making it necessary to do a good sweep before every game. Beyond the tennis court, if you kept to the path, you came at last to a high meadow that looked out toward the ocean to the west with Catalina Island sitting on the horizon like a kind of hazy Never-Neverland.

I enjoyed staying with Max and Mina at Casa Esperanza, though sometimes I was lonely, being the only kid in residence. Mina was like a second mother to me and Max was funny and warm and smart. They were transplants from the East Coast—Max was from an old Irish Catholic Boston family, and Mina from the Upper West Side of Manhattan, where her father had been a successful Broadway producer. They were both part of an Ivy League contingent in Hollywood, a circle of educated Easterners who sought each other out in the provincial wilds of California. Max had gone to Harvard, Mina had been at Vassar, and they often had like-minded exiles over to the house—a few actors like Humphrey Bogart (Phillips Exeter, before he got expelled), but mostly writers, directors, composers and such, a literate, left-leaning crowd who enjoyed laughing at everything California had to offer, including themselves.

The household staff consisted of two live-in positions—Sammy Chang, who was Chinese and inscrutable and served as the all-purpose chef/Man Friday, and an ancient gardener we called "the Professor."

The Professor was Czech, a utopian socialist who had been forced to flee Prague because of his political views when the Nazis invaded. He advocated many ideas that were dear to Mina's heart, such as free love, nudism, and vegetarianism. Unfortunately, he barely spoke a word of English—he and Mina communicated in mangled French—and he was so useless in the garden that she eventually had to hire a Filipino to take up the slack. By the time I began coming to Casa Esperanza, the Professor was well into his seventies and generally could be found wandering the grounds in a forgetful daze with a baffled expression on his face, as though he wasn't entirely certain what strange wind had blown him from Middle Europe to California.

Mina, of course, never considered letting him go, useless or not. She was the sort of person who adopted stray souls, taking them under her wing—and I was one of her strays too, so I appreciated her kindness. There were always odd people coming by the house, swamis and yogis and advanced spiritual types who seemed to spend a great deal of time standing on their heads on the lawn—I learned to stand on my head too, and I rather enjoyed it. Eastern philosophy had been in vogue in Hollywood since the Silent Era and, by the 1950s, we had Paramahansa Yogananda in Pacific Palisades, Krishnamurti in Ojai, and Aldous Huxley in Santa Monica, where he was busy ingesting psychedelic concoctions and knocking on his famous doors of perception.

Max accepted Mina's advanced ideas with a good-natured smile. But he kept to his whisky and soda and both he and I ate meat as often as it could be found at Casa Esperanza—occasionally, he took me down the street to the Bel Air Hotel for a good steak after we'd suffered through too many evenings of vegetables and tofu. "Come on, old man, what do you say we find ourselves a nice sacred cow to eat?" he'd say to me, and off we'd go in a flash in his big old Packard.

I suppose life at Casa Esperanza was fairly eccentric—kooky was the word we used back then. Most of the time I didn't mind kooky, since it offered me quite a bit of unsupervised freedom, but there was a single exception: I was scandalized when it came to Mina swimming in the pool *au naturel*.

"Come in, Jonno!" she would call to me merrily from the water. "We'll be free as fishes, my darling! We have nothing to hide!"

At the age of nine, I certainly had very little to hide, yet I was determined to hide it anyway. It wasn't simply that I was shy, but rather the thought of what my schoolmates at Black Fox would say if they ever found out about such shenanigans.

Deep in my heart, I was terrified of being free as the fishes. Like most children, I was staunchly conservative, doing my best simply to hang on.

*****

I'm not sure how long I would have waited to ask Uncle Max about the Great Saint-Amant, but then Mina had one of her "episodes," as we called them, and for Max and myself, the moment of truth had arrived.

The episode happened on a Sunday morning in May, the first really hot day of the season, more like summer than spring.

Max and I were stretched out in the downstairs library with the Sunday paper—me on the floor with the comics, him on the couch with the arts section—when we heard the sound of running footsteps on the flagstone terrace outside. A moment later, Sammy rushed in the French doors from the outside. I'd never seen him so excited.

"Mr. McCormick! Please, come quickly!" he cried. "It's Mrs. McCormick—she has left the yard without any clothes on!"

We got the full story quickly enough. Apparently, Mina had been swimming in the pool when she decided to leave the grounds and wander through the neighborhood naked. Sammy had tried to stop her, urging her to put on a robe. But Mina refused, insisting that she was "made in God's image," and if human bodies were good enough for God, they should be good enough for the residents of Bel Air.

"Come on, Jonno!" Max cried, springing into action. "We've got to find her!"

We left the property and took different routes through the neighborhood, Sammy, Max, and me—each of us armed with an oversized beach towel that we were prepared to throw around our wandering Godiva should we find her. Of course, I was painfully embarrassed by the whole thing. If *this* ever got back to Black Fox, I might as well slit my wrists.

I jogged up Bella Vista Lane and was coming back on a side street when I found Max in the middle of the road with Mina. He was doing his best to drape a huge blue towel around her, but she seemed to have no idea that she had done anything wrong.

"My dear, darling Mina, you simply can't walk about the neighborhood without your clothes on," Max told her in the patient way one speaks to small children. He added cunningly: "You'll embarrass people, and that's unkind. You don't want to be unkind, do you, Mina?"

"But, Max! It's only a human body," she explained gravely. "Everyone has a body and at least half of them are female bodies just like mine. So it's rather silly for people to be embarrassed, don't you think?"

"Yes, dear. But it just isn't done, you see. Society has certain rules and we have to abide by them."

She gazed at him with compassion. "Oh, Max, don't let them make a prison for you out of all their rules. You're so much better than that."

"But Mina, you must promise me—"

"No, Max. You must forgive me, but I can't promise to do something so silly. Don't you see? I'm a white bird. They can't catch me!"

It would have been funny, I guess, except for the fact that an unpleasant neighbor, a woman who didn't like movie people, had seen Mina wandering about naked and had called the police. Just as Max and Mina were discussing white birds and social norms, a patrol car showed up with two officers inside. Luckily, they recognized Mina Bower, the famous motion picture star, and this made them deferential. I watched as Max used all his charm to persuade the officers to let the matter drop, assuring them that Mina had been under some stress lately and that he would make certain that nothing like this happened again.

Sammy had showed up on the scene by this time as well, and together we led Mina back to the house. But our problems weren't over. Later that night, Mina appeared to emerge from her madness like a sleepwalker waking up, to understand, belatedly, what she had done, that she had walked down the street without a thing on. In an agony of self-recrimination, she tried to swallow a bottle of sleeping pills. Max only managed to stop her in time by rushing through the bathroom door (he had removed the key in an earlier suicide attempt), and grabbing the bottle from her hand just as she was pouring the pills out onto her palm. All this was completed with a great deal of shouting and weeping, a noisy drama that I overheard from my bedroom down the hall. Mina wept hysterically for the rest of the night and in the morning, Max saw no option but to hospitalize her in a place in Santa Barbara where she had been before.

Luckily, Max was between pictures just then, with a break between finishing *The Savage Night* and starting *Blind Alley*, two of his darkest black-and-white film *noirs*, and the following day he drove Mina up the coast to the hospital in Santa Barbara, leaving me in Sammy's care. I spent most of the day by myself on the tennis court by the eucalyptus trees throwing a ball aimlessly against a wooden backboard. When I got bored with that, I invented an imaginary friend and we took a rocket ship journey to Pluto, fighting off green-skinned space aliens the entire way. I was pretty good at make-believe, almost as good as my mother, but even so, there was no way to escape the dull anxiety that hung over everything like a mist, a feeling that the world was out of kilter.

In the evening, Sammy made me dinner and afterwards I fell asleep on the couch in the living room watching TV. I must have slept for several hours because when I woke there was a test pattern on the TV screen, a kind of cross with a circle around it. In those days, TV stations went off the air around midnight with the Star-Spangled Banner playing, a melancholy burst of patriotism for insomniacs. As I lay on the couch rubbing my eyes, I was surprised to hear a rhythmic clicking coming from down the hall. I recognized the sound easily enough—it was a movie projector running film, though it seemed an odd hour for such a thing. I listened for a while, not entirely awake, then I roused myself and went down the hall to investigate.

Max and Mina's library on the ground floor served a double function as a screening room. There was a large blue-green painting of squiggles and pollywog creatures on the far wall (a Miró, though I didn't know that until later) that could be raised on concealed wires to reveal a movie screen underneath. On the opposite wall, a framed Hirschfield sketch of Mina slid aside to reveal a small window that opened to a closet-like room on the other side where the big old 35mm projector was housed, a one-eyed monster with two arms that held the turning reels. Usually Sammy ran the projector, but tonight it appeared as if Max had done the job himself, leaving the closet door half open.

I found Max sitting in the dark on a leather sofa with his feet up on a coffee table and a drink in his hand. He was watching Mina on the screen—a younger black and white version of Mina gorgeously dressed in a slinky old-fashioned gown from the 1930s. Max had the sound turned off, which gave the flickering images on the screen an oddly exaggerated effect, as though you had to strain harder to hear the unspoken words. I deduced quickly enough that the drink in his hand wasn't his first liquid refreshment of the evening. The light from the screen reflected against his upturned face with moving bursts of light and shadow. It was an unnerving sight, frankly, Max in the dark, stewed on whisky, watching the silent image of his wife as she once had been.

I knew the movie well enough. It was *The Romantic Butler*, Max's most famous picture which he had directed in 1937—it had won the award for Best Comedy that year, a category they used to have back when the ceremony was just a dinner party at the Ambassador Hotel. The scene playing was between Mina and William Powell and you could see how funny it was even with the sound turned off. Whatever it was in Mina that made her crazy had also made her a great comic star. I guess these things go hand in hand somehow, the talents and torments that are meted out to us mortals. On the screen, her big waif-like eyes blazed with more energy than what is generally considered a safe voltage for human beings.

Max was so engrossed in his silent viewing of the movie that at first he didn't see me in the doorway.

"Uncle Max?" I said tentatively.

"Oh, Jonno! There you are!" he said brightly, turning my way. Even drunk, Uncle Max was the most polite person I've ever known, the definition of a gentleman. "Just revisiting the past, old man. Hard to believe we were all so bloody young. You remember *The Romantic Butler*, don't you?"

"Sure," I told him.

"Well, it was a bit of fluff, but what the hell. The world liked screwball comedies back then, the sillier the better. It helped people forget bread lines and soup kitchens. Here, I'll turn the damn thing off and we'll have a drink together. What can I get for you, Jonno? Your usual poison?"

"I'll get it," I said after Max struggled unsuccessfully to rise from the sofa. His eloquence improved with alcohol, but gravity took a firmer hold.

I stepped into the closet and switched off the projector, which Sammy had taught me how to run. When I returned to the library, Max was where I'd left him, immobilized on the sofa in the dark. I switched on a floor lamp hoping that light would make things seem more normal—as a child, I had a great urge for normal, a state I always imagined existed in everyone's family except mine. The light revealed what I had already surmised: Max was a mess. His tie was loose, his suit was wrinkled, and his hair was all over the place. Normally, Max was the sort of person who kept above the fray, watching the world's madness from an elegant vantage point. But tonight, the fray had won. He looked positively battered.

"Better make mine a double," he suggested, raising his empty glass. "It'll save your arm from pointless repetition."

Being a well-trained kid, I took Max's glass over to the drink dolly at the side of the room and poured him a shot of Glenlivet, single malt, his usual poison. Only I cheated, giving him quite a lot less than a double, filling his glass with ice from the silver bowl to disguise my subterfuge. I made a Shirley Temple for myself, my favored potion of the moment—grenadine, seltzer, two maraschino cherries, adding a quick shot of vodka into my glass when Max wasn't looking. Not that he would have noticed. All his attention was fixed on the blank white screen at the far end of the room, as though if he stared at it long enough, he might still find a ghostly trace of Mina there.

"Here's your drink, Uncle Max," I said, bringing his glass to the sofa. He turned to me with a sad, hopeful smile.

"Mud in your eye, old man," he said, clinking glasses as I sat down beside him.

"And may the road be long and liquid," I answered, completing one of our drinking couplets. I was definitely a kid who had lived too much in the adult world.

"Oh, Jonno, Jonno!" he said mournfully, shaking his head at the folly of the world. I guess it hadn't been much fun for him today, putting his wife in a loony bin.

"Aunt Mina sure was beautiful back then," I remarked, trying to be upbeat.

"She was a fairy queen, Jonno. She was smart and funny and wonderful. God, how I loved her!" Max took a long swallow from his glass. A normal person would have passed out long ago—there's that word again, "normal"—but Max had a huge capacity for alcohol. I suppose it was a necessary tool for survival back then before the invention of health clubs and bubbly water.

"The problem is, I'm going to have to call Louis B. Mayer in the morning and tell him Mina can't finish the picture she's started," he said. "Metro will need to find another actress, which won't make L.B. happy. They'll have to re-shoot all the scenes she was in and that's expensive. Ten years ago, it wouldn't have mattered—a star like Mina could get away with pretty much anything. But now . . . well, I don't know, Jonno. She has a great many friends in this town, but pictures cost a lot of money and studios won't take a chance on her if this gets out. This could finish her."

"Maybe no one will find out," I said.

Max gave me a sharp look. "Well, L.B. won't tell anybody, that's for sure. He'll make up something, God knows what. How about you, Jonno? Can you keep a secret?"

"Sure," I told him. And I meant it too. I was very good with secrets due to the fact that my mother had a ton of them.

Max kept regarding me. "You mustn't tell anybody at Black Fox. All those kids have parents, and parents like to gossip."

"I won't tell a soul," I promised.

He sighed and turned his gaze back toward the blank screen. "You see, here's the point you need to remember—no matter what happens, you gotta stick with the people you love. If I only teach you one thing in life, old man, I hope I can teach you that. We poor mortals, we've got to be kind to each other. You know that, Jonno, don't you?"

"Sure," I told him.

"Mina's a very wonderful person, but she's fragile and every now and then she breaks. I don't know why she's the way she is, but you have to take the good and the bad with people you love. You can't really separate the two. Do you understand what I'm saying, Jonno?"

I didn't understand, not really. So I waited for more, watching him carefully.

"It's why I can never leave her," he confided. "No matter what."

I took this in, wondering about the *no matter what*. A few months earlier, I had come across Mina in the pool with a young Argentine poet, the two of them in a naked embrace, and I imagined the *no matter what* might veer in this direction. But I didn't want to ask.

Max laughed suddenly. "Did I ever tell you about our first date? I was a junior at Harvard and she'd come up from Vassar for a dance. It was a blind date—a friend set us up together. Do you know what a blind date is?"

I thought for a moment. "Everybody keeps their eyes closed?"

He laughed again, louder than before.

"Oh, Jonno, that's good! . . . no, you keep your eyes open, at least if you're smart. I took Mina to dinner at a little place off Harvard Square. You can't imagine how lovely she was at the age of eighteen. There was always something special about her, a kind of inner sparkle that separated her from the other pretty girls, all those debutantes who only cared about shallow things. I was mad for her, of course. We dated for a few months, but then her parents sent her off on a European tour and we got separated somehow. I didn't see her for nearly five years. That happens, you see. Life has its own way of arranging things. Then I ran into her again in Hollywood—I was just a young director, but she was already a big star. It was Mina who got me my big chance. She convinced L.B. to let me direct her in *The Romantic Butler*, and that was the picture that made me. You can't forget something like that, Jonno, even after things change. I've always loved her, you see. We've never been apart. Except for the war, of course. The goddamn war . . ."

He left that hanging. I knew about the goddamn war because my mother had been in it too and she often spoke to me of what it had been like in Krakow with Nazi tanks clattering down the streets, and later in London when there were bombing raids sometimes twice a night and you never knew if one of those bombs had your name on it.

Max had gone silent just when I was hoping he would tell me more. He had arrived at a stage of drunkenness where his mind was off following things that only he could see. In the end, I had to prompt him. I had to reel him back from wherever he had gone.

"Aunt Mina said I should ask you about something," I began, and then stalled because even now, when we were talking so freely, it was hard to get the words out.

"About what, Jonno?"

"About my father. You know, the Great Saint-Amant. I've been wondering about him, I guess. What he was like, and all that. I was wondering if you knew him."

Max didn't answer right away. He hesitated just as Mina had done. There seemed to be something wrong with Julka Saint-Amant that no one wanted to talk about. I felt Max studying me.

"Look," he said after a while, "I think you need to ask your mother about this."

"But no one ever tells me anything!" I cried, suddenly angry with all the evasions I was getting from the adult world. "I asked Mina, and Mina said to ask you . . . and now you're saying I should ask my mother! But all my mother does is lie!"

Max put his hand on my shoulder. "Jonno, listen to me. These things are complicated. If your mother hasn't told you everything, it's not really a lie. It's because she thinks you're too young to understand. She'll tell you when you're older."

"No she won't! And it's not fair. I want to know about my father and no one'll tell me the truth. Everybody has a father except me, and I can't stand it anymore!"

"Jonno, only your mother can tell you these things."

I turned to him with accusing eyes. "But she won't, she won't! She'll make up something, all she ever gives me is make-believe. You know what she's like, Uncle Max."

I could tell from his expression that he knew exactly what my mother was like. He seemed to come to a decision.

"Okay, old man," he said reluctantly, not really happy about any of this. "If you want the truth, I suppose I'm the guy to give it to you."

"You will?"

"But you have to remember, you asked for it. Are you sure you want to know?"

I nodded.

"All right, then. But it's a long story, and if I'm going to tell it, I need to start at the beginning. I need to tell it so you'll understand."

"I don't mind a long story," I said. And it was true. Growing up in Hollywood, I was big on stories, as long as they had beautiful women, ironic men, and plenty of action. Fortunately, this had all that and more, a steamy saga of long ago.

Of course, I didn't get the whole story that night. It came to me in installments and I didn't get the full version—the one I'm going to tell you (adult, unexpurgated)—until years later when I found Max's journals.

But I should have left it alone, I see that now. I shouldn't have asked about the past, and I shouldn't have listened. For truth is more dangerous than make-believe, and it doesn't always set you free.

Part Two

A Rough Crossing
The North Atlantic, 1943

One

The *RMS Mauretania* sailed after midnight, slipping into the North Atlantic from Clyde Estuary, the secret war-time port in Scotland, and set a zigzag course into a fog bank in order to evade German submarines. It was February, 1943, and the great Cunard liner was blacked-out, not a light showing, only a ghostly shape on dark water. Lieutenant Maxim McCormick was going home.

Max unpacked in his cabin, struggling against a pull of nostalgia so strong it was like a rip tide. The *Mauretania*! The name had been painted off the bow for reasons of war-time security, but as he was boarding an officer on the dock had mentioned which boat it was. With all the ships passing in the night, Max found it incredible that he should be sailing on this ship, a vessel so overloaded with memory it was like a suitcase that wouldn't stay shut.

Max had spent his honeymoon on the *Mauretania*, a pre-war crossing in 1936 from New York to Southampton, a time of laughter and champagne, black ties and evening gowns and rich Americans, proof against the Depression. Now the great ocean liner had been transformed into a troop ship, changed beyond recognition. The porthole windows were painted a black-out gray, far from cheerful, and the carpets had been rolled up to reveal a metal floor.

The walls of his First Class cabin were still paneled with the dark, highly polished mahogany for which the *Mauretania* was famous, making the old ship seem more like a turn-of-the-century men's club than a means of transportation. But now, four rows of bunks took up every available inch of space, transforming what had once been a luxurious stateroom into a crowded dormitory—eight narrow beds and not one of them even slightly comfortable. At least Max had the dormitory to himself, which was luxury enough in this war.

The only improvement Max could see on 1936 was a private bathroom with tub, separated from the main cabin by a metal strip on the floor that was designed to keep bath water from sloshing out into the stateroom. On his honeymoon crossing, he and Mina had needed to go down the corridor, which had been the cause of much hilarity. Built in 1907, the *Mauretania* had few private WC's, even in First Class. The greatest of all the Cunard liners was a floating museum piece of old-world luxury and modern inconvenience.

After he unpacked, Max decided to go on deck. It was late but it seemed somehow obligatory, the first thing people did when they embarked on a sea voyage. It was what he and Mina had done in 1936, setting off from New York on their honeymoon. They had stood on deck with their arms around each other's waist and watched, goofy with happiness, as the Statue of Liberty had disappeared from view. Now, seven years later, wiser and wounded, sailing in the opposite direction, Max slipped on his olive green army greatcoat, found his cane, and left the cabin, hobbling on his bad leg down the long corridor.

The ship had begun to pitch on the ocean swells, forcing Max to lean heavily on his cane. Occasionally he had to reach out with his free hand and steady himself against the corridor wall to keep from falling. The doctor in the field hospital outside of Alexandria had recommended that he use crutches for at least a year, but Max found a cane more stylishly to his taste. If you had the misfortune to get wounded in war, it seemed to him you might as well cling to a few romantic props. Still, his left leg throbbed sharply every time he put weight on it, and it was an effort to maneuver his way through the heavy steel sea door to the deck outside. He felt like an awkward three-legged beast, not exactly Fred Astaire.

For his entire life up to now, Max had been the sort of person people referred to as "young." He had been that "young Harvard fellow," then later (defying his father's wishes to stay in Boston and become a lawyer), he had become that "young Hollywood director." Later still, he was a young married man and then a young lieutenant gone off to war. But being wounded didn't make him feel so young anymore. For the first time in his life, Max felt old. Time had finally caught up with him. Time had finally won.

Using the rail for support, Max climbed a steep flight of outside stairs and made his way limping along the open deck toward the bow. The night was cold and mournful and damp. Beneath him the ship was a living thing, rising and falling, plowing through heavy seas, sending a fine salty spray into his face. He stopped nearly at the front of the ship and leaned against the rail. From where he stood, he could just make out the outlines of two twin-barrel 20mm anti-aircraft guns mounted on a lower deck near the bow. In the last eighteen months he had become accustomed to the sight of large guns, but this was about to change. For Max, the war was over; he reminded himself of this incredible fact again and again, because it had still not completely sunk in. He was going home to California where only movies bombed. Home to Mina, his beautiful, unfaithful wife. Home to the hard push and pull of a career in the movies.

Max pulled up the collar of his coat and lit an English cigarette with the gold lighter Mina had given him on their second anniversary, sheltering the flame against the wind with his cupped hand. *To Max, Forever Mina* she had engraved on the gift. A fine sentiment. But would she love him now, he wondered, returning home with a bad leg? A man who could no longer dance an amusing version of the tango at the Trocadero, or play a game of tennis on the flower-scented courts of Bel Air? Would she still love him, he wondered, if the studios decided he was last year's stuff, no longer the boy genius, and would no longer give him a job?

An Overnight Sensation

Max stood on deck, his eyes gradually adjusting to the darkness. He could just make out the ghostly outline of the ship as it plowed through the waves. He was taking a meditative drag on his cigarette when his eyes drifted upward to the four huge smoke funnels on the highest deck above. The *Mauretania's* smoke funnels were famous, raked backwards against the wind, and had created an entire new look in trans-Atlantic design at the start of the century when they were built. But this was not why Max looked to them now. An improbable memory had just come to mind: a summer dawn in 1936 when he and Mina, drunk on champagne, had stripped naked out of their evening clothes to have sex on a section of the upper deck between the third and fourth funnels, giggling like teenagers and hoping like hell they wouldn't be caught.

What a time that was! Max smiled at the memory. But there was something terribly wrong with the scene in front of him and his smile quickly faded. He wasn't sure at first, because the night was dark enough for possible error. But as his eyes penetrated the darkness, he became convinced that what he was seeing was impossible. The ship's famous smoke funnels were all wrong.

"Bloody hell!" he cried. "What's happened to this god-damn boat?"

It was astonishing, but instead of four funnels, now there were only two. He counted them several times to be sure. One, two. He was sober, there could be no mistake. Had he and

Mina been so drunk they'd seen double? It was possible, he supposed; as a couple, temperance had never been one of their virtues.

Shaken, Max returned inside the ship, stumbling as he made his way along the moving deck, suddenly cold and no longer so happy to reminisce. He closed the heavy sea door against the wind and spray, glad to shut out the night with all its rushing noise. Inside, the ship hummed with a comforting mechanical sound. He set off down one of the long corridors toward the stern where he remembered the existence of a palm court lounge and bar. But nothing was as he remembered it. The *Mauretania*, once the grandest, fastest ship in the water, had been stripped bare. Where was the *fleur de pêcher* marble, the lavish plaster ceilings, the Italian Renaissance smoking room? Had Hitler somehow erased all these fine luxuries?

Max turned a corner and came to a public lounge, the Officers Canteen, according to a sign above the door. But it wasn't any lounge he recalled, or in a place where there had been a lounge before. The tables were bare wood, stained with round circles from countless glasses of beer, and the windows were covered with heavy drapes to keep light from spilling outside. Max walked past a battered upright piano and a handful of passengers and made his way to the bar. He found a sailor bartender in a tan uniform and apron polishing glasses.

The sailor gave a casual salute. "Evening, Lieutenant," he said politely.

Max saluted back, feeling like an imposter. He had gone to war with a camera rather than a gun and had never been entirely at ease in a military guise. He arranged himself on a stool and studied the sailor, wondering how to phrase his next question without seeming either drunk or mad. The bartender was a frail young man with wispy sand-colored hair and thick eyeglasses that gave him a bookish appearance. In another life, another time, he might have been a school teacher in a small rural town.

"Look, sailor," Max said finally, "I happened to notice coming on board earlier that the ship's name has been painted out from the bow."

"Well, yes, sir. They do that, sir, to confuse the Gerries in case we get spotted."

"Right. But this is the *Mauretania*, isn't it? I mean, that's what I was told."

The sailor smiled tolerantly. Too tolerantly, Max feared, accustomed to seeing damaged men returning from the fighting.

"Why, yes, sir. This is indeed the *Mauretania*."

"I ask because I was on the *Mauretania* some years ago, you see, back in thirty-six. My honeymoon, actually. And I can't help but notice how . . . well, how different everything is."

"The war, sir. Very sad."

"Yes, I understand war. We've all had to learn to make do without luxuries. But there are certain changes that are inexplicable . . ."

The bartender had stopped polishing the glass in his hand. "Yes, sir?"

"Look, the *Mauretania* I remember had four smoke funnels. I'm sure of it. They were rather unmistakable, actually—I mean, the damn things were each forty feet high. And now, I was just on deck and there are only two. You see what I mean about inexplicable."

The young man permitted himself a small smile. "Yes, I see your point, sir. The old *Mauretania* had four funnels, yes, indeed, sir. But, of course, this is the new *Mauretania*."

"What are you talking about?" Max stared at the man suspiciously. "How can there be a new *Mauretania*? That's like saying there's a new Grand Canyon."

"Oh, but there is, sir. The old *Mauretania* was decommissioned in thirty-seven. You must have sailed on one of her last voyages, sir. She just got too old—that's the way of the world, isn't it? Things grow old and out of style. The new *Mauretania* was brought into service in thirty-nine, just as the war was starting."

"And they simply named her the *Mauretania*, for the hell of it?"

"Well, not for the hell of it, no, sir. It's a great honor, after all, a tradition."

Max laughed suddenly, brimming over with glee. This was hilarious, the thought of himself mooning with nostalgia for old times, reliving the ghost of his honeymoon voyage, only to discover it wasn't the same bloody ship.

"I feel quite foolish," he admitted.

"I shouldn't let it worry you, sir. There's no reason a Yank could have known about the change of ships, if you don't mind me saying. What can I get you, sir?"

Max paused, undecided. He had intended to ask for a pot of tea. But at the decisive moment, the true nature of his thirst betrayed him. A man who has just embarked on a false journey down memory lane required sustenance.

"Gin," he said. "Better make that a double."

*****

It was nearly two o'clock in the morning and Max's leg was killing him, throbbing in crescendos of pain. He had been on his feet almost continuously since dawn, an exhausting day that had begun at Waterloo Station in London. It was nearly three months now since his Jeep had hit a land mine in North Africa and he was recovering well, a gradual rehabilitation. But after a day like this, standing for hours in endless lines, he was afraid he'd undone all those weeks of healing. Max knew that he should go to bed, but his leg hurt so badly he wasn't certain he could walk. It was easier to remain where he was, propped up on his bar stool. Bar stools were useful that way, supporting a fellow when all other options had failed.

There were only a few other people besides himself, civilian and military, scattered about the Officers Canteen at this late hour. An elderly British couple, tan and fit and tweedy, sat without saying a word to one another at a table not far from the bar. Several tables further on, two young American officers were playing cards, both of them almost comically drunk. Across the room, there was a middle-aged man with an emaciated face who looked like he could be a spy. And finally, at a table near the heavily-curtained windows, an older American officer sat by himself with a glass of beer. As Max watched, the officer slowly filled a pipe, tamped down the tobacco, and lit it in a patient, ritualistic manner that somehow accented the moody boredom of the night.

Max turned back to the bar and asked the bartender for another gin. For weeks now, he had been anticipating the joys of civilian life that were awaiting him. Hot baths, fluffy towels, good martinis, real coffee, clean sheets, sex with one's wife. These were splendid things to look forward to, almost mythical in nature when viewed from the misery of a battlefield. Yet now that the moment was at hand, he felt oddly let down.

Max hadn't enjoyed war, he knew it was a barbaric business. But he had found the spectacle strangely thrilling, the immensity of it—a production a thousand times larger than anything even Cecil B. DeMille might conceive. He had seen great armies in motion, cities turned to rubble, history itself unfolding before his eyes. Now he wondered how was he going to adjust to the petty intrigues of a Hollywood career after witnessing such huge events. It all seemed anti-climactic, horribly small.

Max was slipping into a late-night melancholy, wondering if his best days were behind him, when he looked up and saw a lovely young woman—a girl, really—appear in the doorway to the lounge. After two double gins, she seemed extraordinary, perhaps the most beautiful girl he had ever seen in all his long, difficult, overly-introspective life.

*****

She was nineteen or twenty years old, perhaps older. Max wasn't good with ages, so he couldn't be sure. Her expression was eager yet somehow tentative. She was shy, Max thought, and this appealed to him. There weren't many shy people left in 1943. Shyness, along with modesty, was one of the first casualties of war, lost in a thousand air-raid shelters and sleepless nights, wondering if you would be alive in the morning.

She was decently but poorly dressed in a gray skirt, a dark brown sweater, and a gray woolen cloak that was far from fashionable. Max presumed she must be one of the Displaced Persons on board—DPs, as they were known, refugees from the war. He had seen a group of them earlier on the dock in Scotland as they were boarding, a depressing huddle of humanity talking among themselves in a soft babel of foreign tongues, surrounded by bulging suitcases that were often tied shut with rope. This young girl, however, was far from depressing. Max couldn't take his eyes off her.

Her face was cherubic, a pretty Slavic face with high cheekbones framed by thick dark gold hair that was held by a band at the nape of her neck. A peasant girl, Max decided, full-breasted and frankly sexy. The kind of fresh-faced girl who might dance around the maypole and lie with some lucky country boy in a summer field of tall grass. Her lips were full and sensual, pressed together at the moment in disturbed uncertainty. Lovely as she was, her presence in the Canteen had created something of a problem. Obviously, she did not belong in this part of the ship—and on a British ship, the class system wasn't about to break down simply because of a world war. The girl was only a refugee, one of the gray hordes—there were millions of them in 1943 and she wasn't supposed to be in the Officers Canteen.

Max wasn't the only one staring at her. The two drunk American officers had stopped their game of cards to gape with almost idiotic lust. The gaunt middle-aged civilian who looked like a spy peered up from his book and studied her with eyes that seemed to be photographing her from every angle, as though he might need to make a report about her later. The elderly British couple sniffed with sour disapproval that anyone should be so young and pretty and poor. The girl herself seemed unaware of the small late-night sensation she had caused. At last, gathering her nerve, she walked with purpose to the bar.

The sailor bartender cleared his throat unhappily. "I'm sorry, miss," he said, "but this is the Officers Canteen and you really aren't supposed to be here."

"I wish to purchase a bottle of cognac, please." Her voice was low and she spoke with a foreign cadence. Max couldn't decide what her accent was. He presumed she was from one of those tragic countries on the European map, but which country it was hard to say. She had reached in her cloak pocket for a purse and was awkwardly pulling out coins. "My father, he is sick and has sent me, please, for cognac."

"Miss, I can't serve you here. There's a canteen, I believe, down on D deck—they should be able to help you."

"Yes, but they are closed now. So I came here. My father . . ."

Words failed her. She stopped mid-sentence and looked as though she were about to cry. Max found it unbearable. "Look," he said to the barman. "Why don't you sell her a bottle of cognac? It won't hurt anything, and her father is ill."

"Oh, very well," the barman said reluctantly. "But we don't have cognac. Comes from France, you know. I could give you a bottle of brandy, I suppose. American stuff from New York state."

"Brandy? This is like cognac?"

"I think your father will like it," Max said, deciding to involve himself further in the conversation. She was standing in profile about three feet from his stool, too shy to look at him directly. "New York brandy isn't as good as French cognac," he added, hoping she would turn his way. "But it's drinkable in times of crisis."

"Yes, I will take that, then," she told the barman, still refusing to turn toward Max. "And please, I wish a package of playing cards."

Cards? It seemed an odd request. But then, in the insecure fashion of the poor, she explained herself to the bartender. "My father is bored and I must entertain him."

The sailor reached under the bar and found a bottle for her as well as a sealed package of playing cards. "That will be ten and sixpence, miss."

She had her coins in hand, but she seemed unfamiliar with English currency. "Ten and . . ."

"Ten shillings sixpence . . . no, you see you only have seven shillings and a penny there," he said with growing exasperation when the girl had laid her small offering of coins on the bar. For a young man, he lacked chivalry.

"Here, let me pay," Max said quickly, reaching in his wallet for a pound note. The girl turned his way at last, for just an instant. Her eyes, he saw, were a complicated shade of green, a mix of many colors. Shy as she was, she seemed to take his measure entirely, head to foot. Max had seldom found himself on the receiving end of such a well-focused inspection. Then she looked quickly away.

"I'm very glad to help," he told her. "I'm often without the right change myself."

"Thank you," she murmured.

"It's nothing. I hope your father feels better. Meanwhile, I'm sure there's a doctor aboard if he needs anything."

"No, he will not see a doctor," she answered. "He is only old and tired. We have had a long journey."

"Well, just tell him he'll soon be in America, land of fresh starts."

Max was used to being ironic. Together, he and Mina could put on quite a show of breezy one-liners. But the girl turned and studied him once again with great seriousness, a longer probe than her initial thrust. He found himself wondering what she saw, how he measured up.

"Yes, a fresh start—I would like that very much," she said simply.

"You know, your English is excellent, but I detect an accent. May I ask where you are from?"

"Ah, you wish to know where I am from? I am from nowhere, I'm afraid. A land so far, far away that sometimes I think I only dreamed there ever existed such a place."

The girl smiled mysteriously and Max had the feeling, just for an instant, that she was acting a role, not as innocent or shy as he had first imagined.

"Funny, I'm from a land far, far away myself," he said, hoping to keep her talking. "So you see, we have a lot in common. Perhaps I could buy you a drink. Or a cup of tea," he added, not certain she was old enough to drink.

She appeared to weigh the offer. But she shook her head. "Thank you, but I must go. My father is waiting."

"Well, goodnight, then. And good luck."

Max watched as she took hold of the bottle as though it were a football, tucked it beneath her arm, and turned abruptly from the lounge. The elderly English couple sighed to one another with disapproval. The single man who looked like a spy returned to his book. The two American officers laughed and said something of an obvious sexual nature that Max was glad he couldn't entirely hear. The barman set to work unloading boxes.

As for Lieutenant Maxim McCormick, he finished his glass of gin and tried to write a script in his mind that would account for a beautiful young woman with a complex international accent traveling with her father across the North Atlantic on a cold wartime night.

An Overnight Sensation

He was a married man, twice her age; his interest was merely speculative. But for all his Ivy League education (or perhaps because of it), he missed the point. It had not occurred to him what might have been obvious to someone else: that she had very neatly separated him from ten shillings sixpence to pay for her brandy and cards.

Two

Max settled into his new life at sea. There was something to be said for an ocean voyage, even on a troop ship: a fine freedom to have your life dangling between two points of the compass.

He woke the first morning to find a gray mist over the North Atlantic, a diffuse salty wetness through which the ocean liner traveled, zigzagging endlessly, tramping up and down the gray waves. The itineraries of the great ocean liners were closely guarded state secrets (loose lips sank ships), so it was impossible to get any information about their course, or even their expected date of arrival in New York.

Max overheard one of the passengers say they were heading north into the Arctic Circle to avoid German submarines, but whether this was true, it was impossible to say. They had left Scotland, by his reckoning, on February 8th, and he presumed they would reach America sometime within the next week or two or three. Personally, Max was in no hurry. He was happy to put off the responsibilities that awaited him in California a while longer—work, marriage, and the ambitious person he was obliged to be there.

Three times a day a bugle sounded over the loudspeakers, a military summons to eat. The Officers Mess was a cavernous room with long rows of metal tables from which all pre-war luxuries had been stripped away. The food was always the same: a breakfast of stale buns and tea, lunch with the same buns and bits of greasy sausage, and for dinner a vague kidney stew that never varied, gristly pieces of meat and a few overcooked vegetables that swam in a gloppy brown sauce. Everyone complained, loudly remembering improbable menus from the past— Oysters á la Russe, Poached Salmon with Mousseline Sauce, Filet Mignon Lili, dishes from a world forever gone.

Breakfast, lunch, and dinner were the beats that marked out the slow passage of shipboard time, but the Officers Canteen was where all social life occurred. Max discovered several people he knew onboard, an Air Corps pilot who had been a writer at RKO before the war, and an executive in the steel industry whose wife had been a college friend of Mina's at Vassar. Max remained pleasant but uninviting, using his native New England courtesy as a shield. He wanted this time for himself.

On the second day, the weather began turning bad, with a darkening sky and a cold wind blowing from the northeast. Max spent part of the morning on the open deck bundled up in his heavy coat pacing an athletic circuit around the ship. His English doctor had recommended exercise as part of his rehabilitation, but limping around the deck with his cane, he felt absurdly like Captain Ahab in search of a white whale.

Of course, it wasn't a white whale he was seeking as he made his perambulation about the ship. He was looking for the pretty refugee girl. He told himself he wasn't, but he knew he was.

He found a spot on deck at the rear of the ship from which he could spy down on the war refugees as they gathered below him near the stern. There were about a dozen of them milling about, the men with cigarettes, the women talking among themselves. A solitary old man in a soft cap and baggy clothing stood leaning on the rail, staring meditatively at the ship's wake as it spread out behind him, the flattened highway of water that led back to Europe and the war he was leaving behind. What could he be thinking? Max wondered. What could it be like to lose everything and sail blind to a new land?

The refugees interested Max in some way he couldn't quite pin down. It seemed unfair that he should have so much and they so little, all due to an accident of birth—geography, nothing more. But he didn't see the pretty girl, though he looked for her, nor anyone who could conceivably be her father. It almost seemed to Max that he had imagined her that first night, over-stimulated and more than a little drunk.

*****

On the third afternoon at sea, heavy rain began slanting down from a darkening sky. Max made his way to the Officers

Canteen with a script that Sam Goldwyn had sent him in London, hoping to get some work done.

The lounge was crowded, dense with cigarette smoke, a small world in motion, people and tables all pitching uncomfortably on the waves. The blackout curtains had been pulled back to reveal a row of gray windows streaked with rain. Max was heading toward an empty table when he heard a bullying upper-class British voice call out his name.

"Maxim McCormick! My God, look who's onboard—it's the Hamlet of Hollywood!"

Max pretended not to hear, but it was no good.

"Max, don't let us play the recluse, laddie—you're neither rich nor famous enough to pull it off. Now, stop being stuck up and come on over here. We'll all get plonkers together and have a fabulous time."

It was Shelton Graves, the British actor, and as usual he was drunk. Max had noticed Shelton the day before at dinner and had done his best to avoid him, keeping his head down and thankful to be seated at a different table. Unfortunately, there was no polite way now to get out of sharing a drink, and Max was nothing if not polite.

With a strained smile he went over to where Shelton was playing cards with his American wife, Biff, and an American army captain, a tall, gangly man who was smoking a foul-smelling pipe—it was the pipe-smoking officer he had noticed the first night in the Canteen. There were drinks on the table, a full ashtray, cards that were face up and face down, small piles of chips and money before the different players. From the chaotic array, the stale debris of a long afternoon, it looked as though this group had been camping out here for some time.

"Well, hello, Shelly," Max said, summoning his shield of cordiality. He had directed Shelly in a picture in 1938, but they had never been friends. "What are you doing on a ship to New York? I thought you hated our side of the pond.

"Yes, but the money, laddie! The *money*! They just don't *pay* in England like you brazen Yanks."

"Shelly's doing a movie with Rita Hayworth at Warners," Biff mentioned vaguely as she lit a cigarette. She was a handsome woman, early-forties, with a gravelly smoker's voice. Old Philadelphia money, it was said. She exuded a languid, well-bred boredom.

"It's a *detective* story!" Shelton added, *sotto voce*, pretending to be scandalized by how low he had sunk. "I play a British scoundrel with impeccable manners who has a perfect plan to murder his wealthy wife. Absolute drivel, of course, but an actor has to eat, eh?"

Shelton Graves had the face of a bulldog: a craggy, jowly, time-ravaged face from which two pale blue eyes peered out on the world with a kind of amused bad-boy innocence.

"And what's this cane you're dragging about, laddie?" Shelly demanded as Max lowered himself into a free chair.

"Don't tell me you succumbed to a heroic impulse and got yourself wounded?"

Max obliged with a smile. "Heroic isn't the word I'd use. My Jeep hit a land mine in Egypt."

"Ah! Maxim of Arabia. Bravo! You were fighting Rommel, were you?"

"Hardly. I was following the British Eighth Army about with an Ariflex camera. Filming the war."

"Transforming slaughter into immortal art, I'm sure."

Max shrugged. He and John Huston and a number of other Hollywood directors had been drafted into the army to chronicle the war. It was rumored that Huston was making up scenes, staging reenactments of various battles, but Max had made a point of remaining faithful to actual events. Technically, they were assigned to the Army Signal Corps. In Max's case, his commanding officer was an old friend, a press agent he'd known at Metro, so he had been able pretty much to set his own agenda, go where he wanted.

He'd been lucky, he supposed. He had wanted to see what war was all about, and he'd gotten his wish. He had spent nearly eight months on the Eastern Front in the Soviet Union, taking footage that would be used as propaganda back home, propping up support for our Brave Russian Ally. FDR, who Max had met several times and admired, was struggling to drum up support from a reluctant Congress to send tanks to Stalin. For Max, Leningrad hadn't been a picnic and eventually a touch of frostbite in his hands had made it nearly impossible for him to use a camera. The Sahara, at least, had been warmer.

"It's all part of the historical record," Max explained. "Later generations will be able to marvel at our powers of destruction."

Shelly's pale blue eyes lit up with mischief. "And I'm sure you had a fabulous time getting yourself wounded, didn't you? I can just imagine you lying in the desert looking up at the sky all dreamy-eyed and thinking about God or something. Just like . . . who's that damn character who gets wounded in *War and Peace*?"

"Andre." Max smiled, embarrassed that Shelly in his own mischievous way had pegged him quite so accurately. "But land mines aren't much fun, I can assure you. I was thrown clear. I smashed up my leg a bit, but my driver and sound man were killed."

"Never mind. The women in Hollywood will find you unbearably romantic, and won't that be fun? Speaking of heroes, I presume you know your countryman, Captain Fred Landson here. Biff and I have rather adopted Fred. Biff is just like a blushing school girl where heroic soldiers are concerned—aren't you, Puss?"

"You're drunk," Biff said to her husband, exhaling a thin stream of smoke.

"Of course, I'm drunk! What sane person wouldn't be drunk at a time like this? Come on, Fred, tell this nice director your heroic saga. Maybe he'll make a movie of your life and you'll be famous."

Max reluctantly turned his attention to the American officer who was smoking the pipe. Captain Landson was Max's age, in his early forties, a raw looking man with a bony face and a strange haircut, too short on the sides, that made his ears seem overly large. He sat with all his pipe paraphernalia spread out on the table, studying Max warily.

"Good to meet you, sir," Max said dutifully.

"You might as well skip the sir and call me Fred," said the Captain, friendly enough. "This war's over for both of us, I'm guessing."

Fred offered his hand to shake across the table. But it was the wrong hand, the left rather than the right. Max saw for the first time that Captain Landson's right hand was missing, replaced by a metal hook that jutted out from the sleeve of his uniform. For Max, the missing hand humanized Fred Landson, put him in a new category. It wouldn't be so easy to come home from the war with a frightening metal hook instead of a hand. Something to scare away children. And the girls.

"Come on, Fred, tell Max your story," Shelly bullied.

"Oh, I'm sure Max doesn't want to hear any more war stories," said Fred modestly.

"Fred! What am I going to do with you? This man is a *movie* director—he can make you *famous*, my son. So tell the man how you parachuted into France and blew up that bridge."

"Please, I'm interested," Max lied.

Fred shrugged and never took his eyes off Max while he spoke. He had an odd way of seeming humble and aggressive at the same time.

"Well, it was a cock-up from the start," he said ponderously, warming to his tale. "I should never have been there in the first place—I was with intelligence in London, OSS, not the right guy to lead a team into France. But I was the only one who knew exactly where that bridge was, every darn thing about it, including how it could be blown—a transport bridge just north of Arles that the Gerries were using to bring troops and materiel to the coast. Knock out that bridge and the Gerries would have to use a highway seventy clicks to the north where our planes could bomb 'em. That was the ticket, see. But that bridge . . . that bridge was a son of a gun, I can tell you. Three hundred and thirty-seven feet across a steep gorge with a rough little river underneath. The problem was, the way the land lay, you couldn't even see the bridge from the air. Here, let me show you . . ."

Captain Landson began to rearrange ashtrays and glasses on the table to indicate the difficult geography of the terrain, using his pipe as a substitute for the bridge in question. It was a well-organized but tedious telling of the story, complete with more details than anyone wanted. Shelly wasn't about to sit still for it. He interrupted after only a few minutes.

"Good lord, man! You must learn to tell your tale with more flair!" Shelly cried. "We don't care about the geography. We want the good parts, how you killed a whole squad of Krauts single-handed and lived on bugs and worms in the forest until you were able to escape to the Channel and steal a fishing trawler . . . you see, I've wheedled this all out of him, Max, though it wasn't easy. Fred's a fucking marvel! He's the only one of his squad who made it back alive."

"For chrissake, Shelly, let Fred tell his story in his own way," Biff said, exhaling cigarette smoke. "Don't be such a bully."

"Well, I was lucky, that's all," Fred said with a shrug, picking up the bridge from the table and transforming it back into a pipe in order to have a smoke.

"*Lucky*? No, no, Fred," Shelly objected. "You were more than lucky, that's why they're going to give you that medal thing . . . what do they call it?"

"The Medal of Honor," said Fred. "Of course, it's only the silver medal. You see, Washington needs heroes right now to keep up morale back home, all the sacrifice. So I'm it, that's all. It's nothing special."

"Listen to the man!" Shelly cried. Being a dramatic person himself, he was outraged at Fred's lack of narrative egotism.

"They don't give that medal to just anyone, laddie. Why, you'll be able to run for political office—Americans love their heroes. Davey Crockett, Daniel Boone, and all that. Heaven help us, you could be the next President of the United States!"

It didn't seem likely, the prospect of Fred Landson as the next President of the United States. But Fred nodded seriously and didn't appear to understand that Shelly was making fun of him

"Well, maybe I *will* get into politics," he agreed, puffing on his pipe like a human locomotive. "Why not? If other fellas can do it, why not me?"

"Why not you, indeed?" Shelly cried. "What do you think, Max? You can make a movie of Fred's life, rags to riches, the whole stirring saga. You Yanks like that sort of thing, don't you?"

Shelly was just getting wound up. God only knew what mean-minded drunken nonsense he had in mind. But at just this moment, an amazing change came over Captain Fred Landson. He was staring past Max's left shoulder when all his features seemed to come alive, focusing with single-minded attention, like a hawk who has just spotted a rabbit. Max turned to see what had brought such a change over the war-damaged officer and was surprised to find the pretty refugee girl standing in the doorway, shy yet determined, in the exact spot where she had appeared the other night. She was wearing the same shabby gray skirt and sweater and there was an old man at her side, her father apparently. He was holding onto her arm for support, wheezing in short little gasps. He didn't look well.

The bartender had spotted them as well and was coming their way. Displaced Persons, apparently, weren't any more welcome in the Officers Canteen in the afternoon than they were at night. Sadly, the girl and her father were about to get the boot.

"Well, well!" Shelly said thoughtfully. With his Shakespearian training, he had the knack of changing the quality of his voice in an instant. "I do declare, I sense a damsel in distress. Just waiting, I should think, for one of us to save her. Shall we draw straws? Or shall we butt horns over the darling creature like stags? . . . now, Puss, don't look so concerned," he said to his wife. "A man must have some amusement, after all."

It was Fred Landson who made the first move, rising to his feet, clearly intending some act of chivalry. But the sailor barman had already reached the old man and his daughter.

"Miss, I told you the other night, you can't come in here. I'm sorry, but this lounge is reserved for officers and special guests. You shouldn't even be in this part of the ship—"

"Whoa, there, friend," Fred interrupted, arriving on the scene and putting his good hand on the sailor's shoulder. "It seems to me that if this young lady wants to be here, nobody's going to mind one darn bit. Frankly, it would improve the view considerably, if you see what I'm saying. Where I come from, we believe in hospitality. Are you getting my drift, friend? Or do I need to elaborate?"

The barman was taken aback.

"Captain, I'm sorry, sir, but the regulations—"

"Oh, I get it! Regulations!" Fred's voice purred, the height of reason. He raised the steel hook of his missing hand into the bartender's face so that the point was only a millimeter from his nose. "Do you see this ugly piece of metal?"

"Yes, sir," the bartender managed.

"Let me tell you how I got this. I got this fighting for democracy," Fred told him. "Democracy means everybody is as good as everybody else. It means it doesn't matter jack-doodle if a person is born high or low . . . pardon my French, ma'am," he said apologetically to the young woman, then turned back to the unhappy bartender. "Democracy. That's why we're fighting, friend. And I say they stay, the old man and the girl both. That's my vote, see. But being a reasonable guy, I'm willing to put it up to a show of hands of everybody here. I'll abide by the group decision because that's the right way to do things. So what do you say, pal?"

It was an astonishing speech, pompous yet threatening. Except for the "French"—which in fact wasn't French enough to cause much concern— it was like a bad script from a cheap movie. Max nearly laughed, it was all so overblown and ridiculous. Yet Fred looked like he might use his ghastly hook to gouge the bartender's eyes out and on a military ship, this sort of behavior could end with Fred in the brig. Max rose from the table, thinking he needed to calm things down.

"Look, sailor, Captain Landson has a point," he observed, an unfortunate choice of words under the circumstances. "Why don't you just let the girl and her father stay awhile. What'll it hurt?"

The barman shook his head. "It's not up to me. The regulations—"

"Oh, bugger the regulations!" Shelly said merrily, joining the group in the doorway. "Is my face familiar to you, sailor?"

"Of course, Mr. Graves. Everyone knows—"

"Good, because as it happens, I had lunch with the captain of this vessel at my club in London just before we sailed, and he's a particular friend of mine. Knowing his views on the matter, I'm sure he'd be *most* displeased to see you impeding these fine people, this sweet girl and her dear father who have done so much to strike Hitler right in the seat of his pants, so to speak. You are alive today, sailor, because of heroic partisans like these."

It was all nonsense. Shelly had no reason to believe the girl and the old man had ever been partisans, heroic or otherwise, but meanwhile the barman appeared overwhelmed and confused. He hadn't expected such a fuss over keeping two DPs out of the Officers Canteen.

"Very well, sir," he said unhappily. "As long as you take the responsibility."

"Naturally. *Someone* must take responsibility, I dare say! . . . now come, my girl. You and your father must join us for a drink . . . barkeep, a bottle of Scotch whisky, on the double, if you will."

*****

The father and daughter made about as odd a pair as Max could imagine. Together they were a perfect picture of Beauty and the Beast, a beautiful maiden and a repulsive old man.

The old fellow was emaciated and bent with thinning strands of white hair combed across his skull. His teeth were yellow and crooked and his mouth showed several gaps when he smiled. He was dressed in a shabby blue suit that was at least a size too large, a frayed white shirt, and a maroon bow tie that was stained with the memory of past meals. At least his English was passable.

"Allow me to introduce myself, gentlemen," he said. "I am Count Julka Szopin, in happier times the artistic director of the famous Krakow Opera . . . perhaps you have visited our lovely theater? No? A real jewel box, I assure you, one of the finest opera houses in all Europe. And this is my daughter, Sonya Szopin, the famous singer. Those of us who love her call her Sasha."

"Papa!" cried the girl. "I am not so famous," she told the group apologetically, blushing.

"Oh, yes! Before the war, my Sasha was the most famous voice in all Krakow. She gave song to all our trials and jubilations. You would know her recordings, gentlemen, if you spoke Polish. Our family, of course, has an illustrious history when it comes to music. The surname Szopin, perhaps, is not familiar to you in the Polish spelling. But, aha!—if I give you the French spelling, C-H-O-P-I-N, I think you will know this name, yes? That's right, Frederic Chopin, the great Polish composer, he was our ancestor. My great-great uncle."

"Chopin . . . why, that's swell!" said Fred. "There's nothing like a symphony when you're in the mood."

"Piano, sir. My ancestor wrote for the piano almost exclusively. But this is long ago. Now, alas, we are refugees. You find us, gentlemen, in difficult circumstances. But proud. Oh, yes, very proud indeed."

Shelly could barely contain his glee. He bowed elaborately. "I am honored, Count. As it happens, we are famous artists also. This is Max McCormick, the famous motion picture director. And Captain Landson, the famous American war hero. And I am Shelton Graves, a famous Shakespearian actor—reduced at the moment to mere Hollywood drivel, alas, but still proud also."

The old man had a coughing fit so serious that Max was concerned he might not recover.

"Papa!" the girl cried, patting him on the back.

"I am fine . . . do not be despairing . . . we artists must band together in times of adversity," he proclaimed solemnly when his coughing had subsided.

"Heroic words," said Shelly. "We're going to get along famously   . . . I don't mind saying, I like your spirit. Come, come, sir, let's sit and have a cup or two of liquid consolation."

Shelly managed to pump the old man's hand furiously and kiss the girl's hand in an onslaught of mock chivalry. Fortunately, for the moment they were oblivious of the fact that for Shelly this was all a splendid lark.

"I seek the kind gentleman who gave my daughter money for cognac when she was short," said Chopin's great-great nephew, the Count. "I wish to repay."

"Well, that was me," said Max. "But truly, it's nothing. You must allow that bottle of brandy to be my small gift." Despite himself, it was almost impossible to escape the awful operatic tone that had settled on things.

The old man shook Max's hand energetically. "This is very generous! One day you will come to Poland, to the beautiful city of Krakow, and I will give you a bottle of our wonderful vodka . . ."

"Vodka, did I hear?" Shelly asked, raising a dramatic eyebrow. "What a splendid thing to do to a potato, eh?"

"Holy cow, I've never met a real count before. That's something!" Fred said to the girl, ignoring Shelly's antics. He had placed his metal hook shyly behind his back, which Max found obscurely moving. "So does that make you a countess?"

"Not really," the girl answered modestly. "I'm afraid we have a very large number of counts and countesses in Poland. Too many by far. Really, it does not mean a thing."

"Oh, I don't know about that. And gee, you're a famous singer too!"

"No, I'm afraid my father, he . . . what is the word? . . . he exasperates."

"Exaggerates?" Max suggested, intruding into the conversation.

Her eyes flashed in his direction. Once again, he had a sense of her taking a kind of snapshot of him, taking his measure in a shrewd and disconcerting way.

"Yes, exaggerates. This word is correct. I sang small parts in the opera before the war. But then came the Germans . . . I'm afraid, my career hardly began when it was over."

"Why, gee, you must have been just a little girl before the war!" Fred said gallantly.

"Growing up at the opera, I began very early," Sasha agreed with a smile. "We all took whatever parts were needed. I was onstage by the time I was five years old."

139

Just then, Papa had another of his coughing fits. "Come," said Shelly, "I believe we must get your heroic father to a chair before he collapses."

In this manner, in a babble of voices, Max, Shelly and Captain Landson led the two refugees back to the table where Biff was waiting, smoking a cigarette and looking put out. She shook hands coolly with the old man, nodded even more coolly at his daughter, and they all sat down.

"Ah," said Count Szopin, glancing at the cards and the small piles of money. "You have been playing a game of chance, I see. Which game of chance is it that you play?"

"Poker," said Shelly, giving him a piercing look. "You know this game of chance, do you?"

A cagey smile touched the corners of the old man's lips. "Why, yes. I have been known to try a hand or two at this friendly sport."

Shelly smiled back, just as cagily. "Perhaps you would care to sit in, Count?"

Max cleared his throat. "Shelly, I'm not sure this is such a good idea . . ."

"Nonsense, Max. We're only playing for loose change to pass the time. Fred's beating us all blind, aren't you, Fred? He must have won all of three dollars so far."

"Papa, I don't think you should play," the girl said anxiously.

But the old man brushed her aside. "I must advise you, I am a famous card player in Krakow," he announced grandly. "I do not wish to take your money without warning."

"You see?" Shelly said to Max, just as the bottle of Scotch arrived. "He's a famous card player from Krakow. Better hang onto your wallet, Max."

"Papa . . ."

The old man turned to his daughter and said something sharply in Polish that made her be quiet. Max didn't like anything about this. He was certain the old man couldn't afford to lose money to Shelly, who despite his clownishness was a ruthless player. Max stood up from the table, deciding it would be unbearable to stick around and watch the old fellow get fleeced.

"Aren't you going to play, Max?" Shelly asked, shuffling the deck.

"No, I don't think so. Actually, I came in here to read a script and I think I'd better get to it. I hope you enjoy your game."

Sasha flashed him a curious look and Max had the impression that she intended to say something. But Fred touched her arm and she turned his way instead. "Look, why don't you play with my money," Fred said to the girl, pushing a small stack of chips her way. "Maybe if we play together, we'll bring each other luck."

Fred Landson wasn't an attractive fellow; there was something quite foolish about him. But as far as Max was concerned, he was the only one at the table showing any class. With a curt nod, Max took his script and went off in search of a place to read. He didn't much like cards anyway, and none of this was his problem.

"High card deals," he heard Shelly say behind him.

"And the dealer calls the game," said the Polish Count, the ex-director of the Krakow Opera. It seemed to Max that the old man's English had improved remarkably the moment he started playing poker.

*****

The *Mauretania* groaned and pitched as the bow of the ship broke its way through heavy seas. As the afternoon progressed, many of the passengers disappeared from the Officers Canteen for their own quarters. Max never suffered sea sickness himself; he had spent too many summers of his childhood on the Cape sailing small boats. Sitting alone at his table, he ordered a pot of tea and opened the script of the movie Sam Goldwyn had sent him.

He managed to read for nearly half an hour without retaining a single word. He kept wondering about the girl and her father, hoping they weren't losing too much money. At last, Max gave in to his curiosity and looked over to where the game was in process. He was seated several tables away, but the lounge had cleared out and he had an unobstructed view. To his surprise, the old man appeared flushed with victory. He was sitting behind a pile of chips looking enormously pleased with himself.

"How do you call it? A full house!" the Count cried merrily, slapping down his cards. As Max watched, the girl, Sasha, whispered something urgently into her father's ear. Max hoped she was telling Papa to quit while he was ahead. But the old man shook his head. "No, Lady Luck, she is with me," he announced loudly.

"Lady Luck, indeed," Shelly said drolly, his hilarity momentarily subdued. "If I didn't know better, I'd say there had to be five aces in that pack. Amazing, isn't it, how you happened to have one, Count Szopin."

"Are you suggesting—"

"I'm not suggesting anything at all," Shelly told him. "Still, you don't mind, do you, if we get a new deck from the bar?"

"Of course not," said the old man. "Sasha, be a good girl and bring us fresh cards from the bar, my darling. The old cards, they are not providing much luck for Mr. Graves."

"Perhaps we should just stop the game," Fred suggested. "Hey, I know—what about a spin around the deck?"

"Look, are we playing or not?" Biff demanded. "Personally, I want a chance to win back my money."

"Yes, let's play!" the Count cried recklessly. "Sasha, fresh cards . . ."

Fred was indefatigable. If new cards were required, he would fetch them. But before he could rise, the girl stood first, assuring him that she was happy for the opportunity to stretch her legs.

Max had stopped even pretending to read his script. He watched with interest as Sasha crossed the room toward the bar to do her father's bidding. She moved quickly, absorbed in her thoughts, unaware of Max. The barman gave her a sour look when she arrived at where he was unloading boxes.

"A package of playing cards, please."

"Certainly, miss," the barman said unhappily.

Crossing the room had brought Sasha closer to where Max was sitting. She was only a short distance away now, standing in a three-quarters profile to him. From this angle, Max thought he detected something almost tragic in her face, a depth of feeling he hadn't noticed before. This interested him. As a movie director, he'd met plenty of pretty girls and it had come to bore him, all that well-packaged vanity. But there was a mystery about this girl that he couldn't put a name to, and it held him.

Max watched as the barman gave her a fresh deck of cards. Then an odd thing happened. The barman turned his back and as soon as he wasn't looking, Sasha slipped the deck she had just been handed into a pocket at the side of her gray dress, a narrow slit in the material, and took another pack from her handbag in its place. She did this very smoothly, with the bar hiding her movements from the rest of the room. Max would have missed it if he hadn't been studying her so intently, sitting at an angle where he was able to see the lower part of her body.

It took Max a moment to absorb what he had just witnessed. He was flabbergasted. She had changed the cards! Max's guess was that she had substituted the deck she had bought that first night onboard. The packs were sealed, but seals could be tampered with in the privacy of one's cabin.

Without warning, the girl turned his way to find him watching her. Perhaps she had felt the intensity of his gaze. Her green eyes showed alarm for just an instant before she regained her self-possession. She had to be wondering if he had seen her make the switch. Max smiled enigmatically, deciding not to make it easier for her. She nodded coolly and walked back to the table where her father and the others were waiting. In a moment, the game continued.

Max grinned with unexpected pleasure as he watched the unlikely father-daughter team set to work, separating the other players from their money.

So much for shy innocence.

Max finished his tea quickly and left the Officers Canteen, deciding he'd seen enough human interest for one afternoon. He supposed he should warn the players at Shelly's table of their peril, that Lady Luck had been highjacked and wouldn't be smiling on them any time soon. But he preferred not to get involved. Shelly and Biff were predators themselves, and Fred Landson could look after himself.

Back in his cabin, Max lay on his bunk and laughed for a long time. As usual, he had gotten the whole thing wrong. The Polish Count and his daughter were card sharps, both of them as phony as a three-dollar bill. Boatmen—that was the expression from before the war, professional card slicks who worked the trans-Atlantic liners. Max was delighted.

Best of all, he could stop wondering about her now, who this girl from a land far away might be. The mystery of her had turned out to be rather commonplace, after all.

Perhaps even a bit cheap.

Three

As the days passed—aimless sea days with time to kill, so different from time on land—Sasha and her father were often to be found in the Officers Canteen. Even the sour-faced bartender came to accept them, bowing to the inevitable, that pretty girls made their own rules on a troop ship full of men.

Max watched Sasha's rapid social rise from an amused distance. At first, the old Count was always at her side, generally hanging onto her arm for support. Then Sasha began appearing by herself, leaving Dad below in Steerage. No one regretted the old fellow's absence; it was the girl the men wanted to see, all of them vying to buy her drinks, hoping to make an impression. Sasha soon had first lieutenants, second lieutenants, captains, majors, even a brigadier general in tow. There was no competition and he presumed she would enjoy that. She was the most dazzling female for a thousand miles in any direction.

Of Sasha's suitors, Fred Landson—Captain Hook, as some of the men called him—was clearly the most ardent, lurking nearby whenever she was around, watching her every move with a hungry intensity, as though he wanted to eat her up alive. No one much liked Fred. The other officers thought him an overgrown Boy Scout, a silly fellow with old-fashioned ways who couldn't even swear properly, and it was obvious that Fred didn't stand a chance against the more glamorous applicants for the role of Sasha's lover. By the fourth day at sea, the main contender appeared to be a pilot from Indiana, a dashing young man with jet black hair who had taken the upper hand from an infantry officer, a major, who had initially appeared to be in first place. Sasha treated each of her suitors with grave courtesy, as though determined to keep them all on a string.

Max found it fascinating to watch, the age-old dance of the sexes. He supposed he didn't blame Sasha for basking in the attention. Meanwhile, he was glad to be middle aged and married, only an observer, in no way a player in the game.

Nevertheless, he kept her secret. He didn't tell a soul that she was a cheat, not what she appeared to be. He wasn't sure why he kept his mouth shut, except it was somehow agreeable to know something about her that the others didn't. It created a bond between them, a kind of intimacy. As though they both knew the punch line to the same joke.

*****

One morning after several days at sea, Max was walking past the Officers Canteen when he noticed Sasha at the upright piano with a group of four or five of her admirers gathered around. Apparently, they had coaxed her into giving them a song.

Max had been heading toward the deck for his morning walk, but this was too interesting to pass up. Hoping to escape notice, he slipped into a chair in the back of the room, curious to hear her.

"So, doll, what's it gonna be?" the pilot from Indiana asked, leaning against the piano with his usual self-confidence.

"This is a song from my homeland. Perhaps you will not like it," she answered with a smile. She knew very well that these men would like anything she did.

Fred Landson, who was seated on the far side of the piano, clapped his hands in order to get everyone's attention. "All right! Quiet down, you mugs! She can't sing if you're all making so much noise!"

Sasha placed her hands delicately on the yellowed ivories of the piano. It was a battered old instrument with cigarette burns on the wood that looked as though it had been on the losing end of countless tunes sung at top volume by drunken soldiers on their way to war. Sasha closed her eyes dreamily and let her fingers make a chord. The notes on the old piano were wavery and far from true.

After a brief introduction, she began to sing in a passionate, husky voice that Max found surprisingly low. The song was sad and slow and Slavic, in some minor scale that seemed to Max almost oriental. It was obvious that Sasha had training; she was able to project her voice into every corner of the room, no need for a microphone. But it was an old-fashioned voice. Her tone warbled with unexpected vibrato. It was like listening to a human cello.

Max decided he liked her singing, once he got over the surprise of how different it was from what he had expected. She sang from the heart as though she meant every word. But her voice was unconventional, and this was going to be a problem if she wanted a career in America. Her vibrato reminded him of antique warbles from the Victrola age. No one sang like that anymore. Today girls all tried to sound like the Andrew Sisters, perky and modern.

When she was finished, the men around the piano clapped and cheered.

"Wow! That was something!" Fred declared. "That was really great!"

"More! More!" someone cried.

"How about something jazzy," the pilot suggested. "You know any jazz?"

Sasha laughed. "Jazz? Yes, of course. Poland isn't quite like living on the moon, I know jazz very well. All right, here is another. I think you will know this song. It is called, 'I Am Behaving Well.'"

Max couldn't think of any jazz tune he knew called "I Am Behaving Well," but he listened with the rest of the men as Sasha turned back to the piano. As before, she closed her eyes and her low voice filled the room. But whatever this supposedly American song was, it sounded exactly like the sad, slow, Slavic tune she had sung before, not even slightly like jazz. Pretty as she was, Sasha was going to have a tough time playing music like this once she reached the relentless modernity of New York.

Max wasn't even sure the lyrics were English, though he recognized an occasional word. Still, there was a ghostly familiarity about it, a hint of something he had heard before. "I Am Behaving Well?" Then he got it. It was "Ain't Misbehavin'", though altered to the point where it was barely recognizable. There wasn't a blue note anywhere, nor a hint of rhythm. The result was turgid sentimentality of a middle-European sort that was almost comical.

Max stood and slipped quietly from the room before the song was finished, deciding this was a good moment to make his exit. He didn't want to join the others in forced applause, or be put in the embarrassing position of having someone ask for his opinion. He was a professional, after all; he had little patience with amateurs.

Sasha was an intriguing young woman, as far as he was concerned. But she would be smart to forget music and marry one of the men vying for her attention.

Or maybe she should just stick to cards.

*****

That night after dinner, Fred Landson came walking his way in a purposeful trajectory across the mezzanine lobby outside the Officers Mess.

"Hey, Max, wait up a second, will you?" he called "Look, I saw you were there listening to Sasha this morning. You got away before I could ask you what you thought."

Max smiled. That, of course, had been his intention.

"Well," he said judiciously, "it was great to hear the girl sing. There's something about a young woman at a piano that strikes a chord."

Fred scowled, ignoring the pun. "Yeah, but does she have a future? You know show business, Max. So tell me the truth. Does she have what it takes?"

"What it *takes*? For a career in opera? I really couldn't say."

"Naw, it's not opera she's after. She knows she's missed too many years of training for something serious like that. Because of the war, you see. So she's thinking she'll sing popular stuff. That's her plan, anyway. She thinks she's going to take New York by storm. You think she has a chance?"

"A chance? Sure, she has a chance, Fred. Everybody has a chance. And that's what it is mostly, ninety percent chance. But it's not so easy to take New York by storm. Look, if I were to give her advice, I'd say she should get herself a good teacher when she gets to America, someone who can bring her repertoire up to date and clue her in to modern styles.

Maybe if she studies for a while, she'll get it. But I don't know her well enough to say. You heard her this morning, Fred. What do you think?"

Fred grinned. "Oh, I like her singing! I like everything about her. But I'm a realist, I know how the world works. My guess is that an innocent girl like that isn't going to get anywhere near the big time. A bunch of guys will paw her, that's all. They'll chew her up and toss her out and break her heart. And it's my intention to see that doesn't happen."

Max resisted the temptation to laugh. An innocent girl?

"Well, it's hard to say," he answered vaguely.

"Look, Max, I got a favor to ask you. I'm hoping you'll talk to her, set her straight. She'll listen to you because you're a big shot. I'm not asking you to lie. Just tell her she doesn't have the stuff to make it in show business. Tell her what happens to young girls in New York who don't have someone to look after them, how they end up on the street, all used up."

"Wait a second—you want me to discourage her?"

A cunning look had come into Fred's eye. "Come on, Max, you heard her this morning. She's a great kid, but what she needs is to find a steady fella to marry and give up all this nonsense of being a star."

"And that steady fella is you, I presume?"

"You bet. Sure, I know I'm not a fancy guy. I'm not handsome, I'm a lot older than she is, I have this darn hook for a hand. But I'm ready to settle down and I've got plans, you see. Big plans to make a lot of money. And her being Polish, and all . . . well, it's not going to be so easy for two foreigners with funny accents in America, especially if she's dragging around a sick old father. So I figure she'll settle for someone practical like me, as long as I can snap her up fast before the other guys get to her. All I gotta do is convince her to give up this notion she's going to be a famous singer."

Max's sympathy for Fred was fading quickly. He shook his head. "Well, I don't know, Fred. It's not my style to discourage people from their dreams."

"Come on, Max. All I'm asking is that you talk to her. Tell her the truth, that's all. And put in a word for me while you're at it. Tell her she'd be better off with a solid guy who can take care of her instead of knocking her head up against some dream that's never going to come true. You and me, Max, we know what the world is like. We know what happens to girls like that in big cities."

For Max, the conversation had become distasteful. Only a few hours earlier, he had been thinking the same thing, that the girl would be best off marrying someone like Fred and forgetting her musical ambitions. But now that he had heard Fred put it into words, the whole thing seemed lousy.

Fred moved closer and put his good hand on Max's shoulder. He was taller than Max and there was something aggressive about the hand on his shoulder that Max didn't like. "Just talk to her," he said. "You would be doing me a favor, and who knows? Maybe some day I'll be able to do a favor for you in return."

Max squirmed and shook his head. He had always felt awkward about this sort of thing, people thinking that just because he was a movie director, he could help them break into show business. This had a different twist, to discourage the girl, but he still didn't like it.

"Come on, Max," Fred said quietly, almost a whisper.

"All right," he agreed. "I'll talk to her. I can't guarantee anything, but I'll try."

Fred squeezed Max's shoulder in a friendly manner, but too hard.

"Atta boy, Max. You know, people told me you were a snob. Stuck-up, they said. But you're a regular guy, I see that now."

Fred let go of Max's shoulder. "Thanks, Max. I mean it. I'll tell her to look for you."

Max shook his head after Fred was gone, wondering what he had gotten himself in for.

Damn Fred! he thought angrily as he made his way back to his stateroom. And damn that ridiculous girl!

Four

Max woke the next morning to find the sun had made a remarkable appearance, transforming the North Atlantic into a bright cloudless world of blue: blue sea, blue sky, the sun low on the horizon radiating a warmth that hinted at spring. It was a false spring, the sort of mid-February spell in which a single cloud could bring winter rushing back in an instant. But while it lasted, one should seize the day.

Max was sick of people bothering him and after lunch, he took the script that Sam Goldwyn had sent him in London and wandered out on deck to see if he could find a sunny place where he might read undisturbed. He knew he needed to stop mooning around and get to work.

He'd done his patriotic duty in the war, everyone was proud of him. But he hadn't made a movie for over two years—not a real movie, anyway—and this was a problem. Hollywood had a short memory. You were only as good as your last picture, and if they couldn't even remember your last picture, a director like Max could find himself in trouble. At present, his only prospective employer was Sam Goldwyn, *née* Goldfish —Schmuel Gelbfisz, a Jew from Poland who had dreamed his way to California—a ridiculous individual who was famous for the ways he mangled the English language. Still, as producers went, Goldfish was better than no fish at all.

Max found a make-shift deck chair near the stern of the ship, two dining room chairs facing one another that someone had brought out from inside, and he used them to arrange a small nest for himself behind a lifeboat, covering himself with a blanket from his cabin. Sheltered from the wind, wrapped up in his blanket and overcoat, he was soon snug as could be.

He opened the script with a pencil in hand, prepared to make notes in the margin. The movie was called *The Flower Girl*, a romantic tale of starving artists in Paris in the early nineteenth century, based loosely on Henry Murger's *Scènes de la vie de Bohème*, the story Puccini had used for the source of his opera, *La Bohème*. Like Puccini, Sam Goldwyn was attracted to Murger's autobiographical sketch because it was cheap, in the public domain, a hundred years old, and he didn't have to pay a penny for the rights. Mina was set to play the female lead, Mimi, the dying flower girl who falls in love with the poet, Rodolfo, who was to be played by Robert Taylor. "It'll be the easiest acting job of my career," Mina had written humorously to Max in England. "All I need is to change two letters of my name and learn how to cough!"

Mina had engineered the deal with Sam Goldwyn and Max suspected she was working below her usual salary in return for Sam hiring her husband. This was typical of Mina, how faithful she was in every area except sex. But the script was awful. After reading a dozen pages of turgid dialogue, Max groaned aloud in despair. Still, one had to be practical. If he did a decent job with *The Flower Girl*, he'd be in a position to choose better movies in the future. That was the point on which he needed to concentrate.

Max was determined to take a positive attitude. Yet despite his best intentions, doubt whispered snake-like in his ear. It wasn't only the dreadful script. Somehow the very times had changed while he had been away at war, a new decade in which Max wasn't sure where he fit—the Frumpy Forties, Mina called them, a serious, patriotic time in which people didn't laugh at the same jokes they had before. The world no longer wanted madcap comedies like *The Romantic Butler*, the sophisticated fluff with which he had made his mark in the 1930s.

Max managed to read only twenty pages of *The Flower Girl* before his eyes became impossibly heavy in the pleasant glow of wintry sun. The page swam in his vision, unreal as a mirage. Gradually, his eyes closed, unable to resist the seduction of gravity. The sun made orange patterns on the inside of his eyelids. The ship rocked like a cradle, adding to his languor.

Somewhere in the back of his mind, Max knew he should resist the call of peace. He was a man who must clash horns and struggle. But not today. Today, he refused to struggle. He felt himself slipping downward into sleep, where all doubt and worry drifted away . . .

*****

Max was dreaming he was home in California, floating on his back in his Bel Air pool, when a voice disturbed him.

"Excuse me, this is yours?"

Even in his sleep, Max recognized her voice, a low mezzo-soprano with a foreign cadence. He opened his eyes. It was Sasha, her cheeks flushed from the ocean air. She was dressed in her usual skirt and sweater but now there was a yellow scarf tied around her hair.

"I am sorry to be waking you," she said in her stilted English. "Your book was on the floor. I was afraid it would blow off into the water."

Max sat upright, rousing himself with difficulty from his sun-drenched stupor. The wind had come up since he had fallen asleep. Sasha was holding his script, the life of bohemian Paris according to Sam Goldwyn. Later, reliving this encounter—analyzing his mistakes, pondering how he should have behaved—Max settled upon this as the moment he had gone wrong. He shouldn't have smiled at her. But she stood before him looking so fresh and full of life that he couldn't help himself. The smile came to his lips on its own accord.

"Thanks," he said, taking the script from her hand.

"I hope it is a good book, worth saving from the fishes."

His smile turned into a laugh. "Good? No, I wouldn't say that. It's work, that's all. To be honest, I wouldn't mind if it *did* blow away."

She scowled. "Work is a good thing, if you are lucky to find it. Of course, you are a rich American, so perhaps you are able to spend your life sleeping in the sun."

She had moved so that the sun had put her in silhouette. There was a golden aurora around her head and shoulders. Max had to squint in order to see her.

"And you?" he asked. "You work very hard, I suppose?"

"Yes. My father and I must survive."

"Tell me something," he asked impulsively. "Do you by any chance know the opera *La Bohème*?"

She raised an eyebrow. "Yes, naturally. I like Puccini very much."

"Do you? You see, the reason I ask is because there's a producer in Hollywood named Sam Goldfish who wants to hire me to direct a picture. Years ago, he helped start a very famous studio, Metro-Goldfish-Mayer, but that's another story. Anyway, Sam wants to make *La Bohème* into a movie, but without the music, just as straight drama. Opera's a little highbrow for your average American audience, you see. Do you understand?"

"Yes, I think so. However, *La Bohème* is a good story, even without the music."

"A good story, yes. But here's the rub. Our Mr. Goldfish wants to make some significant changes in the plot. For one, we're going to have a narrator—Puccini himself, the composer in person, played by an actor named Alan Ladd, who's a short little guy who's generally drunk and wouldn't know an opera from an orangutan. Puccini, in the guise of Mr. Ladd, is going to be part of a fun group of starving artists in Paris, all of them in love with Mimi the flower girl. This will provide a chance to depict some good-natured rivalry and allow the actors to crack a lot of bad jokes."

"But this is very wrong! Puccini, he never lived in Paris. He was never poor," Sasha told him earnestly. "He was very successful, almost from the start. And he lived much later than the characters in *La Bohème*. He died in 1924, not so long ago."

Max nodded happily, enjoying the girl's outrage, not to mention her knowledge. "Well, Sam doesn't care so much about historical accuracy. Now here's the good part. In the Goldfish version of *La Bohème*, we're going to improve things a bit. Our lovely flower girl, Mimi, isn't going to die at the end. She's going to get well and live."

Sasha's mouth fell open. "But she dies! That's the whole point of the story, the tragedy. Rodolfo is left all alone. He understands too late that he loves her."

Max's smile was unperturbed. "Yes, but Sam says that Americans want happy endings. Especially with the war going on. So in Sam's version, we're going see our Puccini character, the great composer Alan Ladd, sell his opera, the wonderful story of his good friends in Paris, and after a hugely successful opening night with tons of applause and joyful weeping, he gives Rodolfo the money to take Mimi to a sanitarium in Switzerland. In the last scene, we're going to see Robert Taylor and Mimi in the Alps, living happily ever after with a few goats around them."

The girl stared at him in dismay. "You are joking, I think."

"Not at all. This is the gospel truth." Max handed her back the script she had saved. "So please, do me a favor. Toss it. I'd be fabulously grateful, forever in your debt."

"Now I know for certain you are joking."

"Truly, I am not. I may be dissolute, but I am no shallow jester."

She laughed. "You must excuse my English. What is jester?"

"A clown. Like at the circus."

"Yes, I know the circus. And the other word you use?"

"Dissolute? Never mind that one. You're far too young."

"I'm not young at all," she objected. "I'm as old as the mountains."

"Old as the hills," he corrected.

A shadow seemed to cross her face and for a moment she did in fact look ageless. Max had rarely seen a face that was so changeable, alternating bursts of light and darkness.

"So tell me about yourself," he said. "Let's start with your age. How old are you, Sasha?"

Her eyes flashed. "Why do you wish to know?"

Max shrugged. "I don't know. I'm curious, that's all. You're the sort of girl people get curious about."

Sasha laughed uncomfortably. "Then you must guess. I give nothing away. How old do you think I am?"

Max made a show of studying her from several different angles. "I think you're nineteen, maybe twenty. I think you're a child who got caught in the war and had to grow up fast."

She shook her head. "I am seventeen," she told him. "But I am not a child. I can take care of myself and the people I love."

"I believe you."

"You should believe me. I am poor but I always tell the truth."

"Do you?"

She turned from him and carried his script to the rail. "I'm going to throw your funny *La Bohème* into the water," she promised. "Do you dare me?"

"Sure, I dare you. In fact, I double-dare you."

"Here goes . . . no, I can't."

"Of course, you can. It's total blather. It deserves to be tossed."

"All right." She lowered the script over the rail, dramatically. But then, she couldn't do it after all. With a pretty shrug, she handed him the pages back. "No, I really can't. I've never been able to throw away anything. It's very sad."

"Sad, indeed," Max agreed. With a burst of resolve, he used his cane to rise from his chair and he walked to the rail. He tossed the script overboard, as far into the water as his arm could throw. The pages caught the air, fluttered open and sailed for some distance before disappearing into the churned water at the edge of the wake. It was madness. He knew he was showing off for the girl's benefit, nothing more. Still, he felt a surge of freedom, like a man let out of a dungeon into the sun.

The girl was watching him carefully. "Was that wise?"

"Oh, yes. It's the wisest thing I've done in years. You see how good you are for me, Sasha. Will you marry me?"

Her mouth dropped open in surprise, then she laughed. "You're daft! You know that? Totally bunkers."

"Bonkers," he corrected merrily. "And honestly, it's really the best thing in a marriage for at least one partner to be slightly mad. We'll never be bored, you see. I'll take you to California where everyone is bonkers— it's the very land of bonk. You'll be as happy as a palm tree there, I assure you."

She shook her head in wonderment. "But you don't know anything about me, Mr. McCormick."

"Oh, sure, I do. You're Sasha, the Count's lovely daughter, straight out of a Polish fairy tale. What else is there to know? By the way, the name is Max. In California, only old fogies and studio bosses have last names."

"This is all very well, *Mister* McCormick. However, you can't marry me, because you are married already. To Mina Bower, the most famous actress in the world. That's what Captain Landson told me. You see, I have asked questions about you."

"Have you? Well, I'll get a divorce," he assured her. But his smile now was strained. They were standing side by side at the rail and Max didn't know what to say. After the last few giddy minutes, he felt suddenly awkward. He had meant to avoid the girl, be on guard with her at the very least. Yet here he was showing off and playing the fool, flirting like a youngster.

Sasha turned from him and stared pensively at the ocean horizon, as though affected by his change of mood. "You did not like my singing yesterday," she said after a moment. "I saw you in the back of the room."

Max sighed, remembering his promise to Fred that he would talk with the girl. "Look, Sasha, I'm a professional so I'll tell you the truth. I think you have a hell of a voice, but when you reach New York, you're going to want to find yourself a good teacher for six months or so. What you need most of all is the right repertoire. The thing about America is that everything has to be up to date. You can't sing songs like they were sung twenty years ago. Or even one year ago. You have to sing them like they're sung today. You've got to be the greatest with the latest, that's what it's all about."

"I see," she said. "Yes, I'm sure you are right, Mr. McCormick. But sadly, I am old-fashioned. I prefer the world as it used to be."

Max smiled. "Well, me too. Look, Sasha, to tell the truth, I'm not much in vogue myself right now. But you're young, so I'm sure you'll adapt just fine. My guess is that after a few weeks you'll have New York eating out of your hand."

She turned to face him. "Yes, I have learned what I must do to live. I have not had a choice. Do you think this is bad?"

"No, it's not bad at all. My philosophy is everyone who wants to get ahead, should fight like hell to be king of the mountain. As for the rest of us . . . well, dinosaurs have their good points too."

"I am not sure I understand, Mr. McCormick."

"Good," he said. "You're much better off. But truly, if you don't start calling me Max, I'm going to put you over my knee and spank you."

She laughed. "All right. Now, please, you should sit down, Mr. Max McCormick. You are wounded, no? This is why you say such wild things. I have seen this before. Wounded men talk nonsense."

Max moved back to the arrangement of chairs, feeling suddenly old and disabled. Instinctively, the girl took hold of his arm to help him down into the chair. Her grip was surprisingly sure and strong. Somehow she had turned into his nurse.

"It's handy someone left these chairs here."

"This was me," she told him. "I wished to sit in the sun and be alone."

"Oh, then I've taken your spot!" Chivalrously, he tried to rise and let her have her place back.

"No, please, you must sit. Probably you are a hero like Captain Landson. Will you get a medal too? I think medals are for idiots, to encourage foolish people to die. I despise war!"

"Do you? Well, my story's not nearly as interesting as Fred Landson's. My jeep hit a land mine, that's all. I'm not even a proper soldier." Max pushed the second chair toward her with his cane. "Why don't you sit down, Sasha. You'll make me feel like an old man if you hover above me."

"Perhaps for a moment," she agreed, settling into the chair to face him. "My father will be worried if I'm too long."

"Right. Your father the Count, the director of the Krakow Opera," Max prodded.

She flushed and lowered her eyes. "Why are you so curious about us?" she demanded. "It is not very polite, I think."

"Well, I try to be polite. Honestly, I do. But on a sea voyage, it's set in stone that we all need to behave like busybodies and find out everything we can about our fellow passengers.

I'm afraid you're an enigma, Sasha. Do you understand that word?"

She raised her eyes scornfully. "Yes, of course. It is the same in French, *ènigme*. I grew up at the opera, as I have told you, where we spoke many languages. Along with English, I know French, Italian, German, and some Russian. I may be young, but I am not stupid, Mr. McCormick."

"I didn't think you were. My guess is you're a whole lot more clever than any of your admirers suspect. I doubt if any of them really has a clue about you, do they?"

She met his gaze. "Ah-ha! Yes, I understand now. You saw me that afternoon in the officers' lounge, didn't you? I wasn't sure at first, but now I am. You saw me change the cards."

Max hadn't supposed they would get to this essential point quite so quickly. He nodded. "Sure, I saw you."

"And now you think I am a very bad person."

"Are you? To be honest, I'm not sure I know. So why don't you tell me. Why is it a girl like you cheats at cards?"

"Why do you think we cheat at cards?" she said angrily. "We are desperate, that is why. It is no game, I assure you, to sail across the ocean with less than two English pounds in your pocketbook. But what do you know about these things, Mr. McCormick?"

"I'm not judging you," he said. "I'm just curious, that's all. And your father"

"He is not a count—yes, you are absolutely right. You have watched us carefully and seen all our secrets. He was not even the director of the opera. He was only the proprietor of a small café where the singers used to go after a performance. He is nobody at all. And now he is a sick old man who is hoping we will eat tomorrow. I tell him, Papa, do not play cards, do not pretend you are an aristocrat. I tell him, these people are clever, Papa. They will know. But he is only a foolish old man and he thinks he is doing something to help me. I am sure you must find us pathetic."

Max didn't know quite what to say. "Look, I'm sorry. I have no right to judge your life. I wouldn't even know where to begin."

Sasha stood from her chair and began walking away. Max thought he had lost her. But she went only as far as the ship's rail where she stopped and turned back to him.

"Are you going to tell your friends about us?"

"No, of course not. Among other things, those people aren't my friends. I don't like them a bit."

"I see. And you, Mr. McCormick—why is it you are so nice? Do you expect me to show . . . gratitude? Is that it?"

"No, Sasha," he replied sadly. "You don't need to be even slightly grateful. That's not it at all."

"Then, why?" she demanded.

"Maybe there's no why to it at all."

169

"There's always a why," she insisted. "There's always a price."

"Is there? Well, just call this one a freebie. Call it a going-out-of-business sale."

"I do not understand."

"It doesn't matter, Sasha. Your secret's safe with me. If you don't understand why, just let it be."

She continued to study him. "You are a strange man, Mr. McCormick. But I prefer to pay what I owe."

"All right. How about the answer to a few questions, then? Let's say to settle our debt, I get to ask you three questions."

"Three questions?" she repeated dubiously.

"Precisely. Like a fairy tale. And then I'll turn into a frog and you needn't worry about me ever again."

"A frog?" Sasha's face underwent one of its sudden changes. A smile came onto her face that was like sunshine emerging from a dark cloud. "No, I don't think you are a frog, Mr. McCormick. You are definitely a prince."

"Before you say that, you'd better wait until you hear my questions."

"All right. Ask me."

But suddenly they were no longer alone. A stout, elderly couple came walking up the outside stairs to the deck where Sasha and Max were having their conversation. It was the unpleasant tweedy couple Max had noticed the first night in the bar. They were dressed for a blizzard in scarves and coats, hats and gloves, defying the ocean breeze in order to take their healthful constitutional. Bristling with disapproval, they passed near where Sasha and Max were talking.

"Good afternoon!" Max called after them.

Without answering, the couple continued toward the rear section of the deck that overlooked the stern. Ostensibly, they had come to ponder the hypnotic mystery of the ship's wake, the green and white churning water below, but Max saw them glance back their way from time to time. He rose from where he'd been sitting and joined Sasha at the rail so they could talk without being overheard.

"Okay, here's the first question. We've established that your father owned a small café. How about you? Did you really sing at the Krakow opera?"

"Yes. I grew up at the opera, as I have said—my mother was a singer and as a child I lived with her rather than my father. They were . . . how do you say it?"

"Divorced?"

"They were never married," Sasha said, watching for his reaction. "You are scandalized, I'm sure."

"Oh, not very. Worse things happen in California, I assure you."

"In any case, I sang sometimes in the chorus and small roles. I was hopeful that one day I would have bigger roles. But after 1939, of course nothing was the same."

"And are you related to Frederic Chopin?"

"This is your second question?"

"Sure."

"Then the answer is no. Naturally, not. Szopin is a common name in Poland. This is my father's fantasy. He thinks no one will like us because we are refugees so he tries to find a way so people will think we're special. What is your third question?"

"How did you get out of Poland, Sasha? How in God's name did you and your father get to England?"

"Oh, this is a big question! This is several questions, I think."

"Then tell me just part of the answer."

"Very well. The partisans helped us. You see, there is an underground route from Poland to the south, all the way to Greece. It took many months going from one safe house to another and it was very dangerous." She gazed thoughtfully out to sea, remembering. "Fortunately, my father kept us safe. He is very brave"

"I can see that," Max told her gravely.

"In any case, we made our way to Greece, and from there a fishing boat took us to Lisbon, the open city. In Lisbon we went to the British Consul and I told a big lie. I said we had important information about a terrible weapon the Nazis were building at Wieliczka, the old salt mines outside of Krakow. I said it was an atomic-powered weapon that would change the war. I pretended a German officer had taken me to

Wieliczka to show me the weapon, hoping to impress me. Naturally, the British were very interested and they brought us to England. By the time they realized there wasn't much to my story, we were in London where we wanted to be. And now I know that you are very shocked, Mr. McCormick—a girl whose parents were not married and who tells lies and cheats at cards. But I am not ashamed. We did what we had to in order to be alive."

Max nodded carefully, not sure what he thought. As a New Englander, he'd been taught from an early age that truth was the most basic foundation of a good character. Hollywood had never quite erased his native puritanism. But he had never had to flee Nazi soldiers from Poland to Portugal.

"I think you're an astonishing girl," he decided.

She laughed scornfully. "No, I am not astonishing. I chose to think for myself, that's all. The world did not strike me as such a lovely place that I should do what people pretend is pretty behavior."

"And your mother?" he asked. "Is she alive?"

"Ah! You have asked your three questions, I think! But I will tell you anyway. Like many people in my country, the Germans hanged her. My mother enjoyed life very much, but they hanged her from a lamppost and made me watch as she died. And now you know everything."

"I'm sorry. My God, I shouldn't have asked."

Sasha looked away, dismissively. "It is no matter. She is dead, that's all."

Max was deeply moved by her story. He wanted to tell her that he had grown up easy in Boston and couldn't imagine what it would be like to see your mother hung from a lamppost. But at just that moment, the tweedy elderly woman came walking briskly their way, leaving her husband at the rail.

"I say, aren't you that spiritualist's assistant?" the lady demanded, marching up to Sasha. "The Great Jabolonski? The one who did that séance in Eaton Square?"

"Séance?" said Sasha. "No, I have never been at a séance? You are confusing me with someone else, I think."

"No, I'm not. I remember your face perfectly well. Ever since I first saw you on this ship, I've been certain I'd seen you before. And now it's just come to me where. Diana, that's what you called yourself. You wore that white gown all the men couldn't take their eyes off, the one you could see through when the light was right. You and that old fake, the Great Jabolonski, performed a séance to speak with Emily Ashington's husband who was killed in North Africa. It was December, just before Christmas."

Sasha shook her head. "No, I'm sorry. My name is Sonya, not Diana. I do not know what you are referring to."

"I think you've made a mistake, madam," Max said chivalrously on Sasha's behalf.

"No, I don't think so," said the unpleasant woman. "And you know, there was twenty pounds missing from my handbag that night."

"I am very sorry to hear it," Sasha said loftily. "But I have never been in Eaton Square, nor do I have the slightest idea of this person, the Great Jubilee. You are confusing me with someone else."

The woman put her hands on her hips angrily. "You know, I've never believed in all that séance nonsense, and I think it's a damn shame to take advantage of people like my friend Emily who's lost a husband. I can't prove you took those twenty pounds, but I never forget a face and I'll sure never forget yours, I can tell you that!"

Max intruded once again. "Excuse me, but she's told you twice now, you're confusing her with someone else. Her name is Sonya, not Diana."

"Oh, it's like that, is it?" cried the stout woman.

"Yes, it's like that," he replied. "And now, if you don't mind, we're having a private conversation."

Max watched with some satisfaction as the woman turned red in the face. She made a humphing sound deep in her throat, turned haughtily and walked back to where her husband was waiting unhappily by the rail. Max took Sasha's arm and led her away along the deck toward the top of the stairs.

"Thank you!" she told him. "What a terrible woman! I don't know where she got such an idea! The Great Jabberwocky . . . what an imagination!"

"Jabolonski," Max corrected. "I wouldn't pay any attention to someone like that, Sasha. She's old, probably she doesn't see very well."

"Certainly not!"

At the top of the stairs, Sasha supported Max's arm as he made his way carefully downward, leaning on his cane step by step to the deck below. The afternoon seemed suddenly vast to him and wonderful, a huge vista of sky and ocean with the *Mauretania*, hardly more than a toy, plowing through the white-capped waves.

"Your leg hurts, I am sorry for this," she said when they reached the lower deck.

"It's okay. Maybe it's good to hurt a little. It's a reminder that we're all so damn vulnerable and we need to be kind."

They turned to each other to say goodbye, her green eyes watching him closely. Her lips were so close that Max felt a ridiculous urge to lean forward and kiss her. He resisted, of course, being sensible. Instead he followed his Boston instincts and asked if she would care to go inside for a cup of tea.

"No, I must return to my father," she said. "He is not well. But thank you, Mr. McCormick. You are a nice man. A knight in shining armor, I think."

Max laughed. "Ah, you've just demoted me from a Frog Prince to a knight! But it's a sweet thought. And if you ever run into a dragon that needs slaying, be sure and let me know."

"Oh, I would never kill a dragon!" she told him seriously. "Dragons are my great friends!"

"Are they?"

Her eyes opened very wide and for the moment she seemed much younger than seventeen, only a child.

"May I tell you a secret? When I was little, my mother used to take me to Wawel Castle on Sundays when we didn't have a performance. This is the old royal castle, our most famous place in Krakow—the Germans have made it their headquarters now, but when I was small, the soldiers would open the gates on Sunday so we could go inside to the big cathedral and listen to the archbishop say mass. According to legend, there is a dragon who lives in a cave below the castle and it was to him that I prayed—the dragon, not Jesus and Mary as good girls should. He is my dragon, you see, my guardian, and he watches over me. He has kept me alive. He is why I am different from other people."

"I see. A girl with a dragon. Yes, that's very different indeed."

She nodded. "I will tell you his name, if you like. But it can't be said aloud—I must whisper into your ear."

She leaned closer and Max felt her lips briefly touch his right ear.

"His name is Smok," she whispered. "But you must never tell a soul. It is a very great secret."

"Smok," he repeated. "That's a good name for a dragon."

"Do you promise not to tell?"

"I promise," he agreed. It was ridiculous, but he felt that she had given him an important gift, telling him the name of her dragon. "Look, are you sure you wouldn't care for that cup of tea? We can even get an extra cup for Smok, if you'd like. Though maybe he's the sort of dragon who prefers gin."

Sasha didn't smile. "You are wrong not to take me seriously, Mr. McCormick. But truly, I must go. My father will be worrying. He is old and the trip from Krakow has been hard for him. You must excuse me now."

"Look, Sasha, if I can do anything for your father, I'm in Cabin 139 if you need me. I'm sure there's a doctor onboard. You mustn't hesitate to ask."

Her pretty eyes flashed his way, then she turned and left. Just before she disappeared through the sea door, she stopped by the rail to cast a final look at the ocean, as though she had been struck by a profound thought, offering her profile for him to view. Max knew she was play-acting, putting on a show for his benefit. But he liked her anyway. He knew he shouldn't, but he liked her a lot.

An Overnight Sensation

When he was alone, Max walked toward the bow of the ship and stood with the wind beating fiercely against his face. He was full of the lingering enchantment of the girl: dragons and castles and a phony séance in Eaton Square where a twenty-pound note had been taken from a handbag.

The Great Jabolonski and his lovely daughter! What a pair of scoundrels! He knew he should be outraged. But he wasn't.

Max couldn't stop smiling.

My Awful Hollywood Childhood II:

How I Became a Star

In 1953, when I was ten years old, fate rolled my way and I became a child star in a weekly TV series. A half-century later, I'm still trying to decide if this was good luck, bad luck, or no luck at all.

You'll find me even today—my clean-scrubbed, slightly freckled All-American face—on obscure cable channels of the sort that cater to nostalgia, instant time travel for aging Boomers to revisit their youth. I played Rusty, the younger brother in *What a Life!*—note the exclamation point—a half-hour family sitcom that appeared every Thursday night at seven on CBS. Our sponsor was Lucky Strike cigarettes whose slogan was an odd series of alphabet letters, L.S.M.F.T, that the entire nation back then knew stood for Lucky Strike Means Fine Tobacco.

Such was my personal fifteen minutes—in my case, two years of fame, before the show was cancelled due to scandalous circumstances which I will relate in due time. I had a modest talent for acting, I suppose, though I knew from the start I wasn't destined to be any sort of Laurence Olivier. In my own way, I had been acting as long as I could remember, well before 1953, the sort of kid who had learned early to pretend to be what he was not.

What a Life! came my way because a TV producer, Mort Jenkins, had a case of serious lust for my mother and invited us for lunch at his beach house in the Malibu Colony one Sunday in July. My mother accepted the invitation because she was hoping that Mort could get her a TV show of her own—*The Sonya Saint-Amant Hour*, as she thought of it—coast-to-coast, once a week, preferably Sunday night at eight o'clock.

Lunch with Mort Jenkins was not my idea of a fun afternoon, so I tried to beg off. But my mother wanted me along as protection against lecherous advances and, in the end, I agreed to go. I understood my mother very well. To get her TV show, she needed to flirt, but if I was nearby, the poor guy would be unable to follow up on the invitation and pounce.

We drove to the beach along Sunset Boulevard in my mother's cream-colored 1952 Cadillac convertible, a cutely rounded car with spotted leopard skin upholstery and red tail lights that jutted out behind us, hinting at the rocket-ship fins that were to come later in the decade. I loved seeing my beautiful mother at the wheel (sunglasses, silk scarf tied around her blond hair), knowing we looked just right, the perfect California family having fun in the sun, laughing and sexy and modern for everyone to see. We weren't right at all, of course—we were about as dysfunctional as a family could be.

But no one could tell that as we zipped past in our perfect blur of make-believe.

Mort Jenkins was a plump, roly-poly sort of guy who smoked cigars and was at least six inches shorter than my mother. Still, as producers went, he wasn't such a bad fellow. He laughed a good deal, sometimes at his own expense, and he was very palsy with me, probably hoping that this would improve his chances with my mother. Lunch consisted of hamburgers and corn on the cob which he barbecued himself on the sun deck in front of his house. He and my mother drank French champagne while I sipped on a Royal Crown Cola. I knew I had a job to do, to act as a firewall between Mort and my mother, and I gave it my best shot. To be honest, I'm sure she would have been able to deal with him even if I hadn't been there to chaperone. But it was nice to feel useful.

We were eating our burgers when Mort sprang his surprise.

"You know, I have this idea for a show I've been mulling over," he said casually. (Actually, he had done a lot more than mull. He already had a sponsor, L.S.M.F.T.) My mother perked up, thinking the show was about her. But to both our astonishment, he turned to me. "I think there could be a part in it for a kid just like Jonno here. What do you say, Jonno? Would you like to be a star?"

I stopped munching my hamburger long enough to flash a dumbstruck grin. Of course, I'd like to be a star. Everyone in

California wanted to be a star—college professors, garbage collectors, secretaries, even us kids. If the Pope had lived in L.A., he too would have jumped at the chance to be a star. He would have vacated the Vatican in an instant.

"Gee, sure," I said. Then added, cagily: "Especially if I didn't have to go to school."

Mort laughed. "Well, Jonno, you'd attend a special school at the studio. But you'd like it. Probably more than you like Black Fox." He turned to my mother. "What do you say, Sonya? How about letting me give Jonno a test, see what he looks like on screen? Seriously, he'd be great for the part. The sponsor would have to approve, of course. But I think they'll go for him."

My mother was wearing huge dark glasses because we were outside at the beach on a blazing day. She lit a cigarette and turned to me. I couldn't see her eyes behind the smoky gray-green lenses, but I felt them burning into me. I knew she was disappointed that Mort hadn't offered her what she wanted, *The Sonya Saint-Amant Hour*. But this was nearly as good. I was her pride and joy, I was what she would kill for.

"I don't know, Jonno. Perhaps you wouldn't like leaving your friends at Black Fox?" she said in her low husky voice.

Mind leaving Black Fox? An A-bomb could have wiped that school from the map and it wouldn't have bothered me a bit. But being a California kid, I shrugged, not wanting to appear eager.

"Well, it would only be a screen test," I said. Growing up in Hollywood, I knew all about screen tests. Everyone had them. They weren't a big deal.

Still, I felt my mother studying me from beneath her dark glasses. "Maybe it's not a good idea, Jonno. It would mean you wouldn't have such a normal childhood."

A normal childhood! Right. With my mother the famous sexpot who had an entire calendar year devoted to her nude body. It was an effort to keep a straight face.

"I don't know, Mom. It sounds kind of fun, actually."

Mort laughed. "Oh, you'd have a barrel of fun, Jonno! And you'd earn money, too . . . hey, you could sock it away, put it in a bank account for college. Whad'ya say, Sonya?"

My mother smiled. "Well, why not? I suppose I grew up in the theater too, and it didn't do me any harm. If Jonno wants to be a star, I think that's exactly what he should be!"

I was spoiled rotten, of course. It embarrasses me now. But at the time, I didn't mind a bit.

*****

I did well on the screen test. And because Mort had the hots for my mother, he pushed me over the other contenders and the sponsor agreed that I would be their lucky one.

And so my life changed abruptly. Five mornings a week a car was sent to pick me up—a station wagon, no limousine—

and I was taken to Paramount where *What a Life!* had taken over permanent residence of Stage 17. A sound stage, as you probably know, is essentially a vast empty warehouse with catwalks overhead and lots of hanging bars for lights. On Stage 17, we had an entire make-believe all-American suburban home—a split-level ranch house of the sort that was just becoming popular. Our make-believe house had no ceiling and all the rooms had only three sides, and if you looked out a window, you saw a painted backdrop, paper-mâché trees and plastic grass, all brightly lit in the exaggerated, shadowless glare of TV lighting. Only the white picket fence was real.

We were the Wolper family, and boy, did we have fun! I was Rusty Wolper the youngest—Rusty was supposed to be eight, though I was actually ten. Next came my TV sister, Bunny, who was played by an actress who went by the name of Penny Fox. I discovered her real name years later on a trivia website: Nancy Wasserman. Bunny, her character, was supposed to be eleven, but Penny (as I knew her) was thirteen going on forty. As the two kids of the show, we were thrown together a great deal and even had school together, though we studied different subjects.

Our TV parents were Bill and Susie Wolper. Bill and Susie were played by Don Silver and Nicole Corning respectively—these were their stage names, at least. They probably had real names too somewhere, but I've never had the heart

185

to look them up on the Internet. We had a next-door neighbor as well on the show, Charlie O'Neil, who was supposed to be Irish and was played by an actor named Guy Dearborne. Charlie was always showing up to borrow tools or dream up hare-brained schemes that would backfire and get all of us into a lot of trouble. And last of all, to round out the cast, we had an orange TV cat name Ginger. In fact, there were six cats used on the show, all of them supposed to be Ginger, just in case one of the cats proved uncooperative or got run over by a camera dolly.

Every week my TV family and I got involved in various crazy situations that were designed to last one-half hour. Twenty-three minutes, to be exact, the half hour minus commercials and station breaks. When I started the show, we filmed every week with 35mm cameras just like movies, since this was back in the days before video tape, but by my second year we had begun to use an early taping process called Kinescope.

The work was very boring, actually, repeating scenes again and again. I never had much contact off set with Don and Nicole, my make-believe parents—in real life, neither one of them had much use for children. So Penny, my all-American sister, was my only friend. We played a lot of checkers together, Monopoly, and Clue. She was pretty in a suitably virginal mode—blond ponytail, cute little snub nose—just the way teenage girls wanted to look in 1953. In reality, she was neither stupid nor virginal; she had a very sharp tongue when she wasn't playing cute, and she would end up spending most of the 1970s in rehab. But I'm getting ahead of myself.

In 1953 we were just two child actors, thirteen years old and ten respectively, doing our best to make Lucky Strike proud of our efforts. I liked Penny. We got along just fine. Then an unusual thing happened early that first winter, 1954. I walked into Penny's dressing room one afternoon forgetting to knock first, to find my pretty TV sister oddly positioned on the floor. She had her knees spread, her plaid skirt was up around her waist, and there was an open can of tuna fish between her legs. Ginger, one of the show's six cats, was between her legs sniffing the tuna hesitantly from a few inches away. This particular Ginger's real name was Whiskers—all the cats had their own real names, naturally, and the animal trainer, Bobby Hall, encouraged us to bond with them. For this reason, it wasn't unusual to find Whiskers in Penny's dressing room. But everything else surprised me. I didn't have a clue what she was up to.

Penny shot me a startled look when I walked in, but then she relaxed. "Oh, it's you," she said. "Wasn't my door locked?"

"Gosh, what are you doing with Whiskers?" I asked. I'll never forget the way she looked at me, taking my measure in a cool, practical way that was very different from the helpless manner girls were supposed to have back then.

"I'm trying to get Whiskers to lick me," she replied. "You know."

But I didn't know. I looked at the cat, the can of tuna, Penny's spread knees, and I still didn't get it.

Penny was forced to be more explicit. "I'm, you know, putting tuna on myself. Trying to get him to lick it off. But Whiskers won't do it. He's such a dumb cat."

I was starting to get it now. Though not entirely. Not the whole deal. I thought she wanted to get tickled somehow. Penny laughed at the expression on my face. "Lock the door, Jonno. Don't you . . . you know, ever do things?"

"*Do* things?" My blood was racing. I locked the door. I sensed enormous mysteries were about to be revealed to me. It's just that I didn't have a clue what variety of mysteries they would be. For all I knew, she was going to teach me how to recite the alphabet backwards or corner the real estate market at Monopoly. "What sort of things?"

"You know. With your pee-pee."

"Well, sure," I said, not wanting her to think I was slow. "My pee-pee. You bet."

Her smile became wider and narrower all at once. You might call it a complicated smile.

"You like tuna, don't you, Jonno? I bet you do," she said slyly. "Why don't you come here."

For me, the last part of the puzzle finally slipped into place. I may have been slow, but I was not entirely stupid.

My smile became a little complicated as well. A hopeful smile.

"Meow!" I said obligingly, lowering myself onto my hands and knees.

*****

Thus began my pre-adolescent sex life. Which was a whole lot more interesting, if the truth be known, than my actual adolescent sex life.

I suppose Penny was only a fun-loving California girl, a pleasure-seeker like we all were. But she had been earning a living as a child actress since the age of seven, living a separate existence from the everyday world and the normal limits didn't apply. Lurking behind her façade of snub-nosed cuteness was a bottomless pit of need and desire so great I doubt if she was ever satisfied, always wanting more.

I loved her passionately, of course. We did things together that would be lost to me for another decade, not until Haight-Ashbury, the Summer of Love. Most of our sexual experiments were of an oral nature. Generally, I was called upon (like Whiskers) to use my tongue, though sometimes as a reward, she would use her tongue on me in return. Beyond that, at one time or another I penetrated every orifice of her body with my two inches of perky pre-adolescence (which must have only added to her bottomless yearning). A few years later, I would discover the word nymphomaniac, a word fourteen-year-old boys cherish, and that's how I ended up thinking of Penny most of my adult life. A nympho.

As for myself, all I can say is I enjoyed every moment and I count myself lucky. My only fear back then was that we'd get caught. We became fairly reckless toward the end, tempting fate, sometimes even giving each other hand jobs in the back seat of the company station wagon that drove us home. We were a kind of mutual support system, I guess. It wasn't so easy being two kids on a weird Hollywood TV show, so we stuck together. We gave each other a hand, and any other body part as well that might temporarily put anxiety on hold.

Of course, Penny and I weren't the only ones fooling around on Stage 17. Being older, Penny knew the score better than I did, exactly what was up, and she soon introduced me to the real life of the Wolper family. I discovered that our all-American TV dad, Don Silver, was gayer than carnival in Rio and Penny and I used to spy on him giving blow jobs to a buff young lighting technician in the dark recesses of the sound stage. As for Nicole, our TV mother, she didn't appear to have much of a sex life, as far as we could make out, but she was a serious lush, with bottles hidden all over the place. Penny and I once drained one of her bottles of bourbon and replaced it with cough syrup, a dumb joke, but we thought we were being funny.

The only normal one of us, I think, in that supposedly ultimately normal family, was Guy Dearborne, the next-door neighbor. After *What a Life!* ended, Guy used his money to buy a used car dealership in the Valley and I'm sure he died a rich man, numb and incurious and overweight, all the signs that America mistakes for success.

But I'm digressing. The story I'm telling has little to do with my pre-adolescent sex life, interesting though it might be (it was interesting to me, at least). Yet there's a point I'm rambling toward, a reason for these confessions of early lust. For it was through *What a Life!* that Fred Landson came into my life.

You remember Fred, I hope, last seen on the *Mauretania* hoping to discourage my mother from a singing career. Only now, eleven years later, he was U.S. Congressman Frederick Landson, one of the richest men in California.

*****

Like other sitcoms of the era, *What a Life!* occasionally featured real life celebrities who would make a guest appearance in one of the episodes. I remember Pat Boone coming on our show, and once we even had William Boyd, the silver-haired cowboy who played Hopalong Cassidy. Generally, these celebrities were selling something, their latest song or movie, though sometimes they were just selling themselves. This kind of appearance was considered a good way to goose up the ratings.

And so, a week arrived when the producer (Mort Jenkins, still lusting after my mother) gathered us all together for our usual Monday morning meeting to announce that this week's script would include a brief visit from Congressman Landson. The story would center around Penny, her attempt to win a school contest by writing an essay entitled "Ten Ways to Be a Good Citizen" for her civics class. In the story, Congressman Landson would appear at the end to give the winning prize. Fred had an election coming up in the not too distant future and I'm sure he thought it would be good to appear on a hit series playing himself, showing the electorate just what a fun guy he was. Meanwhile (back to the make-believe story), everyone in the family was trying to help Penny win the essay contest by giving her all sorts of ridiculous advice—Mom, Dad, even Charlie, the neighbor next door. Probably you've seen the show, or a show close enough to it that you can fill in the blanks. In the end, Penny would win the contest, but only because Congressman Landson had such a heart of gold he was able to see through all the shenanigans her family had cooked up to help her.

So this was the story. And though Fred Landson was at the center of things, with his name scattered liberally throughout the script—liberal, of course, being the wrong word to use in connection with Congressman Landson—he appeared for only a few minutes at the end. In practical terms, this meant we filmed most of the show by ourselves and we didn't actually meet him until after lunch on Friday afternoon, the end of our work week.

The Congressman was a powerful man in 1954, famous for his efforts to rid Hollywood of Communism, and I remember a sense of expectancy on the set that day as we waited for him.

Even Penny was curious to meet him. I remember she wouldn't do dirty things with me that morning because she was afraid Fred would sense something un-American about her. Of course, we were all very patriotic back then. We hated Russians because they weren't good people like we were, they didn't believe in God. At Paramount, we had atomic bomb drills every few months in which Penny and I were taught how to hide ourselves beneath the desks of our makeshift classroom in order to be safe from nuclear annihilation. Though we were young, we weren't naïve. We knew it was a dangerous world, and that it was only our constant vigilance that kept America from turning into one big collective farm.

So it was a big deal to have Congressman Landson on our show. The studio sent over a photographer, and there were several reporters on hand as well. Shortly before two in the afternoon, a plain clothes detective showed up on the set to scout out the situation. He spent several minutes giving us all the eyeball and when he decided it was safe, he sent word that the Congressman could make his entrance. I'm not sure what Fred was frightened of, but I guess an important guy like that had to be careful.

Fred appeared at last, tall and bony and grim, dressed in a grey suit. By 1954, Fred no longer had a metal hook where his right hand had been. Instead, he had a plastic hand that was shaped just like a real hand, except he always wore a thin black leather glove over it. Somehow that black leather glove terrified me more than anything else about him. I could barely breathe in his presence. I kept wondering how the fake hand was attached to the stump of his arm, and the very thought of it made me queasy in the stomach.

We staged a small welcoming ceremony in the brightly-lit kitchen of our make-believe split level ranch house. The studio photographer snapped away as Don and Nicole and Guy posed with him and smiled and shook his good hand. Penny and I were required to pose with the Congressman also, though I was reluctant to place myself anywhere near him and had to be coaxed forward.

"Come on, Jonno, don't be shy!" Mort said with a laugh, pushing me toward Fred. Even Mort was nervous. "Congressman, let me introduce you to the youngest member of our cast . . . Jonathan Saint-Amant, who plays Rusty on the show. We all just call him Jonno. You'll never guess who Jonno's mother is. She's Sonya Saint-Amant, the singer."

"Is that so?" he remarked.

I believe I was the only one who was aware of the way Fred's expression changed as he looked at me. His eyes were pale grey, cold as a winter dawn, yet somehow quizzical. He seemed to be staring at me with x-ray vision, like Superman did when he looked at bad people who were trying to conceal things. I had never had anyone look at me with more focused attention, not even Penny when she wanted me to do something dirty to her. Terrible thoughts went through my mind, that maybe he thought I was a Red spy. I couldn't understand why he was looking at me like that otherwise. You have to understand, the Rosenbergs had been electrocuted just a year earlier. I was terrified.

"Well, well. How old are you, Jonno?" he asked quietly. I had to strain to hear him.

"T-t-ten," I stuttered.

"Ten," he repeated. "How about that?" I seemed to fascinate him in some way. But just then Mort brought the director over and they began to discuss the scene that lay ahead. Fred turned away from me to give his attention to the show and for the rest of the afternoon I don't believe he looked at me another time.

I didn't have much to do in that particular episode, for which I was grateful. Penny was the one with the featured part. This meant that I was able to sit off-stage in the semi-darkness behind the cameras among the cables and lights and watch the action from a distance. The final scene had Congressman Landson showing up at the house to give Penny the prize for best essay on how to be a good citizen, despite all the ridiculous things her family had done to help. Fred had a short speech to give with a bit of 1950s morality thrown in, how we can all succeed in our great country America if we only try. Fred didn't do too badly, really. As a politician, he was probably a better actor than the rest of us.

I had to return in front of the cameras for a final shot—our happy family all together, laughing and having fun. Then the director called, "It's a wrap, folks!," and I was never so glad in my life for a show to be over. I retreated back into the shadows as Fred waved in a kind of genial, nonspecific way and told us all to "keep up the good work." I was relieved that he hadn't singled me out again after that first introduction, and that I had managed to escape without saying goodbye.

I was walking back to my dressing room, full of the easy feeling of having the weekend ahead of me, when I felt a grownup tap on the shoulder. It was Congressman Landson's plainclothes cop. I hadn't heard him, so I jumped in surprise.

"Hey, kid, the Congressman wants to have a word with you."

I found myself looking up into a hard, middle aged, pock-marked face that was almost as scary as Congressman

Landson's face. "With me? I . . . I . . . but I have to go change . . . the, uh, the car's waiting for me," I managed.

"It'll just take a minute, kid."

"But the car . . ."

"The car will wait."

The detective put a big meaty hand on my shoulder so I couldn't get away and steered me through the dim squalor of the stage toward the heavy door where a red light would flash when we were filming. Outside, a black Lincoln limousine was waiting in bright sunlight in the alley that passed between the stages. The detective opened the back door of the big car and pushed me inside.

"Well, hello, Jonno," the Congressman said pleasantly as the car door closed behind me. He was sitting with his legs crossed on the back seat in the comfort of the dove gray upholstery. "Come sit by me for a minute, why don't you."

You can imagine how worried I was. There was no one else inside the limousine. Even the chauffeur had stepped out momentarily from his place up front. I kept my eyes on the jump seat that was folded up near the partition to the driver's side of the vehicle. The limousine was so huge my legs only reached halfway across the rear of the car.

"Well, that was sure fun, being on a TV show," the Congressman remarked. "You must have a heck of a time doing this every week."

"Yes, sir," I whispered.

"Nice people, too. Don and Nicole. And Penny . . . now, that's a pretty girl! I bet you guys are good friends!"

Was *that* what this was about, I wondered wildly. That I was doing nasty things with Penny? Maybe he didn't think I was a Russian spy, after all. This was a relief, because I didn't think they electrocuted you for doing dirty deeds with a girl. But it could be bad, nevertheless. I had visions of reform school.

"Sure, Penny's okay," I agreed hastily. "But she's a lot older than me, you know. So we're not, you know, all that close, or anything."

"Would you like a pop, Jonno?" he asked, changing the subject.

This confused me. The very word pop at this moment seemed utter gibberish, disconnected from any tangible sense. "Anyway, I think she has a boyfriend," I said, still trying to diffuse the Penny issue. "I mean, I'm not sure because we're not so close, you see. I mean, she's thirteen."

"Have a root beer, Jonno," Fred said ruthlessly. "You can get me one too. They're in that box in front of you."

"Yes, sir." There was a small ice chest up near the divider where the jump seats were folded. The ice chest was covered with the same dove-colored material as the seats, so I hadn't noticed it at first. I brought us out two cold squat bottles of Dad's Old Fashioned Root Beer. Congressman Landson pointed to where there was an opener on the side of the box and I opened them as well. Perhaps with only one hand, the Congressman had trouble with this sort of chore.

He took a long drink and sighed with pleasure. "I like Dad's," he confided. "It's the only root beer I drink. That's why I keep a box of 'em here in the back seat, just so I can have a cold one whenever I want. It's thirsty work being in politics, I can tell you, Jonno. Giving speeches, meeting a lot of strangers. You have to be on top of your game all the time. Probably a lot of people think I have a cushy job, but it's not so easy to be in the Congress. You have to always be thinking how to protect this great nation from all the dangers out there."

"Yes, sir," I muttered.

"So what do you want to do, Jonno? When you grow up, I mean. You want to be an actor, I suppose?"

"Well, no, sir. What I'm thinking, sir, is I'd like to be a rocket ship pilot."

"A rocket ship pilot? Now, there's a job for the future!"

"You bet," I told him, warming to the subject. "You see, what I'd like to do is build a colony on Mars. We'd all have to live in a big glass bubble, of course, because there's no air on Mars. But we'd have space suits for when we went outside."

The Congressman smiled. "Pretty nifty," he said. "You know, they call Mars the Red Planet. So you'd have to make certain you didn't have any Reds up there."

I understood vaguely that this was meant to be a joke, so I grinned obligingly.

"But that's not what I asked you here to talk about," he went on.

"No, sir," I agreed, staring at my feet. Whatever it was—boffing Penny, the youngest spy in America—I knew I was in for it.

The Congressman let out a sigh like he had been holding his breath. I realized for the first time that this conversation was just as uncomfortable for him as it was for me.

"So you live in Beverly Hills, do you? Just you and your mom?"

"And Claire—she's our maid. Claire's okay, I guess, but she makes me go to bed at nine o'clock, which is a pain in the ass."

He laughed. "Well, you gotta obey the rules in life, it's an important lesson to learn. Now listen to me, Jonno—you can say this Claire of yours is a pain, but not a pain in the you-know-what. We don't use language like that. But of course, you don't know that, do you? You don't have a father to tell you these things."

"No, sir. My father's dead. He was a war hero, you know. A pilot. The Germans shot him down over the English Channel."

Fred's cold gray eyes lit with amusement. "Sure," he said. "A war hero. I remember that now. Did your mother ever mention to you that we're old friends, her and me?"

"Uh, no, sir," I replied honestly. "She never told me that."

"Well, it's a long time ago now, of course. But we are. Old friends, that is. Of course, I'm married now to a very wonderful girl, Debbie. We have two kids, a boy and a girl. But there was a time, you see, when I thought maybe I'd marry your mother. That's why I looked at you so strangely this afternoon when they told me who your mother was. I was thinking that you could almost be my son." Fred gave me a kind of sickly smile. "So I guess it's a small world, isn't it?"

For me, this was a scary revelation. I was awfully glad my mother hadn't married a creepy guy with a bony face and cold gray eyes and a gloved hand. But I tried my best to pretend that it sure was a small world and wasn't it fun.

The smile left his face.

"So, tell me something, Jonno. Who's your mom seeing these days?"

"Seeing?"

"You know what I mean. Your mom always had a lot of men around her. I bet she's seeing someone, isn't she?"

I smiled vaguely. Of course, my mom was seeing someone. In fact, she was seeing several someones just then, juggling a busy calendar. We weren't prudes, my mother and I.

But I wasn't about to give away family secrets, not to Congressman Landson.

"Gee, I don't know," I said, shaking my head. "There's just my mom and me, you know. She misses my father a lot, so she doesn't go out much. I mean, except when she's working."

"She used to be awfully pretty, your mother," he said in a strangled sort of voice, as though her being so pretty was bothersome. "There was a time I couldn't get my mind off her. Do you know what I mean? She was all I could think about. She was like a kind of poison in my blood. The sort of poison that makes you feel good and bad, all at the same time."

Oddly enough, I understood what Fred was saying, even at the age of ten. I wasn't entirely surprised that Fred was obsessed with my mother, for she had that effect on a lot of men. But with Fred, it was spooky, like something buried too long beneath a rock.

"Look, Jonno, I want you to ask your mother to telephone me." He reached into his jacket pocket and handed me a card with a number on it. "Tell your mother this is my private number where she can always reach me. Tell her I need to speak to her as soon as possible. You'll remember, Jonno? You won't let me down?"

He was leaning close and his breath smelled bad. All I wanted was to open the car door and run. Then he put his fake hand on my knee, touching me with his black glove. It took all my will power not to scream.

"Listen to me, Jonno. At first, she's going to laugh. She's going to say, oh, Fred Landson, why should I call him? But you keep at her, you convince her to call me, you got that? Tell her she won't be sorry. Tell her that I can help with Max."

"Max?" I repeated dumbly. I couldn't imagine what any of this might have to do with my Uncle Max.

"That's right, Jonno. You tell her that I can fix things up for Max with HUAC."

He pronounced it, "Who-Ack," and I didn't have a clue of what he was talking about. But I nodded wisely, pretending I did.

"You tell her to call me, son. Don't let me down, boy."

He forced a distracted smile, but I could tell he was far away, not thinking about me at all. Then he let me go, saying I should take my root beer with me since I had only taken a sip.

*****

That year my mother and I existed in different time zones: I was the day shift, early to bed and early to rise, while my mother with her singing career was a creature of the night. Often we met only in passing.

When I got home that evening, she was in the living room with her manager, Sol Weintraub, and Buddy Kanin, the leader of the small orchestra (Buddy Kanin and His Orchestra) who accompanied her on tour. They were all three sitting in clouds of cigarette smoke with sheets of music paper scattered over the coffee table in front of them. I knew better than to interrupt an important meeting of this sort, so I waved from the foot of the stairs and made my way up to my bedroom.

With one thing and another, I didn't have a chance to talk with my mother until nearly eight that night. She was singing at the Macombo, one of the two nightclubs of the time where all the Hollywood people used to go to be seen—the other club was Ciro's. I was already in bed reading science fiction when my mother came in to say goodnight. She was dressed to kill: a slinky black gown, tight against the hips, plunging neckline, low back, long white gloves, high heels, a white mink stole around her bare shoulders, and an array of glittering jewelry, make-believe diamonds that were more sparkly than the real thing. She smelled of some wonderful perfume that evoked the mysteries of the adult world, evenings in expensive nightclubs where I couldn't go.

In 1954, my mother was thirty-one years old and the age suited her, bringing a sophistication that had been lacking before. There was still the faintest trace of foreignness to her that hinted at erotic pleasures good American girls wouldn't even know about, much less be willing to provide. After studying with a voice coach, she had entirely eliminated the last remnants of her Polish accent a number of years earlier. But then, as a deliberate ploy, after much thought, she had brought it back again, ever so slightly—a specially concocted accent that was more French than Polish, and so sexy, deep, and throaty, that it was said that men had to put their hands over their ears to keep from going mad.

She sat down for a moment on the edge of my bed and her smile took on a special warmth.

"Well, Jonno, it seems as though I hardly see you anymore. How was your day?"

"Great, Mom. You know, the usual. We wrapped the week's show ... uh, Mom, I wanted to ask you if I can go to Penny's house tomorrow night. It's going to be a pajama party."

"A pajama party? What's that?"

"Oh, just a bunch of kids sleeping over," I said with a shrug. Actually, I was lying through my teeth. Like mother, like son. There weren't going to be any other kids, only Penny and me, and we were hoping not to wear pajamas at all.

"Hmmm," said my mother, sensing undercurrents of sin. "I don't know. Sleeping over at a girl's house. Penny's quite a lot older than you."

"Oh, her parents are going to be there. I mean, it's no big deal."

This was a lie too. Penny's mother and current stepfather had gone down to Acapulco for the week, enjoying themselves on the money that Penny made for them. My mother studied me with her complex green eyes. I'm sure it worried her that we were so much alike. Meanwhile I put on my Rusty-face, as I thought of it, so innocent and freckly you'd never imagine there was anything between my legs at all.

"Well, I guess it's all right. As long as her parents are there. Do you want me to drive you?"

"It's okay, Mom. Lucky's going to come for me in the afternoon." Lucky was Penny's family's Colored chauffeur "He's going to pick up all the kids, you see," I added for effect. "There are about ten of us."

"And you'll all fit in the back of one limousine?"

"Sure, we'll squeeze in."

My mother smiled. "I'm glad you're having a good time. Well, wish me luck tonight. Sinatra's going to be in the audience. I'm hoping to get him up on stage with me for a number."

"That's great, Mom." I was tempted to let her kiss me and leave without my saying another word. I'm not sure why I felt so reluctant to tell her what had happened that afternoon. But in the end, I figured I needed to do what Fred had told me to do. I eased into the story slowly.

"Something a little funny happened today. There was a guy on the set who said he knew you."

My mother smiled in a conspiratorial manner. "Oh, dear. A guy who says he knows me. This sounds serious!"

"Well, he was the guest star, you see. Congressman Frederick Landson."

"Frederick? Good God, *Fred* was on the show?"

Fred was right. She laughed at his name.

"Yeah, it was just a small part. But at the end of the afternoon, he sent someone for me and I had to get into his car. He wanted me to give you a message."

My mother's laughter faded. "He made you get in his car?"

"Well, I didn't mind. Even though he's a little spooky. He gave me a root beer. He wants you to call him, that's all. That's the message. He gave me a special telephone number too, he says it's a private line."

I reached into my bedside table and found the card he had given me. My mother studied it with a frown.

"Oh, dear!" she said thoughtfully.

"So you know him, huh?"

My mother shook her head and sighed. "No, not well. We were on a ship together once. Somehow he fell in love with me. You can imagine what a surprise it was—I had hardly looked at the poor man twice the entire voyage. I can't imagine what he wants to talk to me about after all these years!"

"Well, there was one other thing," I said reluctantly. "He said something about Max."

"Max?" My mother's eyes opened wider in surprise. "What about Max?"

"He said something about Who-Ack, that he could help you with Max. I didn't really understand. Is it important?"

"Who-Ack? I don't know what he means." Then she seemed to get it. "Oh, yes, *Who-Ack!*" she said more knowingly.

You can imagine how mystified I was. My mother forced a smile.

"Well, it's not important. I'll take care of it, Jonno. Thank you for telling me."

She leaned closer and gave me a delicate kiss, the sort that wouldn't disturb her make-up. Up close, she smelled like a vase full of expensive flowers.

"Are you going to call him?" I asked, my arms around her neck, reluctant to let go.

"Oh, I don't know." She breathed into my cheek and gave me another kiss. "He's rather a bore, really."

"But Uncle Max—"

"Uncle Max is a great deal more clever than Fred Landson, and he can take care of himself very well, darling. So you must promise me not to worry. Do you promise, Jonno?"

"Sure," I told her without enthusiasm. "I won't worry."

She gave me a final kiss and left. But I couldn't keep my promise—I *did* worry. Despite my mother's assurance, I felt something uneasy, something bad moving around the edges of our world. I couldn't quite put a name to it, but I worried that our lives were up in the air with no solid ground anywhere in sight, and that not even my clever mother, with her beauty and many lies, had the power to avert the danger that was rushing our way.

Part Three

Love at Sea
The North Atlantic, 1943

One

Sasha left Max on deck and began her journey into the depths of the *Mauretania* with a feeling that something wonderful had just happened to her.

It wasn't simply that she had enjoyed Max's company; it was as though he had restored a sense of who she was, that she was Sasha, the magical girl, and that the world was full of possibilities. It had been so long since she had felt this way that it took Sasha a moment to understand that she was happy.

But her happiness faded as the central stairway took her corkscrewing downward below waterline into the bowels of the ship. With each step, she felt herself descending from sunlight into airless poverty and worry.

Money was a particular concern at the moment due to a huge gambling loss that Julka had incurred in London. This was infuriating since they had done well with their séances and might have had a nice little nest egg by now. But in his usual fashion, Julka had become carried away by his own success. While Sasha was in Oxford with Edward Harcourt, he had gone to a fancy club in Mayfair with a group of dissolute young men who found him amusing and had lost four hundred pounds at *chemin de fer*. Four hundred pounds, their entire fortune!

What could he have been thinking? It was incredible! *Chemin de fer* was a game where the croupier dealt the cards from an iron shoe leaving no possibility for the sort of sleight of hand in which Julka was so clever. "I'm afraid I had a bit too much champagne," he admitted unhappily after she had returned from her less-than-euphoric weekend with Edward Harcourt. "But don't worry, my darling, I'll win it all back again, I promise."

Sasha didn't think so. In the end, they had fled London with angry creditors on their heels, and she had been forced to sell her few good clothes on Portobello Road to pay for their train tickets to Scotland, the secret estuary hidden from German planes from where the *Mauretania* had sailed. At least, Edward Harcourt had kept his promise to provide visas and tickets to America, though it had taken him more than three months to fulfill his side of the bargain and it had come as an unpleasant surprise that they were to travel in Steerage. Julka had been especially angry their first night on board to discover this slight—as though he had made the sacrifice! Sasha was more philosophical. In truth, she hadn't been especially nice to Edward Harcourt and this was his small revenge. She understood that. She prided herself on being a realist.

Sasha made her way down the central stairway, around and around, running her hand along the banister. She passed through several social layers, through doors that had been designed to separate First Class from Second, and another door still that led to the lowest class of all, Steerage. The British were obsessed with class; it appeared to give their lives meaning, to know precisely where one stood in the pecking order, complete with the appropriate accent. Fortunately, the doors were left unlocked due to wartime considerations and from her first moment onboard, Sasha had refused to allow artificial barriers to stop her from going where she pleased.

She continued downward until she reached F Deck, the lowest passenger level, where she hurried through a long corridor toward her cabin. She and Julka shared quarters with a group of ten sour-smelling Russian Jews, bumpkins from the countryside. The cabin was at the rear of the ship, so close to the giant screws underfoot that the vibration rattled one's teeth. There were twelve bunks crowded into a windowless space with two harsh overhead lights that were left on day and night. Luggage was piled everywhere, taking up every inch of floor space, a chaos of canvas bags and bulging boxes. One almost expected chickens and goats to be milling about.

Sasha squeezed past a group of shapeless women in the aisle who were talking among themselves in Russian and Yiddish. She understood both languages well enough, though she pretended not to. She and Julka had two lower bunks next to one another at the very farthest corner of the cabin. She chased off two young men from her bed, sallow creatures with haunted eyes who were playing cards. "This is my bunk," she said haughtily in English. Without a word, the young men stood and moved their game to a free bunk a few beds away, casting a mournful look behind them in her direction. She doubted if they understood English, but they certainly understood her tone.

Sasha sat on her thin mattress and studied Julka, who was asleep on the next bunk over, lying on his back with a blanket pulled up to his bony chin. His mouth was open and a thin stream of spittle had drooled down his cheek. She couldn't bear to see Julka this way, old and sick and awful. It seemed to Sasha that no matter how desperately she planned, they never got clear of worry. She was suddenly frightened that he lay so still. "Baba, wake up!" she whispered urgently into his ear, using an old childhood term of endearment, her name for him from long ago. She knelt in the aisle by his bunk and took hold of his thin arm. "I'm back . . . oh, please wake up!"

Julka had always refused to name his illness, but she was certain it was consumption. She had seen one of her mother's friends, a ballerina, die of this disease in Krakow. With Julka, the illness had ebbed and flowed ever since they had left Poland. Sometimes he seemed quite all right, but several days before boarding the ship, a new attack had laid him low.

"Oh, wake up! . . . please, please!" she whispered more urgently, pulling on his arm.

At last, he moved. Grudgingly, he showed a faint flicker of life. As she watched, the old man's eyelids fluttered open. He appeared disoriented by dreams and fever.

"Sasha, *c'est toi, ma cherie*?" he asked weakly, turning his head her way. Alone together, they spoke in a patchwork of Polish, French, and English, their private mélange of tongues.

"Yes, it's me," she replied in Polish, irritated by her own relief. "Who else would it be? The Queen of Sheba perhaps?"

He came to his senses slowly. "I was having the most wonderful dream, my darling. It was summer and you were rehearsing *Tosca* with all the theater doors wide open so there would be a breeze. You were in the chorus, a little girl again . . . oh, how pretty you were! I was in the Royal Box watching with a glass of champagne . . . remember how we used to watch rehearsals from the Royal Box? I remember thinking that the war hadn't happened, that the Germans hadn't come—that it was all only a bad dream. Isn't that marvelous?"

"Certainly, Baba. Marvelous!" she answered crossly. "We can just pretend the war never happened. That's the answer, I'm sure."

"You know what else I was remembering? I was remembering the cast party after *La Traviata* closed. You know the production I mean. There was that Czech tenor . . . what was his name?"

Despite her firm intentions to avoid this sort of nostalgia, Sasha smiled wistfully as she remembered the party Julka had in mind. "Piotr," she told him. "He was Russian, though, not Czech. A terrible man, really. He used to touch my bottom

215

whenever he passed by in the corridor. But he was very funny—he used to make me laugh."

"Yes, yes. But do you remember those little cakes we ate at the party? They were a dark chocolate with a kind of creamy filling. I forget now who brought them . . . that must have been nineteen thirty-seven. No, no, I take that back. It was nineteen thirty-five!"

Sasha certainly remembered the dark chocolate cakes with creamy filling. She even remembered who had brought them—Bela, the French horn player who was later hanged. She remembered the Café Chopin, the laughter, the wonderful camaraderie after a production was finished, all the dear people who now were dead. But what did it matter whether it was 1935 or 1937? It was a world they would never see again, and it hurt desperately to dwell on it.

"Come closer," he said. "Sit with me, my darling, for a little while."

With a sigh, Sasha moved from where she was kneeling on the floor and sat on his bed. It was a narrow bed, like hers, and it was remarkable how little space his body occupied. He had become so very thin and insubstantial. His hand was hardly more than a bony claw with bulging blue veins.

"So tell me all the news. Where have you been?" he asked.

"On deck," she answered listlessly. "Trying to figure out how we're going to manage in America with exactly eight pounds sixpence."

"Ah, you worry too much, my dear. New York is going to fall in love with you, just you wait and see. Everything is going to be fine there."

"Oh, you think so, do you?" Julka's optimism had come to annoy her, his total disregard of reality. "Somehow I think New York will not love two foreigners without any money. And please, Baba, do not even think of gambling again."

The old man smiled slyly. "But we're such a good team. You brought our special cards just when they were needed. Come, come—we must have more than eight pounds six pence! I'm sure I won at least ten pounds for us that afternoon."

"Not after I paid back that dull Captain Landson. You remember, in the beginning I was playing with his money."

"Sasha, how silly of you! You could have kept the money and he wouldn't have cared. He is sweet on you, I think. Just like all the men."

"Yes, but that's not how things are done. Men have very definite ideas about these things. If you take their money, they treat you like a whore. We must not gamble again on this ship. Do you hear me? People will become suspicious."

"Yes, yes, my sweet. Don't I always do as you say?"

"Rarely. And this time I'm serious. There is a man who saw me change the cards. The movie director, the man with the sad eyes and the limp."

Julka gave her a knowing look. "Ah! Well, it's a pity he saw you. But, of course, you're very good with men, aren't you? You can make them do what you want. Somehow I think he will not say anything about the cards."

Sasha scowled. "Perhaps," she answered. "But it's tiresome and I don't want to take any more chances."

"You know, I think I remember this movie director," Julka told her dreamily. "Yes, I'm sure I met him in Berlin in 1923. Max Zlinsky . . . you see, I never forget a name. It was at a party at the Metropole. Countess Barazzi was there . . . I believe she and Mr. Zlinsky had a very passionate love affair."

"Not Zlinsky," Sasha scoffed. "His name is McCormack. And I'm sure he's never been to Berlin. You know, when I came in just now, I thought for a moment that you were dead. You will not be enjoying your ridiculous memories if you die on me."

He smiled indulgently. "Sasha, you mustn't worry. I'm going to be my old self again the moment we get to New York. Good food, a little rest . . . you know, I've been thinking of starting a restaurant when we get to America. A little place like the Café Chopin. The only thing we need is a backer. Perhaps your movie director, eh? What do you think, Sasha? Do you think you might convince your Mr. Zlinsky to invest a few zlotys in such a fool-proof idea? It will make us rich a hundred times over!"

Zlotys! It was beyond belief. Sasha would have given him a serious talking to except that at just this moment he had one of his horrible coughing spells. Sasha watched in alarm as the coughing wracked his body. She quickly fetched a bottle of water from beneath her bed and brought it to his lips. Part of the water spilled down his shirt, but he managed to drink a little. When the coughing finally stopped, he was so weak he could only lie on his back.

"Oh, Baba!" she said sadly.

He took several breaths before he was able to speak. "Honestly, my dear, it's just a smoker's cough. Fetch me two of my pills from the blue vial and I'll be fine. You mustn't worry."

Sasha found Julka's pills in the cardboard suitcase beneath his bunk. She was certain they were morphine, though he refused to say. Morphine would make him feel better for a few hours, but she doubted it would help in the long run.

He took the pills with a sip of water and when he was quiet again, she read to him in English from an American book, *Tom Sawyer*, that she had shoplifted from a store in London, hoping to educate them in the ways of their future home.

Julka enjoyed having her read aloud to him. He lay with a dreamy smile listening to her voice until the pills began to work. After a few minutes, his eyes closed and he fell asleep. Sasha put the book down and fought against a strong desire to cry. She was tired and she felt sorry for herself.

Why wasn't there someone to take care of her? Why must she always have to decide what to do for both of them? As she watched, the old man caught his breath in his sleep and didn't exhale.

"Baba! Don't you dare do this to me!" she cried, shaking his thin arm violently. Julka exhaled with a sigh and began breathing again softly. His life seemed to hang by only the slightest breath, a single exhalation from death. It didn't seem possible that he would survive the afternoon.

Two

Sasha lay on her bunk restlessly smoking cigarettes, unable to read, barely able to think, glancing from time to time at Julka in the next bunk. Beneath her, the ship's giant screws churned through the endless ocean, vibrating the hull with a low harmonic drone. With each turn of the screw, she felt herself carried further from everything she knew, propelled across the water toward the terrifying unknown.

Moodily, she stubbed out her cigarette and put the butt in her pocket. It was an American cigarette, Lucky Strike—Fred Landson had bought her an entire pack yesterday in the Canteen, which was nice because she liked good cigarettes and they were expensive.

Thinking of Fred, she glanced at her wristwatch and saw that she must hurry if she were to sneak up to the Officers Canteen to meet Fred at five. It was a date, she supposed. Fred had made a particular point of wishing to see her this afternoon.

Sasha was tempted to stand Fred up. It would be easy enough to claim that a sailor had stopped her from reaching the upper part of the ship where she wasn't supposed to be. She simply wasn't in the mood for Fred today. But in the end, she decided it would be best to meet him after all.

Her life was a work in motion, a ball circling on a roulette wheel. Sasha believed in destiny. She was certain her life would land on a lucky number, as long as she was bold and refused to give an inch to anxiety and doubt.

And so she arranged herself as well as she was able in her one decent outfit. She brushed her hair, studied herself for possible flaws, gave one last look at Julka to make certain he was breathing. Then, ready or not, she took a deep breath and reascended the long flight of stairs, fixing her courage in place like a mask as she made her way upward through the *Mauretania* to the Officer's Canteen.

A girl in her position could not afford to stay in bed while life was waiting, a game that needed to be played.

*****

She found Fred near the windows in a quiet alcove of the Canteen that the regular crowd avoided. After a short time at sea, these things had become well established, certain tables where people gathered and other places where one could be left alone. Sasha knew that Fred had come to this part of the room so he could have her all to himself. She was mildly flattered, she supposed, but not greatly so. It was hard to get worked up about Fred one way or the other.

Nevertheless, she put on her special radiance just for him. She did it automatically while crossing the room in his direction. It was like turning on a switch, lighting herself up from inside. Fred rose from the table smiling when he saw her.

"I am late, Fred, I am very sorry. I hope you have not been waiting," she told him.

"Hey, it's nothing. Gee, you look fine today, Sasha. You look like a million dollars."

"Ah!" she laughed. "A million dollars!"

She supposed it was a nice thing to say. Yet it did not strike her as so romantic, to look at her and think of money. She would rather be compared to a summer's day. Fred's eyes glistened like shiny pebbles as he took her in.

"Say, are you hungry? How about some tea and cookies?" he offered.

"Cookies?" Sasha was momentarily baffled. "Goodness, Fred, what are cookies?"

He grinned. "Gee, don't tell me you don't know what a cookie is? I guess I'd better work on your education a little."

Fred disappeared briefly to the bar and in a few minutes they had a pot of watery tea along with two miniscule cubes of rationed sugar. Chivalrously, Fred insisted that Sasha have his small cube. Cookies turned out to be what Sasha thought of as biscuits—this was the more adult word the British used—not so special after all, hard as rocks. Still, she managed to slip one inside her coat pocket when Fred wasn't looking to take back to Julka.

Fred lit his pipe and sat back in his chair with an air of contentment. Sasha imagined he was more or less the same age as Max, but he seemed much older, almost a different generation.

"So what have you been up to today?" he asked pleasantly.

"Up to?" Sasha still hadn't entirely conquered English idioms, which were often far from logical. In this case, it seemed to her that "up to" implied mischief, getting away with something, and she was momentarily alarmed, wondering what he had found out about her.

"What have you been doing," Fred clarified.

"Oh!" she said with relief. "I've been on my bed reading *Tom Sawyer*. I bought this book in London hoping it would teach me about America."

"Why, sure, Mark Twain is one of our great writers. You know, you sure do impress me, Sasha. I mean, here you are, a girl who spends her money on a book in order to improve her mind. That says something about you."

Sasha smiled, not about to tell Fred that she had stolen the book, which would say a great deal more.

"Look, can I give you a bit of advice about America? A girl like you with so much pluck, you should come west."

"West? Why is that?"

"Well, let me put it this way. The East is fine in its way, but people can be stuck up and unfriendly. They've seen a lot of foreigners over the years—Irish, Italians, Yids, you name it. And they can make it pretty hard for newcomers. In California, people are more open. In California it doesn't matter so much where you come from as long as you've got the determination to succeed. You see what I'm saying?"

"Yes, I do. And I'm grateful for advice," she told him sincerely. "I don't wish to make mistakes when we arrive in America."

He nodded, watching her closely. "You're going to like America, you and your Dad. It's a land of opportunity for people who are willing to work for it, and you're going to do just fine." Fred sucked at his pipe with more than his usual energy. "You know, I'm glad the subject of the future has come up, because that's what I was hoping to talk to you about today. Your future and . . . well, mine."

Oh, dear! Sasha thought. She sensed where this conversation was going and lowered her eyes demurely. She knew how much men liked the illusion of innocence and it was one of her best tricks.

"Look here, Sasha, I want to be honest with you," Fred said in his blustery way, laying his pipe down on the table so that he could concentrate just on her. "I'm forty-five years old and I've been shot up a little, losing a hand and all. The doctors say they can replace this hook back in the States, give me a hand that will look almost like the real thing. Still, I don't expect pretty girls to give a fellow like me a second glance. California girls won't, that's for sure. They're pretty darned spoiled, to tell the truth, the girls back home. They'll want some fellow who looks like a movie star. Someone they can show off to their friends. But of course, a foreign girl like you who's just arrived . . . my guess is you'll see things in a more practical light. When you're a newcomer, well, you got to be realistic, don't you? If you see what I'm saying."

Sasha shook her head. Truly, she didn't see. As far as she could make out, Fred was telling her that he was damaged goods because of his age and missing hand, and she wasn't so wonderful either due to the fact that she was foreign. But was this supposed to be a proposal? If so, she was mystified. As a general rule, she didn't mind receiving proposals. But this was unlike any proposal she had ever imagined.

"Look, here's what I'm saying. I'm not a fancy fellow, Sasha, but I'm solid and I'm intending to be rich. Of course, a lot of guys say they're going to be rich, but I'm not the type who bluffs. I'm the sort who does what he says he's going to do. When I was young, I said to myself, 'Fred, you need to get an education, you need to go to college.' And that's what I did, I didn't just talk about it, see. It was only a small school in Whittier, but I was the first person in my family to graduate from college and it wasn't easy. I had to work two jobs while I was taking classes, and for months at a time I only ate peanut butter sandwiches because that's all I could afford. But I stuck with it because I'm the sort who doesn't give up. Later, when the war broke out, I decided I was going to be an officer, and that wasn't easy either. Look, I'm not bragging, but I want you to know the sort of person I am. So when I tell you I'm going to be rich, you can believe me. I've got a master plan for my life and I intend to follow it, one step after another. Are you getting me?"

"I think so."

Sasha rather liked plans, particularly master plans. And she especially liked master plans that involved getting rich. But then Fred lost her with his next question.

"What do you know about orange trees?"

She laughed. "Orange trees? Goodness! I don't know a thing about orange trees. We don't have them in Poland, I'm afraid."

"Well, we have 'em in Southern California where I come from, I can tell you that. And it's how I'm going to get rich."

Sasha didn't know what to make of this. But she nodded wisely. "Ah, I see. You will be a fruit vendor, Fred?"

He smiled and leaned closer. "I'm going to turn them into houses!"

Sasha was now truly perplexed. She believed in magic, but for the life of her, she couldn't imagine what sort of abracadabra it would take to turn an orange tree into a house. Fred proceeded to explain and for the next half hour, Sasha was regaled with his master plan. She almost believed he might succeed. It was the very fact that Fred wasn't the usual sort of bohemian dreamer she'd known in the past that gave his scheme credibility.

Apparently, Fred's father owned several hundred acres of orange trees in a place called Anaheim that was in the countryside near Los Angeles. Sasha imagined peasants in squat little houses, and horse drawn carts to collect the oranges at harvest time. But Fred was going to do away with the orange trees and the peasants. His plan was to sell off the land and build houses. Hundreds of houses, all the same—three or four models, eight houses to an acre, no money down for vets. After the war, said Fred, as soon as the Yanks walloped the Gerries, there was going to be a boom. And in this boom, folks were going to procreate, multiply like rabbits, and houses were going to be in demand—identical little holes, as Sasha imagined it, where the rabbits might live.

"But that's not all," said Fred. And now his eyes were glowing—for in his way, Sasha saw that Fred was a dreamer too. "You see, all these people in the houses I'm going to build are going to need to shop and eat and buy cars and clothes. So, what I'm going to do, I'm going to build villages where there are only stores. People are going to have to drive to get there, so I'm going to surround these shopping villages with big parking lots, just so everything is very convenient. Can you picture it?"

Sasha couldn't picture it at all. But she smiled and pretended she did. "A shopping village," she said. "I think this is a very original idea, Fred."

"A shopping park, that's what I was thinking of calling it. Maybe there'll be restaurants and movie theaters, too. Banks, even. People will be able to park their cars one time only and get everything they need in a single place. They'll never need to go to the city."

"And you'll own all these stores, Fred?"

"Darn right!" he told her. "Everyone will have to buy everything they want from me. So what do you think of my idea?"

"Well," Sasha said carefully, "it is a very large dream. Of course, the war might last a long time. And perhaps when the war is finally over, there will not be so many people still alive, and they will not have money to buy your houses."

Fred shook his head, confidently. "No, there's going to be a boom, just you wait and see. There was a boom after the last war, we called it the Roaring Twenties. And there will be a boom this time too."

"I hope so, Fred," she told him. *If* America wins the war, she wanted to say, but didn't. Coming from Poland, Sasha had a more pessimistic understanding of how events didn't always work out as you wanted. Americans were astonishingly innocent about these things. They didn't even have to pretend innocence.

"Listen, when you see California, you'll understand," he told her. "You'll see I'm right. I'm going to be rich, Sasha, I promise you. Now, I know you're a bright girl, so I'm guessing you understand why I'm telling you about myself."

"Well, yes, perhaps, I understand just a little," she admitted. "But I'm very young, of course. And I have my father to consider. I would have to think about this very carefully. It is very sudden."

Fred nodded eagerly. "Why, sure it's sudden. And I want you to think about this very carefully. Me, I've been thinking about it ever since I first saw you. The thing about me, I'm a guy who knows what he wants. I'm a guy who makes up his mind quick. And I want to have kids, the whole nine yards. I want to settle down, Sasha. I want some nice little woman to come home to after I've been out there in the world making our bundle. That's the way I see it. Now, I know I'm not handsome, and I'm not so young. But I'm solid, like I've been telling you. I'm a square shooter, Sasha. And your Dad, well, he could come live with us too. I'm not against that. I believe in families sticking together."

"Fred—"

"No, let me finish. Do you know what day it is tomorrow?"

"Day? Tomorrow?"

"Today's February thirteenth. Which means tomorrow is February fourteenth. Valentine's Day. You know about Valentine's Day, I bet?"

"Valentine's Day? This is the day of . . . how do you say, Cupid and his little arrows?"

"You got it. Cupid and his little arrows. What I'm saying is, think real careful about this overnight, talk to your Dad if you want to, and give me your answer tomorrow. It just seems like Valentine's Day is a lucky time for an answer that's going to affect your life and mine. Are you understanding me?"

Sasha was wondering what to make of Fred's proposal when she noticed the unpleasant Englishwoman who had accosted her on deck, the horrid lady from the séance at Eaton Square. She was coming their way, walking through the Canteen with her husband in tow searching for a place to sit. Unfortunately, Sasha remembered her very well. Her name was Mrs. Robbins and as far as Sasha was concerned, the present was quite challenging enough without an old cow appearing from an unwanted corner of one's life to make a fuss.

At first, it didn't seem that Mrs. Robbins would spot her. But then the Englishwoman's eyes turned her way and lit up with a kind of grim satisfaction to see Sasha with yet another man.

Sasha turned to Fred with a frantic smile, sensing it was time to make a quick escape. "Yes, Fred. I will think about what you say. But now, I am starting to worry about my Papa. He's been ill and I need to get back to our cabin. He worries if I am away too long."

"Well, sure, you don't want your father to worry. So we'll meet up here tomorrow, same time, same place. Valentine's Day, right? You'll think over what I've said, okay?"

"Yes, Fred. But really, I must go now."

Fred stood as she rose from the table. With his good hand, he took hold of her hand and pressed meaningfully.

"You know, there's something about you that stirs my soul, Sasha. I just can't get you out of my mind. I swear, you're even better than a million dollars!"

Sasha lowered her eyes demurely, retreating back into her faux innocence. Men were really very stupid. He wanted to fuck her, that was all. Then he wanted her to stay at home, have his children, wash his shirts, cook his meals, and be his unpaid servant. Americans, she observed, were extraordinarily like Poles in this respect.

"Goodbye, Fred," she told him, pulling free.

Sasha hurried from the room, pretending not to notice the unpleasant English couple as she passed within inches of their table. She put a half-smile on her face and set her eyes straight ahead, as though she didn't care. But her stomach was tense and she wanted to scream at the unfairness of it, that a ghost from the past should show up at just this time: twenty pounds stolen from a handbag in Eaton Square, and a horrible woman who was certain to spread malicious gossip about her round the ship.

Three

That night, Sasha tossed restlessly on her bunk as she considered Fred's proposal and debated the question of the right man—which of her suitors she should encourage, who she might snub, and how to do this all quickly before the woman from Eaton Square destroyed her standing on the ship.

Sasha wasn't in much of a romantic mood at the moment; she would have preferred to set the whole matter aside and remain independent. But with Julka to care for and eight pounds sixpence to their name, a man seemed the only practical answer to her worries. She knew she couldn't put off a decision much longer.

But who would it be? Of the lieutenants and captains and majors who were giving her the rush, she knew very well that most of them only wanted a quick tumble, a bit of shipboard frolic before they returned home to their American girlfriends and wives. The only serious candidates, as Sasha saw it, were Fred Landson and Max McCormick, both of whom had pluses in their favor and minuses against.

Fred would be the boring though dependable choice. Fred would protect her, he wouldn't pimp her to the highest bidder as Julka was wont to do. She believed Fred would certainly be rich one day, even if his little houses didn't work out. He had the right sort of dogged determination to make his way in the world. He wouldn't get side tracked by the lure of poetry. He would take care of her. And that would be nice, she thought. To have someone take care of her for a change, rather than the other way around.

Sasha preferred Max, of course. Who wouldn't? Max was handsome and funny, and he was rich already without the need to turn orange trees into houses. She wasn't certain that Max knew he was in love with her yet, but Sasha was confident she could fix this problem. She saw the way he looked at her; she believed he could be won easily enough. But Max had several points against him, potentially even more serious drawbacks than Fred. It had alarmed her this afternoon when he had tossed his movie script into the water. She understood very well why he had done it. Sasha herself was prone to grand gestures. But she didn't need this sort of thing with a man. She couldn't afford another romantic dreamer.

Then there was the fact that Max was married. Sasha had no moral compunctions about involving herself with a married man; her concerns were entirely practical. Everything Sasha knew about men and women she had learned in the dressing rooms backstage at the Krakow Opera where all the girls in the chorus, her mother included, had affairs with married men. The problem was that these affairs never added up to anything. Oh, one enjoyed champagne suppers, sometimes even in restaurants more expensive than the Café Chopin. Clothes were given to you, pieces of jewelry, occasionally you might even be set up in an apartment. But in the finish, the men always returned to their wives and you didn't end up with much. A pretty girl could do quite well in this sort of life while she was in her twenties; but starting around the age of thirty, the whole situation began going downhill, and at forty you were finished. Sasha had seen this happen all too often, forty-year-old women who had once been pretty, selling off their jewelry and coats one by one to make ends meet. She was determined not to let this happen to her.

No, unfortunately Fred was the only intelligent choice. Once they reached New York, Julka would need expensive medical care and a place to rest and she was certain she could get Fred to pay for these things. He was "a family man," as he put it, and being a family man meant taking care of one's ageing parents. Make-believe parents, too, one would hope.

But what about her own dreams? How could she become a famous singer if she was stuck in a one-horse place like Anaheim? Fred hadn't mentioned her singing career once in his not so romantic proposal of marriage. She presumed the omission was deliberate. A man who wished to have a little woman at home to fuck and do his laundry would not want her to have outside interests, much less a career.

There was an alternative choice, of course. She could put both Max and Fred on a kind of flirtatious hold and wait until she reached New York to see if perhaps the right man could be found there. In New York, there would be a larger gene pool than here on the *Mauretania*, plenty of men with lonely hearts and eager penises.

Should she wait? Or was a bird in hand better than an unknown future in the New York bush? Such were Sasha's restless thoughts, spinning round and round. Meanwhile, it was late at night and she was unable to come to a decision.

"I'll decide tomorrow," she said to herself, stubbing out the cigarette she had been smoking and closing her eyes. Tomorrow she would find the ship's doctor for Julka. Tomorrow she would get him some real medicine. Tomorrow everything would fall into place.

Tonight, Sasha wanted only to sleep.

*****

Yet she didn't sleep. She dozed only lightly then woke a short while later without knowing why. The cabin was silent except for the sound of the engine underfoot and heavy snoring from a nearby bunk. Sasha didn't know what time it was, but she sensed it was late. Suddenly she was terrified. She didn't know why, but her heart was pounding.

Instinctively, she turned toward Julka to see if he had woken also. The old man lay on his back with his bony chin protruding upward. One eye was partially open and there was a stillness to him that was profound. Sasha sat up abruptly.

She had seen too much death not to recognize it now, the inert absence of life. But it was too awful, she refused to believe it.

She slipped from her bunk and knelt urgently by his side.

"Baba!" she whispered. "Wake up, Baba!"

She pulled on his arm as she had done earlier in the day, certain he would flutter back to life as he had always done before.

"Baba, you mustn't scare me like this!" she told him, shaking harder. But this time there was no flutter, no breath, nothing at all. She stopped tugging and regarded him closely. It was incredible, but Julka was no longer there. He was gone, simply gone, leaving nothing behind.

Sasha bit her lip so hard she tasted blood. How could he die after all they had gone through together? It didn't seem fair. Not when they were nearly in America, so close to their goal. The prospect of arriving in New York alone filled her with a loneliness so vast she didn't think she could bear it.

She cradled her head against his body and wept as silently as she could, not wanting to wake the others in the cabin. She refused to have them see her naked misery. A small moan escaped her throat and she buried her head in the blanket to stifle it.

Memories rushed by. An afternoon he had taken her to a circus when she was nine or ten . . . her twelfth birthday party at the Café Chopin when he had appeared from the kitchen with a huge cake and thirteen candles . . . the night after the

237

Germans had hung her mother, when they went back to his messy flat off Florianska Street to get drunk on the very last bottle of Scotch whisky in all Krakow . . .

How could a person you love suddenly cease to exist? How could you find yourself so bitterly alone? Sasha wanted to scream against the injustice of it all. But all she could do was cry.

*****

In a better world, Sasha would have continued to mourn the loss of her dearest friend. She would have gladly wept and lain on her bunk in desolation. But eventually her tears stopped and she knew there were things she must do. Already new plans were forming in her mind. A person had to go on. That was the hard truth of it.

And so at last, Sasha stood and took a long breath and set herself in motion. She went down the corridor to the women's restroom, washed her face in the sink and brushed her hair. After studying herself in the mirror, she decided to remain in her cotton nightgown rather than change into her good dress. Under the circumstances, a cotton nightgown would do just fine.

Sasha returned to the cabin and slipped on her gray cloak over her nightgown. She lit a cigarette, inhaled ferociously several times, then stubbed the cigarette out, saving the stub in a small jar under the bed. She supposed that she was as ready as she would ever be.

"*Do widzenia*, Julka," she said softly in her native Polish.

Goodbye. With a gentle stroke of her hand, she closed the single dark eye that been left winkingly open. And that was it, all the mourning that a girl in desperate straits could afford.

Sasha hurried from the cabin with the intention of changing horses, so to speak, in mid-ocean. A dead mount for one that was alive.

But which horse would it be? A practical mount like Fred with his manly determination to earn money and take care of her? Or a romantic, impractical sort of animal with gentle eyes and a sad smile—a show horse who would never pull a plough, and who would almost certainly end up requiring her strength and practicality?

Of course, it was never really in doubt which lover Sasha would choose.

Four

Max was lying awake on his bunk in the dark when he heard a knock on his cabin door. He didn't sleep well these nights, his mind circling in thought. Sleep was one of those things you lost as you grew older and your life became crowded with memory and worry.

He reached for his wristwatch on the table next to his bunk and saw from the green-glowing hands that it was three in the morning. Though he had been awake, it was worrisome to have someone knocking on your door at such an hour.

"Just a minute!" he called. He turned on a light, slipped a robe over his pajamas, and went to the cabin door.

It was Sasha and Max saw immediately that there was something wrong. Her thick dark blonde hair had fallen loose on her shoulders and she looked half-wild. Her face was pale, her lips trembled. She stood in Max's doorway, dramatically posed, a damsel in distress, superbly underdressed. He was aware of these things all at once, a diffuse impression that packed a wallop. Beneath her gray cloak he saw she was wearing a white nightgown. And beneath that, he sensed, there was only her.

"Please!" she said in her low voice. "I'm so sorry to disturb you, but it's my father. I cannot wake him—I shake him, but he will not move. Oh, Mr. McCormick, I am so afraid! I

didn't know who else to turn to. Will you see him, please . . .
will you go to our cabin . . . will you tell me if he is . . . if he
is . . ."

Dead was the word she was seeking, but she couldn't say
it. Max took her arm, guided her to one of the empty beds in
his stateroom, and sat her down.

"All right, you wait here. I'll go to your cabin and check
on him. You'd better give me your key."

"The door is open. You must go down and down the stairs,
all the way to Deck F. The cabin is number 423. It is terrible
there, full of smelly refugees. You must walk past the sleeping people to the bed farthest in back. It is there you'll find
my father."

"Okay," he agreed. "Will you be all right for a few minutes
on your own?"

She looked up bravely with tears in her eyes. "Yes. I will
try," she assured him.

*****

He limped as quickly as he could along the empty corridor
to the stairs, then downward into the ship's lower regions,
holding onto the banister of the stairway as he descended, a
one-legged hobble that he sensed was faintly ridiculous. At
the bottom landing, he made his way along a seemingly

endless corridor until he found the cabin number that Sasha had given him.

Max paused outside the door long enough to catch his breath and suffer an onslaught of second thoughts. What in the world was he doing here? He'd been friendly to the girl, that's all. He hadn't meant to get so involved. Yet he'd committed himself and there was nothing for it now but to continue onward.

Max opened the door and went inside. The cabin was as Sasha had described it: a crowded, windowless space with six sets of bunks beneath two harsh lights. There was raucous snoring coming from several beds. Everyone appeared to be asleep at this hour except an old woman, hardly more than a bundle of clothes, who sat on her upper bunk watching him with suspicious eyes.

He found Sasha's father on a lower bunk in the rear of the cabin lying on his back with his chin jutting upward and one hand trailing onto the floor. Max knew instantly the old fellow was dead. There was something completely different about him, like a shed skin that had been left behind.

It wasn't a pretty sight, a dead old man at this hour of the morning and Max stood for a moment trying to take it in. He supposed someone more clever than himself would be able to divine the meaning of things at such a moment: life, death, the big picture. But Max felt only a dull sorrow.

With a sigh, he lowered himself onto Sasha's empty bunk. His leg throbbed painfully after rushing down six flights of stairs and now that he was here, Max wasn't sure what was required of him. He supposed he should return and inform her that old dad had gone off sailing on the River Styx and wouldn't be returning any time soon, but for the moment he didn't have the strength to climb the stairs. It seemed to him a futile thing to die like this in the middle of an unfinished voyage, far from any port.

Max was tapping his cane lightly on the floor, trying to decide what to do, when the old woman on the upper bunk began to scream. Apparently, she had just noticed that Sasha's father was dead rather than merely sleeping. From her position on the bunk above, she kept screaming and pointing down at the dead man in an accusing manner. A number of the other refugees sat up and now they were all upset, pointing and talking in a babel of languages that Max didn't understand.

A gaunt young man with a half-grown beard climbed down from his bunk. "This old man, he is dead!" he said angrily in heavily-accented English, as though it were somehow Max's fault.

"Yes," Max agreed wearily.

"You must take him away! He is unclean—yes, it is unclean for us to be here with a person who is dead. You must take him quickly!"

Max nodded. It was hard to say why, but he felt a nearly irresistible urge to beat the young man senseless with his cane. He restrained himself, but it was an effort.

"I'll tell you what," he said carefully. "I'm not actually in the business of taking dead people off with me, clean or unclean or in some state in between. But I will go and inform one of the officers, and I'm sure they will do whatever is appropriate. Meanwhile, why don't you make yourself useful, sonny, and see if you can calm down the poor woman making all that noise."

"We are not animals here," the young man told him sullenly. "We will not remain with dead people."

Max sighed, his anger deflated as quickly as it had come. "Yes, yes. Well, I'll see what I can do."

He left the cabin with a murmur of angry voices rising up behind him, a collective outrage that somehow their dignity had been violated by the old man's unwanted death. Sasha and her father had clearly not made friends among their cabinmates. Max walked back along the corridor, his leg hurting with every step, and he began the weary climb upward. All he wanted now was to find someone in authority, report the death, and hand over the responsibility to other people.

Coming up onto the landing on C-Deck, he turned a corner and found himself facing a trim, middle aged officer with graying hair and the stripes of a Lieutenant Commander on his sleeve. Max quickly explained the problem: the dead old fellow below, the others in the cabin who were upset and wanted the body removed as quickly as possible.

"I see," said the officer, fixing Max with his stern eyes. "Well, you'd better wait here, then, Lieutenant. We'll want to talk with you later. Meanwhile, I'll find the ship's doctor."

"Yes, sir," said Max. He found a bench near the elevator where he sat and rested his leg. Ten minutes went by and he thought he'd been forgotten. But then a different officer appeared, a younger man with a slight build, a lieutenant according to his sleeve. He had a folder full of documents in his hand and there was a doctor at his side, a puffy middle aged man with a bushy mustache who carried a black leather bag containing the unappealing tools of his trade. With Max leading the way, the three men returned to the crowded cabin below. Sasha's cabin mates stopped their chattering when they saw Max with two officials, the face of authority.

The doctor knelt by the corpse and pronounced what was obvious: old Julka was gone beyond any hope of revival. While the doctor continued his examination, the British lieutenant pulled Max aside. Seated together on Sasha's bunk, he opened a folder full of papers and flipped through the pages trying to find the old man on the passenger manifest.

"Julka Szopin, you say?"

"Yes, that's the name he told me," Max agreed.

"And he was a friend of yours?"

"I wouldn't say friend exactly. I met him once or twice, that's all. He was traveling with his daughter."

"And her name?"

"Sasha Szopin. Sonya, actually. If you've read your Tolstoy, you'll know that Sasha is a diminutive of Sonya."

"Szopin . . . Szopin," the lieutenant intoned while his finger moved down a list. "No, I don't see it."

"You might try Jabolonski," Max suggested, remembering the British woman's tale of the Great Jabolonski. "I heard someone suggest that he went by that name also, from time to time."

The lieutenant gave Max a speculative look, then returned to his list.

"Ah, yes, here he is, Julka Jabolonski, not Szopin. Well, well, look here—under race, we have him listed as Roma. Imagine that, a bloody Gypsy! I spent time in Eastern Europe before the war. They don't much like Gypsies there, I can assure you."

Max shrugged to disguise a growing unease. It didn't seem possible that Sasha's father could be a Gypsy. The lieutenant kept studying his paperwork. After a moment, his unfriendly eyes turned to Max with curiosity.

"You say he was traveling with his daughter?"

"Yes. His daughter Sonya."

"If you don't mind me asking, how did you meet this girl, Lieutenant? She was traveling in rather a different section of the ship than you."

Max hesitated. He didn't want to give Sasha away, but he didn't see any other choice. "Well, the truth of the matter is she came up to the Officers Canteen from time to time. She's young, her English is nearly perfect—it seemed silly to stand on ceremony just because she was quartered down below."

"I see. Well, that's understandable, I'm sure. What I don't understand is why you keep referring to the girl as his daughter."

"I'm sorry?" Max was tired, he didn't have a clue as to what the man was getting at.

"Because she isn't his daughter, you see," he said.

"Not his daughter?" Max repeated stupidly. "What is she then?"

"She's no relation to him at all. Her name is Sonya Wojtkiewicz. She was born in Krakow, Poland on October 24, 1923. And she's a Jew."

The lieutenant pronounced the word Jew with distaste. When it came to anti-Semitism, the British weren't far behind the rest of Europe.

"It's not possible," Max said. "You have to be mistaken."

"There's no mistake. Believe me, we make certain of these things. We want to know who we're carrying to America."

Max did his best at this late hour to absorb the girl's new identity: Sonya Wojtkiewicz, a Jewish girl without a father who was—with a quick bit of arithmetic—twenty years old rather than seventeen. It was a completely different picture of Sasha than the one he thought he knew.

"I'm afraid she sold you a bill of goods," the British officer told him with a hint of satisfaction. He lowered his voice. "Of course, a Gypsy and a Jew—what can you expect? You can't trust these people, you know. They're tricky. It's in the blood, you see."

Max left the cabin as soon as the doctor and the British lieutenant were finished with him. After the first surprise, a slow anger was burning inside of him. What a fool he'd been! He'd made a lot of allowances for Sasha, after all. He'd kept quiet when he had found her cheating at cards. He didn't care that she was Jewish, he didn't mind that she was three years older than she had pretended to be, it didn't even bother him that the old fellow wasn't her father. But he didn't appreciate being lied to again and again.

Max stomped up the staircase a final time—and it seemed to him that he had stomped up and down these stairs a few too many times tonight. The pain of his hurt leg added to his outrage, his sense of being badly used. His anger grew with every step.

He was determined to give the damn girl a piece of his mind—Sonja Szopin Wojtkiewicz, whoever the hell she was.

But as Max arrived on A-Deck, he paused for a moment to catch his breath and he found himself beset with conflicting emotions.

This was a complicated situation, after all—or at least Max found it complicated, being himself a complicated man. The old fellow had just died, and Max presumed that even if he wasn't her father, she would certainly be upset. Perhaps she was devastated, he couldn't say.

Max didn't want to be heartless. He wanted to be fair. She was alone now, she was vulnerable, and despite his anger, his heart went out to her.

"Damn it all!" he said aloud. He hadn't asked to get ensnared in the girl's drama. Max was ready to have it out with her. But as he came to his cabin door, he didn't have a clue what he was going to say.

Five

Max opened his cabin door to find Sasha apparently asleep, stretched out on his bunk surrounded by seven empty beds. The scene looked absurdly like something from Snow White and the Seven Dwarfs. Or maybe it was Goldilocks and the Three Bears. Max wasn't sure of the right story, but he knew it was a fairy tale.

He sat on the next bunk over, lit one of his English cigarettes, and studied her suspiciously. Sasha was curled up on her side with her cloak gathered around her like a blanket. There were streaks of dry tears down her checks. A single bare leg lay revealed where the cloak had slipped away. The white cotton nightgown had risen above her knee. Her leg was nicely shaped and shown to advantage, perfectly arranged for him to view.

This was an unexpected twist, to find the girl feigning sleep—and the longer he studied her, the more he was certain it was a sham. He'd been prepared to return to his cabin to have it out, a truth telling session in which they would all stop pretending things that weren't true. But instead he found himself treated to an intriguing view of her body. He should have known she would have some card up her sleeve, so to speak—and her leg, Max had to admit, was a pretty good card to play. It was purposefully arranged, he knew that. It was like putting a fly into a stream to see if there were a male trout nearby to take a nibble. Still, though he understood the artfulness of the ploy, he couldn't quite remove his eye from the lure. The problem was that as bait went, Sasha had a provocative leg indeed.

While Max sat smoking, he watched as Sasha's eyes fluttered open, green and curious. After a moment, she sat up, covered her leg more modestly with her nightgown, and looked at him.

"I wasn't sleeping," she admitted. Her voice was curiously empty of emotion. "I just couldn't bear to be awake." She lowered her eyes. "Did you see my father?" she asked quietly.

"Your father? Well, he's dead," Max answered. "You knew that before you sent me down there. It's very sad to lose a father, of course. The problem is, we only have one father to lose, don't we? I mean, fathers don't grow on trees."

Her face remained expressionless. "May I have a cigarette, please?"

Max offered her a Player's from his case. She held it to her lips while he lit it for her with his lighter.

"These cigarettes are very good," she told him, inhaling deeply. "In Poland we were smoking sawdust wrapped in paper that we tore from books. It was not very good."

"Let's talk about your father, Sasha. There are matters to arrange."

"God, I hate this war!" she said evasively, exhaling a long stream of smoke. "I still dream about 1939 when the Nazis were outside Krakow. Every day the guns came closer and there was nothing we could do to save ourselves. It was like waiting for the guillotine, wondering what the Nazis would do to us when they arrived."

Max watched her, fascinated, wondering what card she would play next. First a bare leg, and now Krakow 1939. She seemed to be trying different approaches, seeing what kind of leverage she could get on him.

He smiled warily. "Sasha, I know the war hasn't been easy. I take my hat off to you for getting this far. Truly, I do."

She blew smoke in his direction. "Do you? What do you know about these things, Max McCormick from Holly-wood?"

"Well, of course, I've seen a few things myself," he replied. "For instance, I saw the Siege of Leningrad. That wasn't a piece of cake, I assure you. Nor was getting blown up by a land mine on the road to Alexandria. But I don't mean to compare my experience to yours. I'm not even sure what the point of it would be."

She shook her head vaguely and looked away. "I'm sorry. You have tried to be helpful, and I am grateful. Perhaps you will do one more thing for me and notify the ship's authorities about my father. I don't have the heart for this myself. I would only cry."

"Yes, I'm sure you were very fond of your father, Sasha. As a matter of fact, I have already notified the authorities. I found one of the officers and the ship's doctor and we all went down to your cabin to have a look. As I said, he was dead, all right, your father. A very dead father, indeed."

Sasha kept inhaling compulsively on her cigarette. "Ah, I see. You have found me out again," she said after a moment. "You're very good at that, it seems."

Max laughed bitterly. "What? You think you can hide these things? They had all the information from your papers. Julka wasn't your father, he was a Gypsy, no relation to you at all. I have to admit, that came as something of a shock, after all your talk about dear old papa always worrying when you were away too long. Incidentally, Miss Wojtkiewicz, you aren't quite a blushing seventeen after all—you're three years older. I imagine you lost count."

Sasha stared at him. "Yes, I understand perfectly. They told you all my secrets and now you are disillusioned. I am sorry. Men prefer illusions, I know that very well. You prefer an innocent young girl who will speak to you nicely about Puccini. You see, all I did was give you what you wanted. Did they tell you that I am . . . that I am . . ."

"Jewish?" Max said with a smile. "Naturally. I have to say, that's one part of your secret life that doesn't bother me. I'm what's known in America as a flaming liberal—I don't care a fig about someone's race. I'm only sorry you told me a lot of nonsense about going to the cathedral in Wawel Castle and praying to Jesus and Mary . . . or maybe it was your dragon you prayed to, I forget. With all the stories you tell, it's hard to keep anything straight."

Sasha looked away. "Well, I didn't like being a Jew. And I didn't see why I had to be one, if I didn't want to."

"What? You think you can simply tell a bunch of lies and pretend to be whatever you choose? Is that it?"

"Yes, that is it exactly. And Julka and I chose to be alive." Sasha carefully stubbed out her half-smoked cigarette in the ashtray on the side table by the bunk. "May I keep this for later?" she asked, holding up the butt.

"Of course. It's yours entirely, every last puff."

She stood from the bunk, gathered her cloak around her body, and walked to the cabin door.

"Goodbye, Mr. McCormick. Thank you for letting me stay here. I knew there were people who needed to be told, but I couldn't bear to do it myself."

"Wait a second, where are you going?"

"Down to where I belong. You don't like me and perhaps you are right. You are a decent man and I have disappointed you."

"Hold on. I think you owe me a few answers. Why in God's name did you pretend that Julka was your father?"

"Why do you think? It was for protection, so that men like you would treat me with regard, not just some easy prey. But you will not understand this, Mr. McCormick. How can you? You have had a very different life. Julka was my dearest friend and I loved him very much. We traveled many miles together and we nearly died together many times. Incidentally, I am not actually Jewish," she added, raising her eyes to him.

Max was astounded that this was the one part of her tall tale that appeared to cause her worry.

"Sasha, believe me, I couldn't be bothered less if you're Hindu. You could be Zoroastrian, for all I care."

"No, this is important, and I wish you to know the truth. I am . . . well, I am half-Jewish. My mother was Jewish, but my father was not. He was a young Gentile, an artist. She was a model for him, you see. I have never been in a synagogue in my life. We were bohemians, my mother and I, free of bourgeois prejudice. The only religion I know is music."

"For chrissake!" Max swore, inappropriately.

"And now I will say goodbye. I think you will be very glad not to see me anymore."

She was right. Max wanted her to go. Yet, at the same time, he couldn't bear the idea of her leaving.

"Wait a minute, Sasha. Look, I have a good bottle of English gin in my duffel bag—I was saving it as a present for someone in California, but maybe this is a good time to break it open. You've had a bad shock."

She stood by the door shaking her head.

"Come on, stay and have a drink. You look like you can use one. We'll get tipsy and you can tell me the real story of your life."

"Why do you care?"

"Because I'm curious. And I bet the real story of your life is even more interesting than the made up one. Don't you want someone to know the real you?"

She kept shaking her head. "Julka understood me very well."

"I'm sure he did."

"No, you understand nothing," she said bitterly, lowering her eyes to the floor. "How could you? He was only . . ."

Sasha stopped, biting her lip. Up to this moment, her composure had seemed the most remarkable part of the conversation. She had appeared to Max a tough cookie. But now he understood that she was not composed at all. She was close to bursting apart.

"Only what?" Max pressed.

Tears began flooding from her eyes. "He was only a weak, silly old man!" she shouted at him suddenly. "Yes, goddamn you! He lived in a dream world! A foolish old Gypsy—he didn't mind what we did, if we lied or stole, and sometimes he said I should be with men, if that would help us! Is this the truth you want so much, Mr. McCormick? Well, now you know. He was a wicked old man! But I loved him and now he's gone and I . . . I have no one!"

As Max watched her, she broke. She simply broke. Max looked on with sympathy, but from a certain emotional distance. Perhaps even now, nothing would have happened between them that morning. But just then, the *Mauretania* hit a swell that sent the ship yawing wildly from side to side.

"Oh, God!" Sasha cried, reaching to the wall to keep from falling. "When will this horrible night end?"

She tried to make her way to the door, but Max took her arm.

"Sasha, for chrissake, where the hell are you going to go? Stay here, at least for a while."

"I wish I were dead!"

"No, you don't," he assured her. "You're only being dramatic. Now, why don't you sit down and we'll—"

Just then the lights inside the *Mauretania* flickered off, leaving them in darkness. It was only a few seconds and then they blinked back on. But Sasha cried out, startled, and by the time the lights were on again, somehow she was in his arms. Max was never sure afterwards how this happened, if he had reached out and pulled her to him, or whether she had simply fallen his way. It didn't matter. From the moment he held her, Max knew he wasn't going to let her go.

Sasha cried hot tears onto his neck. Her hair tickled his cheek as he held her. It was hard to say why, but this ticklishness was almost unbearably intimate. It filled Max with an overwhelming sense of absurdity and tenderness, all mixed together. He held her awkwardly, not certain what to do with his hands.

"I don't know what's to become of me!" she cried. "I'm so frightened!"

"Shh!" he comforted. He stroked her hair, he kissed the tears falling on her cheeks. He could feel her heartbeat and breath. It seemed to him that he was holding life itself—everything that was warm, fragile, vulnerable, and impossibly foolish.

Then, somewhere in all the comforting, he found he was no longer kissing her tears and hair, he was kissing her lips. Her mouth was wet with saliva and mucous, eager for love, kissing him passionately in return.

"No, we'd better not," Max said, breaking away. He knew he shouldn't do this. He loved his wife and his life was complicated enough without adding extra complications. But there are times when the ship has already sailed and there's no going back.

"Oh, don't stop," she cried. "Please, won't you pretend that you love me? Just for tonight?"

Somehow that seemed all right, if they were only pretending. His hands moved of their own accord along the curve of her back until they found the hem of her nightgown, her bare legs. She was naked underneath, warm to touch. She tore at his belt buckle while he stripped her nightgown off over her head.

An Overnight Sensation

As love went, what happened that early morning was not a thing of beauty. He saw himself briefly as though from a celestial view: a ridiculous figure, a wounded middle aged man with a limp, his olive green trousers down around his ankles and an erection jutting upward between the parting of his regulation army shirt. Here was the human comedy in all its undeniable force. Together they crashed down onto his bunk in a tangle of limbs.

Comedy or not, still it was astonishing, the power of lust and exhaustion at four o'clock in the morning. The night was overwhelming and human beings required comfort. By the time Max slipped inside of her, he had forgotten that it was only make-believe.

Six

For Max, what happened between himself and Sasha that morning on the North Atlantic was a revelation, beyond anything he had ever known, more than sex, a kind of annihilation. All he wanted was to plunge himself into her again and again.

There was little conversation between them. He didn't tell her amusing anecdotes about his childhood. They weren't suddenly best friends. They didn't discuss literature or Broadway plays. He wasn't even sure he especially liked her. They simply tore at each other as though the world were ending.

Hours later—how many hours, it was hard to say—Max found himself entwined with Sasha on his narrow bunk in a tangle of sheets. She had fallen asleep with her head on his shoulder, her right arm flung across his chest, her leg resting on his thigh, the bend of her knee touching the small sticky thing that his penis had become. She was snoring gently, and though Max was the sort of romantic who generally shunned women who snored, he found it didn't bother him this morning in the least. In the new intimacy of their bodies, after all the penetrations, a snore was nothing to worry about.

He was too wound up for sleep. He had never before been in such state of post-coital grace, in some nether world where everything was imbued with a slightly fuzzy radiance.

All he needed was a cigarette for there to be absolute perfection. Gently, he slipped himself free of Sasha's body in order to find his silver case on the side table. She moaned softly, then turned over and was asleep again instantly.

Max found a cigarette and put its perfect whiteness to his lips. He sat naked, smoking on the edge of the bed, and studied the smooth bare contours of Sasha's shoulders with proprietary interest. He liked her shoulders. He felt a wild urge to lick them with his tongue, blade to blade. Perhaps next time.

Exhaling smoke, Max picked up his wristwatch that had fallen onto the cabin floor in some moment of passion. It was ten minutes to nine. The night was over. A winter's dawn would be breaking on the North Atlantic, God's daily orgasm of morning light, and Max decided impulsively that he must see it, a final greedy splurge of poetry to delight his senses.

He dressed quietly so as not to wake Sasha, recovering pieces of clothing from far flung corners of the room, and hobbled out on deck. Dawn came late at this latitude, at this time of year, and the sky was just turning gray with a fine vapor in the air that wasn't quite rain. What a miracle, Max thought, to make love so fabulously then walk outside on the deck of a mighty ship and breathe the salty dampness of the North Atlantic into one's lungs. How lucky he was to be alive!

Max made his way along the deck toward the bow, where the wind was blowing stronger. Ahead somewhere over the horizon, across the gray waves, lay America.

America!

Max felt a wrinkle of concern touch his perfect happiness. America meant the future, plans and movie work, California and Mina . . .

"Ah, there's the laddie!" a British voice called out behind him. "Happy Valentine's Day, Max!"

It was Shelton Graves with his wife, Biff. Max turned and stared, unable at first to reply. He saw himself suddenly as they must see him: unshaved, slack-jawed, loose-limbed from spent passion, played out from lack of sleep.

"Valentine's Day?" he repeated stupidly.

"Yes, laddie, it's February 14th. And you look like something the cat dragged home, don't you, Maxie?"

"Valentine's Day!" Max repeated a second time. An absurd grin lit up his unshaved face. "My God, you're right! It's Valentine's Day!"

Shelly kept studying Max with predatory interest. "You know, if I didn't know what a prude you were, I'd say you got lucky last night. What do you think, Puss? Did our Maxie get lucky last night?"

Biff puffed on her cigarette and looked at him with her hard, dark eyes. "I don't know. Did you get lucky, Max?"

He kept grinning, unable to restrain himself. "I'm always lucky at sea," he told them. "It's only on land that I have trouble." It didn't mean a thing, it was utter gibberish. But lacking meaning, it was the sort of comment that might, with a little luck, be taken as clever.

Fred Landson came around the deck just then looking very eagle-eyed and sharply pressed for such an early hour.

"Ah, look what we have here—it's our heroic hero," Shelly remarked unpleasantly. "Our most earnest Boy Scout."

Fred didn't appear to notice Shelly's sarcasm. "Say, have you seen Sasha?" he asked. "I just heard that her father died. The old guy passed away last night, and Sasha didn't spend the night in her cabin. I went down there to ask about her and no one knows where she is."

Shelly shook his head. "Don't look at me? I don't know where that girl spent the night. Gracious me! She certainly wasn't in my bed! How about you Max? She's not in your bed, is she?"

Max squirmed under the question, but was saved from answering by Fred. "I've got to find her," Fred said. "I bet that poor girl is devastated!"

"Oh, the poo' wittle thing!" Biff said in vicious baby talk.

"Well, she's bound to show up sooner or later," Shelly said, offering around his case of cigarettes. "Girls like that always do. Unless she's thrown herself into the ocean, of course, in a tragic fit of grief. What do you think, Max? Is she the sort of girl to make a dramatic gesture?"

Max shook his head vaguely and accepted one of Shelly's cigarettes. Fred took a cigarette too, foregoing his usual pipe as perhaps too difficult to light on a windy stretch of deck. Biff lit up one of her Chesterfields and they all blew smoke at each other. World war would have been unthinkable without tobacco. Without tobacco, everyone would have simply shrugged their shoulders and gone home.

"Look, Max, you didn't see her last night, did you?" Fred asked, getting back to his main preoccupation. "In the Canteen, I mean? Or with one of the fellows?"

Max was starting to feel rotten, sensing he had gotten in the way of Cupid's rightful arrows. He should have stayed clear, he saw that now. Here, obviously, was a man with serious intent who might actually take care of the girl.

And meanwhile he hadn't answered the question. Had he seen Sasha? He wanted to howl with laughter. The problem for Max was that he believed in truthfulness. Honest work. Honest men. Honest answers. So what in the world was he going to say to Fred?

"No, Fred," he answered after only the smallest hesitation. "No, I didn't see her."

Fred scowled. "Well, maybe I'll go below and see if anyone's seen her there."

"Yes, be sure to let us know when you find her," Shelly said. "We don't want any lost girls, do we, Max?"

Fred gave a dispirited wave with his iron hook and walked away.

"What an idiot!" Biff remarked thoughtfully, watching him go.

"Look, I'm feeling a little green around the gills," Max said. "I think I'd better go lie down."

"You do indeed look a little green, laddie—doesn't he, Puss?"

Biff gave him a continental kiss on the cheek as he was leaving. "Look, if you want to get really lucky, come and visit me some night," she whispered into his ear.

Max backed away with a strained smile. It was impossible to know if Biff had just made a pass at him, or if she was only being ironic in some oblique way. Either way, he hated it. He made his way back inside the ship in a gloomy mood. It was astonishing to Max how a few minutes with Shelly and Biff had sucked away the magic of the morning. He stumbled down the corridor trying to get his thoughts into working order. The encounter with Fred had reminded him that he had responsibilities, the happiness of other people's lives to consider, and he must decide something fast. He didn't want to lead Sasha on. He didn't want her thinking they might have a future when they clearly didn't. He needed to be fair to her. He needed to tell her that he didn't intend to leave his wife, and that he would be heading to California as quickly as he could arrange it once they docked in New York.

This is what Max intended to say. He had the very words on his tongue. But he opened the cabin door and found her sitting up in bed, smoking a cigarette, hugging her knees, with her thick dark blonde hair spilled over her shoulders and the sheet dropped away so that he could see her now-familiar breasts and nipples.

Even standing across the room, Max could taste the complex sweetness of her.

To his surprise, he saw that she had been crying. With a small self-conscious laugh, she wiped the tears from her cheeks with the back of her hand.

"I was on deck," he said, leaving the question of tears alone.

"Yes, I supposed that was where you were. What is happening?"

"Oh, nothing important. Just the endless human comedy. *Veni, vidi, vici.* Fortunately, we have better things to do."

She smiled. A smile of complicit mischief, a smile only lovers know.

"I think you are a little crazy. What is this *veni, vidi, vici.*"

"You didn't study Latin? I came, I saw, I conquered. Such is the story of man. I'm going to have to teach you history, Sasha."

"Perhaps I can teach you a few things, Mr. McCormick."

Suddenly he was almost dizzy with joy. Probably he was only punch-drunk from a night of no sleep, yet he felt wonderful looking at her and knowing that in a moment he was going to take her in his arms.

"You know something, I've just figured out the secret of love," he told her eagerly. "Do you know what love is, Sasha?"

She shook her head, laughing at how eccentric he was.

"Love is being with someone who makes you see how beautiful the world is."

Sasha continued to shake her head. "The world is beautiful? . . . no, I don't think so. I think you have had some of your famous gin on deck and you are perhaps a little fuddled."

He approached the bunk and took her hands. Her nails were slightly chewed, not entirely elegant.

"Oh, yes, the world is beautiful, Sasha. You're beautiful. . . I'm beautiful. We're all so goddamn beautiful I want to write a poem . . . or listen to you sing a sad Polish song!"

Sasha laughed. Of course, she knew he was wrong. She knew what love was. It wasn't being with someone who made you feel how beautiful the world was.

She could have told him about Julka, how the two of them had curled together for warmth in a forest outside of Bucharest one winter's night to keep, quite literally, from freezing to death. That was love. Or how when she had been ill in

Bulgaria, her teeth chattering, so sick she wanted to die, Julka had cleaned her bed pan full of shit. That was love also.

No, the world was not "beautiful," and two people would be foolish to tell each other so. It amazed her that someone could arrive at Max's age and still be such a child. And yet he was wonderful and kind, and suddenly she wanted him very much.

Her smile was simultaneously shy and dazzling. She pulled back the blanket to let him in.

"Happy Valentine's Day!" he said, going to her. "Oh, I'm going to pierce you to the core, you beautiful girl!"

Seven

And so it began, Max and Sasha's grand love affair. But their time together was brief. They had precisely three days before the *Mauretania* reached New York and reality resumed its usual hold. It wasn't much, seventy-two hours, only the length of a long weekend. Yet at the time it seemed to last forever.

They made love continually, romping from one bunk to another, top and lower. By the time it was over, there wasn't one of those eight bunks without a memory. Sexually speaking, they established a physical intimacy so final that for Max it was difficult to imagine ever being apart.

Yet they had little else in common. Max never tried to talk to her about the usual subjects men and women discussed in his social circle— literature, art, movies, socialism, capitalism, Jung versus Freud. With Sasha, there wasn't even Hollywood gossip to fall back on. They had no common ground at all.

Later, in his years of remembering, Max was certain they must have talked, though he couldn't remember many of the words. Naturally, he was curious about her. But if he asked about her past, then she would ask about his, and before you knew it, they would both be a thousand miles away in their separate histories.

That was the usual thing, in Max's experience, what couples did when they first got together: they told each other the stories of their lives. But he didn't want to do it. He didn't want to know about the men Sasha had seduced, or had been seduced by. And for his part, he didn't want to tell her all his over-told anecdotes of prep school and college, and how he had broken his father's heart by going to Hollywood rather than settling down in Boston as the earnest young attorney everyone had always assumed Max would be. And most of all, he didn't want to talk about Mina. He didn't want that subject even to come up.

Sasha managed to hide in his cabin for the entire three days, with Max bringing back food from the kitchen when they were hungry, claiming he had a sick friend. The food never varied: the same greasy buns in the morning, buns and sausage for lunch, and at night the same kidney stew in gloppy brown sauce. Sometimes Max gave Sasha his portion, amazed to see her eat up every oily bite.

"Where do you put it?" he wondered, watching her wipe up the sauce with stale bread. "How do you stay so thin?"

"I've learned to eat when I can, my darling. You wouldn't have lasted a day in Nazi Poland," she taunted.

"You're right," he agreed. "I wouldn't."

She laughed, seeing the thoughtful expression that came to his face. She had never known anyone who thought so much about everything. "But it's all right, because I would

270

take care of you," she assured him. "I would keep you safe from those Nazi beasts. You need me, my darling Mr. McCormack. You are a dreamer, so you must have someone practical like me."

"But you're a dreamer too, Sasha. Look at you," he said. "Why, you've dreamed your way to America."

She smiled happily but kept back the truth: she had schemed her way to America, which wasn't quite the same thing.

It seemed they were always laughing during those three days. Yet for Sasha, Max was as foreign as she was to him. She was in awe of him, just a little, because he was so smart and cultivated, and also very rich by her standards. But sex was democratic and quickly broke down the barriers between them. Sasha had never before experienced sex like she did with Max. In the past, she had used sex to get what she needed; she had learned early in life that it was advantageous to be a pretty woman. But she had always held herself in reserve. She had looked on, play acting for effect.

And now look at me! she told herself. I am in love. At last this miracle has happened to me!

She forgot her caution. She was certain that Max loved her in return and that no woman would ever succeed in making this complicated man happy except herself.

As for the future, it was natural to fantasize while lying in his arms, post-coital, pretending to be asleep.

She imagined a safe harbor, a house in California where Max would keep her. Sometimes in her imagination the house resembled a French chateau, at other times it was like photographs she had seen of English manner houses with their great lawns. There would be sunlight and palm trees and always enough to eat. Even with caution thrown to the winds, Sasha was practical enough to understand that Max wasn't going to leave his wife. But this didn't bother her unduly. Men had mistresses, after all. And perhaps these things didn't need to end as badly as she had always imagined.

Who could say? Perhaps it was better to be Max's mistress than his wife. She got the best part of him that way. Max was an artist, after all. A cinema director. And from her childhood, Sasha knew that great artists didn't write great operas for their wives. They reserved their best work for fallen women like herself.

*****

At least once a day, usually toward sunset, Max and Sasha left their love nest to walk on deck. Generally, they headed up to the highest reaches of the ship near the *Mauretania's* two smoke funnels, hoping to avoid anyone they knew. Nevertheless, people spotted them together from time to time—Biff and Shelly, another time the aircraft executive who had married Mina's friend. Max was aware of their curious glances, but he no longer cared.

But then one time they encountered Fred Landson while they were heading up a flight of outside stairs and he was going down, and this was awkward. Fred stopped long enough to give them a glowering look, then he hurried by.

"Oh, dear!" Sasha said, pausing on the higher deck. "I was supposed to meet Fred in the Officers Canteen and give him an answer. But it completely slipped my mind."

"What sort of answer?"

"He wanted to know if I would marry him. It wasn't such a romantic proposal, I'm afraid. But it was terrible of me to forget. He must be very angry."

"Ah, well, poor Fred," Max said complacently.

"But I wonder what made him ask to marry me? I never gave him encouragement."

"You didn't need to, Sasha. You're a great prize, you see. All the men are hungry for you. You're the veritable Christmas goose."

She smiled. "I'm not sure I wish to be a Christmas goose. Perhaps I have my own mind."

"Perhaps you do," he agreed. "I've noticed it, actually, that mind of yours. You're not even slightly stupid."

"This is a compliment?"

"Sure it is. I like smart girls. Smart girls are sexy."

They laughed and moved on, hand in hand, and didn't give Fred another thought. It wasn't that they were callous, but their happiness insulated them from the world, enwrapping them in a bubble that only had room for two. Fred's anger or disappointment—whatever it might be —was impossibly distant. Almost unimaginable to two people swept away in the first burning fascination of love.

*****

"We are causing gossip," Sasha said to Max the following evening after Shelly and Biff had spotted them on their high perch for the second day in a row. "A very big scandal, I think. They are wondering what your lovely wife will say."

"Do you mind?"

"No. Why should I? I am nobody. I do not know these people or care what they think about me. But it is different for you, Max."

"To hell with them," he said blithely.

"You don't mind? Maybe one of these nice people will write a secret letter. 'Dear Miss Mina, I feel obligated to inform you that your handsome husband he is making the time with a little Polish number, very shocking.'"

He laughed at her English. "I still say, the hell with it. Mina's had plenty of affairs. It's my turn, that's all."

Sasha raised her eyes. "You have not told me this. That Mina has affairs."

"Oh, well . . . it's not important." He sighed wishing this subject hadn't come up. "It's difficult to talk about, Sasha. Mina's a free spirit and perhaps a little mad. She doesn't understand the usual limits. But that's who she is and I've learned to accept it. She likes being married, but she refuses to let it clip her wings."

"And you accept this?"

Max shrugged. The truth was something only a Hollywood couple would understand: that as a great star, Mina was more important than Max and therefore called the shots. This had changed somewhat over the years as she had come to rely on him, but her independence was never in doubt. Mina was the queen who set the rules and Max was only the consort; if he wished to be with her, he had no choice but to go along.

Sasha took the cigarette from his mouth, had a puff, then returned it to him. They had taken to sharing smoke in this way.

"You love her very much," she told him.

Max shrugged again, fighting off a vague irritation. Up to now, he had done his best to avoid the topic of his marriage. But of course, it was inevitable. Didn't Sasha have a right to ask such things? Hadn't he given her this right?

"Yes, I love her very much," he agreed. "She's funny and smart and neurotic and terribly kind. Maybe that's what I like best about her, how genuinely kind she is."

"And she's very beautiful," Sasha added. "And she's famous, and she's rich. Do you live in a big house?"

"It's big enough, I suppose." Max sighed again, thinking of the upkeep, the need to always make so much money. "Too damn big, if you want to know the truth."

"In the town of Los Angeles?"

"Well, Los Angeles isn't much of a town. It's more a huge sprawl. We live on a hilltop in a part of the city called Bel Air. Sasha, can we not talk about this right now?"

"Yes, I understand, Max."

"I know we need to talk about these things later. But just not now."

"I said yes, I understand."

"Do you?"

She nodded. "Of course. You love your wife. You are having an affair. I am a big girl, Max. I think maybe it is you who are the child."

This made Max hesitate. They were standing on their favorite high deck by the smoke funnels with a gray horizon darkening all around. Max wanted to say something comforting to Sasha, but he didn't know what it would be. Sasha looked at him and laughed, seeing his struggle.

"It's all right, Max. You know what I am going to do?"

"What are you going to do?" he answered with a smile.

"I am going to . . . tickle you!" she cried merrily, reaching with her fingers to the part of his waist, the sides, where he was most ticklish. It was ridiculous, but Max was very ticklish, and so was she. They had taken to having tickle fights in Max's cabin, generally without a thing on. In this case, Sasha soon had Max howling with laughter. But then he turned and chased her around the two smokestacks, hobbling after her with his cane.

"I'm going to catch you!" he cried, as they ran around the huge funnels. "And when I do, look out!"

"No, no!" she screamed with laughter. "I am too fast for you!"

"Here I come!"

Of course, Max caught her in the end. She let him. And their tickle fight soon took on a different meaning, leading them back down to the cabin. In this manner, laughing and kissing, they chased away the shadows that were never far away—the past, the future, every moment but now.

They were very different from one another, about as ill-suited a couple as you might ever imagine. And yet something had brought them together; something more than sex, more even than mere chance. They clung to one another with all their might. It was as though they were shipwrecked together. They transformed the *Mauretania* into a desert island for two.

But, mile after mile, New York pressed inevitably closer, and for Max and Sasha, their three days of love and cigarettes were almost at an end.

*****

The *Mauretania* was due to arrive in New York at seven in the morning. Max woke before dawn, too agitated to sleep. He left Sasha in bed, bundled up in his warmest clothes, and made his way outside to the deck. The sky and sea were black all around him. A steady wind was blowing over the bow, cold and salty and wet. It was after six, but it could just as easily have been midnight.

At first, he didn't see any sign of land. Then he saw a light on the horizon, Ambrose Light, the first visible sign of the New World flashing red and green in the pre-dawn darkness. It was a thrilling sight. Max stood on deck and imagined all the immigrants who had seen this famous light before him, and all the soldiers returning home from foreign wars.

Soon the twinkling lights of Long Island come into view. They passed Sandy Hook and the *Mauretania* slipped into the Lower Bay, heading toward Quarantine on the northwest corner of Staten Island. No one else was on deck; Max had America all to himself. As he stood watching, the eastern horizon become translucent with the break of day.

Well, he thought, here I am, back in the land of the free. But it was also the land where decisions couldn't be put off much longer. He had no idea what he was going to do with Sasha and Mina. Not to mention Sam Goldwyn, who was expecting him to direct a picture Max wasn't certain he wanted to make. At least he would have a few days in New York to mull things over. Mina was in California shooting a picture and he would have perhaps a week before he saw her. Who could say what miracle might come along to rescue him during this time, some Ambrose Light that would flash and make things clear.

Eeny, meeney, miney, moe, Max thought with a smile. He loved Sasha, he loved Mina . . . catch a tiger by the toe. Could he have them both, he wondered? Two tigers rather than one? (No, said the New England moralist. Human beings are put on this earth to make difficult choices, to suffer, to renounce.)

Max was lighting his second cigarette of the day, when he heard Sasha coming up behind him. He felt her physical presence even before he heard her.

"I woke and you were not there," she said sleepily.

She was all bundled up, wrapped in her cloak and a blanket as well. Max took her in his arms and kissed the top of her head.

"Welcome to America," he said slyly.

"Oh! Is that America?" She was suddenly awake, seeing land all around.

"Look over there. What do you see?" He pointed across the water at the distant skyline of Lower Manhattan, only just visible in the morning mist. The city looked like an impressionist painting from this distance, an impossible enchantment of towers reaching into the sky.

"Oh, it's New York!" Sasha cried, as though the city had not existed until she had named it.

Max laughed. "In a few hours we're going to be in a room at the Plaza," he told her. "It's a nice old hotel overlooking Central Park. We'll have room service bring us breakfast as we lie decadently in bed. Would you like that?"

"Oh, yes! But deca . . . what was that word again? This means the number ten, yes?"

"Decade means ten," he explained. "But decadent . . . well, I think it might be best to show you this in person. In the act, as it were."

"Ah!" Her eyes gleamed full of mischief. "This means you wish to have your way with me, I think."

He laughed. He hadn't meant that at all, but he was willing to pretend he did. He had pictured more the two of them sprawled across a comfortable queen-sized bed having all the long conversations that they'd been putting off.

"Very good," said Sasha. "But before you have your way with me, you must tell me this. What do they eat for breakfast in America?"

"Eggs and bacon and pancakes with maple syrup. All sorts of nice things."

"Pancakes! What are pancakes?"

Max saw he was going to enjoy being Sasha's guide to the New World. It was fun describing pancakes to someone so brand new. Still, she was doubtful.

"Don't they have ration books in this lovely land of America?"

"Well, sure," he agreed. "But I think at the Plaza we'll manage. I happen to know the *maitre 'd* of the restaurant."

"And where will we eat dinner tonight, Max?"

"Let's see. How about Delmonico's? Would you like that?"

"Is it a good restaurant? Is it very expensive?"

"Absolutely!" he assured her, laughing again. "How can you always be thinking about food, my love?"

She turned away from him in order to watch a launch that was coming their way across the water from the direction of the Hudson River. A small frown had settled on her face.

"You don't know what it was like in Krakow. We did not go to Delmonico's. We ate cats when we were lucky enough to find one, and rats sometimes when we were desperate."

"You're right, I can't imagine that," he agreed gently. "I'm a spoiled Yank, I admit it. Just like you're going to be, now that you're here in the land of milk and ulcers. Before you know it, you'll forget what it was like to be hungry and frightened. You'll find new things to fret over, like the mean-ing of life. Just you wait."

"You always joke, Max," she said, moving out of his em-brace. Suddenly she was all arms and elbows, prickly.

"What's the matter? Do you want a cigarette?"

"No. You smoke too much. Nothing's the matter."

"Tobacco's good for your digestion, all the doctors say so. Let's not have our first quarrel on such a memorable morning. Tell me what's the matter?"

Sasha stared at the city across the water. "Now that we are in New York, perhaps you will not want me anymore. I only wish to tell you, you do not owe me anything. From the start, I always knew you were married."

"Look, Sasha, I tell you what," Max said after a moment. "Mina's in California doing a picture, so let's hide in the Plaza for a few days and give ourselves a little breathing room. We'll keep our clothes on, at least some of the time, and have some good long talks about the future. We'll eat pancakes and see where it leads us."

For Max, this seemed a reasonable approach. A bit of breathing room, a few days to make rational choices. But there was no breathing room, they were already out of time.

Max was looking into her green eyes, trying to understand the alarmed expression he saw there, when he heard a familiar voice cry out his name.

"Max!" a woman cried. "Max! Down here!"

An Overnight Sensation

The launch that Sasha had been watching earlier had pulled up to the side of the *Mauretania*. Max peered over the rail to see a woman standing on the deck of the small boat. She was waving upward excitedly to where he stood. Max knew her very well. She was slim and sophisticated, dressed expensively in a long sable coat that was open to reveal a black evening dress. She looked as though she had come directly from some fashionable all-night party.

It was Mina.

"Max!" she shouted. "Surprise, darling!"

Eight

Sasha stood stricken, like a deer caught in headlights. The blood had left her face, even her lips were pale. She knew much better than Max how quickly, and without warning, reversals of fortune can arrive.

"I'll deal with this," Max told her.

"Yes? And how will you deal with this?" Her voice was strained, almost unrecognizable.

"Look, I'll go talk to Mina. I'll meet you back at the cabin."

She shook her head. "No, I will not wait in your cabin. I will be in *my* cabin. If you wish to find me, you will find me there."

"All right," he agreed. "Your cabin, then."

He started to leave, but he couldn't bear it. He turned back to look at her standing by the ship's rail, the New York skyline rising up behind her like the painted backdrop to a play.

"Go, Max. Go to your wife," she said scornfully.

He didn't blame her. It was a cheap situation. Unhappy with himself, Max made his way inside the ship and down the central stairway to the Embarkation Lounge three decks below where the launch would unload. He didn't have a clue what he was going to say to Mina. It was all happening too quickly to sort out.

An Overnight Sensation

The Embarkation Lounge was a large windowless area crowded full of people he didn't know. Max's eyes took in an indistinct blur of uniforms: dark blue uniforms of officers from the *Mauretania*, olive green uniforms of the American military officials who had arrived on the pilot boat. Flash bulbs began exploding nearby. Where there were cameras, he knew Mina wouldn't be far away, and that's where he found her. She was the center of a group of men paying homage. It was a typical Mina moment.

She saw Max and waved extravagantly. "Max!" she cried. "Oh, Max!" She broke free of the group surrounding her and flowed his way, smiling tearfully. The crowd parted for her passage. In a moment she was in his arms broadcasting a scent of familiar perfume.

"Oh, Max! Darling! I hope you're not mad at me for showing up like a bad penny!"

They kissed delicately, a public kiss with flashbulbs going off all around, camera lenses pointed their way in order to record a patriotic moment for tomorrow's newspapers, a reunion that would bring tears to many an American eye, the limping soldier returning to his famous wife.

"I know this is horribly vulgar," she whispered. "You hate photographers, my darling, and I don't blame you. But it was the only way I could get on board the pilot boat to surprise you. Tell me you don't mind."

"I don't mind."

"Really, truly? You're not just saying it?"

"No, I'm awfully glad to see you, Mina. But what about your movie in California?"

"The picture's been delayed. You'll never guess why? Shirley Temple came down with chicken pox."

"But Shirley's not in your picture, is she?"

"No, but Van Johnson is. He's in both movies, you see. And he caught Shirley's chicken pox, so now he's spotted like a leopard and absolutely furious. He swears he'll never work with a child actress again. Meanwhile, my movie had to be delayed until he's better."

"Well, a pox on both their houses."

Mina laughed. "Oh, Max! You haven't changed at all!" She stepped back to take him in. "Except you've lost weight and you look tired. Does your leg hurt?"

"Only when there's a typhoon," he told her.

They could go on like this for hours with a jaunty repartee that camouflaged more dangerous matters. On screen, her presence was large and electric, but in fact Mina Bower was a petite woman, barely five foot four, a waif with a sweet oval face. Her natural hair color was brunette, though this changed from picture to picture, depending on her role. Today she was platinum blonde, what he could see of it. It seemed to Max too bright, almost strident. But he didn't care about her hair color. They studied each other fondly, for it had been a long separation. Along with her black evening dress and sable coat, she wore a slightly daffy hat with a brim that was turned up. Daffy hats had always been an essential part of Mina's public persona.

"How are you, really?" he asked.

"Oh, I've been surviving, I suppose. You know how it is, darling . . . pretending to be all these different people I'm not. Sometimes I feel so stretched thin. Everybody wants something from me, and I only want my Max."

On impulse, he kissed her and she kissed him back, and this time it wasn't just a photo opportunity for the press. She broke away, laughing delightedly.

"Oh, you're back, Max! You're truly back! And you're going to love Hollywood, I promise, how it's changed since you've been gone. Everybody's there now. Thomas Mann, Stravinsky. Rachmaninoff's in Beverly Hills, and I understand Brahms is due to arrive any day. You're going to be as happy as a pearl, my darling," she assured him, "surrounded by all that culture."

He smiled sadly. It was good to see Mina. They understood the same jokes, they were from the same world. They fit together like a hand in a glove. But he felt a sharp pang thinking of Sasha waiting in her cabin. Somehow, without intending it—in his usual fashion, without even quite knowing how it had happened—Max sensed a decision had already been made.

*****

Mina always attracted a frenzy of attention when they were in public together. Normally Max didn't mind that. It allowed him to stand aside and watch from the sidelines at industry functions, an anonymous part of Mina's entourage, only the husband. But he found it unpleasant now. He waited impatiently as a naval press officer cornered her to ask if they might set up a photo shoot later in the week. The Navy wanted to pose Mina on the deck of a battleship in a skimpy outfit, the sort of photo, he assured her, that would be a great morale booster for the boys overseas.

Max glanced at his watch and saw it was twenty minutes since he had left Sasha on deck. She would be worrying, of course, wondering what was going on. Whatever happened, he needed to find a way to return to her so they could talk.

Mina was saying something, and he'd been so far off in his thoughts that he hadn't noticed.

"I'm sorry, darling, what was that?"

"Are you all right, Max?" Mina was studying him with a sympathetic expression.

"It's my leg," he told her, smiling as he lied. "Typhoons aside, it starts hurting like a son of a bitch when I stand too long."

"Oh, Max! You should have said something earlier! Let's get you to a chair!"

Mina made her excuses to the press officer and led Max toward a sofa at the edge of the room. Max sensed that she was going to enjoy his being wounded. In the past, he'd always been the one to take care of her, but now the tables were turned. It was a chance for revenge, he supposed.

"Oh, Max! Let's get you off your poor old leg, darling. We'll go back to your cabin—can you make it that far? You can lie down and rest. I'm sure it's going to be a while before we get past Quarantine and pull up at the pier. You're glad to be home, aren't you? Oh, Max, I was so crazy without you. Tell me you're glad!"

"Of course, I'm glad. You're my darling and I've missed you unbearably."

He did love Mina—he'd always told Sasha that, and it was true. But he had to get free of her for ten minutes. He couldn't leave Sasha dangling.

"Look, I'll go back to my cabin and pack," he told her. "You'd better stay here and deal with your fans or they'll start a riot for want of you. I'll only be a few minutes."

"Are you sure you can manage?"

"Darling, my leg is feeling much better."

He was about to give Mina a reassuring kiss when he was surprised to see Sasha in the crowd. She hadn't waited in her cabin after all. She had brushed her hair and put on make-up and was wearing her good gray dress, the one that she had worn the afternoon he spotted her cheating at cards. She was coming his way, staring at Max as though there were no one else in the room. Perhaps, he thought, this was best after all.

He pulled gently on Mina's arm to turn her toward Sasha. "Darling," he said, "I'd like you to meet someone."

*****

Max understood from Mina's expression that the cat was out of the bag. Of course, she had known from the start. She couldn't help but know. She had seen him and Sasha together on deck before they had become aware that they were being watched. Mina would have a very clear idea of what it meant for her husband to be standing on deck with a pretty girl before seven in the morning.

Max watched Mina's face as she gave Sasha her best smile.

"Mina, this is my friend, Sasha," he said, making the introduction. "Sasha's from Poland . . . Sasha, this is my wife Mina."

Sasha was not as poised as Mina, and Max expected that—except when Mina was falling apart, she was the most poised person he had ever known. As for Sasha, her face became suddenly flushed with unnatural color and her lower lip seemed about to tremble. She had been staring only at Max, fixated, but now, making an effort, she turned to Mina.

"I'm so pleased to meet you," Mina said. Sasha appeared dumbstruck as she accepted Mina's offered hand. "How pretty you are!" Mina went on blithely, pretending there was no awkwardness. "And what a lovely name, Sasha! Is this your first trip to America?"

"Yes," Sasha managed faintly.

"Sasha's traveling with the group of refugees who are onboard," Max said, speaking for her. "She's had a difficult journey from Krakow. I'm afraid her . . ." Max hesitated, trying to decide how he would describe Julka. "Her father died on the way over, only a few nights ago."

"Oh! How awful! You poor thing!"

"Her father was Julka Szopin, the director of the Krakow Opera," Max added, as though this detail made the situation more understandable.

"Ah!" said Mina. "You know, I think I remember reading about him. Szopin . . . this is such a familiar name. Wasn't there an article about him a few years ago in the *Times*, Max?"

"You know, I believe there was. The partisans helped Sasha and her father get away south through Eastern Europe to Greece. It's quite a story. They escaped Poland without much more than the clothes on their back."

For Max, it was a very strange conversation. Perhaps the oddest conversation he had ever had. Sasha kept staring at him, searching his eyes, seeking some clue as to what he was talking about.

Impulsively, Mina took Sasha's hand.

"My God, your father's dead and here you're arriving in New York for the first time with nothing! Oh, Max, we absolutely must do everything we can to help Sasha!"

"Exactly," he agreed.

"She can stay with us!"

"Well, I was thinking more of the Evangeline House, down on 13th Street," Max said delicately.

"Oh, yes, that's a very nice hotel. For women only, very safe. Quite a number of actresses live there. But, Max, Sasha's going to need money!"

"Yes, of course, and we'll give her some," he said. "I've already made arrangements about her father."

"Oh, yes!" Mina agreed.

Sasha was turning back and forth from one to the other as though they were both mad. Unlike Max and Mina, she had never found herself in a sophisticated comedy before. Undeterred, Max continued to extemporize, chattering away like a maniac. He believed that as long as he kept talking, they would all somehow get through this. He spoke about their crossing, the unusually fine weather they'd had in the middle of the voyage. He hardly knew what he was saying, but somehow the inanity worked as a kind of sedative. Even Sasha appeared to relax, not such a deer fixed in headlights.

"Darling, why don't you finish packing," Mina told him finally. "I'll stay here with Sasha—perhaps we can find a place to have a cup of tea."

"Right!" he said eagerly. "Sasha can show you the Officers Canteen!"

He kissed Mina on the cheek, smiled hopelessly at Sasha, and hobbled away on his cane. The moment he was alone, all of Max's brightness vanished. He deflated like a spent balloon. As social events went, he would be happy never to repeat a meeting like that ever again.

He made his way back up the staircase to his cabin, glad for the way his leg hurt with every step. The pain was a welcome distraction and he was certain it served him right.

*****

Max packed as quickly as he could, wondering the entire time what Mina and Sasha were talking about in his absence. He was certain Mina would be kind, for she would understand from the start that she held the winning hand. Beyond that, kindness was at the center of Mina's wounded nature. Still, the conversation worried him, and he didn't linger.

It took Max nearly twenty minutes to throw his things into two suitcases and arrange to have them taken on shore, and then another fifteen minutes to find the ship's doctor one last time and make certain everything was in order for Julka's remains. It seemed important to him that this should be taken care of, that Sasha wouldn't need to worry about it. By the time he was finished, the *Mauretania* had passed Quarantine on Staten Island and two tugboats were pulling them slowly on their final approach to the dock in midtown Manhattan. Limping hurriedly to the Officers Canteen, he caught sight of the Empire State Building floating past hardly more than a dozen blocks away. This was one of the extraordinary things about arriving by ship in New York, to sail directly into midtown Manhattan only a short walk from Sardi's and the theater district. Already Max could hear cars honking in the distance, the indefinable city music of traffic and motion, the restless energy of New York.

The ship was bustling with activity, everyone in a hurry, excited that they were finally in America safe from the long reach of war. Max stopped at the door to the Canteen and watched Mina and Sasha together for a moment before they saw him. They were the only two people in the room, seated at a table by a window, smoking cigarettes and talking in low voices as the wharfs and docks of 10th Avenue moved slowly behind them on the other side of the glass. Anyone coming upon two women like this would have thought they were the best of friends.

As Max watched, Mina laughed at something Sasha had just said. And though Sasha didn't quite laugh in return, she smiled. Mina reached out impulsively and took Sasha's hand in a gesture of camaraderie that Max found disturbing. He was glad to see them getting along, but he didn't quite want them to become long-lost sisters.

Sasha saw Max and her smile faded. Her eyes followed him as he crossed the room.

"Ah, here you are!" Mina said cheerfully.

Yes, here he was, he thought. He pulled up a third chair and did his best imitation of an innocuously helpful American male.

"Well, I spoke with the ship's doctor about your father, Sasha, and I have everything arranged. There's quite a pretty old cemetery in Queens —all the paperwork will be sent to me, along with the expenses. Unless you'd like to do something else, of course."

Sasha appeared bewildered. "Queens? I did not think you had royalty in this country."

Mina and Max smiled, though Mina's smile was more sincere. Sasha was awfully green when it came to New York City, and being green in a city like New York could be a problem. Max explained that Queens was a district of New York, something that people here called a borough, but she stared at him with a dazed expression and he wasn't sure she was quite visualizing the geography involved. Clearly, one of the first things Sasha would need in the New World was a map.

"Would you like us to arrange a small service for your father, dear?" Mina asked gently.

Sasha's eyes filled with tears. But she shook her head. "I don't know, it doesn't really matter," she murmured.

"Oh, look! We're almost at the pier!" Mina said brightly, looking out the window at the city drifting past. "You know, I think I'd better go find the ladies room. I always hate going down gangplanks with a full bladder."

Max smiled uncomfortably. As it happened, Mina had a bladder like a camel, one of the few women he had ever known who wasn't always running off to the powder room. With her unerring tack, she was simply giving him and Sasha a few moments to say goodbye. It was a generous gesture. Yet, when they were alone, neither Max nor Sasha knew what to say. He watched Sasha study her fingernails, refusing to look at him. Everything he'd been thinking to tell her seemed inadequate.

"I thought we'd have more time," he said finally. "You understand, don't you? It's the oldest joke in the book, I'm afraid. I'm a married man."

Sasha nodded miserably.

"Sasha, please, look at me."

"I don't have to look at you to understand. Of course, I understand, Max. Really, I do. And she is very nice, your wife. I am quite certain she knows about us. I would not be so nice myself in her position."

"Well, that's Mina. She doesn't take the usual narrow viewpoint of things."

"Yes, she's very nice," Sasha said again, but a knife-like edge had crept into her voice. "And you've known her for a long time. I am only a recent arrival."

This was true, of course. Sasha couldn't compete with the sheer weight of time, the common background he and Mina shared.

Max said only, "It's good to know someone for a long time, Sasha. The years add up to something. It's like . . . well, it's like building a house. To be honest, I'm not sure I have the energy to start from scratch again."

Her eyes flashed up at him. "No, love is not like building a house," she said angrily. "Love isn't like that at all. Love comes in an instant. And it goes in an instant, too!"

"Sasha . . ."

"I understand," she interrupted, not letting him speak. "Yes, you've known Mina for a very long time. But there's new love, also. There's meeting someone and falling in love for the first time."

Max hesitated. "Look," he said, "we had three days together that I'll never forget. To be honest, I don't know what would have happened if Mina hadn't shown up like this. But seeing her, I understand my life is with her."

"Yes, naturally. Max, I told you I am not a child. I always knew you would not leave your wife, but I thought . . . oh, I was so stupid!" she cried bitterly, looking away.

"What did you think? Tell me?"

"I was a fool, that's all! What does it matter?"

"Sasha, look at me."

"I am looking at you. I can see you very well."

"No you can't. You're staring at your damn fingernails."

She turned and stared at him with mute accusation. Her eyes were burning with anger and unshed tears. "I thought you would take care of me! Oh, Max, don't you understand? A rich man can have both his wife and a woman like me also. You can put me in a small house nearby and visit when you like. There doesn't have to be a choice between one and the other."

Max was frankly aghast when he understood what she had in mind. "Sasha, I'm from Boston! We just don't do things that way. You're in America now, and we're not as sophisticated as you Europeans."

"You don't love me, that's all!"

He sighed, suddenly exhausted by the ordeal. "Of course, I love you. How could I not love you? We're just not going to be together, that's all. It's not in the cards."

"Ah! Cards! That is what this is all about, I think. I am not good enough for you!"

Max had not meant to use the word cards. It was an unfortunate choice. "No, it's not that," he said.

"Then why? Don't I have a right for happiness too?"

"Listen to me, Sasha. You're going to find the right guy. Believe me, the moment you step off this ship, you're going to be surrounded by so many guys, your head's going to spin."

"Oh, you think all men are the same? You think any man will do?"

"Oh, Sasha . . ." There were a lot of things Max might have said, but he knew it wasn't any use. This wasn't the sort of conversation where a rational argument would win the day. Meanwhile, Mina wouldn't be in the ladies' room forever. The minutes were slipping away and there were practical things he needed to discuss.

"Look, we don't have much time. I am going to take care of you. Of course, I am. Did Mina give you money?"

"Yes. She was very generous."

"Well, here's some more, the rest of my English pounds. You can change them at a bank," he told her, pulling out his wallet.

"I don't want your money."

"Yes, you do. New York is a fine city, you're going to love it. But they don't give things away for free. Here, take this— it's sixty-five pounds. Did Mina give you our phone number in Los Angeles?"

"Yes."

"Good. I want you to call if you need more money, or anything at all. Do you understand?"

She shook her head. Tears were running freely down her cheeks. "No, I don't understand. I don't understand anything."

"That's all right. Understanding isn't essential. What's essential is getting through this. Now, I'm going to give you another telephone number. This is for an old friend of mine by the name of Nathan Cunningham. Nate and I went to prep school together and he happens to be my attorney as well as my oldest friend. He lives in Connecticut, but he has an office here in New York. I've written down both numbers. As soon as you get settled somewhere, I want you to give Nate a call and tell him where you are. I'll arrange it with Nate so that he'll give you money whenever you need it. Are you listening to me?"

Sasha nodded, but she was crying in earnest now and couldn't speak. Max was watching her helplessly when Mina returned from the ladies' room. Perhaps she sensed it wasn't a good idea to leave them alone any longer. Her expression deepened when she saw that Sasha was crying. But in her decent way, she left the matter alone. She didn't ask the meaning of the tears.

And so it was that the *Mauretania* slipped into its berth at the end of West 50th Street and came inch by inch to a stop. Gangplanks soon connected the giant superstructure of the ship with solid land. A loud speaker crackled and came to life, full of useful announcements. United States citizens were asked to disembark first, leaving foreigners such as Sasha on board for a while longer.

The goodbye Max said to Sasha was brisk, friendly, efficient, and utterly ruthless. He knew it was not his finest hour . . . but what could he do? Mina did her best to make things easier. She helped him maneuver the gangplank, she held his arm when he had trouble on the slant that led downward to the wharf, he felt her presence every moment.

There were more reporters on the wharf with cameras and flashbulbs at the ready to record Max's first hesitant steps on dry land. The next day, when Max saw the photographs in the papers, Mina was dazzling, as she always was in public, broadcasting a thousand watts of glamour, while he appeared shrunken beside her, a dim male figure with a cane and a wooden expression. Max wasn't proud of himself. At least he didn't stumble. That was the best he could manage for his inelegant exit from Sasha's life.

What had he done wrong? he wondered. Max couldn't say exactly. He hadn't meant to hurt her, he hadn't meant to love her. He hadn't meant anything at all, he had only opened the door to his cabin when she knocked, a damsel in distress. Each step of the way, he had tried to do his best. And yet now, walking away, he felt the unbearable weight of failure, the sure knowledge that he was utterly in the wrong.

Just before leaving the pier to enter the customs building, Max stopped and looked up at the high deck near the bow of the ship. He knew he would find Sasha there, and he wasn't wrong. She was standing alone at the very spot where they had stood together at dawn discussing breakfast at the Plaza Hotel, a breakfast that would never be. From where Max stood on the wharf, Sasha was only a small figure looking down on him, watching as he walked away. He couldn't see the expression on her face, but he knew that she was crying.

Mina led Max onward, through customs toward the limousine that waited for them outside on the busy New York street to take them to the St. Regis where she had made a reservation. Max was relieved it wouldn't be the Plaza; life had its small mercies after all.

Just as they were settling into the upholstery of the comfortable car, she took his hand and said something that Max would remember throughout the remaining years of his life, because, brief as it was, it was one of the few direct comments she ever made about his affair with Sasha.

"It's all right, Max," she told him. Her voice was gentle and enormously kind. "It's best in life that we love one another. Love is never wrong."

Love is never wrong?

Max wasn't sure about that. He felt wrong. But he loved Mina for saying it. You had to be a saint, he supposed, to look at love that way.

Or, like Mina, simply a little mad.

My Awful Hollywood Childhood III:

A Ghost from the Past
Los Angeles, 1954

I remember the day the past found us.

It was an overcast Saturday in 1954, dull and gray. Penny was in Palm Springs with her parents and I had time on my hands, nothing to do until Monday. It was early afternoon, but my mother was still asleep in her bedroom, door closed, curtains shut. By 1954 she seldom rose before noon, what with the vodka, the sleeping pills, and late nights on the town.

I was in the backyard shooting baskets into the hoop above the garage door, doing my best not to make too much noise, when I was surprised to hear a stranger call my name.

"Hey, you must be Jonathan . . . hey, Jonathan, over here!"

I turned with the basketball clutched to my stomach and saw a man looking at me from the far side of the wrought iron gate that closed off the backyard from the street. He was nobody I had ever seen before, so utterly non-descript that it's hard to describe him: tallish, thinish, middle-aged, dressed in a wrinkled brown suit and a brown city hat pulled down low on his forehead.

It sounds snobbish to say, but I knew from the start that he wasn't our kind of person—a Hollywood kind, someone in show business. He wasn't the sort of glamour-puss who usually appeared at our door.

"Hey, is your mother home, kid?" he called through the gate. "I've been ringing the doorbell, but there's no answer. I need to speak to her."

"Is she expecting you?" I asked dubiously

"Sure she is. Hey, Jonathan, open the gate. I gotta talk to you."

I frowned. No one I wanted to know called me Jonathan and I certainly wasn't going to let him in. But then something unpleasant happened. He was leaning on the gate when it sprang open of its own accord. Life's like that sometimes. On bad days, even inanimate objects work against you.

"Oh, wow, look at that—abracadabra!" he said with a smarmy sort of smile. He opened the latch and stepped through. "Don't look so worried, kid—your mother and me, we're old friends. We go way back to before you were born. Did she ever tell you about the time she spent in New York?"

"A little," I answered reluctantly.

His suit jacket fluttered open as he walked up the driveway and I saw there was a gun in a holster on his hip. It was one more thing not to like about him.

"So you're playing basketball, huh? That's not too much fun all by yourself. Do you know how to play Horse?"

"Are you a cop?"

"Hey, you're a sharp kid. I *used* to be a cop, a New York City detective. But these days I'm a private eye. You ever watch TV shows about private eyes? There's more money in it, see. And the babes, they just about drop dead at the sight of you. Maybe you'll be a gumshoe when you grow up, Jonathan. Whad'ya think? Would you like that?"

I stared at him and didn't answer. Actually, a career as a private eye had a certain appeal, as long as I could do it off planet. Jonno Saint-Amant, Boy Detective from Pluto.

"So let's play Horse," he said cheerfully, ignoring my silence. "I bet I can beat you. Gimme the ball and I'll go first."

"My mother wouldn't like me playing basketball with a stranger," I told him. I felt a little silly saying it, like a simpy rich kid. But I said it anyway.

He laughed. "Like I keep telling you, I'm not a stranger—your mother and me go way back. I'm Ricky, by the way. Ricky Bolano. You can ask her about me. Come on, let's play ball."

I'd never heard her mention any Ricky Bolano, but he grabbed the basketball from where I was hugging it against my stomach and began shooting hoops. He was good, I have to give him that. He got a basket on the first try.

"Okay, so I'm an 'h'," he said, handing me back the ball. "Now you go."

I didn't like it, but I couldn't think of anything to do except play Horse. I missed my first shot and he told me to take a second try, then a third. He called it a handicap because he was older. I made a basket on the fourth try and he took the ball from me. We played in silence a few more rounds, until he was an "hor" and I was an "ho." Then he kept hold of the ball and turned to me.

"So Jonathan, let's get down to cases. Where's your mom?"

"She's not home," I lied.

"Really? When will she be back, do you think?"

"I don't know. Maybe not for a few days. You see, she's on tour."

"On *tour*? And she just leaves you on your own?"

"I'm not on my own. Claire's here to take care of me. Claire's our maid."

"Oh, she leaves you with the maid. You know something, Jonathan, I don't think so. I think you're lying through your teeth. Like I said, I used to be a cop so I'm pretty good at knowing when people are lying."

"I'm not lying," I lied. "My mother's not home and I think you should go now. She wouldn't like it that I let a stranger into the backyard."

"You're not listening to me, kid. I told you I'm an old pal."

"I don't believe you, and I don't like you either!" My whole body was trembling, I was so scared. But I wasn't about to back down. "You don't know my mother. And you'd better leave before I go inside and call a real cop."

He grinned. "Well, well, a tough guy! Imagine that."

"I'm tough enough," I assured him. "So give me back my basketball and go away."

He only smiled. "Oh, yeah? You think you're so tough you can take your ball back? Somehow I don't think so, kid."

It was a nasty situation and I'm not sure how it would have ended, except my mother appeared at just that moment in a pink dressing gown, a cigarette in one hand, walking angrily our way from the back door near the kitchen. She must have gotten out of bed and seen us through the window.

"Who the hell are you? How dare you come into our yard?" she demanded, bearing down on us. "Jonno, go inside. I'll take care of this."

I didn't go anywhere, of course. I stayed right there in case my protection was needed. There was a baseball bat on the lawn about a dozen feet from where I was standing. I thought it would make a good weapon, if I could get to it before Ricky Bolano reached for his gun and shot me dead.

"Don't you remember me, Sonya?" the man asked. "Gee, my feelings are hurt. I sure remember *you*."

"I have never seen you before in my life!" My mother was a hellcat when her temper was up and she was spitting mad. "Now get the hell off my property. I have already called the police and they will be here in a moment."

His smile was unperturbed. "Oh, I don't think you've called the cops, Sonya. You don't like cops, I remember. You don't like them at all. Come on, surely you remember me. Ricky Bolano. How about Lieutenant Bolano? We got real close there for just a little while."

"Jonno, go inside, please, and telephone the police," she said without turning from him.

"Don't do that, kid. It would be a mistake. How about a certain movie theater on Sixth Avenue, New York City, spring of 1943? Is this starting to ring any bells, doll? Of course, you weren't a fancy lady back then. You were something else that I won't even mention with your kid standing nearby."

My mother had opened her mouth to say something unpleasant, but the words, whatever they were, died unspoken. In other circumstances it would have been almost comical to watch, the change that came over her. She simply froze.

"*Yeah!*" he said watching her. "I see it's coming back now. Memory's a funny thing, isn't it? There are good memories and bad memories, and some memories that won't wash away no matter how hard you try."

"What do you want?" my mother demanded. She was struggling to gain possession of herself, but her voice wasn't entirely steady.

"I tell you what. Why don't you invite me inside and offer me a drink. You and me, we have things to discuss. Things that maybe you don't want your boy to hear."

"All right," she agreed, frowning hard. "We don't have anything to discuss, Mr. Bolano. But you might as well come inside." She was back in control of herself, almost icy calm. "Jonno, it's all right, I do know this man—I didn't recognize him at first because it's been some years. I'd like you to go to your room for a while. I'll be fine, I promise you."

"Mom, I think I'd better stay, just in case."

"Jonno, please do what I say. Go to your room. I want to talk to Mr. Bolano alone."

I don't think in my entire life she had ever sent me to my room before. I was spoiled rotten, as I've mentioned previously. So it had some weight, telling me now. Surprise value.

I watched as she led the ex-cop from New York through the backyard toward the sunroom at the rear of the house. When their backs were turned, I picked up the baseball bat from the lawn and walked toward the living room, as though I were planning to go upstairs to my room. But it was only an acting job, like something I might have done on Stage 17. As soon as I was sure they couldn't see me, I got down on my hands and knees and crawled back around the rear of the house toward the sunroom, using a hedge to conceal myself.

I wasn't about to let my mother face Ricky Bolano alone. I knew she needed me. Besides, I was curious to know what this was all about.

*****

The sunroom was my mother's favorite room in the house. It was a symbol, I think, of how far she'd come in life, to have a useless room with sliding doors and plenty of glass overlooking a swimming pool.

There was a wet bar in the sunroom and wrought iron chairs with yellow pads and matching side tables that were covered with glass. Several potted palms were scattered about and there was an out of control bougainvillea that had taken over an entire corner of the room. The bougainvillea served as my cover. I was able to crawl along the outside wall until I found a perch just below an open window where I could peer in through the glass, past a misty tangle of pink flowers, and see what was going on inside.

I watched my mother at the wet bar as she made a bourbon and water for Ricky Bolano. He sat in one of the wrought iron chairs with his legs crossed and his hat balanced on his knee.

"Say, you're looking good, Sonya," he told her. "Though not as good as you looked back there in forty-three. Guess you're not getting any younger, huh?"

"What do you want?" my mother demanded, handing him his bourbon.

"Aren't you going to join me? Everybody in town says you're a lush. You see, I've been keeping an eye on you. I have a whole file in my office labeled Sonya Saint-Amant."

"Why are you here, Mr. Bolano?"

"*Mister* Bolano! Well, well! The last time we met we weren't so formal, if I recall. You know something, Sonya, there've been times over the years, I've listened to your records and seen you in movies, and I've thought to myself, I knew that girl before Hollywood ever heard of her, before she turned into a fancy piece of tail. When she was just a Polack fresh off the boat. It's kind of interesting how the world turns. I bet you never thought you'd see me again, did you?"

"Please get to the point, Mr. Bolano."

"Oh, I bet you can guess why I'm here. It's money, of course. What else would it be? A little cash and the past can be forgotten. Poof! It can go away. Like magic."

"How much money?" she asked contemptuously.

"Ten grand will do the trick. I wouldn't want to be greedy."

My mother didn't speak for a moment. I could almost see her wheels turning, weighing her choices. "Ten thousand dollars is a lot of money."

"No, I don't think so. Ten grand is chicken feed for someone like you, Sonya. Someone with a secret like you have. A secret that would bring down the whole house of cards. I'd think for someone like you, ten grand is fucking cheap."

My mother turned her back to him and walked toward the bougainvillea, so close to where I was kneeling on the other side of the glass that I thought she might see me. But then she turned and paced back the other way toward the wet bar. She looked like a caged animal. I watched as she poured herself a shot of vodka and drank it down in a single swallow.

"All right," she said, turning back to him. "Since I don't have any choice, I guess I'll have to do it. But I need to know this is the end of it. You're going to have to give me some guarantee that once you're paid, I'll never see you again."

He stood up from where he was sitting and pointed a finger at her chest. "Let's get something straight, doll—I don't have to give you shit. You know why? Because I hold all the cards. I've got everything and you've got nothing. Still, I'm willing to be nice so here's what I'll do. I'll give you my word."

"Your word!"

"That's right. I give you my word that ten grand will keep me good and quiet. And if my word ain't good enough, that's too damn bad. You should count yourself lucky. Normally, I don't even give that much to cheap whores like you."

Without warning, my mother slapped him hard across the face. In the movies, gentlemen who get slapped by a lady turn red with embarrassment, rub their cheek and walk away. But Ricky Bolano was no gentleman. He staggered backward because my mother had hit him hard. But then he recovered and slapped her in return with the back of his hand, hard enough to send her reeling against the wet bar. She tumbled against a drink trolley full of bottles. The collision sent a bottle of rye crashing to the flagstone floor where it shattered into a hundred pieces.

I'd seen all I cared to.

"YEEAAAHHH!" I screamed, setting myself in motion. I rushed through the screen door with the baseball bat raised over my head. "YEEAAAHHH, you fucking creep, you leave my mother alone!"

I swung the bat down hard, but Ricky jumped backward just in time to dodge the blow. The bat came down on the coffee table, shattering the glass surface. "YEEAAAHHH!" I cried again, my crazed war cry. I was raising the bat again, determined to kill him, when I felt my mother grab me around the waist from behind.

"No, Jonno, don't!" She struggled to get me under control. It wasn't easy, even for her, because I was wound up. "It's all right, Jonno. It's all right," she kept saying.

For a few moments I was literally blind with rage. I came to my senses, more or less—what passes for sense in California—to find my mother had taken away the baseball bat and was holding me fast. Ricky had moved back against the bougainvillea as far as he could to get away from me. His gun was out, pointed in my direction, an ugly pistol with a square barrel. We were all breathing hard.

"Put your gun away, Mr. Bolano," my mother told him. "You'll get your money, ten thousand dollars. But I don't have it in the house. You must let me have a few days."

"I'll give you until Monday," he said. "Got it? Monday. That's it, doll, then I go to the newspapers, end of story.

Meanwhile, keep that crazy kid off me. Jesus, that fucking kid's dangerous! He tried to kill me!"

"Mr. Bolano, I am the one who is dangerous," my mother assured him. "Now, please leave my house. I will have the money for you on Wednesday afternoon and if I ever see you again after that, I promise I will kill you."

Ricky laughed, but it was an uneasy laugh, far from merry. "All right, Sonya. I'll go along. Wednesday afternoon it is. But don't fuck with me or you'll regret it. I have copies of that arrest report, and if there's any trouble on Wednesday they'll be sent to certain publications. You understand what I'm saying?"

"I understand very well. I will give you the money on Wednesday and we will be finished with this. Now, goodbye, Mr. Bolano."

He gave a kind of ironic wink that didn't quite come off. Then he left the room, making his exit through the main part of the house. When we heard the front door open and close, I turned into my mother's arms and she held me while my fury broke—all the crazed energy that had led me to the edge of homicide—and I began to sob.

"It's all right, darling," she told me, rubbing my back, kissing the top of my head. "You are my brave, brave little man, my knight in shining armor. And now you mustn't worry because I will come up with a plan."

An Overnight Sensation

My mother was very good with plans, I knew that. She had planned her way out of Nazi Poland at the height of the war and made her way to California. I knew in my heart that a second rate ex-cop from New York City was no match for her.

My crying gradually stopped.

"Mom," I said when I could talk again, "tell me about New York. What happened there?"

She shook her head and walked away without answering. Undeterred, I followed her inside the house. Our maid, Claire, was off for the weekend—I'd lied about that to Ricky Bolano—and I wasn't sure if my mother was going for a broom to clean up the mess in the sunroom or heading to the living room where there was another bar, another bottle. It was the living room. I watched as she poured herself a glass of vodka and took it to one of the sofas by the fireplace.

I sat across from her on a facing sofa. "Mom," I said again, patiently: "Tell me about New York."

She took a big swallow of vodka and her eyes were far away. I waited, not saying a word. I knew she would end up telling me the story because she was a great egoist—total narcissism, if you want the truth—and egoists always tell their story if you wait long enough. Their stories are all they've got, and they're fascinated by them.

I found a cigarette and lit it for her and put it between her fingers.

"Oh, Jonno! New York nearly broke me," she said after a while. "It was the worst time I ever had."

"Worse even than getting out of Krakow in the war?"

"Yes, it was," she answered. The smoke from her cigarette drifted like an uneasy spirit, making wispy circles in the air. "Worse even than Krakow. In a different way . . ."

Part Four

A New World
New York, 1943

One

Anger swept Sasha off the *Mauretania*, from the wharf on the Hudson River into the spires of midtown Manhattan.

She was angry at Julka for dying, angry at Max for abandoning her, and angry at herself for being such a fool. She had let her guard down for an instant, and look what happened.

Never again, she vowed. Never, never again.

She stomped her way up West 50th Street with such dark purpose that even the sailors on leave sensed it was best to give this unsmiling girl a wide berth. But Sasha had never seen a city like New York and after walking only a few blocks, the rage that had carried her this far evaporated, leaving only bewilderment in its place.

She stopped on the sidewalk and looked around, amazed to find herself on a narrow street with buildings that were like steep cliffs rising at a dizzy angle into the sky. Cars and people rushed by, everyone in a hurry. She had no idea where she was, or where she was going. Alice recently arrived in Wonderland could not have been more lost than Sasha at this moment, gaping up at the enormous buildings with her battered suitcase in hand.

Now that she had come to a stop, a sailor shouted at her from the window of a passing taxi, "Hey, there, doll!" Sasha didn't know New York, but she knew men, their keen animal sense of when a woman was vulnerable and might be cut off from the pack. She set off walking again with a purposeful stride, pretending she had somewhere to go.

She came to a street corner with a sign that said 50th St on one side and 8th Ave on the other. But where was 50th St? And what sort of avenue was 8th Avenue? These names might just have well been hieroglyphics as far as Sasha was concerned. She didn't have a clue.

"You look a little lost, dearie," she heard a stranger say. "Can I help you find where you're going?"

Sasha was about to rush on, terrified. But she saw it was only an old lady dressed in a shapeless grey coat. Sasha decided to trust her.

"I am trying to find the square called Times," she said. It was simply the first name that came to mind, a place Sasha had heard about in New York. She didn't want to sound like someone who didn't know anything.

"Times Square? You sure you want to go there, dearie?"

"Yes, I do. You see, my husband is meeting me," she added, a small creative flourish.

"Well, you go down this block to Seventh Avenue. Then you turn right and go all the way to Forty-Second Street . . . you sure you're all right?"

"Yes, yes . . . oh, thank you!" Sasha rushed off. She had heard of Forty-Second Street and this seemed even better than Times Square, a famous boulevard. She decided she would find a café where she might have a coffee and a small pastry because it was afternoon and she had eaten nothing all day. Afterwards, she would find a taxi to take her to the hotel for women that Max had recommended, the Evangeline House.

Sasha made her way to 42nd Street by staying close to the buildings and keeping her eyes fixed on the small patch of sidewalk directly in front of her. New York was more than she could absorb all at once. What a city it was! Everything seemed in motion, all at once. Loud music and the hot aromas of cooking food came at her through open doors. Smoke was pouring up from the very asphalt, from the gutters and man-holes. It was like walking through hell. The entire city seemed to be filled with sailors, all of them calling and whistling at her, but Sasha put her head down and kept moving.

She reached 42nd Street, but now that she was here, she felt too shy to enter one of the bright cafes as she had in-tended. She decided she would eat later. However, the sailors who were trying to pick her up had given her a new thought. Max, of course, wanted her to stay at the Evangeline House—that would suit him nicely, wouldn't it, a hotel for women! But it was men who liked her, not women, and if she were to survive in this new world, she needed to play her best card. A hotel for women would be of no use to her now.

Sasha turned and carried her suitcase back to where she had noticed the awning for a hotel that looked quite cosmo-politan and grand. It was called the Hotel Jefferson and it seemed to Sasha that the proximity to a famous location such as Times Square made it a desirable address. This would be helpful, she believed, in order to establish her new life. The name Jefferson was somehow familiar, and she assumed it must be a fine establishment indeed for its name to be known even to her, a newcomer in this terrible land.

*****

The lobby was small and dusty and smelled of stale cigar smoke. A small, pale man with sunken cheeks sat behind a counter that was guarded by a metal grille. He wore a green eye shade, a vest, and a shirt and tie that weren't entirely clean.

"Yeah?" he asked, seeing Sasha. "I'm the manager here, how can I help you?"

"I wish a room, please."

He stared at her uncertainly. Apparently, girls like Sasha did not often arrive at the Hotel Jefferson asking for accommodations.

"A room," she repeated, not certain if her English had been faulty. "You have rooms, yes?"

The man nodded. "Sure," he said. "We got rooms. For the night, the week, or by the month. We even got rooms by the hour, but that will cost you. A special surcharge, I guess you could call it."

Sasha didn't like his manner. However, now that she was here, she didn't want to look for a new hotel. She very badly wanted the protection of four walls and a door that she could close behind her.

"A week, I think. After that I will decide if I wish to stay longer."

"I can give you a room in the front, $15 a week. Or one in the back for $12."

"I will take the expensive room," she told him. This was foolish, simply an assertion of pride.

"Okay. That'll be $15 in advance. The bathroom's down the hall, there's no cooking in the rooms, no loud noise, and no heavy drinking." He paused and gave her a lingering look. "And no visitors of the opposite sex unless you give me that special surcharge I mentioned. We can talk about that if you like. I might even be able to help you arrange things, if you understand my meaning."

"There will be no visitors of the opposite sex," Sasha told him primly. She handed him the money and he gave her a registration form to fill out. She felt his eyes inspecting her as she wrote down her name.

"So, you've only just arrived in our fair city, I'm guessing," he said.

"I am from Poland," she told him, putting on her haughtiest tone. "I am here waiting for my husband, who is a fighter pilot. When he arrives, we will be going to California."

"Oh, I see. You're a Polack, huh?"

"No, Poland," she repeated, not understanding the word he had used. "I have just arrived on the boat."

"Yeah, I got it. A Polack right off the boat. By the way, I can't help noticing what a nice wedding ring you *don't* have on your left hand, missy."

Instinctively, Sasha hid her hand inside her cloak. But the damage had already been done.

"Rings are easily lost in a war," she told him, knowing it would be wiser to keep her mouth shut. "But you wouldn't know about war."

"War? Oh, yesseree, I've been in a war. Not this one, though. You should have been in France in 1918 if you want to talk about war. Look, a word of advice, missy. If you want to pull the marriage stunt, at least get yourself a ring to go with your story. You can go to one of the pawn shops on Eighth Avenue. The yids over there will set you up in style. Make you respectable quick as a blink to a blind horse. My name's Bill, by the way. Bill McSorrenson. If you have any problems, any of the guys try to bother you, you just let me know." Bill rang the bell on his desk with a decisive slap of his hand. "Henry will show you to your room."

Henry the bellboy appeared at Sasha's elbow. He was an old black man, lanky and bent. His skin was dark as midnight and he seemed to sag everywhere. Sasha had never seen a black man this close before and he frightened her. He was dressed in a shabby uniform that was too short in the arms and legs, a red jacket with useless brass buttons, and a small pill box hat perched on his head. He tried to take her suitcase, but Sasha thought he might steal from her, so she held on tightly to the handle and wouldn't let go.

Henry only shrugged. "Follow me, please."

He led the way into a creaky old elevator that was barely large enough for two people. The cage rose fitfully into the upper reaches of the building.

"Well, ain't life surprising? A girl like you showing up," he said vaguely, inspecting her in what Sasha took as an insolent manner.

Sasha didn't grace this comment with an answer. Indeed, she wasn't certain she had understood every word. People in New York spoke very quickly and used expressions she had never heard before. They arrived on the sixth floor and Henry led the way down to the hall, whistling tunelessly and jangling a room key in his hand. They passed an open door through which Sasha had a glimpse of a grotesquely fat woman who was sitting on a bed in only her underwear, a bra and a half-slip that didn't entirely contain her. There was a bottle in her hand and she grinned as Sasha hurried on by.

"That's Baby," the bellboy said as they continued toward her room. "Don't pay her any mind. Baby drinks a bit and sometimes she wanders the hallways. But she won't give you no trouble, long as you keep your door locked at night."

"Oh!" said Sasha, wondering what sort of place she had come to.

Henry showed her the hall bathroom and then led the way to Room 624, unlocking the door and standing aside for her to enter. It was only a small room: a single bed, a sink in one corner that had yellow water stains in the enamel, a scratched wooden wardrobe, a night table with a lamp, an upholstered armchair of some indeterminate color that had a cigarette burn on one arm. There was a paper shade on a roller covering a window, and when Sasha raised it, she found she had a view through dirty glass onto 48th Street. Everything about the room was sad and poor and defeated. With a sinking feeling, she understood that this would be her fate also, unless she managed to improve her situation.

Henry was standing by the door holding her key. She reached for it, but he moved his hand away.

"You need to give me a dollar first."

"Why?" she challenged.

He grinned. Though he was old, his teeth were very white against the blackness of his skin. "In this country it's called a tip. You'll get used to it here. No tip, no service."

"A dollar is too much money. I will give you something less."

"Better make it a dollar," he said. "You're going to need a friend here, believe me. You don't want to get off to a bad start."

She snorted with displeasure. "And for a dollar, you will be my friend, I suppose?"

"That's right. And you'll be glad of it."

With a sigh, Sasha found a dollar bill and handed it to him. Henry gave her the key, made a ridiculous little salute, then backed out of the room, closing the door behind him. With trembling hands, she turned the latch to lock herself in.

As soon as she was alone, Sasha threw herself onto the bed and sobbed.

Two

On her third day in America, a gray New York afternoon, Sasha took a taxi to a cemetery in Queens and watched as two workmen lowered Julka's coffin into the ground. She supposed she should be grateful to Max for arranging the small ceremony, but all she felt was such sorrow so crushing it was hard even to breathe.

The cemetery in Queens was enormous, a vast city of death with tombstones and monuments stretching out as far as the eye could see. Sasha stood by the open grave as a minister of some sort, a small white-haired man dressed in black, read meaningless words from the Bible. Sasha had no idea what his denomination might be, but she didn't imagine Julka would find solace in these English words from a foreign Bible. She barely listened to the short service. It seemed to her a terrible fate to be buried in this unfriendly land of Queens, so far from home.

Afterwards, the minister asked if she would like to come back to his rectory for a cup of coffee. He appeared uncomfortable with her, as though he knew his service was unsatisfactory. Perhaps he meant well, but Sasha told him no. She preferred to remain alone by the grave.

There was a bench nearby on the cemetery grounds where Sasha sat for a long time with no particular thoughts or emotions. She was simply empty and tired. In the distance, she could see the harsh, geometrical skyline of Manhattan through the bare branches of a wintry tree. As far as she was concerned, Julka was the lucky one. He had escaped in time, while America was only a fantasy; he had been spared the necessity of figuring out how to make a life here.

It was dark by the time Sasha returned to the Hotel Jefferson. She rode the creaky elevator to the sixth floor, unlocked the door to her little cubicle, and sat on her narrow bed with such a sense of oppression that she couldn't imagine how she was going to last another day.

If Julka were here, even this dreadful hotel would have been bearable. They had been in worse places, after all. But when there were two of you, you could keep your spirits up. They would have made a joke of it. She would have said something like, "Well, it's not the Ritz, is it?" And he? What would Julka have answered to make her laugh? Probably he would have said something extremely silly: "No, it's not the Ritz, my dear—it's the Fritz!"

Yes, welcome to the Fritz! That was exactly Julka's sense of humor, nonsensical. But how they would have laughed!

Sasha could hardly bear to think about it, her darling Julka. Her last connection to Krakow, forever gone.

*****

An Overnight Sensation

For nearly two weeks, Sasha barely left her room. She stayed in bed, kept her door locked, and shut out the city as best as she could. For the first time in her life, she was too shy to face the world. She only wanted to hide. New York terrified her. The angular buildings, the angry roar of traffic, the people themselves who bustled by. There was nothing soft in this city, nothing kind, nothing familiar.

If it hadn't been for the need to eat, Sasha might have never left the safety of her room. She made quick forays into the neighborhood, generally late at night when she felt more hidden. There was a delicatessen on 8th Avenue where she shopped, bringing back food to her room.

Delicate female creatures in misery are supposed to pine away, but Sasha's grief left her ravenous. Her stomach was like an empty pit that refused to be filled, no matter what she put into it. She didn't have a ration card which meant there were a number of things she was unable to buy, such as meat and butter and milk. But she filled up on everything else she could lay her hands on. She wasn't particular. She simply wanted to feed herself mechanically without end. The motion itself was soothing.

Ten days passed in this fashion: eating badly, sleeping, crying much of the time. She knew that eventually she would need to earn money, and perhaps this would rouse her. Yet even this could be put off due to Max's generosity—guilt money, as she saw it. She presumed she had a month or two before the question of money would need to be seriously considered. But then, of course, she could simply go to Max's attorney, his old school friend, and ask for more. She had his address on a piece of paper in her suitcase.

Toward the end of Sasha's second week in America, a vague restlessness took hold and she began to make longer explorations of the nearby streets. She never went far. She didn't have a map, she had no idea how the streets were laid out, so she was careful to memorize certain buildings and billboards, landmarks that would lead her back to the safety of her room. In this way, she covered only a limited midtown area that went as far as 50th Street to the north, 32nd Street to the south, and eastward to First Avenue. She never turned her steps westward to the Hudson and the wharf where the *Mauretania* had docked, for that was somehow forbidden territory.

Sasha's restless walks were only a form of pacing, allowing her inner drama to play out. The motion was lulling, one foot after another, and while she walked, songs from her childhood often came to mind, old lullabies. There was one song in particular that her mother had liked to sing, a nursery rhyme about a cat name Grisha who was such a bad hunter he could never catch a mouse. It was a silly song, really, with a silly little melody, yet Sasha couldn't get it out of her head.

There was an old singing exercise Sasha remembered from her earliest lessons where you breathed deeply, allowing the diaphragm to expand, and then you released the air slowly with your lips closed, letting it vibrate your head with sound, a kind of intense humming. Sasha found herself doing this now on her long walks, breathing and humming that childish song about Grisha the cat, letting it fill up the inside of her head as loudly as if it were a Beethoven symphony.

In this way Sasha began to sing again, though it was music no one could hear except herself. She loved the silly melody about Grisha the cat. And how telling it was that the mouse always got away! This was a Polish song, of course, in which cats were failures just like everybody else. American cats, she sensed, would be more successful, eating mouse-steak morning, noon, and night.

There always came a point in the song about Grisha the cat when Sasha began to cry. She just couldn't bear it, the song was so nostalgic and sad. That poor, poor cat!

Sasha sensed that music was the one thing that might save her. But for the time being, it didn't seem a promising avenue, not when she couldn't even get through a nursery rhyme without a torrent of tears.

*****

Even in despair, Sasha was practical enough to keep track of her money. During their last moments aboard the *Mauretania*, Max had given her all his cash, exactly sixty-five pounds. Sasha had a small amount of English money herself, twelve pounds three shillings and sixpence—a bit more than she had told Julka—and Mina had given her $259 American dollars. Adding these sums together, she possessed a grand total of seventy-seven pounds three shillings and sixpence and $259 American dollars. In 1943 there was a bit less than four pounds to the dollar, which meant she had arrived in America with a fortune of approximately $519 plus loose change

After two weeks at the Hotel Jefferson, this amount had decreased by $56—$30 for rent, $21 for food, and $5 for taxis back and forth to the cemetery in Queens. For Sasha, this was still an astonishing sum, more than she had ever possessed at one time in her entire life. As far as money was concerned, she had no fears for the future. But then something remarkable happened. On the fifteenth day, she woke in the morning, ate a bagel covered with sticky strawberry jam, and promptly threw-up her entire breakfast into the sink.

At first she believed it was only an upset stomach from eating badly and she bought fruit that day, an orange and two bananas, determined on a healthier diet. But the next morning she threw up again, this time even more wretchedly than before. She threw up all morning long, then felt better for a few hours, and then became sick again in the afternoon.

By evening, Sasha suspected the worst: she was pregnant. She didn't want any part of it, she tried to tell herself it couldn't be true. Yet it seemed somehow appropriate, punishment for her foolishness. God's little joke on wayward girls.

On top of all the throwing up, her nipples had begun to be sore, and this was something every girl backstage at the Krakow opera had warned her about, a sure way to know if you were in that sad, sniggering condition to which women who defied conventions were prone. Examining herself in the mirror, it seemed to Sasha that her breasts were larger, swollen with some new energy of motherly intent.

Sasha had learned about these matters in the backstage dressing rooms of her childhood. Every topic had always come back to sex: how to get it, how to avoid it, how to recognize when you were pregnant, and what to do if you wished to rid yourself of the results. It was all a funny joke, except when it happened to you.

She began to do some elementary arithmetic in her head. Her last menstrual period had come in England a week before boarding the *Mauretania*. She remembered that very well because there had been a bombing raid that night and she had been stuck in an air-raid shelter, the Piccadilly Circus underground station. It was approximately two weeks later, the early morning hours of Valentine's Day, February 14th, that she'd had sex with Max the first time. Valentine's Day had become part of their private mythology, Cupid's silly arrows, something to smile over.

But Sasha wasn't smiling now.

They had arrived in New York four days later and now she had been at the Hotel Jefferson sixteen days. Which meant, mathematically speaking, that she very well *could* be pregnant. The collective wisdom of the Krakow Opera was that a girl could experience morning sickness within a single week of conceiving, though this varied from case to case. Some women didn't get sick at all, and with others the nausea happened quite a bit later.

Sasha was still pondering these matters one day later—her seventeenth day in New York—when her menstrual period appeared to begin. For an entire morning, she was almost her old self again, so great was her relief. But then after only a few hours, the flow of blood stopped as suddenly as it had begun and didn't continue, not even when she performed strenuous knee bends in her room. Unfortunately, she knew about this also from the talk backstage, that in many cases pregnant women experience light spotting after they've been knocked up. A bit of comic relief, smiles all around, only for nature to have the last laugh after all.

For Sasha, this clinched it. No doctor needed to tell her what her body (and Max) had done to her.

She was pregnant.

And she didn't have a clue what she was going to do.

*****

An Overnight Sensation

On the afternoon when Sasha finally admitted to herself that she was pregnant, she decided to visit the Plaza Hotel, the fine place Max would have taken her for a pancake breakfast if only his wife hadn't arrived.

She was certain that the Plaza couldn't be as grand as the expensive hotels she had glimpsed in London, the Dorchester and the Connaught. Sasha was prepared to sneer. But she wanted to see it anyway, the alternate life she might have had. There was a tattered telephone book by the pay phone in the lobby downstairs and this supplied her with the address.

"All right! Let's see this wonderful hotel!" she said to herself. She dressed with care, studying herself in the mirror and making a subtle application of lipstick and make-up. Fortunately, she still looked good. She didn't *look* pregnant. Youth was on her side, the ultimate camouflage.

"I'm a very pretty girl," she said to the mirror. If she could simply hang on to that single fact, everything might still work out for her.

When Sasha was ready, she left her room, locked the door, and made her way through the dreary hotel lobby into the hard-etched New York afternoon.

Life was stirring inside of her. Sasha was ready for an adventure.

Three

Fifth Avenue was wide and pleasant, and it became increasingly pleasant the further Sasha walked uptown. She passed great department stores and glittering shop windows that were full of lovely things. The buildings themselves were towers of stone and glass, glistening in the afternoon sun like pillars of salt.

Sasha had never seen such crowds. Fifth Avenue rushed against her, as though she were caught in a current going the wrong way. At one busy intersection, she was nearly mowed down by a large woman in a fur coat who came stepping out of a taxi with great purpose and marched across the sidewalk toward one of the luxurious stores. The woman had a teenage girl in tow who Sasha imagined might be her daughter. Their trajectory took them only inches from Sasha, but they continued their private conversation as though she didn't exist.

"I simply *refuse* to go to Connecticut this weekend," the girl was complaining. "I'd rather die, I swear, than endure another dull dinner with the Markham's."

"My dear, Helen, you *can't* get out of it, that's all there is to it," the older woman answered. "Anyway, Charles is coming down from Choate . . ."

They were gone as suddenly as they had appeared, vanishing through a revolving door without once looking Sasha's way. The store they entered was called Saks & Company and there were exquisite dresses in the windows, gloves and hats and fur coats and a great variety of fine things. Sasha found herself wondering where Connecticut might be and what was this thing called Choate.

She continued walking, but more slowly than before. The fragmentary encounter disturbed her, the glimpse of the wealthy woman and her daughter. It brought home her own crushing unimportance as an outsider in a city she didn't know. Wouldn't it be lovely, Sasha thought, if all she had to complain about was going to this place called Connecticut and having dinner with the Markham's?

After several blocks, Sasha gazed up from her musings to see a hotel across the street. She knew immediately that this was the Plaza even before she read the name on the awning. The façade resembled pictures she had seen of great chateaux in France, only it was elongated upward as New York buildings tended to be. The building had a lovely air of elegance, and it hinted at even more luxuries inside: soft beds, smiling faces, bathtubs with hot water, people with money. In a hotel like this, you wouldn't see fat women in their underwear with bottles in their hand.

The hotel was situated on a wide, clean corner on Fifth Avenue bordered by a huge park on 59th Street, a park whose boundaries she could not yet fathom. Sasha crossed the avenue to the edge of the park and found a bench in the sun from where she could sit and study the hotel more closely. Her eye traveled upward to the metallic green roof that sat on the building like a kind of cap. Sasha presumed the best rooms would be up high with stunning views of the park below. This was where Max would have taken her. There was a particular corner window whose glass reflected the sun, blazing back at her like a star, and Sasha had the fancy that this might have been *her* room, *her* window . . . if only Mina hadn't appeared at such an unlucky moment, changing everything. She might be sitting there now, at this very moment, surrounded by comfort and security, adored by a rich man.

The memory of Max came rushing back: his gentleness, the kindness in his eyes, his aura of culture and intelligence. She had come so close to winning him, yet here she was, cast out, on a public bench on the street. Sasha stared miserably upward at the room that might have been hers, so absorbed in her enormous failure that she didn't realize there were tears streaking down her face. She only became aware that she was crying when she heard a man's voice on the bench next to her.

"Excuse me, may I offer you a handkerchief?"

Sasha turned to discover she was sharing the bench with a well-dressed man of perhaps forty. He was handsome in a somewhat rough and tumble way. That was the first thing she noticed about him, a good-natured manliness that exuded self-confidence. He had black hair slicked back from his forehead in a style more reminiscent of the 1930s than the 1940s, yet it suited him. His eyes were prominent, very dark, almost black, and he was studying her with a keen look of intelligence. His chin was too small, and this architectural failure kept him from being conventionally handsome. Yet the total effect was somehow attractive. He was deeply sun-tanned, and this added to her sense of the exotic.

"Go ahead, blow your nose," he told her, pressing a clean white handkerchief into her hand. "It'll do you good."

"Oh, I couldn't, really."

"Sure, you can. Come on, you'll feel better."

The second thing Sasha noticed about the man on her bench, after the fact that he was handsome, was that he was expensively dressed. He wore a gray vicuna overcoat that struck her as perhaps the nicest, softest overcoat she had ever seen. There was a blatant atmosphere of money about him; but it was new money, she sensed, rather than old.

Beneath his outer garment, she could see a grey pinstriped suit that even from the hint of what was showing revealed itself as superbly well-tailored, the best wool money might buy. His tie was silk, a rich burgundy color, and there was a subtle pattern on it that suggested exclusive schools and clubs. Yet Sasha wasn't fooled. From the start, she had him pegged. She had encountered this type before, his European equivalent. With a wardrobe this flashy, he was no gentleman. This was a gangster.

"Go ahead," he said again. "Don't worry about the hanky. I got a dozen more where that came from. It don't matter a bit. Give yourself a good blow. It'll clear out your head and you'll be able to think straight. That's a girl . . ."

His speech was common. It wasn't the patrician way Max spoke. He watched with clinical interest as Sasha wiped her eyes and blew her nose.

"No, no, keep the hanky," he told her when she tried, with an apologetic smile, to return it to him. "Think of it as a souvenir of a chance meeting."

"Thank you. You're very kind. I . . . you see, I've had a . . ."

But what had she had? A shock? A broken heart? A failure at the Gaming Table of Life? Sasha wanted to offer some abbreviated explanation of why she was crying, but had become momentarily befuddled, not quite sure how much she wanted to say. The man laughed in a good-natured way.

"Hey, don't worry about it. Listen, I understand completely," he said. "You'll get over him, believe me. That's the crazy thing about love. This time next year you won't even remember his name."

Sasha managed a smile that still had a few tears in it. "Am I that obvious?" she asked.

"Well, sure. Why else would a pretty girl be sitting on a park bench crying if not for a man . . . go ahead, one more blow and you'll be free of this guy forever. Give it a good honk, why don't you."

It was ridiculous, this insistence that she blow her nose, treating her like she was a little girl. Yet she found his easy manners attractive and she did exactly what he said.

"You feel better now?" he asked.

She nodded.

"I guess this is where he's staying, huh? This gentleman of yours who broke your heart. Upstairs in the Plaza?"

"Yes, this is where he likes to stay," Sasha answered. "But now he is in California with his wife."

Sasha knew it was incautious to say such a thing to a stranger. But in an odd way, he had won her trust.

The man laughed gaily. "Ah-ha! The wife! The plot thickens! I imagine you didn't know about her until it was too late."

She shook her head sadly. "No, I knew about her very well. I was stupid. I have only myself to blame."

He nodded seriously. "Well, welcome to life. You know what I think? I don't think you're stupid at all. You see, it's the smart people who know when they've been chumps—stupid people, they never find that out, they never get wise to themselves. How old are you, by the way?"

It wasn't a polite question for a stranger to ask a woman he had just met. But she told him anyway, more or less.

"Eighteen," she said, deciding on a number.

"Eighteen!" he repeated with a smile. "Well, there you are. Eighteen is exactly the right age for people to get their hearts broken. I had a broken heart myself at that age, and I'm forever grateful for it. It gave me a chance to wise up and I never made that particular mistake again. I doubt if you will either. You're no bimbo, I can see that."

Sasha found herself regarding him more closely. He was an attractive man, there was no denying the fact. It was hard not to feel a certain thrill at finding herself the object of his scrutiny. She liked his air of confidence and ease, and his vicuna coat was so luscious, she had to resist the urge to touch it. But she wished he wouldn't use words like bimbo. She only had a hazy idea of what bimbo meant, but she was certain it was crass.

"You know something, your English is real good," he said. "But I detect an accent. Very attractive, really, in a young woman. So where are you from?"

On the spur of the moment, Sasha decided to switch nationalities. She'd been in America long enough to realize that being a Polack was not necessarily an asset.

"I'm French," she told him.

"No kidding? Gay-Paree, huh?"

"Well, not Paris, exactly. Only a small village in the south."

"A country girl!" He nodded with approval. "You know, I could tell that. There's something just a little fresh about you.

Me, I grew up in Pittsburg. My folks came over from Lithuania before I was born, but I always thought of myself as just plain American. To tell the truth, I don't even speak the old language, not a word of it. One day your kids will be like that too."

"Will they?" Sasha asked thoughtfully, remembering the alien presence in her womb.

"Sure. That's how it is in America. So tell me, how long have you been in our fair country?"

"Only a few weeks," Sasha told him. "I . . . you see, I escaped from the Nazis. I stole a small boat and sailed across the Channel to England."

"My God, all by yourself?"

"No, my father was with me. We were determined to make our way to freedom. But he was wounded by a German soldier and he died on the crossing. I had to sail through the night by myself with sharks everywhere."

"Sharks in the English Channel? No kidding!"

"Well, they were only small sharks. But they were very frightening. I was certain they wished to eat me."

The man raised an eyebrow and studied her with new interest. "Sounds like you been through it. You've seen a lot, I guess."

Sasha nodded demurely. "Yes," she said. "I've seen a lot."

"You got family here, I imagine?"

She shook her head, feeling suddenly so vulnerable she didn't trust herself to speak.

He didn't speak either for a moment, but continued to study her with his keen eyes. Apparently, she was not the usual sort of pretty girl one met on a park bench.

"Look," he said after a moment, "why don't you let me buy you a cup of tea. We'll go across the street to the Palm Court. You'll like the Plaza more from the inside than the out. They have some nice little sandwiches and cakes."

The main events of our lives so often rest on the merest accident. Sasha would have gladly gone with this man to the Palm Court. She was inclined to like him, and one didn't get an invitation to the Plaza every day. But at the mention of nice little sandwiches and cakes, her stomach did a flip-flop and all her nausea returned, threatening to overwhelm her. With the nausea, she remembered the cause of it too. Suddenly the attentions of an attractive, well-dressed man seemed too much, too soon, more than she could deal with.

"Thank you, but I can't," she told him hurriedly, standing up from the bench. "I really must go."

"Are you sure?" he asked, standing also. "I promise, tea at the Palm Court is a New York ritual, not to be missed. And if your young man happens to hear about it, you can bet that he'll be eaten alive with jealousy."

Sasha managed a laugh. She wished she could stay and have tea. But she was afraid she was about to throw up all over him.

"No, I must go," she said. "But thank you very much. You've been very kind."

He shrugged good-naturedly. "Well, good luck to you, then. Who knows, maybe we'll meet again. New York is a big city, but it's surprising how you bump into people."

Sasha sensed that if she had managed to delay their parting even for a moment, he would have asked for her address and a more concrete opportunity to meet again. She would have liked that. In an indefinite way, she enjoyed his company. But delay was impossible. She hurried off without even shaking hands.

She managed to get as far as 57th Street before throwing up into a trash basket on the corner. The people on the street surged around her, while Sasha stood with her head over the bin, wretchedly embarrassed.

*****

But this was only the start of a bad afternoon. When Sasha returned to the Hotel Jefferson, she discovered that she had been robbed. The door to her room was ajar, the drawers of her dresser pulled open, her clothes and underwear thrown everywhere. It was as though a tornado of malice had swept through her belongings.

Sasha let out a string of Polish swear words, every terrible word she knew. But swearing didn't help. At last, with a groan of resignation, she got on her hands and knees to gather her things and see what was missing. Luckily, she'd had her money and papers with her in her handbag, for she had learned early in life to keep valuables close at hand, trusting no one.

It wasn't until she looked inside the wardrobe that Sasha realized her battered old suitcase was gone. She searched the room to be certain, but it was nowhere. The suitcase itself was replaceable, nothing special. But in it she had kept a few important things from her old life that she hadn't wanted to unpack, including the single photograph she possessed of her mother and a long-ago menu from the Café Chopin, the occasion of her twelfth birthday. Julka and all her friends from the opera company had written humorous comments on the yellowing paper, and for Sasha, these mementos were more precious than any amount of money.

"Oh!" she cried in despair. A second wave of anger rushed over her, one that was even stronger than the first. Grabbing her handbag, she marched from her room down the hall and rang for the elevator. The elevator was busy, so she took the stairs, charging quickly down all six flights, round and around. She burst through a door into the lobby, where the manager was seated at his desk studying a racing form.

"Someone has robbed me!" Sasha cried. "They have taken my suitcase and I demand to have it back!"

"Whoa, whoa, whoa, little lady," the manager said. "Let's start this from the beginning. A little more slowly, if you don't mind."

"I have been most terribly robbed!" Sasha was so furious she could barely speak English. "I am out just now and when I get back my suitcase is gone."

"Your suitcase is missing, huh?"

"Yes, that is what I'm telling you. And I demand to have it back!"

"Look, I don't know a thing about this. Maybe you left your door unlocked. Maybe you got careless."

"This is your responsibility!" Sasha shouted. "This is your fault! And now you must find my suitcase or I will go to the police. I will tell them that you rob people here at this terrible hotel!"

"The police, huh? I'm not sure I like your insinuation. You think maybe *I* took your damn suitcase?"

Sasha saw she was getting nowhere. She took a breath and tried to slow down. "No, of course not," she agreed. "But I demand you get my belongings back."

"Look here, you've caused trouble from the moment you arrived."

347

"*Me*?" Sasha cried in astonishment. "You . . . you are a big liar!"

"Oh, yeah? You know something, I've had complaints about you, that you've been soliciting men in the hallways. We don't allow that sort of thing at the Jefferson. If you want to be a working girl, that's your business. But you're going to have to do it some place else."

The accusation was so outrageous, Sasha hardly knew what to say. "Who told you this lie?" she demanded. "Who told you that I am speaking to men in the hallway?"

The manager leaned back in his chair and crossed his arms. "I'm not at liberty to say. And I'm afraid I'm going to have to ask you to leave. I don't like foreigners coming over here and causing trouble. You should have stayed where you belong, girlie. So I'll give you half an hour to pack and then *I'm* going to call the cops if you're still hanging round."

"Leave? I have paid for an entire week! You must give me a refund then."

He shook his head. "Nope. We don't give refunds to people who are in abeyance of the law. If you don't want no trouble, you just clear out, and do it quick."

This was so unfair that Sasha wanted to grab the man by his scrawny neck. But he sat protected behind a metal grille and she knew better than to make a scene. Coming from Poland, she knew first-hand that life was seldom fair. She was only surprised to encounter such unfairness so quickly in America, the promised land.

"I see," she said coldly. "All right, then, I'll go. This is a horrible hotel anyway. You are all drunks and crooks."

"Yeah, yeah," the manager said, looking back at his racing form. "You've just used up five minutes. Now you've got twenty-five minutes before I call the cops."

Sasha stared at him. She had intended to take the elevator upstairs to pack her few belongings, but now she changed her mind. She no longer had a suitcase to pack and her clothes were easily replaceable—underwear, an old dressing gown, a shabby dress from England that had seen better days. She was wearing her one decent outfit, and she had her handbag with her money and papers.

Without another word, Sasha turned with her head held high and stepped out onto the sidewalk into the early evening. It was satisfying to show the awful man how little she cared.

She walked angrily for several blocks before stopping so suddenly that a woman bumped up against her from behind and had to step around. Sasha had just remembered the piece of paper she had with the name and telephone number of Max's attorney in New York, the old school friend she was supposed to call for money. The paper had been inside the suitcase with the photograph of her mother and the menu from the Café Chopin. She had always supposed she would call Max's attorney when her money was gone, but now he was lost to her as well. She had never even bothered to remember his name.

Standing on the sidewalk, Sasha felt as though she were in freefall with nothing to hang onto. Old clothes didn't matter, but money most certainly did. In an instant, her situation was completely changed.

Could she return to the hotel and cause such a fuss that the manager would somehow get her suitcase back? Surely he had an idea who had robbed her. She would threaten him, she would let him know what she was capable of, a girl who had escaped the Nazis.

Yet even in her anger, Sasha knew it was hopeless. She had met low, stupid men like the hotel manager before. They were a universal breed and she knew her threats would only make him more stubborn. After storming out in such a grand manner, she hated the idea of returning to the hotel. Pride was all she had left. Everything else had been taken from her.

Her thoughts circled round and round, like a ball spinning on a roulette wheel. She knew, of course, that she could locate Max in California if she put her mind to it. She could telephone and ask him to give her the attorney's name again. But this was even less appealing than returning to the Hotel Jefferson to demand her suitcase back. She thought she would rather die.

"I don't need Max!" Sasha told herself. "I don't need his money. And I don't need his attorney either!"

An Overnight Sensation

Sasha took a deep breath and she felt something return to her that had been lost, some vital part of herself that had slipped away in New York.

It was a blessing not to have Max's money to fall back on. She saw that now. Max's money had made her helpless. Now she truly had no one except herself. But that had always been her main strength.

Sasha resumed walking through the edge of the theater district toward the East Side. The evening streets were crowded with people getting off work, everyone heading to dinner, going home. The lights of the city came on one by one, illuminating billboards and store windows, for there was no blackout in the strange city, not even during a time of war.

Sasha had no idea where she was going or what she would do. She didn't even know where she would spend the night. But she knew she had resources at her command. She was clever, she was pretty, and anger had finally roused her to do battle. She was ready to let New York know that a girl of destiny had arrived.

By the time Sasha reached Fifth Avenue, she had already dreamed up the first sweet notions of a plan.

Four

Sasha arrived at the Plaza Hotel by taxi on the afternoon of Monday, March 12, 1943, two days after she had been thrown out of the Hotel Jefferson, accused of soliciting men in the hallways,

She had been busy during those two days, reinventing herself.

Sasha stepped from the cab in a fashionable dress of gray silk that had small polka dots on it, black high heeled shoes, nylon stockings, a glossy black leather handbag over her shoulder, a hat with a brim that dipped down low over her face, and a sumptuously soft gray rabbit skin coat. The doorman hurried to take her valise: an elegant little bag made from a tapestry material with leather trim. The suitcase contained her one other outfit, a slinky black cocktail dress that might serve for a variety of situations, day or night.

As Sasha walked into the lobby of the Plaza Hotel, she was astonished at what a change of wardrobe could do. She was no longer invisible. Suddenly she was an attractive, well-dressed young woman in an expensive hotel. Every male eye followed her for a beat longer than was entirely proper. Only she knew the truth, that beneath her fancy new wardrobe she wore a pair of ragged underwear and a brassiere that was held together with a safety pin. Sasha was so nervous she could barely breathe.

Would they know she was a fraud? Would they somehow smell her out, that she wasn't their kind? Sasha had never felt quite so self-conscious and shy. But she forced herself onward across a dark red carpet toward a front desk of dark oak. A young assistant manager smiled demurely in a most attractive way. Sasha believed he was the first man she had met since she turned thirteen who didn't sneak a look at her breasts. What a difference this was from the Hotel Jefferson! It was like arriving in an alternate universe.

But she could barely speak.

"Do you . . ." Her voice faltered and she had to clear her throat. "Do you have a room, please? I wish to stay a week, perhaps longer."

"Do you have a reservation, ma'am?"

"No, I am afraid I have left this to the last minute. I have only just learned that my brother is arriving from London and I am hoping to meet him." Once she started her tale, imagination came to the rescue and her words came more easily. "He is a pilot in the Free French Army and we have not seen each other since the Nazis marched into Paris, so I wish to see him very much. It is quite sudden, but I am hoping you will have room for me."

The assistant manager nodded sympathetically. It would take a very hard-hearted fellow indeed not to help a pretty girl who hadn't seen her brother since the Nazis marched into Paris.

"Let me see what I can do," he said earnestly, thumbing through a huge ledger. "Hmm . . . yes, I think we're going to be able to accommodate you. Would a suite on the tenth floor be suitable?"

Her eyes turned slightly tragic: a young woman who had suffered the vicissitudes of war and had known sorrow. "Perhaps you have something more modest? I don't need quite so large a room."

"Yes, I see!" said the young man, entirely won to her cause. "I'm sure I can find something."

She was already in love with this wonderful hotel. She felt every inch a princess. Nevertheless, she arranged for the cheapest single room that was available, not wishing to overplay her hand. In fact, the quality of the room itself wasn't important, only the fact of its location. Even the cheapest room at the Plaza was expensive, $17 a night, which was a considerable amount for lodging in 1943.

She registered as Sonya Chopin and supplied a home address in Paris, a street and a number she cheerfully invented: 2132 Avenue Louis XIV. Why not? There *had* to be an Avenue Louis XIV in Paris, didn't there? And if there wasn't, how could anyone check with the Nazis in residence?

She assumed the beautifully behaved people at the Plaza would require money in advance, but when she took out her purse to pay, the assistant manager made a little bow and said payment at this time was not necessary. They would put a bill in her box. How wonderful it was to be rich! Even to pretend to be rich was wonderful. It was such a kinder and more trusting world than life among the poor.

Sasha followed the bellboy to her new room. For $17 a night she found herself on the third floor with a sunless view onto 58th Street, a narrow canyon of buildings that comprised the wrong side of the Plaza Hotel. Her room was hardly more than a cubbyhole, only slightly larger than what she'd had at the Jefferson: a single bed, a small desk, an armchair, a bedside table with a lamp. But the sheets were clean, the bed was soft, the carpet was marvelous on her bare feet, and the door closed with a satisfyingly solid click. Best of all, she had her own small bathroom with a tub, all the hot water a person could want, and soft white towels whose touch against her skin was so delicious the pleasure was almost sexual. The room had a radio, a closet, a telephone, a room service menu, and various bells she could ring to summon a maid, a valet, or a waiter.

Sasha unpacked quickly the scant contents of her suitcase. Then she closed the curtains, made certain that the door was locked, and spilled out what remained of her money onto the bed to make a count. She arranged the bills according to their denomination, put the coins in careful stacks, and hovered over her fortune with the stealthy greed of a Polish peasant.

After changing her English pounds at a bank on Madison Avenue and paying for two nights at a modest hotel on Lexington Avenue, she had possessed a grand total of $443.57— what remained of her own few pounds and the money that Max and Mina had given her on the ship. For Sasha, this was an astonishing amount, and when she tried to translate the sum into zlotys, she soon got lost in zeroes. With $443.57, her mother would have regarded herself as a millionaire.

But that was before her strategic shopping trip to Saks & Company, the department store where she had nearly been run over by a wealthy mother with her teenage daughter. In a single frantic afternoon, she had purchased her new wardrobe—two separate outfits, hat, coat, handbag, shoes, and valise—for $183.23. It was a terrifying amount to spend in one afternoon, but it was essential to her plan that she look good. She shoplifted the nylon stockings, slipping them into her bag, but she hadn't dared to try her sleight of hand on the larger items. This left her $260.34, and with $6.20 spent on food and the taxi that had brought her to the Plaza, she now had $254.14 spread out before her on the bed, her entire treasure.

There was a pen and pad on the small desk in her room, and Sasha did some quick arithmetic—never her strongest subject in her make-shift education backstage at the Krakow Opera. At $17 per night, $254.14 meant that she could spend fifteen days at the Plaza before her money ran out (fourteen, really, two weeks). But this didn't take food into account. She planned to eat sparingly, but she had to eat something. And there might be hotel tax as well, she wasn't sure. Plus, she still had one more thing to do to complete her transformation. She needed to have her hair done.

Sasha felt sick with indecision, wondering what was more important: additional days at the hotel or a new hair style.

How could you decide something like that?

The thought of a further raid on her treasury caused a physical onslaught of pure anxiety. This whole venture could so easily turn out badly. But what choice did she have? She couldn't come this far and not continue to the end.

*****

She found a beauty salon around the corner on Sixth Avenue where she could have her hair cut and styled for $20.

Sasha had worn her hair long since childhood; it reached almost to her waist when she let it down. But she knew this was hopelessly old-fashioned, not how a smart young woman in New York City was supposed to look. Even Max, who often told her how much he loved her hair, once mentioned that she looked like a pretty peasant girl at harvest time right out of some middle-European fairy tale. Max seemed to think this was a compliment, but Sasha couldn't afford to be a pretty peasant girl in a middle-European fairy tale any longer. She watched bravely in the mirror as her thick dark gold hair fell in clumps to the floor.

She was cut, shampooed, curled, styled, combed, put under a hair dryer, and cut some more. Two hours later she emerged from the salon with her hair in the latest perky style hanging just above her shoulders, the ends curled upward in a wave. Her new hair bounced and glistened. The hairdresser said she looked just like someone named Lana Turner, and that she was pretty enough to go to Hollywood and be a star. Sasha wasn't sure. She nearly wept at the sight of her hair on the salon floor. But it was too late for second thoughts.

On her way back to Fifth Avenue, she stopped and spent another $7 on make-up, shampoo, conditioner, and the curlers the hairdresser had said were essential for her new hair. The money was positively pouring out.

Sasha returned to her room at the Plaza, locked the door, and repeated the ritual of counting her dwindling fortune on her bed.

Now she had $227.14. Divided by $17, the price of the room, this meant that she only had thirteen days to live at the Plaza.

But now, realistically, she had to consider food. If she budgeted $3 a day on food and assorted extras, that added up to $39 over thirteen days . . . which meant in fact that she had eleven days before she was out on the street.

Call it a week and a half.

An Overnight Sensation

Sasha felt a new surge of panic, wondering again if she wasn't making a huge mistake. But she refused to think about it. There was no time to worry, only time to do.

She was pregnant, her money was nearly gone, and the clock was ticking.

Five

Sasha's plan was not complex, but it contained several aspects.

First and foremost, she required a rich husband who would become (with some fiddling of dates) the father of her child. This was the main purpose of the Plaza Hotel. She was on a fishing expedition, offering herself as bait for the right wealthy gentleman to snap at, with a concealed hook to hold him fast. She knew it was a shabby trick—Sasha never fooled herself about these things. But what alternative did she have? On her budget, a husband was simply a forgone conclusion, a requirement that could not be avoided.

The second part of her plan was to become a famous singer as quickly as possible. She was willing to start modestly, possibly in a theater, perhaps in a club—Sasha was flexible, as long as whatever role she found led to stardom. Singing suited Sasha in every way. She loved music, she loved the dramatic feeling of pouring herself into a song. And of course, she loved applause.

Throughout her childhood, she had imagined she would sing opera, because that was what she knew. But Sasha was too knowledgeable about the demands of serious music to fool herself. She had already lost too many years to the war. Realistically, all that was open to her now was popular music.

With her classical training, she assumed it would be easy enough to pull off.

Of course, she knew popular music would have its own demands. She would need to learn a new repertoire, meet the right people. The whole thing could take a few months. Three months, say. At which point, of course, her money would be long gone. But this was where the rich husband came in.

And so, her two-pronged plan seemed to Sasha quite perfect, one that covered all contingencies. A rich husband, a glamorous job as a musical star. And if the husband turned out to be less than ideal, chosen in haste, she could always deal with that when she was securely established on stage.

Why not? This was America, land of opportunity.

*****

Sasha set to work. For the rest of the afternoon, she sat in the deliciously hot water of her bathtub and practiced scales, using the tiled walls to enclose the sound. It was more than two years since she'd had the leisure to do vocal exercises, so she began slowly, working at first with open vowels, simple scales, then progressing to thirds and fifths and arpeggios.

She found that her voice was still intact, waiting like a treasure that had been put away safely in a box. Perhaps not as strong as it would need to be in order to sing over a full orchestra in an opera hall. But strong enough.

"I will be a great success!" she told herself boldly . . . with only a small whisper of doubt nagging about the edges.

The following morning, Sasha woke languidly, bought coffee and a roll from a delicatessen she had discovered on 6th Avenue, determined not to waste money on expensive meals at the hotel, and she returned to her room with all the morning newspapers under her arm. She was pleased when her breakfast remained in her stomach. She hoped the awful nausea was over. She simply couldn't afford it.

She spent another hour in her bathroom with the door closed doing her singing exercises, then progressing to a few of her favorite arias, from Puccini and Verdi. Once this was finished, she spent the rest of the morning reading the theatrical and entertainment sections of the New York newspapers, educating herself as to what sort of music was performed here.

Sasha had confided her purpose to the newspaper seller on 6th Avenue, a funny little man with glasses, letting him know that she was a singer looking for work, and he had recommended a publication called *Variety* that he said all the actors and actresses and singers read each week as though it were the Bible. *Variety*, she saw, was a goldmine of information, with listings of auditions and casting calls.

After some careful study, Sasha settled on her first audition, a casting call this very afternoon at the St. James Theater for a new play with an unusual name that Sasha wasn't certain how to pronounce. She wasn't even certain if the name was in English, for it wasn't like anything Sasha had ever heard.

"Ooh . . . kla . . . hoo . . . ma," she said aloud experimentally. She didn't imagine she had it right, but at least it seemed to her that none of the other girls trying out would know how to say it either.

Oklahoma! It looked odd in print. But Sasha rather liked the exclamation point at the end. She took that as an optimistic sign.

*****

With destiny calling, Sasha dressed carefully in her black cocktail dress, nylon stockings, her new hat, new shoes, and splendid rabbit coat.

Before leaving the mirror, she practiced a mysterious smile until she was certain she was irresistible. Who could resist a smile like that? Who wouldn't want to solve the mystery of the girl in the rabbit coat?

She swept out of the Plaza Hotel like a visiting dignitary, bestowing her smile on the doorman. Nevertheless, she declined his offer to put her into a cab, telling him it was such a fine day she believed she would walk.

It wasn't a fine day at all—the afternoon had turned cold and bleak— but Sasha was afraid that a cab would be expensive. Her new high heeled shoes began to pinch within a few blocks, and by the time she had arrived at the St. James Theater on West 44th Street, her feet were pure misery. To her surprise, there was an enormous line of men and women who had come for the audition, a line so long it trailed outside the stage door for almost half a block. This was discouraging. Sasha had expected a few people, but nothing like such a crowd. As she took her place in line, she was glad to see that none of the other girls looked like they had a new wardrobe from Saks & Company. Most of them were rather shabby, in dresses that appeared comfortable but were far from stylish. Many were neither young nor particularly pretty. Sasha felt a surge of confidence at seeing the poor state of the competition

The girl ahead of her in line turned and smiled. "Hey there, how you doing?" she asked.

"I am doing fine, I think," Sasha replied.

"So you're here to try out for the chorus, huh?"

"Well, yes. If that is what they are auditioning for. I would rather have a better part than the chorus, of course, if I can get it."

"Wouldn't we all?" the girl said cheerfully. She was blond and almost pretty, but her face was too narrow, her skin was freckly and somehow the effect was almost spinsterish for such a young woman, rather plain. Her teeth weren't very good either, Sasha noticed. "I'm Jill, by the way," said the girl, offering her hand. Her manners were very direct. "Who are you?"

"I am Sonya Chopin. Please, will you tell me what this play is about, 'Ook-la-hoo-ma'? Do you know anything about it?"

"'Ook-la-hoo-ma!'" Jill repeated with a laugh. "What a hoot! Oklahoma, girl! That's how you say it. I guess, you're not from around here, are you? Jeepers, where did you come from? The moon?"

"Europe," Sasha replied with dignity.

"Oh," said Jill, her smile fading. "Well, I guess that explains it. How long have you been here?"

"Two weeks. And I need a job."

Jill looked her over, up and down. "You've never been on a New York audition before, I guess?"

"No," Sasha admitted.

"Well, next time don't come quite so dolled up. They want you to look good, of course, but not like some useless society dame. They want to know you're not afraid to sweat a little and work."

Sasha made note of this information. "Thank you . . . thank you, very much. I will remember this."

"Did you bring some sheet music along? They're going to ask you to sing something."

Sasha shook her head. "I did not know this. There will be a piano accompanist?"

"Yeah. A piano player, sure."

"Then I will ask him to play an aria from an opera, something every accompanist will know."

"From an *opera*?" the girl cried. "You're an opera singer?"

"Well, yes," Sasha answered. "I was with the Krakow Opera."

"Krakow as in Poland? You're a *Polish* opera singer?"

Sasha didn't know it, but Jill would be dining out on this story for weeks. The Polish opera singer who had dropped down from the moon.

"Actually, I'm French," Sasha said, remembering who she was supposed to be. "Unfortunately, I was caught in Poland when the war began, and it was difficult to escape."

"Hey, I'm sure you can sing circles around the rest of us," Jill said pleasantly. "But you want to make sure you don't warble or anything, if you know what I mean. I mean, you're supposed to be a cowgirl for this musical. You know what a cowgirl is, I hope."

"A girl who . . . milks cows?"

"Not exactly, Sonya."

Fortunately, Sasha waited nearly an hour in line, long enough for a rudimentary education in cowgirls and cowboys. Jill was awfully nice and did her best to be helpful—a fact which seemed astonishing to Sasha under the circumstances, since they would be competing against one another for a job.

As the line moved forward gradually, Sasha learned that *Oklahoma!* was set to open at the end of the month and they were auditioning for several vacant places in the chorus. Normally this was late to join a Broadway production, only a few weeks before the opening, but one girl had left to accept a role in Hollywood, a male dancer had been drafted into the army, and a second girl had suffered a breakdown on hearing that her boyfriend had just been killed in the South Pacific. This was the scuttlebutt, anyway, as Jill called it, the gossip coming through the grapevine, and Sasha paid careful attention to every detail, as though she might be tested later.

Sasha and Jill had become chummy by the time they passed at last through the stage door into the theater itself, such good friends that Sasha began to fantasize how nice it would be if they were hired together. A production assistant took her name down on a list. For Sasha, it was pleasantly familiar to be backstage in a theater again. The St. James was quite a different sort of theater from what she had known in Krakow, yet there were certain things—a musty smell of scenery paint on muslin flats, the dreary greenish paint in the backstage hallways that the audience would never see, a sense of expectation over everything—that gave Sasha a jolt of memory so strong it was like coming home.

Sasha watched from the wings as Jill went on stage first to do her audition. Sadly, the girl wasn't very good. She told the pianist in the orchestra pit that she would do "They Can't Take That Away From Me" in E-flat, but when Jill began to sing, her voice was very thin, almost brash. It seemed to Sasha that her pronunciation wasn't very good either. Every time she came to the line, "no, no they can't take that away from me," she pronounced "can't" as "c'aint." To Sasha's ears, this was far from elegant and quite inexcusable. She had learned the importance of clear diction early in her childhood from strict teachers who would rap your knuckles with their baton if you sang like that.

And yet, when Jill was finished, a man's voice from the half-dimmed auditorium said, "Very good, Miss . . . Miss Jill Parker, right? You look familiar somehow."

"I was in the chorus of *Junior Miss* at the Lyceum, Mr. Hammerstein. Maybe you saw me in that."

"You know, I think I did. So tell me, what have you been doing since?"

Jill rattled off a number of different plays and revues that Sasha had never heard of. When she was finished, Mr. Hammerstein, the man in the auditorium, told her to leave her contact information with the production assistant and they would call her back for a separate dance audition that would be held later on in the week. After a bit of pleasant chatter back and forth, Jill left the stage and it was Sasha's turn.

The stage lights were momentarily blinding as Sasha walked out onto center stage. She stood with the warm beam of many lights upon her— footlights, lights on a metal bar overhead, a theatrical glow of pure illumination that was like no other glow in the world.

Sasha hadn't stood center stage in a theater since Krakow, and she found herself literally paralyzed with memory. She couldn't breathe, she could barely move. Ghosts swarmed around her. There were a half dozen people gathered in the fourth and fifth rows, only half-visible through the glare, and Sasha became aware that one of the men was asking her a question.

She cleared her throat with an effort. "I'm sorry?"

"I'm asking what you'd like to sing for us, Miss . . . Chopin, is it?"

"Yes, that's right . . ."

Sasha struggled to get the words out. What music had she decided upon? She couldn't remember. All she could think of was Nazi soldiers flooding down the aisles. All she could think of was *Carmen*.

"Miss Chopin, are you all right?"

"Yes, yes . . . I'm sorry. You see, I've just come from Europe and I haven't any sheet music. But I would like to do the 'Toreador Song' from *Carmen*."

"From *Carmen*?" one of the voices asked. "The opera, you mean?"

"Yes, yes, the opera. I'm an opera singer, you see. I was a member of the Krakow Opera company . . . I'm, uh, French, actually, but I got caught in Poland when the war started. But yes, if you could let me sing the 'Toreador Song,' please . . . in re-minor."

"D minor," she heard someone say in the auditorium, translating her request into English. There was some whispered discussion among the half-seen people in the fourth and fifth rows. Finally she heard a voice, louder than the others say, "Look, I would like to hear her sing *Carmen*. Why not? Let's give her a chance."

Then another voice: "All right, Miss Chopin. Would you take off your hat please? We'd like to see your face better . . . Tom, think you can play the 'Toreador Song'?"

"Sure, I guess I can fake it," said the piano player from the orchestra pit.

"Okay. Go ahead, Miss Chopin."

Sasha took off her new hat, held it nervously by the rim in front of her with both hands. She hadn't expected to feel this way, the crushing familiarity of standing on a stage. *Carmen*! Sasha wanted to howl in grief. But now Tom the piano player was playing a make-shift introduction, arriving quickly at an exaggerated dominant-7th chord that was supposed to lead her into the tune.

Her mouth was dry, she wasn't sure she could sing. Yet she couldn't simply stand there, making a fool of herself.

So Sasha sang. Silently at first, barely a whisper from her moving lips. But by the second line, the sound grew louder, more confident, until it filled the auditorium like a cry. She sang the "Toreador Song" so close to tears that the melody wept. She turned it into the saddest song there ever was. No one had ever sung Bizet like this, it was unthinkable. And yet no one in the fourth and fifth rows stirred a muscle. She held them mesmerized. It wasn't like watching someone sing; it was more like seeing an acrobat on a high wire who you were certain was about to fall. She missed a number of notes altogether; it had been too long since she had trained and practiced. Her voice careened and missed in wild abandonment, and sometimes hit notes that were so beautiful the sound was like a beam of sunlight shining down from an opening in a cloud. As for Sasha, all she wanted was to cry.

When she came to the end, the small audience sat silent and stunned, unable to move. Sasha laughed nervously and wiped a tear from her eye with the back of her hand.

At last, a man with short dark hair and a square face stood from his seat. It was Oscar Hammerstein. Sasha had no idea who he was, but he seemed to be in charge.

"Well, well, that was extraordinary, Miss Chopin. Truly extraordinary. Your voice isn't quite right for *Oklahoma*, but my suggestion is that you try over at the Met. You might want to get yourself a teacher first for a few months. I can tell that you've had a good deal of training, but you're a little out of practice, yes?"

"Yes. The war, you see . . ." Sasha managed.

"Yes, I do see. And I wish you all the luck in the world, my dear. My God, with a voice like yours . . . as I say, with a teacher for a few months, I expect we'll be hearing a great deal from you in the future. Now perhaps we'd better go on to the next singer since we're running late."

Sasha remained where she was on stage, too overwhelmed to move.

"Miss Chopin, this way please," said the assistant who was keeping track of all the names.

"Don't you want me to come back for a dance audition?" Sasha asked.

"Miss Chopin, they don't think you're right for *Oklahoma*. Now if you'll step off the stage please, it's getting late and we still have twenty-five people behind you."

Sasha's legs were wobbly as she walked off stage. She felt off-balance, as though she were drunk. Earlier, she had made arrangements to have a cup of coffee with Jill afterwards, but now she only wanted to escape. Fortunately, Jill was standing outside the stage door with her back to Sasha, and she was able to sneak off in the other direction without the girl spotting her.

The afternoon seemed colder and grayer than when she had gone inside the theater. Sasha walked at a fast pace down West 44th Street until she reached 7th Avenue. At which point she broke into a run, thinking only to get away, to put as much distance between herself and the St. James Theater as she could manage in new high-heeled shoes that were positively killing her feet.

Six

Sasha wallowed in misery all that evening, certain that no one in the history of the world had ever suffered such humiliation as she.

She blamed no one but herself, she knew her failure at the St. James Theater was her own fault. She hadn't been prepared. She hadn't even known that Oklahoma was a principality located somewhere in the primitive regions of the country between New York and California, a place of cowgirls and cowmen, not until Jill, the girl ahead of her in line, had informed her.

But Sasha wasn't to be defeated so easily. The following day, full of new resolve, she rose to have her usual bout of morning sickness, then spent the rest of the morning by the radio in her room with a pen and a piece of paper jotting down the names of every song that struck her fancy. She knew she needed a more modern repertoire if she were to conquer New York.

After several hours of listening to the radio, she came up with two songs she liked well enough to learn. One was called "Don't Sit Under the Apple Tree," sung by the Andrew Sisters—a cute number, she thought, just the thing for her voice. The second was "Blue Skies," an old Irving Berlin tune that Frank Sinatra had re-recorded recently with Tommy Dorsey.

And of course, she already knew "Ain't Misbehaving." With three popular songs at her command, she believed she would be in a better position to audition again.

In the afternoon, she took the Fifth Avenue bus to 14th Street, to a music store she had found in the phone book, where she bought sheet music for "Don't Sit Under the Apple Tree," "Ain't Misbehaving," and "Blue Skies" for 75 cents each—$2.25 in all from her dwindling treasury. Returning to the Plaza, she spent the rest of the day rehearsing in the tiled enclosure of her bathroom. She began with scales and all the warm-up vocal exercises she could remember from her long-ago lessons. She knew very well that she had missed a number of notes at the St. James and she was determined that this should never happen again.

On her fourth day at the Plaza, newly energized, Sasha bought a pair of comfortable dance shoes at a store on 7th Avenue that specialized in theatrical wear (another $6 from the treasury) and she was ready to try her luck again.

She managed to fit in two auditions that day, one for a Broadway musical, the other for a review at a posh nightclub. She sang the song about the apple tree for the Broadway audition and the other about not behaving badly at the nightclub. Unfortunately, when it came to apples, she lacked the coy Yankee innocence necessary to make the song work. "Ain't Misbehaving" was even worse. To her surprise, the rehearsal pianist played it twice as fast as she had ever sung it before, transforming the tune back into the up-tempo number it was meant to be. From the opening bars of the introduction she never quite managed to catch up. It was as though the train had left the station without her. The whole thing came out so badly that there was sniggering among the other singers waiting their turn to audition.

The next day was Friday (her fifth day at the Plaza, the clock running), and Sasha showed up bravely at two more auditions, sporting a brittle smile that was set on her face like a mask. Both auditions were for nightclub reviews, and, for the second of these, she managed a fair enough version of "Blue Skies" for the director to ask to see her dance. This was where disaster struck: a required high kick sent her crashing off-balance onto her rear end on the hard stage floor, to the sound of more sniggering from the other girls waiting in line. Years ago, Sasha had had a number of dance lessons, elementary ballet, but nothing that had prepared her for a high kick.

Despite the rejections, Sasha kept at it doggedly, going from one audition to another with a determined smile fixed on her face. She had several near misses, directors who asked her to sing a second number, sometimes a third, and who often stared at her in a puzzled way, as though they couldn't quite figure out what there was about her that was subtly wrong.

She just didn't fit. Her voice was too operatic for Broadway, yet not operatic enough for opera. She didn't have an ear for jazz, she didn't understand the streetwise rhythms of the

New World. Everything about her proclaimed that she was an outsider, someone who didn't know the rules—who didn't even know the game everyone else was playing. Even her good looks worked against her. Directors wanted pretty girls for their chorus lines, but not girls quite as pretty as Sasha, whose looks would steal too much attention from the stars.

Sasha struggled to keep her spirits up. Certainly, the auditions brought offers of a more carnal kind—New York men might be all business when it came to money, but they weren't entirely blind to sex. At one audition, a man in a business suit came up to her afterwards with a leer in his eye and suggested they go out and have a drink together to talk over her career. But he had whisky on his breath, a wedding ring on his finger, and he didn't bother to disguise his visual interest in her breasts. At another audition, an assistant director made her a straight-forward offer, a guaranteed place in the chorus in exchange for an hour with him in an empty dressing room. Traipsing about the city, Sasha received two or three such proposals a day, which she turned down with the haughtiness of a queen.

But then one afternoon, Sasha was the last girl to audition for a revue at a club on West 52nd Street and she met someone with a more interesting proposition. It was her third audition that day and she didn't do well. Exhausted and discouraged, she was gathering her things to leave when the young pianist who had accompanied her hurried over.

"Hey, hold on a second. Look, can I be honest? You have a terrific voice," he told her. "It's just you don't know how to use it. Plus, you don't know a thing about rhythm. You're singing on the beat, you see. And that's as square as a wheat field in Kansas."

Sasha hadn't eaten since breakfast, her feet were killing her, and there were tears gathering in her eyes from the discouragement of another wasted day. She looked up to find a gawky young man with a bad complexion peering down at her with a concerned look on his face. Everything about him was odd. He wore thick glasses with huge rectangular frames, his hair was wild, his suit wrinkled, and his breath smelled of onion and garlic.

"A wheat field in Kansas?" she repeated, dumbfounded. She really didn't have a clue what he was talking about.

"Look, forget Kansas, that's not the important point. You're not going to cry, are you? I have a phobia about girls who cry."

She shook her head.

"Good. I tell you what, why don't we get together some time and I can show you some things."

A square wheat field in an unknown American state might be a mystery, but Sasha had a very good idea now where this conversation was headed. "Ah! I have had such offers before!" she said wisely.

"No, hey, it's not what you're thinking. I mean, sure, you're gorgeous, but I'm immune to that stuff. I'm a genius, you see. So I need to keep my focus."

Sasha smiled very slightly. "A genius?"

"Sure, I am. But let's talk about you. You have a classical background, don't you?"

"Yes, I have sung opera," she told him.

"I thought so. But you've never sung popular music or jazz?"

She shook her head.

"And you're not from around here, that's obvious. You don't know the scene. Look, what I'm saying is we could work together a few mornings when I'm free and I'd be glad to teach you stuff about music, what you need to know."

Sasha paused to study this young American specimen more closely. He was nearly her age, perhaps a year or two older. He was an odd duck, certainly. There was something almost goofy about him. But he had played the piano very nicely for her audition and he had an appealing smile. In rapid fire, he told her that his name was Dave Lubowitz, though he was considering changing this to Dave Delirio for stage purposes—what did she think? He was currently a student at the Institute of Music Art at Columbia University, and he played piano at the nightclub in order to pay his tuition. His ambition was to write great jazz symphonies that would combine the old forms of Brahms and Beethoven with the new sensibilities of Duke Ellington and Billie Holiday.

Sasha had never heard of this Institute of Music Art, which three years later would be renamed the Juilliard School of Music, but she sensed that Dave Lubowitz was rather nice in his odd way. She had always had a weak spot for music students, especially the starving kind who had to support themselves by playing piano in seedy nightclubs while they aspired to become great composers.

"Yes, I know I have much to learn," she admitted. "But I have no money to pay for lessons. I am afraid I am very poor."

"Oh, that's okay, I don't care about money. It's music that interests me. So what do you say? Why don't you let me teach you about jazz?"

Sasha doubted that music was his only interest. She recognized all the signs of an awkward young man who had fallen for her. Yet he seemed harmless enough and it was an offer that was hard to refuse.

"Well, perhaps we could give these lessons a try," she agreed. "Though I'm sure you are very busy, and I don't wish to take you from your studies."

He assured her that his studies meant nothing in comparison to the joy he would feel to be in her presence, and they made a date to meet at the nightclub the following morning. The club would be closed at that time, but the owner wouldn't mind if they used the piano to rehearse.

And so Sasha began her informal study of jazz. The club was only a fifteen-minute walk from the Plaza, so it was convenient for her spend a few hours with Dave each morning before she went on to her daily auditions. They began with rhythm, clapping out various beats together. Sasha thought she knew how to count time, but this wasn't like any time she had counted before. Once they got the main beats established—the down beats—they moved on to the back beats, and soon Dave had her clapping eighth notes, sixteenth notes, triplets, then missing beats entirely, creating strange syncopations. Little by little, he taught her the trick of staying off the beat, of being ahead of the beat, or behind the beat, but never on the beat, because that was square—that mysterious wheat field in Kansas again.

He called it swing time, and for Sasha it was a revelation. Swing time was the pulse of New York, the sound of the New World, and once Sasha got it, she felt it everywhere around her: in the jackhammers tearing up the pavement, in the way Colored people walked down 7th Avenue, in the fast motion that comprised Manhattan. Once she was able to clap out swing rhythms with her hands, Dave let her sing. He worked on her phrasing, her breathing, and finally the emotional delivery of a song.

He found a Jerome Kern-Richard Rodgers tune for her, "Little Girl Blue," and assured her that when she got this one right, she'd make people cry.

"You see, Sasha, here's the deal—you're a torch singer," he told her. "That's where your talent lies, and once you get it, you're going to be a star."

Sasha frowned. "Wait, please. I don't understand this. Torch . . . what is this thing?"

"Torch singer? You've never heard that expression?"

"Torch is like a flame, yes? A big candle?"

"Yeah, a flame, sure, that's it. 'My old flame, I don't even remember her name,'" he sang. Then stopped, seeing the confusion on her face. "Look, it's only an expression. When people talk about someone they like, they sometimes use the word flame—my old flame—because love is hot, right?"

"And you get burned," Sasha added.

He laughed. "Yeah, you got that right. Now look, there's two types of music these days. There's cool music, Bee-Bop—that's what I like to play. And then there's hot music. That's what you do. You're a hot singer, you're burning up. That's why you're a torch singer. Do you understand what I'm saying?"

"I think so. But I'm not sure."

"Well, here's some examples. Edith Piaf, the French singer. And Marlene Dietrich. They're torch singers, though in different ways."

"I have heard of Marlene Dietrich," Sasha told him. "She was in a movie I saw before the war, about a professor and a night club singer."

"The Blue Angel? There, you see, that's just it. That's a torch singer. Hot stuff. Just what you are."

Sasha frowned. "You mean, I should only sing ballads?"

"No, it's not that. Ballads are fine, and you should do a lot of them. But you can do up-tempo songs as well, if you do 'em right. It's not the speed, it's the delivery. It's the emotional sizzle you put into the song."

The lessons progressed in this fashion day by day, a combination of jazz theory, clapping out rhythms, and singing instruction of a very different kind than Sasha had ever received in her childhood. There was no immediate pay-off in terms of work for the lessons would take time to sink in, to become a natural part of her style. Still, she was grateful to Dave and she knew she was lucky to have a teacher. He brought her up to date, musically speaking. He brought her from the Old World to the New.

Of course, Dave wanted more from her than music. She let him kiss her once after one of the morning lessons, and another time she allowed him to put his clammy hand beneath her bra. He was grateful for these favors; he assured her that one day he would write a great symphony in honor of her right nipple. But she was careful not to let things go too far. He had no interest for her as a potential lover—he was too earnest, too gawky, and far too young. More importantly, he was poor as a church mouse, barely able to feed himself after paying his expenses at the Institute of Music Art, the school that was not quite yet Juilliard. He wasn't even entirely healthy—he'd been kept out of the army due to occasional fits of epilepsy, and this was worrisome as well.

When it came to men, Sasha had clear ideas of what she wanted. She didn't want a gangster, like the man she had met on the park bench, or a music student who was as poor as she was. Of course, it wasn't a mere date she was after, nor a friendly fling: with her clock running, Sasha was seeking nothing less than the father of her child.

And who would he be? Established, that went without saying. Wealthy. Elegant. Well-educated, please. No fool, if she could help it. But not so smart that he might do the right sort of arithmetic and figure out the precise parameters of nine months.

Fortunately, the Plaza Hotel appeared full of men of exactly this sort. She only had to snare one into her bed and do it quickly.

Seven

When Sasha wasn't throwing up in the toilet, or attending auditions, or studying jazz music with Dave Lubowitz, she spent every moment of her time trolling the corridors and public rooms of the Plaza for the man who would save her.

The contenders came and went: tall men, short men, plump men, thin. Men in three-piece suits. Men who looked like bankers. Men who looked as though they had never worked a day in all their lucky lives. And of course, in 1943 there were plenty of soldiers in uniform—at the Plaza, these were generally officers rather than the enlisted variety.

The lobby was Sasha's preferred hunting ground. There was a small red velvet settee near a potted palm in one corner of the room not far from the front entrance where she liked to set herself up for an hour or so at a time, pretending to be waiting for a friend. She held a newspaper for a prop and kept one leg crossed with her skirt carefully raised to show a few inches of ankle.

Sasha missed very little from her vantage point on the red settee. She witnessed quarrels between husbands and wives, parents and children. She saw guests checking in and guests checking out, often with dozens of pieces of luggage that kept the bellboys running back and forth. There were beautiful young women (the competition) and ugly old hags who looked like they had tons of money or nobody would put up with them. There were those who seemed as though they had been coming to the Plaza for years, who carried themselves with an aura of ease and entitlement, and others who appeared even more intimidated than Sasha.

After a while, she could distinguish between those who were coming in from the country—Connecticut and such, Sasha knew where that was now—and those who lived in New York. There was also a California contingent and a Florida crowd who could be spotted by their winter suntans. But Sasha's focus was on the passing men, any likely candidate between the age of thirty and fifty who appeared financially secure and romantically inclined, the sort who might appreciate a woman such as herself and not be afraid to take a nibble at the bait.

For all her sitting and observing, Sasha got very little in return. She knew that men were looking at her out of the corner of their eyes, sizing her up, the married men in particular. But the Plaza was a polite sort of place where people apparently didn't approach strangers. Of course, many of the best possibilities, males from the top-of-the-food-chain, had women close at hand—wives, mothers, daughters, dates. By the end of her first week, Sasha had received only one serious nibble, a somewhat eccentric gentleman in his mid-forties who Sasha imagined had imbibed a few drinks.

"I don't mean to alarm you, ma'am, but you don't happen to know the time, do you?" the man said, coming over to her settee. His clothes appeared to be of the best quality, but his accent was unusual, and his necktie was askew.

"I'm sorry, I don't carry a clock," Sasha told him.

"A *clock*!" The man grinned impishly. "Oh, I like that! Tick-tock, tick-tock . . . just like the crocodile in *Peter Pan*."

Sasha didn't know what he meant. She had never heard of Peter Pan and had no immediate thought of crocodiles. Still, there was something about the disheveled man that made her smile.

"Normally, I don't carry a clock either," he confided. "Where I come from in Mississippi, time doesn't really matter. But then I wrote a book, very stupidly, and got myself plucked up and plopped down here in this cold, cold city without a sweet love to keep me warm."

"Then you're a—"A writer, Sasha meant to say. But he wouldn't let her finish.

"Yes, a fish out of water," he said sadly. "A flounder who has floundered. A sole in need. And you, you're a princess, aren't you?"

Sasha laughed. She liked this funny man, even though he reeked of whisky. He would have been right at home backstage at the Krakow Opera. "No, actually I'm not a princess, I'm afraid."

"Oh, but you are!" he said, lurching closer. "You know what you are, my radiant one? You're the first girl I've seen in this hard city with poetry in her eyes."

Sasha liked that. She liked being a girl with poetry in her eyes. Who could say how such an encounter might have progressed? An author would have suited her very well, especially the kind who could afford to stay at the Plaza. But just then the gentleman sighed and shook his head.

"Oh, damn! Here's my publisher! Well, I must be off, princess. I'm catching the train to California tonight. Can't be put off, I'm afraid . . . lord, you're lovely! My God, another missed chance . . ."

The author from Mississippi shrugged and turned away, muttering vague, not entirely comprehensible sentiments of loss. Sasha watched as he joined a short bald man who had just walked into the lobby and together they turned a corner and disappeared.

And that was it, the sum total of her success after one week at the Plaza Hotel, $17 a day, the clock running: no job, no man. Later that evening, Sasha walked to the delicatessen she frequented on Sixth Avenue and had a lonely sandwich at one of the tables. When she returned to the Plaza, her first hotel bill was waiting in her box when she asked for her key. The amount due was $124.84.

Unfortunately, $17 a night added up quickly, particularly with tax. Sasha paid on the spot, wishing to put this unpleasant reminder behind her.

Returning to her room, Sasha locked her door, set all her remaining money out on her bed, and made her ritual count. She counted twice to make sure: she had exactly $81.32 left from her original fortune. A physical assault of panic squeezed her chest and throat. $81.32! It was less than she had imagined.

At this rate, she would come up short for next week's hotel bill. Perhaps they would accept a partial payment with promises of funds that were soon to arrive. With a pretty smile, it might be possible to cajole a few days of credit from the nice people at the Plaza. But then she would be out on the street.

"And then what will happen to me?" Sasha wondered. She curled up in bed in a self-comforting fetal position, but worries assaulted her and she was unable to sleep.

*****

Another week passed, her second week at the Plaza, with more music lessons but no work and no gentleman on her hook. On Monday afternoon, her second hotel bill was in her box when she returned to the hotel discouraged after yet another rejection for the chorus in a Broadway musical. The bill was for the same amount, $124.84, which was sixty dollars more than she possessed. Sasha put on her best smile as she accepted the dreadful piece of paper from the man at the desk.

"Oh, dear, I must go to the bank!" she told him, deciding to deal with half-payments and promises at a future time. "Perhaps I can give this to you tomorrow?"

"Of course, madam," he answered politely.

Sasha left the front desk knowing the desk clerk would be less polite tomorrow, and less polite still the day after that. She knew very well how these things worked. In the absence of paying work, she needed to find a suitably wealthy man and do it now. There was no time to waste.

On the following morning, Dave Lubowitz, her music teacher, had an examination at his school so they couldn't meet for their usual lesson. Sasha decided to show herself for breakfast at the Palm Court—coffee and toast, the cheapest items on the menu, but nevertheless a splurge at $1.25. Still, the price of hiding in her room seemed greater still.

The Palm Court was airy and open, separated from the lobby by a hedge of potted palms. Sasha sat at a table with a red rose in a vase and a white cloth and silverware that was heavy and satisfying to hold. A waiter in a white jacket brought her real coffee and real butter. The butter came in beautiful little balls that sat on shavings of ice, exactly two butter balls due to rationing—a lucky sign, she thought, promising male prospects. There was a delicious fruit preserve as well, raspberry jam. "Oh, don't let me be sick!" Sasha prayed. "I swear, I'd rather die than throw up this lovely breakfast!"

She was self-conscious, seated alone at a table as though she didn't have a friend in the world. Worse, she was surrounded on all sides by women of various sizes and ages: young women, old women, plain and pretty, children too, but hardly a man in sight. Sasha pretended to be engrossed in her newspaper while she inspected the room. Wasn't there a man anywhere in this group of cows? Yes! Suddenly she spotted one. A young man, too. Or relatively young, as things went in the Palm Court. Mid-thirties and rather attractive with dark, thinning hair and a round, moonish face. He was seated by himself several tables away beneath the bough of a potted palm, dressed in a naval uniform, crisp and white. Sasha liked naval officers. All that salt and sea stirred the sexual appetites, she knew for a fact.

Oh, yes, now he had spotted her! He was looking. Trying to pretend he wasn't, but definitely he saw her, absorbing her youth and loveliness . . . and now he was undressing her, she was certain of it. And why not? Mental nudity was free, Sasha didn't mind.

How could she encourage him without seeming to be too forward?

She glanced up from her paper in an abstracted way, as though she were trying to spot the waiter. But instead, quite accidentally, her eyes chanced to meet the eyes of the young naval officer. Sasha smiled pleasantly and he smiled back. As smiles went, these were of an insipid sort. Merely a kind of mutual acknowledgment that it was a fine morning. *A fine morning for fucking!* Sasha articulated silently, sending the thought out as mental telepathy across the room. *A fine morning for making a young maid pregnant, my dear aristocratic naval officer!*

Sasha had it all worked out. They would have three days together, fucking like mad. (Sasha knew all about three days together, fucking like mad.) But this time out, on the fourth day they would marry, and the fifth day he would be sent to sea, so sadly . . . to the Pearl Islands, or wherever it was the Americans went to fight their war. And then, alas, a month later she would receive a letter from the government: "Your brave husband has sunk to the bottom of the ocean with the fishes, dear Madam. Leaving you a respectable widow, you'll be happy to know, with a very generous pension . . ."

It didn't seem much of a challenge, a lonely sailor home after months at sea. How could he resist a girl like Sasha? But then a horrible thing happened. An unpleasant young woman with two nasty children joined the officer at his table. The faithless man quickly looked away, no more smiles to spare across the room.

Sasha was furious. It seemed to her almost as though he had led her on, promising an early death and sizeable pension in a most despicably dishonest manner. A girl really had to look out for herself!

Retreating back into her newspaper, Sasha was reading about a dishonest politician in a place called Tammany Hall when a foul smell drifted across the room. Someone nearby had just lit a cigar. Sasha glanced about and soon discovered the source: an overweight man with a red face, white hair, and a big belly standing in the lobby on the far side of the potted palms with an enormous cigar in his mouth. Normally, Sasha didn't mind cigar smoke. But this morning the sweet, cloying aroma caused her entire stomach to convulse, threatening to propel the rich butter and raspberry preserves outward in a kind of volcanic eruption.

Gagging and holding a napkin over her mouth, Sasha rose so abruptly she sent her chair flying backward. Without pausing for a second, she made a run for the public bathroom on the ground floor, arriving just in time.

*****

For the rest of the morning, Sasha was so sick she could do nothing but lie on her bed and hope she wouldn't need to dash to the toilet bowl still another time. But by the afternoon, the nausea finally subsided. Sasha took a hot bath, then dressed and went downstairs to try again.

An Overnight Sensation

She had decided upon a new strategy, to find a place where alcohol was served. It was obvious, now that she thought about it. Liquor loosened the tongue, removed inhibitions, would make even the most bashful American man lustful as a bull. Sasha had been wasting her time posing on the red settee in the lobby and in the Palm Court. What she needed was a bar.

Fortunately, she knew where such a bar might be found. By four in the afternoon, freshly bathed and full of purpose, Sasha brought a magazine, a pen, and some hotel writing paper down to the Oak Bar on the ground floor. The room was Germanic, though no one would have used that adjective in 1943: a high wooden ceiling and wood paneled walls that were so dark and heavy they were almost black. Oak, Sasha presumed. The bar wasn't crowded this time of the afternoon and she sat at a table near a tall window that looked out upon 59th Street and Central Park, arranging herself comfortably with her paper and pen in order to write a letter. In her experience, men couldn't resist women who looked as though they were in the act of poetic creation. As she waited to order, Sasha posed in profile with the pen raised slightly from the paper, as though she had just been struck by a profound thought. It was such a good pose, it was a pity, really, that she didn't have a soul on the entire planet to write a letter to.

"Dear Julka," she began at last, putting the tip of the pen to the paper. "Oh, my darling, you are probably looking down at me right now shaking your dear old head. I tell you, New York is a horrible place, not at all what we imagined. I would give twenty years of my life, I promise you, just to be back in Krakow for a single day with all our friends . . ."

"Yes, Miss, can I help you?" said the bartender coming over. He was an Irishman with a meaty face who looked as though he had been in the Oak Bar since the start of time.

"I would like a dry sherry, please," she said pleasantly. She had seen a menu outside, so she was prepared for the bartender's question. A sherry would set her back financially slightly more than beer, but beer didn't seem very romantic.

"Are you expecting someone to join you, Miss?"

"No," she told him. "I thought I'd sit here awhile and write a letter."

"I'm sorry, Miss, but unaccompanied women are not allowed in the bar."

Sasha peered up into the man's face, confused, not quite understanding what he was getting at. There was something hard and stubborn in the bartender's eyes.

"I'm sorry. I'm staying here at the hotel. I'd like a sherry, please..."

He told her again, as plainly as possible: unaccompanied women were not allowed in the bar and, if Sasha was not expecting someone to join her, she must leave. Though Sasha didn't know it, the Oak Bar was notorious for this old-fashioned rule that prohibited unaccompanied women, a rule that wouldn't be lifted until the 1970s.

"But this is the most ridiculous thing I've ever heard!" she complained.

"Yes, ma'am," said the bartender.

"I'm going to complain to the management."

"Yes, ma'am. But this is a respectable establishment and I'm afraid you will have to leave."

Sasha was stunned. *A respectable establishment*! She wanted to tell him that at the Café Chopin on Florianska Street a woman could sit with a sherry as long as she liked. But in the end, she simply gathered up her writing material and magazine with as much dignity as she could muster and walked out of the Oak Bar with her head held high.

She made her way back into the hotel lobby and found her old seat on the velvet settee. Sasha's anger grew as she sat stewing over this latest rejection. It was barbaric that a woman couldn't sit by herself writing a letter. She thought of all the clever things she might have said to the bartender. "Excuse me, but I come from a civilized country where women are treated properly, and people do not think all the time about sex!"

As Sasha sat pouting, she became aware of a man who was studying her from a dozen feet away. He was of uncertain age and appearance, a tall man with wavy brown hair wearing a brown suit. Sasha looked away quickly, not wanting to make eye contact. Still, it was nice to have a man finally notice her and she couldn't resist another look.

At first, she couldn't find him. He wasn't in the same place as before. Then she spotted his brown suit, this time closer to the front door. He seemed to be waiting for someone and, since he was looking the other way, Sasha was able to study him more closely. He had broad shoulders. She didn't think he was handsome, but he looked solid and strong. A rich industrialist, she decided. The sort of man who knew his own mind, who had very definite ideas about how things should be.

A rich industrialist would do. Why not?

The man's eyes began roving across the room, moving her way until he found her watching him. Sasha lowered her eyes . . . but not quite immediately. She needed to hurry up this game. And so for the briefest moment she met his gaze directly, and let implications fly. Just as she looked away, she saw the hint of a satisfied smile come to his face.

She didn't need to look at him anymore. She knew he would be coming over with some excuse to talk to her. All she had to do was wait. But then there was a commotion at the front door and she glanced up to see what was going on. Two army officers in olive green uniforms had just come tumbling into the lobby. They were drunk and quarrelling loudly.

"Look, you lousy son of a bitch, you keep your goddamn hands off my girl!" one of them was saying. "Find your own girl, why don'cha!"

The other officer was even more drunk. He staggered and nearly collided with a sofa. "Screw you, Jack!" he said. "It's not my fault you have bad taste in broads!"

This was scandalous talk for the Plaza lobby. A respectable establishment indeed! The two soldiers appeared ready to start slugging each other. But then, to Sasha's surprise, the man in the brown suit hurried over and pulled them apart. "Whoa, gentlemen!" he said with calm authority. "This is no way to behave." In a moment, two other men appeared and they assisted the man in the brown suit, the three of them working together to get the drunken soldiers out of the lobby through a door into another room.

Sasha digested these facts quickly. The man in the brown suit who had smiled at her was not a wealthy industrialist after all. He was a hotel detective!

She had . . . it was incredible! . . . she had been about to try her luck at seducing the hotel detective!

She stood quickly and fled the hotel by the side entrance to 58th Street, knowing she had to be gone before the detective returned. It was late afternoon with a darkening sky overhead. Sasha couldn't bear her awful ignorance any longer. She headed off blindly down Fifth Avenue without the slightest idea where she was going.

Eight

Stupid, stupid, stupid! Sasha told herself angrily as she trudged down Fifth Avenue.

She had done everything wrong, she saw that now. She should have gone to the Evangeline House, the hotel that Max had recommended. She should have saved her money. It was unbelievable how she had made a mess of everything. And now she had a hotel bill she couldn't pay and she didn't know what to do.

Why am I like this? she wondered. Why am I such a fool?

Sasha walked for such a long time that she came at last to the end of Fifth Avenue, arriving at a small park where there was an arch that resembled pictures she had seen of the Arc de Triomphe in Paris. Night had fallen and the street lights sparkled in the mist. It was warm for the time of year, but a light drizzle had begun to fall.

Leaving the square, Sasha walked westward until she came to Sixth Avenue, a name she recognized even though it was a very different sort of Sixth Avenue than the one uptown near the Plaza. There were low buildings, only two or three stories high, with small shops on the ground floors and inexpensive restaurants. After a few blocks, the rain began coming down harder and she ducked inside a movie theater, paying fifty cents to escape into a double feature. She was exhausted and she didn't think she could walk another step.

The first movie was a comedy about a group of college kids who didn't appear to have a care in the world except to win an important football game. Sasha barely followed the story, but it was soothing to sit in the dark and forget herself for a while.

The second movie came as a shock. It was a comedy as well, but this one stared Mina Bower and Ronald Coleman. It was very strange to see Max's wife in black and white on the big screen. Everything about her was beautiful and sophisticated. And her clothes!—in every scene she wore a different extravagant outfit. Seeing Mina made Sasha understand just how shabby Max must have found her, the refugee girl from Poland. There was no comparison between herself and this fairy-like creature who smiled and laughed and said witty things on the huge screen. The photography itself made everything magical. Mina seemed to glow bigger than life with a kind of black and white phosphorescence.

The story was about a book editor (Mina) who had to deal with a successful writer (Ronald Coleman) in order to get the writer to finish his book. Of course, all sorts of comic twists occurred and the two of them, after a rocky start, ended up falling in love.

The theater wasn't crowded. Sasha was sitting in a row by herself absorbed in the movie when she became aware that a man in a raincoat had taken the seat next to her.

"I've been watching you," he whispered hoarsely. "I'll give you five dollars if you touch my cock."

Sasha turned and regarded the man coldly. He was a harmless looking fellow, not very large; neither young nor old, rich nor poor, so entirely average she would have barely noticed him in a crowd. It was strange how everyone believed she was a prostitute. Perhaps they knew something about her that she didn't know. Perhaps they were right.

"Ten dollars," she told him after a moment.

"That's a lot of money for a hand-job."

"I won't do it for less."

"Okay," he agreed. "Don't get mad. But for ten dollars, I want you to suck me. You have to suck me off."

"Twenty dollars," she told him.

"Twenty!"

"Yes, for that you must give me twenty dollars. And you must give it to me first, in advance."

"All right," he said, after he had studied her for a moment. "You're a pretty girl."

"Yes, I'm a pretty girl," she agreed, taking his money. The man opened his raincoat, unbuttoned his trousers, and she lowered her head onto his lap.

An Overnight Sensation

Sasha knew she was a very bad person to do such a thing. She was ashamed and defiant at the same time. The man's penis was rubbery and smelled of sweat and urine and she only wanted to have it be over quickly. Yet she had a disturbing sense of déjà vu, something she couldn't at first place, that this had happened before. It was a memory she had forced from her mind. Then it came to her: kneeling in the snow near the Bulgarian border while two German border guards put their cocks in her mouth, one after the other, with Julka standing nearby with his back turned so he wouldn't have to watch.

The memory was so awful that Sasha stopped what she was doing and turned her head away, unable to continue.

"For chrissake, don't stop now!" the man in the raincoat hissed at her.

"I can't!"

"Sure you can. Unless you want to give me back my twenty bucks!"

What choice did she have? She needed the money desperately, just as in 1941 on the Bulgarian border she needed not to die. With loathing, Sasha took the man's penis back into her mouth. She did her work methodically, pumping up and down with her hand as she listened to Mina's voice coming from the screen, speaking words that had become meaningless sound. It took the man a long while to come. He seemed intent on getting his money's worth. But she managed the trick eventually, his little spurt of biology filling her mouth.

401

Twenty dollars, she reminded herself, spitting out his sperm onto the darkened floor. With twenty dollars she would have an additional night at the Plaza, plus food for one day. A girl in her situation had to do what was necessary.

The moment she was finished, Sasha intended to take her money and leave, for she didn't want to see the man when the lights came on. But to her surprise, he reached out and held onto her arm.

"Not so fast, sister," he said in a very different sort of voice than he had used before. He flashed a badge at her with his free hand. "Guess what, girlie? You're under arrest."

Sasha didn't know it yet, but she had just met Detective Ricky Bolano of the NYPD, whose specialty was vice in all its many forms.

Nine

Detective Bolano led Sasha from the theater toward a squad car that was waiting at the curb outside, keeping a tight grip on her arm so she couldn't run away.

On the sidewalk, rain was falling heavily from a milky black sky. A young couple beneath an umbrella turned to stare at her curiously as she was led away. Sasha kept her eyes lowered as the detective pushed her into the back seat of the squad car and slipped in next to her. A second cop, a uniformed officer in front, steered them out into the traffic.

"You can give me back my twenty bucks now," the detective told her, grinning. "Guys like me, we're so handsome, girls do it for free. Ain't that right, Ed."

"Right as rain, Ricky," the uniformed man in the front answered.

Sasha stared out the rain-streaked window at the blur of city lights and pretended not to hear them. She was too miserable even to be angry. She had never felt so utterly defeated in her life.

"Oh, you're stuck up, are you?" Detective Bolano said with a laugh. "Maybe you think you're too good to be a whore, is that it? Well, doll, let me clue you in. You suck a guy's dick in a movie theater and that makes you about as low-down as whores get. So get your nose out of the air and fork over the fucking money before I lose my patience."

Sasha turned to the detective with as much contempt in her face as she could muster. She hadn't seen him properly in the theater. He was a lanky man with an unpleasant wolfish face and dark circles beneath his eyes, maybe forty. If Sasha had taken a better look at him in the theater, she would have left him alone. Without a word, she opened her handbag and gave him back his twenty-dollar bill.

"Hey, I did you a favor, so don't be so unfriendly," he told her. "There are some girls working this neighborhood who would cut you to pieces if they'd seen you moving into their turf. So take my advice and peddle your ass somewhere else. A girl like you—you could make big dough uptown, I'm thinking. A lot of guys would like to fuck you. Isn't that right, Ed?"

The cop in the front seat looked at her from his rearview mirror. "Sure, they'd fuck you. If they didn't mind getting the clap."

Sasha turned away, fighting back tears.

"I tell you what," the detective said, putting his hand on her knee. "Maybe we don't have to go to the slammer after all. I'll take you to an apartment I know where I can do you proper, then I'll let you go. That way we'll both be happy. Whad'ya say?"

Sasha shook her head.

"What was that?"

"No," she told him. "*No!*"

"Well, well. Whad'ya think of that? This doll seems to think she's too good for us, Ed. Whad'ya think we should do with her?"

"Come on, let's just take her in," Ed said.

"Just take her in? What's wrong with you, Ed? This here's a quality piece of ass."

"For chrissake, Ricky, let's just book her and call it a damn night."

Sasha listened with an increasing sense of detachment as the two policemen discussed what they were going to do to her. She felt only a deepening numbness. Still, she was glad when the uniformed officer, Ed, won the debate. They decided not to rape her after all, or beat her up. Instead, they drove her to a brightly lit building where she was fingerprinted and photographed and put inside a jail cell that was crowded with other women, all of them prostitutes and drunks.

*****

Sasha survived her night in a New York City jail by shutting down her vital functions, thinking nothing, feeling nothing, retreating into a state where she was absent, not really there at all. She even managed to sleep for several hours, finding space on a bunk that became vacant at two in the morning when one of the women began screaming so violently that at last an officer came into the cell and led her away. Sasha had learned to sleep in difficult places while moving south through Eastern Europe on the run from the Germans. It came in handy now.

In the morning, a food cart was wheeled by, the women were given coffee and toast, and then they were all released without further explanation. Sasha's handbag, shoes, and hat were returned to her at the main desk and she found herself outside the police station on a narrow street that was unfamiliar. She had no idea where she was. Normally, she would have taken a bus back to her hotel—Sasha was quite familiar with New York's public transportation by now—but she was too dispirited to ask directions, and too tired to care about her budget, so she waved down a taxi instead.

The rain had stopped overnight, but the morning was sullen and gray. It was hard to imagine that there could be further misfortune in store for her, but as the taxi approached the Plaza Hotel from Columbus Circle, Sasha opened her bag to discover that her money was gone. Someone at the police station had robbed her—whether it was the detective who had arrested her or someone at the main desk, she couldn't say. What mattered was that she didn't have a cent and she had no idea what she was going to do. She asked the taxi driver to cross Fifth Avenue and let her off on the far corner rather than at the entrance to the hotel.

She studied the driver from the rear seat, wondering how best to approach him. He was an overweight man with dark bushy hair and a pencil stuck behind one ear. Perhaps he was a family man, perhaps he would show some pity. She smiled at him anxiously when he turned to her for his money, $1.15 on the meter.

"I am afraid a most terrible thing has happened—I have been robbed," she told him. "I thought I had money, but I do not. I am so sorry, but I cannot pay you. I do not know what to do."

For a New York taxi driver, he took the news well. He didn't shout, he didn't abuse her. Instead, he told her calmly that he was going to call over the cop on the corner and have her arrested unless she managed to find $1.15 quick.

"Oh, please, Mr. Driver! I have already been in jail, you see, where you picked me up—it is a long story, but I am innocent, truly. And it is the police who have robbed me," Sasha told him tearfully. "I am so sorry but the police in this city, they are terrible crooks. You have a kind face, and I will be so very grateful if you will please let me go."

The driver shook his head in disgust. "Oh, get out, for chrissake! Jeez! Just fucking *go*!"

Sasha hurried from the taxi before he could change his mind and watched as he sped away. She had suffered so many calamities, one after the other, that she had momentarily lost confidence. It seemed to her that she was spinning downward out of control; every move she made only took her to some worse place. She crossed Fifth Avenue to Central Park thinking she would walk on one of the paths until she figured out how she was going to survive in New York without a penny. But when she reached the corner, she came to the very bench where she had sat two weeks earlier, gazing up at the hotel, and she found herself too discouraged to walk another step.

Sasha collapsed onto a free corner of the bench, buried her face in her hands, and wept freely. She sat and cried for some time, oblivious to the city around her. But as before, when she was here two weeks ago, she gradually became aware of a man next to her who was attempting to press a handkerchief in her hand.

"Go on," he said, "blow your nose. Good thing I happened to be in the neighborhood, isn't it?"

Incredibly, it was the same man. The same flashy dresser she had taken for a gangster. They were side by side on the same bench. Only the handkerchief was different.

Sasha didn't know it, but life had just backed up to offer her a second chance.

*****

"This is getting to be a bad habit, my dear," said the flashy gentleman. "I'm not sure I approve, frankly, having you bawl your eyes out on my lucky bench."

"Well, it's not *my* lucky bench!" Sasha cried.

"Yeah, I can see that. Now be a good girl and blow your nose. Come on, we can't have pretty girls like you crying their eyes out every time a fella needs somewhere to sit down."

Sasha became aware that the man was dressed in a dove-gray suit that looked even more expensive than what he had been wearing two weeks ago. As she was observing him, absorbing his aura of money, the sun broke through a cloud and shone down a beam of sunlight upon her. It was as though God Himself wished to show her to advantage.

"There, there," said the man, studying her hard. "I hope this isn't about the same fella. No guy deserves Noah's Flood."

"No, it's not anyone, it's *me!*" she cried passionately. "I'm so stupid! That's all. I never learn! I just want to die!"

The man nodded thoughtfully. "Well, you could always jump in the river and drown. That would be reasonably quick."

"Yes! I will! That's exactly what I'll do!"

"Good. As it happens, you have two different rivers to choose from and neither of them are far. There's the East River and the Hudson. I can get you a cab if you want, or you can walk. We're about an equal distance between them, so you'll just have to decide which one you prefer."

Sasha peered into his face, aware that he was making fun of her. "What are you doing here again?" she asked unkindly. "You must have a lot of time on your hands to sit on park benches all day long."

"Hmmm, and I was just thinking the same thing about you. I told you, this is my lucky bench. I once made a million dollars on this bench, if you must know, and I'm hoping lightning will strike again. I'm superstitious, frankly, and I have a very big deal cooking at just this moment that could use some luck. So that's what I'm doing here. Now the question is what are *you* doing on *my* bench. One time, well, that could just be coincidence. But two times . . . tell me something, my wet friend, what sign are you?"

Normally a phrase like "a million dollars" would have gotten Sasha's full attention, but not today. Today she was too upset and everything he said merely irritated her.

"What do you mean, what sign am I?"

"Astrological sign," he answered mildly. "Come on, my dear, you'd better tell me your birthday."

"You're very nosy, aren't you? November fourteenth, if it's any of your business. I'm Scorpio." Sasha knew all about astrological signs from the Krakow Opera, but she had never been much impressed by such parlor games.

An Overnight Sensation

The man regarded her with such quiet intensity that Sasha's tears gradually subsided and she found herself regarding him in return. His face was rugged and lined in a way that struck Sasha as even more uncouth than when she had seen him before. He was good looking but coarse. Clearly he spent too much time in the sun, which Sasha associated with manual labor. He was older than she had thought, perhaps fifty.

But what had he said about a million dollars?

"Well, well," he said thoughtfully. "Scorpio. I don't mind telling you, I generally avoid Scorpio like the plague. You're a serious case, I can see that. You'd better tell me what your problem is, and tell it to me straight. If it's not some guy— and I believe you're telling the truth there, for those aren't guy tears you're crying . . . if it's not a guy, what is it then? Do you have an incurable disease?"

"No, I *don't* have an incurable disease!" Sasha was incensed at the thought. Although it seemed to her, on further consideration, that being pregnant might fit this category very well. "Anyway, you wouldn't believe me if I told you the truth. It's too awful."

"Go ahead and try me. What do you have to lose? Perhaps I'll have some good advice for you. If not, there's always your choice of rivers."

Sasha laughed bitterly. The situation, running into the same man twice on the same bench, was so ridiculous that she

411

felt an odd intimacy with him. She was inclined to tell him the truth . . . or at least an edited version thereof.

"I am going to be living on the street, I think, by tomorrow at the latest," she said. "That's my first problem. I am about to be without a home."

"Then you don't have any money?"

"No."

"Where are you living now?"

She nodded at the building across the street. "The Plaza."

He laughed. "Let me make sure I got this right. You don't have any money, but you're living at the Plaza?"

"Yes, I decided to move there after I saw you last. I had two hundred dollars and I thought why not see what life might have in store for me there."

"Ah-ha! Yeah, I get it. But with two hundred bucks you could have gone to the Y or found a nice boarding house. Did you consider that?"

"Yes," she agreed. "But I preferred to gamble. I knew nothing very wonderful would happen to me at a boarding house. So I thought, all right, I have enough money for a week or two at the Plaza. Why not take a chance?"

The man smiled. "I have to tell you, this is a pretty good story. And I'm a man who hears a lot of stories. So you thought you'd stake yourself to a few weeks at the Plaza. But what did you think would happen? Did you think you'd meet some rich guy? Is that what this is all about?"

She gave him a scornful look. "I don't care about rich men," she said, with not quite the same honesty that had guided her up to now. "It is my tragedy that I love only poor men. Or complicated men who are married."

"Still, you need someone to pay the bills, don't you?"

"Yes, I do," she admitted. "But it is only a temporary need so I can achieve my Great Goal."

"Ah! Well, that's different! You're on a quest, are you? What is your Great Goal, if you don't mind me asking?"

"I'm not sure I will tell you, because you will laugh."

"No. I want to assure you, my dear, that I never, never laugh at Great Goals."

"All right. I am going to be a famous singer. Not just any sort of singer, but a singer who makes people weep and cry for joy."

The man nodded. Sasha noticed that indeed he was not laughing.

"Then you're a singer, huh? You have training?"

"I trained as an opera singer. In Krakow, Poland."

"An opera singer! You don't say? In Poland? But you're French, aren't you? That's what you told me last time."

Sasha was glad to be reminded. "Yes, I'm French. But my mother was a famous opera singer and we were touring in Poland when the war broke out." This was at odds with the story she had told him last time, that she had escaped in a boat from

France with her father across the English Channel, but the man didn't appear to notice. Or care.

"This is very, very interesting," he said. "So you want to be an opera singer in America?

"No. It is too late for this, I think. I have missed too many years of training. I think it is better now for me to sing popular songs. But this has been a problem, too."

Sasha went on to recount at some length her misadventures auditioning for Broadway shows. The man listened carefully and with an air of both sympathy and understanding, which led her to describe her problems with her voice and her lack of repertoire, and most of all her lack of experience with American songs. Finally, she told him how she'd been robbed, a final catastrophe in a long string of bad luck, leaving her without a cent. A few lies were necessary to make the story more sympathetic—she omitted any mention of movie theaters, oral sex, and a night spent in jail, claiming someone had plucked her purse from her handbag in a crowded Fifth Avenue bus.

"Well, luck works in odds ways," the man said thought-fully, when she came to a pause. "And who knows? Maybe your luck is about to change."

"No, I don't think so," she told him bitterly, close once again to tears. "I only had two weeks and I wasted them. And now I am going to be living on the street, and I don't think people will be so eager to hire me then."

"Oh, I don't know. A girl like you. I don't think you'll be on the street long."

She shook her head. "No, I am out of steam. I think maybe I should go to one of your rivers and end it."

He raised an eyebrow. "You're serious?"

She shook her head. "But what else is there for me? You are very kind to listen to my sad story, but I am bored with it, and I think most people will be bored as well. This is a city, I think, that prefers success to failure."

"Yeah, you got that right. But at your age, you got yourself a little leeway, see. You're just paying your dues, it's no big thing. Of course, you're discouraged right now, but you can't really call it failure."

"Can't I?"

"No. You know, it's a funny thing, but we've talked for some time now and you've never asked me what I do. Why don't you go ahead and ask."

Sasha laughed bleakly. "All right. Who are you, Mr. Mystery Man on the bench? What do you do?"

"My name is Zachary Wise. Does that ring any bells?"

"No, I'm sorry."

"Well, take a guess, then. What do you think I do?"

Sasha smiled. She thought, of course, that he was a gangster of the most blatant kind. But this seemed rude to say.

"I think you are . . . a gentleman crook," she answered, adding, as was her habit, romantic luster to the literal truth.

"A famous cat burglar. I think you are sitting on this park bench because you are planning a very big robbery at the Plaza. You're casing the joint, as they say in the books. Probably you're planning to steal some rich old woman's jewels. But it's all right, I don't mind. I won't give you away, I promise."

Zachary Wise stared at Sasha in astonishment. His mouth fell open. He was truly speechless. Then he began to laugh. He howled with laughter. He couldn't stop.

"Oh!" he said when he could speak again. "That is really, really good! No, no, my dear young woman. I admit, you're close in an odd way, but you missed the mark. A cat burglar! I like *that*! As it happens, I own a movie studio in Hollywood. It's not the biggest studio in town, but it's not the smallest either."

"Oh, I see," Sasha told him contritely. It was a lovely thing to say, *I own a movie studio*, absolute magic. If it were true. She managed a misty smile. "I'm sorry I was so rude."

"No, don't be sorry. I haven't had a laugh like that in years. Look, let's get down to cases here. You're a singer, and I happen to be looking for a singer for a certain part. It's a small part, but it will be noticeable. You see, this may be your lucky bench after all. I tell you what. Why don't you let me take you to Hollywood and give you a screen test."

"Hollywood?" Sasha repeated.

"You've heard of Hollywood, I presume?"

"Yes, but—"

"No, let's have no buts about it, my dear. Now, I'm not guaranteeing anything, mind you. It's not every day I come across the same beautiful young woman twice on my lucky bench, but business is business and either you'll look good on screen or you won't—and if you don't, I can't use you. Still, for a girl like you, I think it would be worth the gamble. So what do you say? Yes or no?"

"Well, yes, of course. But—"

"*But*? There's that word again, my least favorite word in the English language. No, my dear, we can't have any more buts. Look, I have business in New York until the middle of next week and I'll have my secretary get an extra ticket for the Coast. We'll take the Super Chief together on Wednesday. Meanwhile, you can use the time to buy some clothes. I'm going to want you to look decent when you reach California."

"But . . . but I can't even pay my hotel bill!" Sasha cried before he could interrupt again. "How can I buy clothes? How can I go to California when I don't have any money?"

Zachary Wise gazed at her sternly and shook his head, obviously disappointed with his new protégée. "Look, you're not to worry about money. I'm going to take care of everything. Please repeat after me. Money . . . come on, say the word, don't be shy. *Money*."

"Money," she repeated dutifully.

"Grows."

"*Grows*."

"On trees.

"*On trees*."

"In California."

"*In California*."

"Now say the whole thing. Start to finish."

"Money grows on trees in California."

"No, no. You gotta say it like you mean it. We can't have any half-measures with a thing like this. In Hollywood, there's only room for true believers."

Sasha threw her head back and laughed. She could barely stop laughing long enough to say what the lovely movie man wanted. But she managed in the end. She said it passionately, from the depths of her heart:

"*Money . . . grows . . . on . . . trees . . . in California!*"

She knew she had found her place at last. She had arrived among her own kind.

Ten

The rest, as they say, is history.

In the Hollywood of that golden era, some girls got discovered in elevators, others at Schwab's, but for Sasha it was a park bench. The publicity department at Zachary's studio liked this twist and made quite a thing of it. It was said that in the following year, 1944, a whole new crop of girls tried their luck on park benches, hoping to repeat the miracle. What they found I can't say. Maybe they met Prince Charming, or more likely a pigeon in search of crumbs.

I only know about Sasha. She got lucky. On the following Wednesday, she boarded the Super Chief to Los Angeles and watched from her train window as America opened up before her, a huge landscape of prairies, mountains, and deserts that led to California on the farthest shore. Sasha had her own sleeping compartment due to the fact that Zachary Wise was a married man with three children. Still, there was plenty of time for romance in the wide hinterland between New York and Los Angeles and they became lovers soon enough. Zachary visited Sasha's sleeping compartment often, at night and sometimes in the afternoon, filling time as the train whistle blew its lonely cry through small towns and fields beneath the vast American sky.

In Hollywood, Zachary set Sasha up in a small but fashionable apartment on Fountain Avenue within walking distance of Sunset Boulevard. Sasha did a screen test and Zachary was pleased with her. He was a superstitious man, as he had told her. It was said he ruled his movie empire with an iron fist and a host of fortune tellers, and that if you wanted your movie to get a green light, you had better hope the tea leaves were right. In this case, he was soon convinced that his lucky bench had worked its charm once again, bringing him exactly what he wanted: the perfect girl for the perfect role in the perfect movie that would earn him a new fortune to add to the fortune he already had.

The movie was called *Underground*, a war story about the French resistance. Sasha's part was exactly two minutes and twelve seconds long. She appeared for only a single song, but it was the kind of song to launch a career. Her moment came toward the end of the movie, at a point in the story when a group of freedom fighters, certain they are about to die, gather in a tavern in a small but atmospheric French village in order to make a final toast. It's in this tavern that one of the village girls, a patriot, stands and sings to the hushed room, accompanied on a tinkly piano by one of the resistance fighters who happens to play exquisitely well.

Sasha was the village girl with the angelic voice, and it was her luck that, though this was a small part, it was a cathartic moment in the film that was designed (milked, one might say) to leave not a single eye dry. Her second piece of luck was the song itself. It was called "I Believe in Tomorrow" and it was written specifically for Sasha's voice. It was more than a song, it was an anthem that stole the show, a sentimental fountain of tears in which war-weary America could sob its heart out yet find hope in the future. Sasha sang it straight on the beat in four-four time without a single syncopation or jazzy innuendo, and so, as it turned out, she didn't much need her lessons in swing time. She simply sang her heart out, with tears in her eyes, belting out the lyrics with her low, passionate voice, her lovely head uplifted to a celestial klieg light that appeared in the smoky tavern to make sure she was properly photographed. There were violins as well, gorgeous strings that swelled up from nowhere, an orchestra under the direction of Dmitri Tiompkin. "I Believe in Tomorrow" made Sasha an instant star. Even today when people think of the movie *Underground*, it's this song that comes to mind, not the unfortunate actors who were furious at finding themselves upstaged by an unknown girl.

She was given a new name, Sonya Saint-Amant, to go with her new glamorous personality. The name was the creation of a dreamer in Zachary's publicity department, a heavy-drinking Catholic who liked the idea of saints and who believed "amant" would suitably imply the act of love. The only problem for Sasha was that despite all her newfound success—glamour, money, and an American bathroom that her darling

Julka would not have been able to imagine—she could not stop the biological process taking place within her body. To her surprise, Sasha found that she wanted her baby fiercely, with an animal intent that rose from the deepest part of her being. She wanted something of her own that no one could take from her, a family. What she needed now was to corral a husband and do it quickly. The morning sickness had stopped soon after she arrived in Los Angeles, but her stomach was starting to show.

She knew she had to face Zachary with the happy news, she couldn't put it off any longer. He'd had his way with her and now must marry her, that was all there was to it. Fortunately, Zachary's current wife was an old cow, forty years old if she was a day. It didn't seem possible that Zachary wouldn't prefer to be with her.

The important talk took place in Zachary's huge office at his studio complex in Burbank nearly a month after she had arrived in Los Angeles. Sasha sat in a black leather armchair facing him across a huge marble slab that served as his desk. In California, Zachary wore gaudy sports shirts open at the collar that Sasha found distasteful. He sat in a kind of throne, a black leather chair that was twice the size of hers, with floor to ceiling windows behind him and the shaggy green heads of two palm trees in the near distance.

"And how's my beautiful good-luck girl?" he asked with his usual charm.

"Fine, Zach. Except . . . well, I have to tell you, there's one problem."

"No! We can't have any problems, my pet. You must tell me about this quickly and I'll wave my magic wand and make it go away."

She forced a smile. "Well, it's not really that sort of problem, Zach. And really, I don't want it to go away. Actually, I am very happy. I am . . . well, the truth of the matter is I am pregnant."

He nodded sagely, holding the palms of his hands together in a kind of silent prayer. "I see."

"Oh, darling, it's good news, really! I want to have your child, Zach. I don't mind. We'll have to do something, of course."

"*Do* something? Well, yes, I see that. What sort of something do you have in mind?"

There was a cold glint in Zachary's eyes that took Sasha by surprise. Still, she gushed onward.

"Oh, I hope you're pleased, darling. You know what I want . . . I want to be with you, that's all. I want us to be a family. Oh, I know you're married, but she can't love you the way I do. Say you'll leave her, Zach. Say you'll be with me and I'll be the best wife to you that you could ever want."

The great man laughed gently. "Sasha, Sasha, just listen to you—you're the child, my pet, and I love you for it, truly I do. I've never met someone who's so jaded and innocent, both at the same time. You're one of a kind and I'm never going to let you go. But I'm not going to divorce my wife and marry you. And please don't think I'm so innocent myself as to believe that I have made you pregnant."

"But, Zach—"

He held up a hand to stop her from speaking. "Sasha, please, let's not play games. I must tell you, hotel maids are quite willing to talk if a private detective slips them a little money, even maids at the Plaza. And they have quite a story to tell, these maids who cleaned up your room, about the girl on the third floor who threw-up every morning into her toilet . . . yes, don't look so shocked. Of course, I hired detectives to tell me what they could find out about you. I like mystery girls as well as the next man, but I'm not such an idiot as to get involved without knowing what I am getting involved with."

"Zach, I swear—"

"Sasha, you don't need to swear anything. I've known all about this pregnancy of yours from the start and I've been wondering when you'd try to pull this stunt. I'm not a fool, my dear. Now, I don't know who the man is, and frankly I don't care to find out. But you aren't to see him again. I'm about to invest a good deal of money in you, and I don't want some idiot from the past showing up making trouble. Is that perfectly clear?"

"Yes, Zach, but—"

"No buts, please. Now, listen carefully. Everything is going to be all right. You don't have to pretend anything, I like you just the way you are. Things are going to continue exactly as they have between us. You're my most adorable love and I'm going to take excellent care of you."

Sasha was in shock. Her mouth opened, her face turned blotchy red, and for a moment she didn't look at all pretty. "But I'm pregnant!" she cried. "And I don't have a husband! How can anything go on like it has before? What am I going to do?"

Zachary came out from behind his huge desk and led Sasha to a more intimate corner of the office, a sofa where he took her hand and sat next to her.

"I have it all arranged and you aren't to worry a bit. Of course, you must have a husband. He will be dead, that's all. A dead war hero, I think, will be just the thing. A French flyer will do the trick perfectly. He can even be Polish if you prefer. One of those glamorous foreign volunteer types with the RAF. Shot down over the channel. I'll put my publicity department on it and we'll work out the details. Everyone will be most sympathetic. It will only add to the sense of romance about you."

"But won't people want to see a marriage license?"

Zachary kissed her hand. "Oh, I don't think so. It's astonishing what people will believe, as long as you manage to keep a straight face. Still, we'll get you a license, a ring. We'll arrange matters in England, fix up the proper documents there in case someone checks. Don't you worry your head over it. This will be much better in the end, for you to be married but without the inconvenience of a husband. Dead war heroes really are the answer to a girl's prayer."

Sasha stared at Zachary as though he were mad. She herself was almost entirely self-invented; she had been fiddling with her biography since childhood, one revision after another. Yet this was more incredible still, the grand scope of Hollywood make-believe.

"But can we get away with it, Zach?"

He smiled. "Of course we can get away with it. You and me, my darling, we're magicians. We're the ones who create the dreams that other people live by."

"Yes, Zach, but—"

"My girl, I'm going to spank you if you don't rid yourself of that terrible word. We can be whatever we set our hearts to be. There are no limits for dreamers."

"Yes, I'm sure you're right—"

"Don't you dare say that b-word! I'm serious. Repeat after me. We . . . say it, my dear."

"We."

"*Can be.*"

"Can be."

"*Whatever.*"

"Whatever."

"*We set our hearts.*"

"We set our hearts."

"*To be.*"

"To be."

"*There are no limits for dreamers.*"

"There are no limits for dreamers."

Zachary was paternalistic, a god in his own world who was accustomed to being obeyed. He had three different movie productions to attend to and a famous actor with his agent waiting in the reception area to see him. Nevertheless, he took the time to have Sasha repeat her catechism before he let her leave.

We can be whatever we set our hearts to be. There are no limits for dreamers!

Oddly, Sasha had suspected this truth already: that imagination conquers all, if you have the nerve for it.

And if you're lucky.

*****

And so it seemed that Sasha's dreams had come true: fame, fortune, a hit song on the radio, and a make-believe husband, too.

But the human heart is insatiable—Sasha's heart—and now that she had everything, she was already wanting more. She was lonely in California despite her new success. There was a chill beneath the sunshine, a whisper of something cold and predatory.

As her pregnancy progressed, Sasha retreated into a kind of purdah, hiding from the world in her Fountain Avenue apartment. Zachary insisted on this, saying that the sight of her swollen stomach wouldn't do a thing for her image as a sex goddess. Sasha knew he was right. Glamour was a sleight-of-hand—a card trick—in which the facts of life needed to be carefully hidden from view. Nevertheless, the baby wasn't due until November and as the months went by, she was increasingly impatient for her forced solitude to end.

Once a day, defying Zachary's orders, Sasha tied a scarf around her head, hid herself behind a pair of dark glasses, and walked to Schwab's Pharmacy on Sunset Boulevard a few blocks away. Schwab's was a popular meeting spot for movie people and Sasha enjoyed sitting on a stool at the soda fountain watching the bustle of busy Hollywood insiders come and go. Friends ran into one another with a good deal of laughter and noise, then hurried off self-importantly to their various destinations. Everyone seemed to know one another and be on the best of terms. Only Sasha was alone. She knew no one, and no one took any particular notice of her—an overweight pregnant woman sitting by herself at the counter.

Many women are beautiful in pregnancy, but Sasha was not. She had gained weight everywhere, even her face and arms were bloated. She felt like an ungainly cow, larger every day. Yet she couldn't stop eating, gobbling up everything in sight. Ice cream was her new passion. Sitting at the counter at Schwab's, hot fudge sundaes had become the high point of her day, eagerly awaited, better than sex—an astonishing concoction of vanilla ice cream (two scoops), hot chocolate syrup, a mountain of whip cream, nuts, and a bright red maraschino cherry on top.

Sasha especially loved the maraschino cherry, which she always ate first. The bright red cherry seemed almost a metaphor for Southern California: garishly eye-catching, yet somehow unfulfilling.

Each afternoon as she walked to Schwab's, she told herself that today she would be strong; she would resist the fatal lure of the hot fudge sundae and have perhaps a nice dish of cottage cheese instead. Zachary, alarmed at the weight she had gained, had recommended cottage cheese as a sensible dietetic choice. But it was no use. When the man at the counter came to take her order, the words seemed to pop into her mouth of their own accord. "I think I'll try one of those lovely fudge sundaes, please. Just a small one."

Of course, there was really only one size for hot fudge sundaes at Schwab's: gigantic. She knew what a weak person she was. But what other pleasures did she have?

Sasha was devoutly eating her sundae one afternoon in early October, eight months pregnant, carving at the ice cream with her spoon as though it were a piece of sculpture, when she was startled to see Max McCormick walk into Schwab's from the street. Her breath caught in her throat; her spoon froze midway to her mouth. For months she had been preparing herself for such an encounter, knowing that Hollywood was a surprisingly small town and that it was inevitable their paths would cross. She had prepared clever things to say, even the twinkle of recognition that would come to her eye: ironic, amused, but guarded. A look designed to show Max that she was his equal now, someone who had made her way to Hollywood on her own terms. But now that she saw him, she was unable to do anything but gape.

Luckily, Max didn't see her. He was with another man—the writer, Budd Schulberg—and together they walked to the counter at the front of the store where Max bought a newspaper and a pack of cigarettes, Pall Mall. He looked good—buoyant, charming, even more handsome than she remembered. He was dressed in a tan suit and tie and his jacket was open in a casual sort of way that was boyishly attractive. Sasha turned away, hoping he wouldn't recognize her. Not now, not today—not when she was puffy and pregnant and halfway through the messy remains of a huge hot fudge sundae she knew she shouldn't be eating.

She lowered her eyes and waited in suspense while Max paid for the cigarettes and then took a moment to chat with another man who had just come in the door from Sunset Boulevard. She could only hear part of what he was saying—

something about a picture he was about to start next week at Warner's—but his voice was so deeply familiar, it seemed almost to bore a tunnel into her soul. She didn't let out her breathe until he was gone. Disgusted with herself, she pushed the half-finished ice cream off to the far side of the counter. Thank God, he hadn't seen her. Not like this. When they met again, she intended to be slim and glamorous and fully in control.

Sasha walked home slowly along Fountain Avenue, a street of stubby palm trees and white stucco buildings with red-tiled roofs. Most of the buildings were small apartment complexes of three or four units that tended to have over-produced names like Villa Zanzibar or Casa Encantada. Sasha's building called itself Villa del Mar, though it wasn't much of a villa and they were quite a few miles from the mar. Moodily, Sasha walked through the front gate, past an insipid patch of lawn, and up the steps to her apartment on the second floor. Once inside, she settled on the sofa in her living room, folded her arms over her huge stomach, and stared emptily out the front window at the pale, foreign afternoon.

She had hardly thought of Max during her time in New York; she had been too busy trying to survive. But now memories from the *Mauretania* rushed by: the touch of his lips, the gentle way he had of taking her hand, how they had laughed and laughed at nothing at all . . . simply the magic of being alive.

She loved Max. She saw that now. He was the thing that was missing from her life, what she needed to be happy. The next time they met, she would be ready. She wouldn't be eating a huge dish of ice cream.

Sasha felt better now that she had a plan. A plan meant that you had turned the chaos of life into a narrative. A plan meant that there was a way forward. She would win Max all over again, she knew she would. Max was the love of her life, and though at the moment she was another man's mistress—and he another woman's man—she believed with all her heart that she would have him in the end.

How could there be any other outcome? In Hollywood it was written in the stars that love—after a few initial difficulties to stir the plot—must triumph in the end.

The days passed quickly, the final weeks of Sasha's pregnancy, and she found herself filled with a new confidence. She was no longer lonely. Each morning she woke to the warm scent of flowers and fresh mown lawn and she told herself not to worry.

Happy endings were what Hollywood was all about.

Why come to this awful place otherwise?

Epilogue

Max Gets His Star
Los Angeles, 1986

In 1986, thirty years after his death, Max finally got his star on Hollywood Boulevard.

He was more famous after his death than when he had been alive. His reputation began its upward climb in the 1960s, starting in France where a new wave of filmmakers were inspired by the black and white *noir* crime thrillers he'd done at Warner Brothers after the war—B pictures, at the time, but now a new generation decided they were art. Soon all the critics were calling Max a genius and his pictures were studied in college courses.

Fame is fickle that way. It can hit you when you're young (as it hit me, over the head like a baseball bat). Or when you're old and no longer care. Or many years after you've been killed in a double murder/suicide on a stormy St. Valentine's Day night from hell.

Even after he was famous, Max didn't get his star on the Hollywood Walk of Fame right away. It was delayed for political reasons. He had been uncooperative with HUAC, the House Un-American Activities Committee, and even by 1986, the Hollywood Chamber of Commerce was slow to take a chance on someone who might once have been pink. So I was surprised to receive a letter from the Chamber informing me that a five-pointed star honoring the motion picture director Max McCormick would be embedded in the sidewalk near the intersection of Hollywood Boulevard and Gower Street at a small ceremony on May 21, 1986, with an invitation for me to attend. I was invited because I was Max's closest surviving relative. His son.

I was in Greece that year, on the island of Crete, and I hesitated as to whether I would go. I didn't like Los Angeles anymore. It was a place I avoided. Meanwhile, spring was lovely on Crete, I had a little house with a verandah on a hill above the sea, and I wasn't in the mood to fly halfway around the world for what promised to be a silly sort of event. The very thought of the Hollywood Chamber of Commerce, the kind of people they would be, made me open a fresh bottle of retsina and sit on my verandah and sigh.

But Max! It was years too late to give him the honor he deserved. The whole thing was absurd, a star on the Hollywood Walk of Fame!

But how could I not go?

*****

I flew into L.A. on a Wednesday night, rented a car at the airport, and checked into the Beverly Hilton Hotel. In my childhood, my mother and I had often eaten at Trader Vics on the ground floor of the Hilton, but other than that the city seemed entirely foreign to me. More foreign, really, than Athens or Paris, the ex-pat places that comprised my adult life. I was forty-three years old that year, but returning to the scene of my childhood made me feel ancient, like something left over from the age of dinosaurs.

The ceremony was to be held at 2 o'clock the following afternoon. A young woman named Kirsten from the Chamber of Commerce phoned my hotel and offered to pick me up, but I said I would make my way to Hollywood Boulevard on my own. I wanted my own wheels handy in case I needed to make a quick escape. By 1986, Hollywood was in love with itself more than ever. Everything was hyped and inflated and soggy with self-admiration. All the movie studios had a Department of Nostalgia. Personally, I was cynical about the whole thing.

So, I was surprised when I arrived and saw Max's star in the sidewalk to find myself deeply moved. The star was a kind of pink stone rimmed with brass and there was an emblem of an old-fashioned movie camera beneath his name.

Max McCormick, 1899 - 1956, it said. Motion Picture Director.

Seeing his name there, and the finality of the dates, I could barely hold back my tears.

There weren't many people at the ceremony, because even though his movies were taught in college courses, Max wasn't

Elvis Presley or even Francis the Talking Mule. The young woman from the Chamber of Commerce, Kirsten, was there with one of her assistants, an eager-beaver sort of guy who kept grinning idiotically whenever he caught my eye. There was an older man in a suit and maybe three other people, none of whom I knew. We all stood in a circle around Max's star. Several people snapped photos. At one point a group of Japanese tourists wandered by to see who was being honored, but they didn't recognize the name Max McCormick and they quickly moved on.

Kirsten gave a little talk about Max's career that lasted maybe ten minutes. She spoke about the different movies Max had directed, and how there had been an enormous change in style from the early pictures he had made before World War Two—madcap comedies like *The Romantic Butler*—to the stark, black and white thrillers he had done after the war.

I stood with my head bowed, like I was at a funeral, and I didn't follow much of the talk because I was trying so hard not to cry. When she was finished, Kirsten flashed a bright smile in my direction and told the small gathering that they were honored today to have Max McCormick's son, Jonathan Saint-Amant, with them on the sidewalk. She asked if I wanted to say anything about Max, but I shook my head. I was wearing dark glasses and I hoped nobody could tell how close I was to falling apart.

And that was it. Kirsten invited me to a late lunch at Musso and Frank's down the street, but I said thank you, no. The idea of waxing nostalgic for another second more made me want to howl.

I hurried off on foot down Hollywood Boulevard because I had one more destination in mind before I drove back to the hotel: my mother's star, which had been set in the sidewalk some years earlier, in 1974. It's strange to have your parents' stars underfoot on a street full of tourists and prostitutes rather than up in the night sky where stars belong. But I had learned long ago that a sense of absurdity is a necessary tool of survival in L.A.

I found my mother near Cahuenga Boulevard between Lassie and Ronald Reagan, which is the sort of surreal juxtaposition you'll find on Hollywood Boulevard. My mother's five-pointed star was pink like Max's, and rimmed with brass, and underneath her name there was an engraving of an old-fashioned gramophone to indicate that she had been a singer:

SONYA SAINT-AMANT
1924 -1956

I stood by her marker with a sick smile on my face. It hurt to see her there, but it was funny, too. The joke was that the dates were wrong! It was crazy, but even in death, my mother had managed a final lie.

I was laughing—the sort of laugh that could change to tears in an instant—when I heard a voice beside me.

"Now, that's something. It's not often you see a guy standing at his mother's memorial laughing his head off!"

I looked up sharply to find the older man in the suit who I had noticed earlier at Max's ceremony. He was in his late fifties with short silver hair and there was an air of self-confidence about him that worried me. I didn't like it that he had followed me here from Gower Street.

"So, Jonathan," he said comfortably, as though we were friends. "You came a long way for this, didn't you? All the way from Greece, I understand. Has it helped put all those old ghosts behind you?"

"Who are you?" I managed.

He pulled out his wallet and showed me a badge with a five-pointed star that was almost like the stars that were embedded in the sidewalk, only this one was smaller and it wasn't pink. "Detective Jerry Floyd, L.A. County Sheriff's Department."

I did my best to smile. A man without a care.

"So what's the deal, Sheriff? You're a nostalgia buff?"

He shook his head. "Naw, I'm on the job. Cold cases, that's my department. Interesting work, really. It's like being an historian, going back in time. And sometimes it sure is fun to nail a killer who thought he'd got away with something long ago."

He grinned and seemed almost boyish for someone his age and in his profession. "Come on, Jonathan, let me buy you a drink. I know a bar not far from here. I can tell just by looking at you that your mouth is dry."

*****

We sat across from one another in a booth at a bar called Tully's. It was dark and anonymous and sad, like all the bars on Hollywood Boulevard in the afternoon. There was cigarette smoke in the air and a TV set showing a baseball game. Two men at the bar were arguing loudly about whether Cary Grant had been in *The Philadelphia Story*, or Jimmy Stewart. Otherwise, the place was nearly empty.

I had a vodka tonic and Detective Floyd had a Corona, which he drank from the bottle with a squeeze of lime.

"So you're reopening that old case," I said, as though I found it amusing. "My mother and Max and poor Fred Landson. Valentine's Day night, 1956. You're not a historian, Detective. You're an archeologist."

He smiled. "Actually, the case was never closed. Only put to sleep, you might say. There's no statute of limitations on murder, of course. And there were just too many loose ends."

"The Beverly Hills police were satisfied at the time."

"Well, sure, the BHPD. What can I say? They weren't the sharpest blades on the block. They're more professional now, of course. They have to be. But nineteen fifty-six! . . . man, that was back at the dawn of modern forensics! A small department like Beverly Hills just didn't have the expertise. And then the three bodies were cremated before anyone had a chance to take a serious look."

"Cremation was what Max wanted," I said. "He'd left instructions about that in his will. As for my mother and Fred . . . I don't really know what they wanted. Of course, I was very young at the time."

"Advanced for your years, though. Wouldn't you say?"

I shrugged. "It doesn't seem like a difficult crime to understand. Fred had been obsessed with my mother for years, ever since they'd met on the *Mauretania*. He couldn't bear walking in on her and Max in bed together. So he went crazy and shot them, and then turned his gun on himself. End of story. What is it about this that bothers you?"

Detective Jerry Floyd leaned forward and spoke in a stage whisper: "There were too many bullets. *That's* what bothers me."

I stared at him. "What do you mean?"

"The slugs they found in the upstairs bedroom. Even without modern forensics, the BHPD went through the wreckage of the fire carefully and they found a total of ten slugs. There were four 9mm bullets that had been fired from Congressman Landson's gun—a German Luger he'd brought home from the war. And then there were six .22 caliber bullets that came from a small Smith & Wesson revolver. That's a whole lot of fire from two different guns. And it doesn't really square with the simple scenario you've just mentioned—a jealous guy shooting his girl and her lover, then killing himself."

"Well, I don't know," I said warily.

"In your statement at the time, Jonathan, you said you woke up in your bedroom and heard two shots. Is that right?"

"That's what I remember, anyway. And then of course there was a third shot, when Fred shot his brains out. I was there when it happened, not a pretty thing to witness."

"And the six shots from the .22? You didn't hear them?"

"I guess not. I was sleeping pretty soundly."

"I guess you were," the detective said, nodding sagely.

"Look, I was twelve years old and I was totally freaked-out!" I was starting to be angry. "The way I understand it— what the police said back then—was that my mother had a small revolver in her bedside table, and she tried to defend herself. Maybe she fired a few times and missed. She wasn't exactly Wyatt Earp. Even if Fred took a few hits, a .22 wasn't necessarily going to kill him."

"But that's not what you said in your statement, Jonathan. Believe me, I've gone over those old documents very carefully. You never said that Fred was wounded."

"How could I tell? He was sitting in a chair. He could have been bleeding all over the carpet for all I knew."

"Okay, but here's another question. What about the fourth 9mm slug they found? That shot came from the Luger and it would have been loud. You've accounted for three shots, but not the last one. Why didn't you hear the fourth shot, Jonathan?"

I shook my head in exasperation. "Look, detective, if you read those old documents, then you'll know that I was completely traumatized by the events that night. I was nearly catatonic. I couldn't even speak for several weeks. I don't know what I heard and what I didn't. I was twelve years old, for chrissake! I have no idea what really happened."

The detective took a swig of Corona and put the bottle down on the table. "Tell me about the fire, Jonathan? How did you start that?"

"It's in the report," I said wearily. "I've gone over this dozens of times."

"Sure. But indulge me. Tell me one more time."

I closed my eyes. I tried to think. I tried to remember what I'd said.

"I don't know for sure. There was a candle burning close to the canopy, the gauzy material that came down around my mother's bed. One second I was looking at her, the way she just lay there dead. Then suddenly there were flames everywhere. I must have moved the canopy, pushed it against the flame. But I don't really remember. I've blocked it out."

"How convenient. First a convenient fire to destroy the evidence, and now you're claiming a convenient case of amnesia as to how it started. Is that it?"

"It's not what I'm *claiming*," I said angrily. "It's what three different psychiatrists said who examined me afterwards. The human brain does funny tricks in moments of extreme trauma. At this point, thirty years later, I'm not even sure how much of that night I dreamed and how much was real. I'm sorry, detective, but I was only a kid."

"Right, only a kid!" he repeated. "But then of course, you were a pretty good actor back then, weren't you? A child actor. You were on TV."

I shrugged, but my heart was racing. I had been waiting for this confrontation for thirty years, some cop taking another look, edging too close to the truth. I thought I was prepared with the right answers. But now that it was happening, I was so tense I couldn't think. I tried to remind myself that this cold case detective didn't know anything for certain. He was only guessing.

But his next question edged closer still. "Did you ever hear your mother mention an ex-New York City cop by the name of Ricky Bolano?"

I shook my head. "Ricky Bolano? No, that doesn't ring a bell."

"Lieutenant Ricky Bolano. He was dirty. A vice cop in New York who was on the take. Not an upstanding fellow.

Eventually the NYPD let him go, though they did it on the quiet, not wanting to draw attention to their own dirty laundry. Ricky ended up as a private eye in L.A. He did most of his work for *Confidential* magazine, finding out people's secrets. Until he ended up dead one night in Coldwater Canyon. I have a suspicion he was blackmailing your mother."

I kept shaking my head, hoping my hands weren't shaking also. I had never known that Ricky had worked for *Confidential*. This was news to me, a strange twist from the past. But it made sense in a weird way. Meanwhile, Detective Floyd was starting to scare the hell out of me, how much he knew.

"No, I'm sorry," I told him. "I've never heard of Ricky Bolano. And I'm sure I would have known if my mother was being blackmailed. But she wasn't. It just never happened."

"You and your mother were close, weren't you?"

"I suppose. In some ways."

"Would you describe her as a woman with secrets?"

I smiled. I wanted to howl with laughter. *Secrets?* But I controlled myself.

"If my mother had secrets, she never told me," I answered. "Why should she? I was just a kid at the time."

"So you keep saying. Tell me about Mina Bower. I've never had a real good fix on her. Did she know Max and your mother were fucking?"

I knew Detective Floyd had used the word fuck deliberately to make me angry, hoping it would jar loose new information. It was only a ploy. But I didn't like it anyway.

I took a breath to calm down. "Sure, Mina knew. It would have been hard to miss, and she wasn't stupid."

"And she accepted it? She wasn't jealous? You people in Hollywood, I guess you're more sophisticated than the rest of us."

"Exactly," I told him.

I relaxed several degrees. Detective Floyd had been getting hot, skirting closer to the truth than anyone had ever come before. But now the cold case man was getting colder.

"You think maybe Mina barged into the bedroom that night and killed Max and my mother?" I asked with a smile. "And then she gunned down Fred Landson, too, just for the hell of it?"

"The thought has crossed my mind. Mina wasn't in her right mind, was she? She had to be hospitalized several times in Santa Barbara."

"You've done your homework, Detective. I'll give you that. But no, there wasn't a violent bone in Mina's body. And she was never jealous of Max and my mother. When it came to sex, Mina had advanced ideas. She had her Summer of Love about a decade earlier than the rest of us. She was a free spirit."

"And you lived with her after your mother and Max were killed?"

"That's right. Mina was always a second mother to me, so it was natural that I should go live with her afterward. Look, Detective, I wish I could be more helpful. But like I've told you, I was twelve years old that night and I just don't remember anything more. Now to tell the truth, I'm still jet-lagged after my flight and I wouldn't mind getting back to my hotel to lie down. I came to see Max get his star, that's all. Not to revisit the worst night of my life."

The detective sat for a moment studying me hard. I felt entirely exposed, naked under his gaze. I was certain he was about to handcuff me and read me my rights. But then he nodded. He didn't have anything after all. He was only fishing.

"Well, okay, Jonathan. Sure, I understand. How long are you going to be in town?"

I had planned to spend a week in California, perhaps drive up the coast to Big Sur. But suddenly I couldn't wait to get away.

"I'm flying back to Greece tomorrow," I told him. "But I'll leave my address. And if you think of any more questions, please feel free to write."

"Oh, I'll feel free, all right." He pointed a finger at me, like it was a gun. "And actually, I have your address. Interpol has been very cooperative. I'll know where to find you."

"Good!" I said brightly, rising from the booth, doing my best imitation of a man with an easy conscience.

I stumbled against an empty table as I walked out of the bar, clumsy with nerves, knowing the cop's eyes were on me each step of the way.

*****

I fled. L.A. to London, London to Athens, the overnight ferry from Piraeus to Crete. It was expensive to change flights at the last moment, but I didn't care. I only wanted to get away.

I kept thinking about the cold case detective from the Sheriff's Department, telling myself he didn't have a clue as to what had really happened on Valentine's Day, 1956. The evidence was lost, if it had ever existed, swept away by fire and by time. All the players were dead. Except for me. I was the last man standing.

I reached my home on the beach, a little cove on the southwest side of the island, nearly thirty-six hours after leaving Los Angeles and I slept for an entire day to catch up. I kept waking and remembering, then sleeping again. When I woke the final time, it was late afternoon and the sun was low on what we ex-pats like to call the wine-red sea. That's an exaggeration. The color of the sea is more a deep blue, touched by whatever is happening in the sky. But poetry is in the air here, and in Greece, Homer is never far away.

I poured myself a glass of cold retsina—white wine with a hint of pine tar that you need to develop a taste for—and I stepped out onto my flagstone verandah. The beach was empty except for two young women who were coming out of the water. They were naked, which is how foreigners generally swim in my little cove—those few who find their way here, for I am off the beaten path. One of the girls was blonde and the other brunette and they both were deeply tanned, head to foot. I sensed they were Scandinavian, early twenties. Young people from northern Europe often make a pilgrimage to Greece, where the beer is cheap and the sun lightens their native melancholia. I watched idly as they dried themselves and got into their clothes.

It occurred to me that I was finally ready to tell my tale. I needed to let it out from where it had been hidden all these years, a restless genie in a bottle. The real story of my mother and Max and Fred Landson, and that son of a bitch Ricky Bolano from New York. Maybe I would turn it into a book. I could almost see the dust jacket: A lurid tale of blackmail and murder, and how it had all come to a climax on a dark and stormy night in 1956.

The more I thought about it, the more the idea of a tell-all book appealed to me. Perhaps it would set me free from the past. Perhaps I would send a copy to Detective Jerry Floyd.

Though maybe not.

In any case, I'm the sort of person who likes to think about books that I may (or may not) write someday. It's an idle way to fill time, and I am nothing if not idle. I was smiling, standing with my glass of retsina, as the two young women came walking up from the cove carrying their beach bags. The path brought them nearly to the edge of the verandah and as they moved closer, I saw that they were both very pretty. Long legs, soft smiles, their bodies aglow with the animal magic of youth.

The title of the book I wanted to write came to me just as they were climbing past the flowering bougainvillea near my front gate. *An Almost Perfect Ending*. I liked that. The suggestion of irony, the mirage of happiness that remains always out of reach: Hollywood in the Golden Age, and how we wished so desperately to outrun the shadows that were chasing us.

"Hello, there!" I called to the girls in English, the international language. "Have a nice swim?"

"It was wonderful!" said the brunette happily, a little breathless from the climb. "What a lovely house you have!"

"It's paradise," I replied. "Sorrow is forbidden in this cove. And no one ever grows old."

"You are American, I think," the blonde girl remarked astutely.

"Yes, I used to be. And you? . . . I sense a country far away beyond the sea."

"Denmark," they said, both at the same time.

They laughed. I was a good deal older than they were, but I had a beach house, an easy smile, and I'm sure they thought I was a character.

I invited them in for a drink, and they accepted. I'm incorrigible, I admit it. It's bred in the bone, my roots. Raised on swashbucklers, suckled on the California sun, child of desperate pleasures.

The blonde Danish girl had a little snub nose that reminded me of Penny, my long-ago love. Looking at her, I felt such a sharp stab of loss that I could hardly bear it.

"I'll get us a bite to eat," I said gently, leading them inside the cool shadows of the house. "Give me a moment and I'll make up some tuna. I know an old recipe I think you'll like . . ."

"We will help," said the blonde girl, in her slightly stilted English.

"We are very good in the kitchen," said the brunette.

"I bet you are," I told them. "I bet you're good anywhere."

And they were. They were perfect.

And we were happy together, for a while. In our paradise by the sea.

Coming Soon!

An Almost Perfect Ending
The Torch Singer
Book Two

By Robert Westbrook

Book Two, *An Almost Perfect Ending*, the continuation of *The Torch Singer* saga, opens with Sonya Saint-Amant at the height of her career—a glittering, triumphant appearance at Ciro's, the clubhouse for the stars in 1950s Hollywood where everyone wants to claim her as their friend.

But in 1954, popular music is undergoing a revolution in which all but the biggest stars will be cast aside. With her looks and popularity fading, Sonya believes she has come up with the perfect plan to save her career . . . if only she can maneuver a tricky path through the many dangers that beset her, a vortex of politics, sex, blackmail, and murder . . .

For more information
visit: www.SpeakingVolumes.us